Summer STORM

HOLLYWOOD CONNECTIONS BOOK THREE

LILY ALEXANDER

Summer Storm
Hollywood Connections Book Three

Copyright © 2021 by Lily Alexander

All rights reserved.

This book is a work of fiction. Names, characters, businesses, places, events, locales, and incidents are either the products of the author's imagination or used in a fictitious manner. Any resemblance to actual persons, living or dead, or actual events is purely coincidental.

ISBN: 978-1-7345686-8-4 (Ebook)
ISBN: 978-1-7345686-9-1 (Paperback)

Cover Design: Annie Anderson / Tattered Quill Designs
Interior Design: Stephanie Anderson, Alt 19 Creative
Edited by: Abby at Abby Content Editing
Proofreading by: H. C. Bentley

*For everyone who had the courage to grow up and become
who they truly are, and those who will get there some day.
It's a process. But you aren't alone. <3*

CHAPTER ONE

Trina

STILL PANTING, I rolled off of my mattress. Happy endorphins rushed through my blood as I pulled on the t-shirt and shorts I'd discarded a few minutes earlier.

I felt a bit low-class having invited someone over with nothing in my apartment but packed-up boxes and a mattress on the floor. The quick tumble with the cute blond had been worth it, though.

"Sorry about the bed."

"No biggie, I understand completely. You're ready to get out of town." He winked at me as he discreetly tucked the condom into a tissue before pulling his pants up.

It wasn't originally on my agenda, but the hookup with a man I found on a dating app while eating pickles over my kitchen sink had certainly given me a second wind for packing.

I dashed into the bathroom to use the toilet, expecting him to be gone when I came back out. Instead, I found him in my kitchen with a glass of water raised to his mouth.

Hoping he'd get the hint, I grabbed a box and some bubble wrap so I could pack up my dishes. In a dismissive tone, I said, "That was great, thanks..." His name escaped me, but honestly, it didn't really matter.

"Yeah, it was. I'm glad you swiped." He rinsed the glass, setting it on the towel next to the sink before casually sauntering off toward my bathroom.

Annoyed, I went into the living room to get a marker. As I considered how best to kick him out, a knock came from the door.

Through the peep-hole, I saw my boss. I didn't have any desire to be seen post-orgasm messy, but I didn't have much choice. I gave my clothes a quick tug to straighten them and fluffed my hair with my hands, inhaling a deep breath to steel myself before pulling open the door.

"Hey, Sasha. This is a surprise." I forced a smile as she looked me up and down, a disgusted frown pulling at her mouth.

As usual, she was dressed in expensive business attire, heels, and full makeup. It exhausted me to think about how much effort she put into getting ready every single day.

"Sorry to interrupt. I wanted to be sure you hit the ground running once you get to Birmingham." She thrust a handful of files at me. "I trust you'll maintain the same quality of work without my direct supervision." Condescension dripped from her words.

Once, I admired this woman. Years ago, when I first started working for her, we'd been something like friends. When she'd realized I wasn't interested in playing her corporate, mean-girl politics, our relationship quickly cooled. We were still cordial, but that was about it. The nicest thing she'd ever done for me was get me the transfer back to Birmingham. I could guarantee there was something in it for her; I just had no idea what it might be. Yet. Maybe it was simply getting me out of her general vicinity.

I didn't care. I was going *home.*

"Of course." I backed up, gesturing to the chaos of boxes in my living room. "Would, uh… would you like to come in?"

Her nose wrinkled, the disgust at the prospect of entering my chaotic apartment obvious. Her face went blank as she saw something behind me, however, and her face transformed completely.

I glanced over my shoulder, finding the object of her focus. He appeared as stricken as she was. I suddenly felt nauseous.

"Jesse? You son of a *bitch,*" Sasha cursed, pushing her way past me as she stalked into my apartment. Before I could process what was happening, she'd reached my kitchen and was hurling my plates at him, the cheap ceramic shattering loudly on the tile floor. "What the hell is this?"

"Oh wow, Sasha? Hey, stop!" He warded off the dishes with his arms, blocking them from hitting his face.

I hated to be impressed, but her aim was actually quite good.

Foolishly, I stepped between them. I didn't even *like* the dishes they were breaking, but for some reason, I was still compelled to intervene.

Her vitriol turned my way.

"*You.* How *could* you?"

I stopped moving, cursing myself for not at least putting on some flip-flops. Bare feet plus broken ceramic were not a good combination. I carefully picked my way across the tile floor on my tip-toes, hands raised.

"Sasha, listen—" Another dish crashed on the tile as he attempted to explain.

"We talked about this, Jesse! You promised! And with my *employee*? Are you *kidding* me?"

Taking advantage of her diverted attention, I grabbed my shoes from the living room, glad to put some distance between us.

The pieces were all coming together. A wave of hot shame washed over me. I'd *never* knowingly sleep with someone who wasn't single. My face burned, the negative emotion quickly turning into anger.

"Hang on. You're dating Sasha?"

They both looked over at me, Jesse with fear in his wide eyes, Sasha with murderous rage.

"You didn't know?" Sasha accused. "This is disgusting, Trina."

Her tone ignited my own fury. I didn't need or want her judgement on my personal life.

"Listen, I met him an hour ago on MatchMaker. How would I have *any* idea he was involved with you? His profile says *single.*"

Sasha stomped her foot as she let out a shriek, grabbing the water glass to chuck at him, as it was the nearest thing to grab. It hit the wall with a hollow crunch.

"You promised you would quit that damn app months ago!"

She snatched his arm and pulled him through my apartment.

"Good luck on your move," he said, sheepishly waving a second before she yanked him out the door, slamming it behind them.

The absolute *audacity* the man had.

I stood there for a few long moments, replaying what had just happened, blinking through the confusion.

"Holy shit," I breathed out, a giggle following my words. Shaking my head, I grabbed the broom and got to work cleaning up the disaster in my tiny kitchen.

Once the broken shards were all swept up, I abandoned the few remaining pieces of the set to a box without wrapping them. I would get myself better ones in Birmingham. The leftovers were now destined for the thrift store, with the other stuff I didn't want to pack. I didn't want any part of that energy following me back home to Birmingham.

Hopefully, this was my last city change. I couldn't come up with a single reason it wouldn't be, but life sometimes threw curveballs. Obviously.

My moving container was set to arrive in the morning. This was my third move in five years and while I was getting to be a pro at it, there were always some unavoidable kinks.

Like the disaster hookup I just had.

I was still in shock over my random app hookup turning out to be Sasha's boyfriend.

What a jerk.

No doubt, there would be consequences for me at work because of it, even though I'd done nothing wrong.

My phone alerted me from the floor next to my mattress. I smiled, seeing my best friend Addison's avatar on the screen.

An electric buzz blossomed in my chest. She and I were platonic soul mates, lucky enough to find one another during an intro to biology class our first semester at college. Her BFF stress level spidey-senses must have been tingling.

A: You all done packing? Sitting down for a minute?

I chuckled, spying little holes in the walls from where my artwork once hung. I ignored the urge to spackle the holes and flopped onto my mattress.

T: Yep, as good as it gets for now. I gotta load the container in the a.m. and clean. I'll call you from the road. I've got a story to tell you.
A: Oh, man. Those are my favorite conversations. Get a shower and rest!
T: Yes, ma'am.

I set the phone down and went into the bathroom, amused by the sight of my disheveled reflection in the glass shower enclosure. My pixie-short curls were wild and there was a super sexy smear of dirt down the whole right side of my face.

Me, from a few hours ago, had no idea how the last-minute romp would end up. My stomach dipped for a moment as I recalled the expression on my boss' face. So much for cordial working relationships.

My phone beeped with one more message.

A: 69 hours left!

"Sixty-nine hours," I muttered as I stripped off my dirty clothes before climbing under the steamy spray. I was perpetually a teenager as far as my dirty mind and sense of humor. To myself, I uttered, *"That's what she said."*

CHAPTER TWO

Trina

DROVE THROUGH THE first place I could for coffee and got on the highway before I dialed Addison.

"Good morning, sunshine," she answered on the second ring. It was clear she'd been waiting for my call. "Are you headed this way?"

"Yes, girl. I cannot *wait* to see your face."

"Me freaking too."

"How are we going to celebrate my homecoming?" I teased.

"I thought throwing a barbecue was the only way to celebrate? Seriously, what other options do I have?"

"None, I guess. Meat cooked over a fire, booze, and potato salad sound exactly right. Just don't make me a Jell-o mold."

Addison made a gagging noise. "No problem. My aunt used to make this weird salad with green Jell-o, canned pears, mayonnaise, and shredded cheddar every time the family got together. Why? Who eats that?"

"*Nobody.* So gross." My whole body relaxed as I laughed with my friend. "You ready to hear what happened the other night?"

"I'm a little pissed you've left me hanging this long, so yes." She giggled.

"Well, I decided I needed one final *hurrah* before I left Memphis, so I swiped on a handsome guy on MatchMaker."

"Let me guess, he was a catfish?"

I laughed at my friend. If only. That would have been much less dramatic.

"No, he was actually really cute. You gonna let me tell this story?"

"Sorry, sorry."

"Anyway, he came over, we had our fun, it was fine. While I'm trying to get him to leave, my boss stops by to fling some files at me."

"She did not. Why did she go to your house? Couldn't she email them to you?"

"Girl, I have no idea, but here's where it got *weird.* She sees the dude in my kitchen and barges in, cursing at him."

Addison gasped. "Oh, no."

"Oh *yes.* Jesse from MatchMaker knows Sasha. Like they're... *together* or something."

"What the hell, Trina? What did you do?"

I passed a slow-moving van, then set my cruise control before I got a ticket.

"Well, nothing at first, but she started hurling my dishes at him before eventually hauling his ass out my front door. I don't even know what to say about it other than I feel bad. It wasn't my fault, but I just know she's going to find a way to retaliate at work."

"What can she do, other than make your life miserable? She doesn't have legal grounds for much. You were at home and had no way to know who he was."

"I know, but she's sneaky. I'm not putting anything past her."

Addison laughed. "I cannot believe your last hookup in Memphis was your boss's boyfriend. You have absolute shit luck with men, my friend."

I joined her, tears leaking from the corners of my eyes.

"Me neither. Oh, my God. What is my life?"

We giggled for a while, in full agreement about how ridiculous such a situation was.

"Should I get you a set of dishes as a housewarming gift?"

"Yes, please. She broke everything except a few bowls, salad plates, and mugs. She was *big* mad."

"I can't blame her, but damn. That's violent."

We chatted for a few more minutes before I hung up, promising to stay up all night talking to her once I arrived if she wanted me to.

I drank my coffee, singing along to the radio as my tires ate up the miles between Memphis and Birmingham.

PULLING INTO THE long-term efficiency motel after the uneventful four-hour drive was painfully anti-climactic. Not that I needed fanfare and balloons, but my excitement just deflated without any kind of satisfying resolution.

I was reminded of a couple of my past dates, as a matter of fact.

The kind older gentleman at the front desk told me my company had reserved the room through the end of the month. I hoped I'd be out long before then, though I was glad for the cushion. Couch surfing with Addison was an option, but one I'd rather not resort to unless absolutely necessary.

Card key in hand, I made my way around the complex, parking in front of the door for my room. I grabbed a few bags from the car, dropping them on the concrete so I could unlock the door. I used one of my bags to prop it open while I took a good look around.

The room was cool and clean, if a bit outdated. There was a queen bed next to a small round table with two chairs. A small bank of countertop with tiny appliances made up the kitchenette area. It was nothing fancy, but the microwave worked and the fridge was cold. To my surprise, the bathroom was on the larger side, with a full-sized tub. I was pleased to find they'd provided a huge stack of towels.

After bringing in my luggage, plus my few odds and ends of value, walking space was limited. It would do until

I could find a permanent place. Which hopefully would be as close to immediately as possible.

"Home, sweet home," I murmured to myself.

Trying to make it a little more inviting for sleep, I put a pillow I'd brought with me on the bed. After pulling off the dated bedspread, folding it neatly, and stashing it in the small closet, I unzipped my sleeping bag and laid it on top of the sheets, then pulled a couple of my own blankets over the top.

"You're a weirdo… Trina Lee," I sang to myself in the tune of *The Grinch*.

The last thing I needed was to deal with bedbugs or other people's body fluids. I didn't care if my unconventional bedding was strange as long as it allowed me to sleep at night.

I'd texted Addison both when I hit town and after checking in. She told me to meet her at her place when I was ready. Wasting no time, I drove over to her apartment as soon as I'd finished unloading my car and getting the bed ready for later.

I cranked the music up and rolled my windows down, accepting the early summer heat as a small price to pay for the slice of joy being in my favorite city brought me.

My bestie must have been watching for me because she bounced down the wooden stairs outside her little garage-top apartment, throwing herself into my arms the moment I got out of my little car.

"You made it!"

"Thank God that's over with." I squeezed her back as tightly as she was hugging me.

"Was the drive bad?" she asked, gesturing for me to follow her.

"Nah. No traffic or anything, just my ass going numb from sitting for four solid hours."

"Are you hungry? I'm guessing you grabbed a coffee and muffin or something when you left, but nothing substantial."

As usual, her insight into my complicated brain amused me.

"I can *always* eat, you know that."

Addison's cozy apartment was refreshingly cool after baking in the midday sun. All the heavy curtains were closed to help keep the heat down. The darkness was comforting. The tension I'd been carrying in my shoulders unraveled, my chest loosening as I breathed in the familiar citrus tea scent of my bestie's home.

"Of course I do. Why do you think I asked you to text me when you hit the city limits? I had to get provisions."

A buffet of my favorite foods awaited me on her coffee table. I welled up with grateful tears.

"Aw, you thoughtful bitch. Thank you, this is amazing."

"There are ice cream sandwiches from Big Spoon in the freezer, too. Do you want water or sweet tea to drink? Something stronger?"

I settled into one of the cushions of the love seat, debating where to start with the finger foods.

"Sweet tea. It'll go better with the grease." I dunked a deep-fried pickle slice in ranch dressing before dropping it into my waiting mouth. I was rewarded with a salty crunch, which led me to do a little happy dance in my seat as my friend joined me with our drinks.

"They don't have fried pickles in Memphis? I find that hard to believe."

"They don't have *these* fried pickles. Or *that* ice cream. Or *those* ridiculously good chicken bite things. Or *you*." I jostled her shoulder playfully as she pulled an assortment of our favorite goodies onto a paper plate for herself.

"True. What are we watching?"

"*Destiny Falls*? I'm behind a bunch of episodes because I was packing."

The star of the show, Devon Greene, was the older brother of Addison's boyfriend, Dennis. She'd spent some time in California with Devon, along with other members of Dennis' extended family. I wasn't sure that fact would ever stop being both awesome plus a little weird to me.

My BFF and I curled into her love seat, snacking while enjoying our favorite supernatural drama. By the time we'd completely caught up on the available episodes, I was highly unmotivated to remove my tired carcass from Addison's loveseat.

"You could always sleep here." Addison yawned as she gathered up some of our trash.

"I could. I didn't bring anything with me, though."

"Terrible planning on your part, but still, not a deal-breaker. I have clothes. Probably even a new toothbrush. I promise not to kick you too much if you sleep over. No promises about snuggling though." She mimed zombie arms, puckering her lips, chasing me across the living room.

"Stop being a bad influence." I laughed at my friend's silliness, not at all motivated to keep arguing with her. The foreign motel held absolutely no appeal compared to my bestie's cozy apartment. "You'll see me plenty! I'm *back*, Ads. *Permanently.* No more long-distance drama. We're doing this in person from here on out if I have anything to say about it."

Addison hugged me. "Thank goodness, too. This whole being separated thing was for the birds." She tilted her head. "You know you want to stay. Come on." Addison grabbed me by the hand, pulling me toward her bedroom.

While I stood staring, my best friend collected clothes for me to sleep in and led me to the bathroom.

"Fine, fine. You win. What are you doing tomorrow?"

She shrugged, producing a new toothbrush from a drawer. We squeezed together in front of her bathroom sink to go through a quick face washing and teeth brushing routine. Our familiar bedtime routine was like a cozy blanket for my soul.

"After my run? No idea."

"I'm *not* going with you."

She laughed at my horrified expression. "I'm well aware. I'll make coffee and send you on your way before I even consider lacing my shoes up. Work for you?"

I scoffed as she left me alone to get changed.

"It blows my mind how you still go every weekend," I called.

"I've done it for years. One little car backing into me shouldn't stop such a good habit."

"Yes, it *should*!"

While she'd only been a little banged up from the slow impact, we'd been on the phone at the time. The sound of the tires squealing, plus how shocky she sounded afterward, was not something I ever wanted to repeat.

Once I was all settled into one side of her comfortable bed, my body relaxed, sinking into the pillow top.

"That was the best possible homecoming I could have asked for. Thank you. You know I love you."

"Aw, so sweet. You're welcome, bestie," Addison said, covering a yawn with her hand as she turned off the light.

I needlessly worried it would be hard for me to actually fall asleep. Within a minute, I was out hard, dreaming of the donut and latte I was going to enjoy on my back to the motel while my crazy best friend was out running.

CHAPTER THREE

Dallas

"**Y**OU DON'T HAVE to," my mother said, eyes glossy. "You can stay here as long as you need to. It's not a problem."

The need to have this conversation had been making me itchy for weeks. Now that it was finally happening, my heart was pounding behind my ribs and my hands were sweating.

I wasn't necessarily afraid of my mother's reaction, though I did feel anxious about taking a tangible step into my future by committing to stay in town. Plus, I knew it would make her sad. Which was the last thing I wanted.

"I know, Ma. But it's time. I need my own space." I gestured to my current work area, which was her kitchen table.

The table we always ate dinner around, especially when company came over. The place where I'd done all my homework as a kid. The spot my brothers and I traded some of the best insults. Where I'd had some of the most important conversations of my life. Dad sat us all down at one point for *the big talk* right where I currently puzzled through shipping manifests and cursed my way through emails.

I alternated my time between the kitchen, my childhood full-sized bed, and the porch. I often felt like I was in someone's way, even when my parents were in a different part of the house.

This house would always be my home, but it was time for me to have my own place.

As if she'd heard my thoughts, Mom said, "You're not taking up too much space here, honey. Ever. There were four of you at one point, remember? I could hardly hear myself think, let alone keep food in the fridge, especially when you all brought friends over. Whatever made you leave… well, I'm pretty sure you and Dennis have worked out your issues for the most part." Her expression sought out some kind of confirmation, so I nodded.

"We have." Work would be very awkward every day otherwise.

My brother Dennis and I ran one branch of a charitable foundation here in Alabama. Our location focused on animal-related projects; shelters, bedding, food. Our other two brothers, Devon and Daniel, managed a newer branch in California which centered around sustainable organic pantry items. It was us, my warehouse staff, plus Dennis' girlfriend, Addison. She probably deserved top billing now, since I was in the warehouse all the time while Dennis was working in the field, building animal shelters. She managed all the things that kept the business going day-to-day. She and I had managed to become close friends as well, which surprised us both while annoying my brother.

Thanks to Addison, my brother and I hashed out a long-standing issue between us about the reason I'd left. Apparently, a massive misunderstanding drove an unspoken wedge between us. His ex had refused his marriage proposal, then made a false claim about how I'd tried to seduce her. In response, I'd left home, believing I was the problem and it was the right thing to do.

Three years, I'd been gone. Time enough to screw up my life in several new and exciting ways, all on my own.

"Either way," Mom continued, breaking my train of thought. "I need you to know we love having you home. If you need some more time to get your feet back under you, we're happy to help. You're no trouble." Mom reached out to squeeze one of my hands.

I'd been back for the better part of a year already; while my parents were good about treating me like an adult, it was time to spread my wings. My childhood bedroom had served me well, but it was time to move on. As far as being no trouble… I wasn't sure my mom ever saw the bad sides of her kids and such a statement proved it. Trouble seemed to follow me around, no matter how hard I tried to avoid it.

"I appreciate it, Mom. I should find my own place, though. I want to—I've never had one before. Not with paperwork in my name, at least. For a guy approaching mid-twenties, it feels like something I should tackle."

Her smile was radiant as she placed her palm on my cheek. "I love you to the moon and back, Dallas Kyle. If it's time for you to fly the nest again, I'll have to let you go. I know it's been a big step for you to come home. I'm so proud of you."

Those words would never stop bringing every single emotion to the surface, right where they were exposed and vulnerable. I swallowed hard, trying to clear the lump in my throat. "Thanks, Ma."

"Alright then. Go see some places. If you're willing to sign a lease that will keep you here in Birmingham, I can breathe a little easier."

Guilt rose in my chest, thick and sour. "I'm sorry, Ma—"

"No, no. None of that. I swear I'm not trying to make you feel bad, baby. I just missed you so much when you were gone. I can't help worrying you'll go again." Her clear blue eyes cut right through me. Her lips tilted. "If you do, that's perfectly alright too. You have to live *your* life. You were always here for things when we needed you. I want you to know we can be here for you the same way if you need us." She blinked a few times to clear her tears away before they fell.

"Ma, I know. I swear." My throat was clogging up. No part of this conversation was going the way I'd thought it would.

Mom was the one person who knew the whole story around both why I'd left and why I'd come back. It was likely Dad knew by extension, although we'd never talked about it directly.

Telling my mother I'd fallen for and stayed with a man who drank away our money, threw punches, and blamed me for everything that went wrong in our lives while generally making me feel like I was nothing had been a humbling experience. In true Shelley Greene form, she'd gotten a little misty-eyed, hugged me tight, and told me she loved me. Then… she'd asked where to find him so they could have a conversation.

I knew my southern mother well enough to understand her *speaking* to him might involve an accident involving his skull and a large cast-iron skillet, so I asked her to let it be. She was disappointed but honored my request. At least, as far as I knew.

Somehow, Mom always managed to get the dirt on whatever one of us was going through. Sometimes, we were pretty awful about talking to one another, but we all loved her for being our soft place to land.

"I'm not going anywhere, Ma. Not for a while. Where would I go? There's nothing to go back to and I don't have a reason to stay away. Reggie and I…" I shook my head, my ex's name bitter in my mouth. "We're done. For good, I promise. No more worrying, alright? No more crying. I may not be here for dinner every night, but I'll be somewhere close by."

"Okay." Turning her emotions around, she put on a bright smile and clapped her hands once. "Go take some tours. Find a good one, okay? Don't settle. Never settle, baby."

None of us deserved her. Thankfully, she loved us all with her whole heart, anyway. My brothers and I had certainly put her through the wringer over the years. Every last one of us caused trouble. There wasn't a single time our parents hadn't been there for us when things went to shit. It was a gift I didn't take for granted.

"I got it. Believe it or not, I'm pretty good with money. I paid attention when Daniel went on his tangents about it." Of my three older brothers, Daniel was the businessman. He even had a fancy degree to prove it. Dennis may have sunk his whole heart and soul into running the foundation, but Daniel was our numbers guy.

"You never once let any of your work with the foundation slide when you were away, either. Of course you listened to your brother about money. He's impossible not to hear when he starts talking dollars and cents because—"

"He always makes sense," I finished her pun. "I know, Ma.

Her levity vanished, replaced by heavy empathy. I looked away after a moment, her stare was so powerful.

"Besides, I know *you* were always good with money, baby."

The intense urge to re-explain how the reason I'd had to borrow money a few times had nothing to do with me and everything to do with Reggie's anger issues rose in me. His need to feel important led to buying useless things we couldn't afford. Not that she didn't already know, because we'd already been through all the details before. Regardless, guilt would always lay thick across the memories of having to call home for money to be sure rent was paid.

Her clever eyes watched me battle with myself, but she stopped when I really started to squirm. "Dallas. I *know*. It's okay."

I nodded tightly. "It's not okay, Ma. But I'll make it right." I was paying them back bit by bit and wouldn't stop until my debt was gone.

"You know I don't give a single shit about the money, Dallas Kyle." She leaned back in her chair, crossing her arms, which was a warning she was getting irritated.

"*I do*, Ma."

We stared each other down for a long moment.

"Alright."

Pleased she understood my need to pay them back, or at least not arguing with me about it, I got to my feet.

"I need to go. I have an appointment in half an hour."

She stood as well, following me through the house toward the front door.

"Alright. Honey…" She heaved a breath, squeezing her eyes closed for a moment as though sending up a prayer. Whatever it was she'd decided not to say hung between us. "Please, be careful."

Her hands were linked together at her chest, her mouth pulled into a tight line. She hated my motorcycle. Unless she was my passenger, anyway, which I found endless joy in teasing her about.

"I always am, Ma, you know that. I pretend you're riding with me. I love you." I dipped down to kiss her cheek before opening the front door. "I'll see you later. Don't worry, okay?"

"Impossible," she scoffed. "And I know that's a damned lie, you ride completely different when I'm with you. But be careful anyway."

"Well, *try* not to worry, then? For me? It gives you wrinkles." I snapped on my helmet, giving her what I hoped was a reassuring smile to go with the sarcasm. She'd bestowed many gifts on her children, snark being one.

"Are you *trying* to get hurt, son? Are you saying I look *old*?" Her fingers probed her face carefully.

I winked at her again, our mutual humor having lightened the mood considerably. "I'd never say that, Ma. I enjoy my heart beating on the inside of my ribcage."

"Good boy. I'll do my best not to worry, you do your best to be safe."

"Deal." I crossed to where my motorcycle was parked.

As I drove away from my childhood home, emotion made my chest tight. Per tradition, Mom waved, waiting on the porch until I was out of sight.

It wasn't the first time I'd moved away, but this time was different.

I wasn't leaving to disappear this time. I was staying close by and didn't have an expiration date lingering somewhere on my timeline.

Most importantly, this time, I was doing it for me.

CHAPTER FOUR

Dallas

I FOLLOWED THE BLEACH-BLONDE leasing agent through the apartment. At least this time she was restraining herself from flirting heavily like she had when I toured a similar unit in another building a couple of weeks ago. I didn't mind the flirting; she just wasn't my type.

"Over here we have the master suite. It's, of course, larger than the other bedrooms. It also has the best view."

The expansive bedroom overlooked a small man-made lake, complete with a walking path and a playground for children at one end. The bathroom boasted a massive tub separate from the slate walk-in shower. Everything in the recently completed space was done in ultra-modern black and chrome with icy blue accents.

I'd toured a handful of different places around the city, but this was the one I liked most. Something about it lifted the weight I carried around on my shoulders, allowing me to breathe.

"Thank you, Candace."

She smiled brightly at me, leaving behind a tiny smear of crimson lipstick on her teeth. "Of course. I'll let you have a wander. I'll be out in the hallway when you're ready."

"I appreciate it."

Her high heels clicked against the dark hardwood floors as she crossed through the living room.

The floor-plan was open concept, with the main living space and kitchen flowing together as one great room. On either end of the apartment were the larger bedrooms. There was a short hallway with a half-bath and smaller third bedroom between the living area and smaller suite.

There was absolutely no reason for me to be considering a three-bedroom apartment. Unfortunately, they didn't have any smaller units opening up for at least six months and I was ready to move. I didn't love the idea of having to get a roommate, though it was the best option if I committed to the one-year lease. I could manage on my own, but it would be extremely tight. It was possible I'd have to lobby for a raise at work. Not that I was undeserving, but it would never be my favorite conversation to have with my brothers.

Walking through the space, I breathed in the unmistakable scent of fresh paint and new carpeting. My fingertips grazed the countertops as I went.

This was the place for me, I was sure of it. I just had to figure out how to make it work.

After one last longing look, I joined Candace in the hallway.

"So? What do we think about this one? I know the killer view is hard to say no to." A hopeful expression brightened her face as she led me back through the hallway toward the elevators.

"It's too much apartment for me if I'm being honest."

Her face fell, but she schooled it quickly. "Well, that's too bad. Is the rent an issue?"

The elevator door opened with a *ding.* I put my hand out to keep the doors from closing as she got in.

"It's part of it. I don't need three bedrooms. I love the area and that unit in particular feels like a good fit. I have some details to consider."

Candace tapped a lacquered fingernail on her teeth as the elevator descended. When the doors opened again, she gestured for me to follow her.

"Come with me. Let's see what we can do to get you into that apartment."

I pasted on a patient smile to cover my discomfort. Sitting in a leasing agent's office was just about as enticing as shopping for a used car or having some dental work done. It was necessary, but not something I would ever get excited about.

The vinyl of the chair was cold even through my jeans as I took a seat in her frigid office. I guess it was good to know the air conditioning for the building worked, if a little too well.

"Sorry about the temperature. For some reason, this office is linked to the same thermostat as the resident gym. I freeze while they still complain it's too hot." She pulled a cardigan off the back of her chair, slipping it over the shoulders of her blouse before taking her seat.

"No problem."

"Alright, let's see. We've got your application, everything was great there. Same with your deposit approval and references." She dragged out the *s* as she scrolled on her computer. "Ah! There it is. I knew we had a promotion going on."

"Promotion?" I leaned forward, unable to resist the lure of her excitement. Plus, I was just as much of a sucker for a deal as the next guy.

"Yes, we've got a new resident credit I can apply. Maybe..." she pulled a calculator across the desktop and tapped on the numbers, then went back to the computer. "...yes, I can also offer an additional break if you sign today for a full year."

Candace leaned sideways in her chair, peering over my shoulder to be sure nobody was lingering outside her office door.

"I'm not supposed to stack these things," she spoke in a loud whisper, giving a dramatic wink. "But something tells me you're an *excellent* tenant."

"I like to think so." I hoped my smile came across reassuring instead of maniacal. "I'm sure I can provide more references if needed."

"No need. The new resident promo is two months' free rent." Breath stalled in my throat. "Signing for a full year today essentially knocks off another full month."

My mind reeled as I considered the number. It was manageable. I could cut some expenses to make it work. That place could be mine. If I decided to find a roommate, it might be comfortable, even.

"You drive a hard bargain, Candace."

She smiled brightly, the smear of lipstick faded to a small pink stain on her teeth. She turned the calculator in my direction. "This would be the new monthly rent on your unit if you sign before you leave here today."

The number, which was significantly lower than we'd briefly discussed after I toured a similar unit in another building, had me transfixed.

I must have made some kind of noise, because she asked, "Are you about to become the newest resident at Shadow Lakes, Mr. Greene?"

Impulse drove me to pull one of the pens out of the waiting cup at the edge of her desk. My heart was pounding, but I didn't feel the sense of foreboding that usually showed up when I was about to make a terrible decision. Instead, I felt excitement.

"It's starting to seem that way, Candace."

"Fantastic, let me get your paperwork all set up."

My hands were damp as I signed the documents. All in all, it wasn't a painful process, though it was time-consuming.

She gave me a refresher on all of the building rules and amenities before handing over a set of keys.

My keys.

I'd never had keys of my own before. Copies of copies and shared keychains, sure, but these were all mine.

"I'm so pleased this worked out." She traded me for the check and shook my hand.

"Me, too. Thank you for all your help."

"My pleasure, Dallas. You can move in whenever you're ready."

"I appreciate your help, Candace."

"I'm always available if you need anything." She winked in a way that suggested she meant for personal as well as for business as she handed me her card.

I wouldn't be taking her up on it.

The metal was a pleasant weight in my palm as I thanked her again. Once she'd returned to her office, I let out a heavy breath, excitement electrifying my body.

I stopped by the unit one more time before heading back to my parents' house to start packing. I'd soften the blow for my mother with dinner out. She was well aware this was coming, but no doubt the confirmation would hit her a bit more gently over her favorite chocolate cake. She'd gotten extra attached since I came back home.

For the first time, I had a place I was looking forward to calling my own. I'd been the roommate, the sub-let, the boyfriend. This place belonged to *me*.

It was a heady feeling, and I was pretty sure the weight of the keys in my pocket was the only thing keeping my feet on the ground as I crossed the parking lot.

CHAPTER FIVE

Trina

AS PROMISED, TO celebrate my homecoming, Addison was throwing me a barbecue.

She was setting everything up in the long driveway and detached garage under her apartment. Her sweet landlords even gave their permission for us to spread into their yard if we needed to. I honestly didn't care if we had to sit on top of one another inside her adorable little one-bedroom. I was just glad to be back.

The plan was to eat plenty of food, play some music, and get drunk. I was going to celebrate my ass off that I'd finally made it back to Birmingham.

Addison's face scrunched on the other end of the video call as she puzzled out some details about the party.

"I need to pick up the stuff for the sides, but that's it."

"What about meat?"

"Dennis said he would take care of it."

"Drinks?"

"Dallas is on drinks."

"Plates? Napkins? Silverware?"

Addison skewered me with a glare through the phone. "*Trina*. I've got it taken care of."

I threw my hands up in surrender. "Fine, fine. Just trying to be helpful."

She rolled her eyes at me as she stood up, moving around her living room. "Well, stop. You're the guest of honor! Sit back and enjoy yourself. You don't have to organize your own party."

I snorted. I wasn't sure how *not* to be the one in charge of the organization, but I'd give it my best shot.

"When are you going to the store?"

"I'm getting my shoes right now. I'll come pick you up."

"Thank God." I gave a bounce, the stiff mattress on the motel bed barely moving. "I'll be ready."

I hung up, hurrying to put on my sandals while double-checking the contents of my purse. I threw together an overnight bag, because chances were very good I would be passing out on my bestie's couch if the party went well.

By the time Addison arrived, I'd nibbled a thumbnail down to a nub. This last move had left me with very little patience.

She drove us to the store in her little sedan, the pair of us wandering the aisles the same way we'd done a hundred times in college. We ended up with at least a dozen things we didn't need, but tossing random items at one another was a game we couldn't resist playing. She threw a package of peppermint hard candies at me, so I tossed a bag of white chocolate chips at her. I had no idea what to even do with the turnip she'd chucked at my head. I'd fired back with a cucumber so large it could classify as a deadly weapon.

It made us both laugh until we couldn't breathe, especially when Addison held up a pair of interestingly curved Japanese eggplants to go with it. Our giggles prompted an older lady to shake her head at us, but we both saw her grin as she walked away, and *that* only made us laugh harder. Grocery store Granny knew *exactly* what was up.

What should have been a quick run to the store turned into a full dramatic production, making us later than expected getting back to her place.

"The only thing requiring any effort is potato salad. Can you manage to just sit on my couch while I get it ready?" Addison asked as we hauled bags up the staircase to her apartment.

I snorted. "Unlikely."

Her long, wavy braid snaked along her back as she shook her head at me. "I figured as much."

Once we were inside with the groceries sorted out, she gave me the task of putting together a music play-list for the party to distract me until the potatoes and eggs were done boiling.

My bestie knew all too well I needed a tactile project to keep me occupied.

I adored her.

As I loaded in a bunch of songs, mostly ones from our college years, a nostalgic smile crossed my face. I reveled in the memories that surfaced of the pair of us dancing and laughing while the music played in the background.

"Alright, come peel," Addison called, dragging me from my reverie.

"How many?" I stared at the massive mixing bowl full of eggs.

"All of them."

"Seriously? There are three dozen eggs here, Ads. How much potato salad are you making, exactly? We only have so many people coming over, you know. Are you sure you want me to peel this many?"

She lifted an eyebrow, hip checking me. There was limited counter space in her little kitchen, but we'd made do with less plenty of times.

"*All* of them. I need some for the potato salad. I'm also making Angel Eggs."

I paused, a warm egg clutched in my fingers. "You are?"

"I am." Her smirk was adorable. She picked up a small jar of capers, motioning with it to the dill growing from a tiny pot in her window.

Addison's special twist on Deviled Eggs was one of my favorite snacks. No matter how hard I tried, I could never make them like she did. She'd invented them one afternoon in our dorm room and we'd never made them any other way since.

"I fucking *love* you."

Her mouth quirked up. "I know. Hey! Not so tight!" She choked on a laugh, accepting my very enthusiastic, if graceless, hug.

Once I released her, I happily peeled eggs until my fingertips were sore from sharp shell edges while she diced potatoes. Addison was preparing the largest batch of potato salad I'd ever seen outside of a restaurant kitchen, but I wasn't about to complain.

"Alright. Swap?"

"Sure." I dried my hands on one of her tea towels, tossing it over my shoulder when I was done for later use.

"You, my feral friend, look downright domestic." She grinned at me.

"Shush."

Sunlight streamed in the windows, how much I'd missed this pressing on my heart. Moments like these were everything I'd been lacking while I lived away from my best friend. Silly trips to the store, bumping into one another in the kitchen, kidding around, and trading insults.

It was damn good to be home.

THERE WAS NOTHING the Greene brothers weren't good at, apparently.

After Addison put the finishing touches on my Angel Eggs, we stashed everything in an ancient fridge down in the garage. While we discussed the merits of disposable tablecloths and folding chairs, Dennis backed down the long driveway in his massive black pickup truck. He was hauling coolers full of meat, plus a shiny new grill to cook it all on.

"Damn, girl. Pretty truck-and-shovel guy sure does have all the bases covered."

Addison giggled, a bashful expression on her face. I loved seeing her in love with such a genuine, good man.

"How long are you going to call him that?"

I raised an eyebrow at her, playful indignation setting in.

"Why would there be a time limit to calling him that? It's who he *is*." It would always be, at least in my mind.

Addison's former fiancé had left her the day of their wedding. Dennis had been his best man. He'd been sure to inform me of his usefulness that day by not only disowning the defective groom, but also offering use of his truck and shovel should I need them. In the end, I avoided murdering the runaway groom, though the knowledge Dennis possessed the tools to help me out if I snapped had endeared him to me. Well, and how he came to adore Addison, of course.

"You could call him by his *name*," Addison argued with a grin.

"Ugh. Fine." I got a sharp elbow in the ribs for my attitude. "Hey!"

"You deserved it and you know it."

I shrugged, earning me a hearty dose of hairy eyeball from my best friend.

Without waiting for direction, Dennis lowered the tail-gate. He slid the large coolers down the bed, lifting them out by himself with a simple flex of tanned forearms.

"Hey, you." Addison approached him with a bright grin.

"Hey." He dipped down for a kiss while I politely glanced away.

Once they separated, I joked, "Truck, shovel, and now grill? You're the most well-equipped man I've ever met." I winked at Addison. "Or so I hear."

"Oh, my God." Addison blushed bright red, too amused to resist giggling, though I could tell she wanted to be frustrated with me. I was, and always had been, the inappropriate friend. There shouldn't ever be any surprise when I said something outrageous.

Dennis's lips quirked into a smirk. "Always nice to see you, Trina."

I snorted. He was very methodical with the limited words he used, but he was clearly amused. I appreciated his compliment.

"Dallas should be right behind me. Where can I park the truck after we get it unloaded?"

Addison gestured vaguely to the street. "Anywhere is fine. I let the neighbors know what was going on and invited them over for a drink to make any inconvenience up to them."

Southern manners were something else. When I first came to Alabama for college, the politeness had taken me by surprise for a while. Once I'd realized people weren't trying to pull one over on me and were being genuine with their kindness, everything changed. My east-coast mind had been thoroughly blown.

I was betting the neighbors were mostly retirees, like her landlords. Still, they were more than welcome to come over if they wanted. The more the merrier, as far as I was concerned. The guest list, as it stood, was small but mighty. Aside from all the food Addison had prepared, Dennis brought three separate coolers. I was fairly certain we were going to be positively swimming in leftovers. You wouldn't hear any complaints from me about it, though.

As if to prove so, my stomach growled.

"I'm going to start putting out the finger foods," I proclaimed, leaving Dennis and Addison to give one another googly eyes.

"Save some of the Angel Eggs for other people," she warned.

I blew raspberries at my friend with my tongue. "We'll see. You made those for *me*. I am the guest of honor, am I not?"

She shook her finger at me in threat but never broke eye contact with Dennis. They were disgustingly happy. It simultaneously thrilled me for her and grossed me out a little. It also made me feel a kind of longing I hadn't known was inside me. I was quick to push this particular sensation as far down as I could.

Addison transformed as many things as possible into a flat surface inside the garage. There was a door on top of sawhorses with a plastic cover for all of the side dishes. The workbench had been cleared off for use as a buffet. The washer and dryer got covered in old towels with giant plastic tubs as a station for used dishes. Folding chairs lined one wall, ready for duty. An assortment of card tables had been borrowed to be set up as needed.

My bestie was freaking *good* at this.

I dumped bags of chips into plastic bowls in a rainbow of colors, snacking as I went.

As Dennis predicted, his brother, Dallas, rolled into the driveway a couple of minutes later on his motorcycle. Parking off to the side, he dismounted with a smooth glide, stashing his helmet and jacket in one of the saddlebags.

It was impossible not to see the resemblance in their features, though Dallas immediately struck me as much more easy-going than his older brother. His plain jeans and t-shirt were much better fitted to his body than anything I could ever hope to own, his easy smile hard not to respond to. In another reality, he might be just my type.

"Welcome home." He grinned, catching me staring.

"Thanks."

He approached me with a hand extended. "I'm Dallas."

"Trina."

"So, you're the bar I've been held to."

"Sorry?" I pulled my hand back after he shook it.

"Addison and I are friends. But you're the *best* friend." He cocked his head off to the side, his blue eyes sparkled as he took me in. "You set a high bar."

"Ah." Flattered, I cocked my hip and put my hand on it. "Well, a girl needs standards. Thanks for coming."

"The pleasure is all mine."

Dallas left me to help his brother offload the grill from the bed of his truck and retrieve a stunning amount of liquor from the back seat.

I caught myself staring for a second time while he paused mid-stride, frowning at something on his phone. I forced myself to find a task to complete before he caught me watching. Again.

I wasn't after a man, especially not one that had complicated ties to my best friend. Nothing was holding me back from looking though, and Greene men's asses in tight jeans were pretty epic to stare at.

It was going to be a great day.

CHAPTER SIX

Dallas

"YOU SHOULD TRY one of these," Trina said, shoving a platter full of hard-boiled eggs in my direction.

Not long after I'd arrived, Dennis lit the grill and started cooking. Other guests began to arrive as he cooked his first batch of meat, so I made myself useful by putting drinks into the coolers. My brother diverted me away from the grill when I wandered toward him, asking me to find him some aluminum foil. Addison already had it covered though, so I'd ended up in the garage where Trina was organizing side dishes.

"Angel Eggs?" I recognized Addison's handiwork, happily taking one and dropping it into my mouth. After I'd chewed the tangy treat, I said, "They're great." They were also a welcome distraction after the strange text from an unknown number that made my gut churn.

Trina's dark, almond-shaped eyes were wide as she gave an exaggerated gasp, clutching at invisible pearls. "She made my eggs for you?"

A chuckle rumbled in my throat after I swallowed the egg half. Her horror was only half pretend, I realized. "Sorry. Should I have kept that information to myself? I didn't realize they were proprietary. I can always start over and fake surprise at how delicious they are. Want me to?"

She sagged a bit, waving her hand. "Nah, cat's out of the bag now, so no point. I appreciate the offer though." Her lips wore a playful smile. "What did she make them for? The last time you ate them, I mean."

"She brought them over to my folks' house for brunch a while back."

Trina tapped at her full bottom lip with a fingertip. "I'll allow it."

"Thank goodness." I swiped at my brow with the back of my hand in exaggerated relief before taking another egg. I winked at her as I bit into it, making her snort a sharp laugh.

"Addison told me we'd get along." She sounded mildly surprised. Her hand strayed to her short, spiky hair, shifting a few curls around her face.

I reached for a clean plate, the eggs having stirred my appetite.

"She told me we were two peas in a pod," I agreed, adding a few more eggs onto the plate before moving down the line to an assortment of chips. Past those, there were foil containers with the cooked meat.

"Huh." Trina prepared a bun with lettuce and tomatoes for her burger, one eyebrow raised the whole time. She looked across the driveway to where Addison was keeping Dennis company at the grill. I followed her gaze.

My brother was maneuvering the remaining meat across the fire with oversized tongs as Addison gestured with her hands, laughing as she told a story.

"They're pretty disgusting, aren't they?" Trina's grin took the sting out of the insult.

"Definitely." Plate in hand, I followed her to one of the tables. "Well then, fellow pea, what is it you do for work?"

"Graphic and web design. For marketing purposes, mostly."

"Sounds… complicated."

"I've been doing it so long it doesn't feel that way, but I suppose. What part of things do you run at the foundation?"

"Mostly I'm the warehouse manager. I'm still taking care of the website too." I dipped in for a bite of my burger as she nodded.

"Sounds like it's doing well?"

"We've had a couple of good years."

"Addison almost didn't apply." Trina tossed a chip in her mouth, shaking her head as if still frustrated with her friend over it.

"She mentioned it. Thanks for twisting her arm."

Trina shrugged as she chewed. "Wasn't too hard. She was pretty stuck after…" Her thoughtful gaze met mine, and even though she didn't say it, I knew what she was referring to. Being left at the altar by your fiancé for your own sister would be enough to derail anyone's life track. "I was super happy to find her this cute apartment. I knew she'd find a job one way or another."

"This place was a hidden gem. While I was apartment hunting, I realized pretty fast I could either have what I was looking for or what I could afford, but not both."

"Oh my God, same." Her forearms hit the tabletop, illustrating her exasperation. "I'm having the worst luck right now. Did you find a place, then?"

I nodded, goosebumps of awareness tingling across my arms. "I did. It's more than I need, but I love it."

"Think some happy housing thoughts my way, if you don't mind. My company has me put up in a motel for now. I'd love to find something permanent sooner rather than later, though."

"Sure thing." I didn't know her well, but I got the feeling we were fairly compatible as far as personalities went. I filed the information away, knowing I was headed for some roommate interviews I didn't want to do. If I had someone in my back pocket as a possibility, it wouldn't be a bad thing.

Dennis was calling my name, gesturing with a platter stacked with meat. I inferred he wanted my help to shuttle another round of food from the grill to the garage. Who was going to eat it all was the million-dollar question.

"Nice talking to you, Dallas." Trina smiled at me as

she straightened the skirt on her short sundress. "Thanks for joining me."

"My pleasure, Trina." I tossed her a wink out of habit. She laughed at me while shaking her head.

"You boys just can't control it, can you?" She dumped our dirty plates in a large trash bin, sundress flouncing around her body as she moved. It was a great dress.

"What's that?" I asked, pausing outside the garage door.

"Your charm. Is it DNA encoded?" She propped a hand on her hip, sass abounding.

"You bet." I winked again, exaggerating it for humor value.

"Ridiculous." Her bright chuckle followed her as she made her way to one of the drink coolers.

"Don't start," I warned Dennis, seeing the question written on his face as I joined him at the grill.

"She's single."

I kept my face impassive as I stared at him.

Unfazed, my brother shrugged. "Just saying."

My dating preferences ran more male than female, but I didn't discount anyone based on gender; I was equal opportunity in that regard. Attractive is attractive. If I have chemistry with someone, I'm open to giving things a shot. Regardless, I wasn't looking for anything at all at the moment, serious or otherwise.

"Not a priority right now," I told my brother. "Besides, what if we hooked up and it didn't work out? It would be awkward for everyone."

Dennis grunted, indicating he was finished with the conversation, but my point was taken. I took the platter of meat to the garage, shaking my head.

She was definitely pretty, but that was not a road I needed to go down any time soon. I couldn't even manage an occasional casual hookup very well. It probably didn't help that I'd been living with my parents.

As the day faded into evening, some of the neighbors joined the celebration. Plenty of the food was getting eaten, much to Addison's relief. The sheer size of the potato salad container had stunned me when I'd first seen it.

Trina was loosening up quite a bit, thanks to a couple of cocktails. She was dancing her way between small clusters of people, her smile broad, her bright tropical-themed cup perpetually full.

More than once, she'd hugged Addison, a progressively slurry, "I love you, bitch!" falling from her lips.

I could relate to the relief of having returned home, which honestly surprised me. I found myself enamored by the amusing antics of Addison's pixie-like friend from the sidelines while she enjoyed her party.

"She's fine," Addison assured me, both of us watching Trina gyrate to the music all by herself near a portable fire pit. It was getting late, and the crowd had thinned. Trina's petite body swayed to the rhythm, her head thrown back, eyes closed.

"She's happy to be back, I take it?"

Addison snorted. "What gave it away? Her telling every-one—*loudly*—at least a dozen times?"

"Something like that." I'd been nursing the same warm beer for more than an hour, and it was finally empty. "Need a drink?"

"No, thanks." Addison glanced around, lips lifting when she found my brother leaning up against the edge of the garage, not far from where Trina was dancing. I noticed his attention was split between his girlfriend and Trina since the grilling was done.

"Let me know when you're ready to shut it down for the night. I'll be happy to bounce people right out of your driveway." I was smaller than my brother but very capable of what I was offering.

Her hazel eyes landed on mine. "I appreciate it. Pretty sure we're good for now. Do you think the fire is enough? It's cooling down…" She surveyed the remaining crowd before allowing her eyes to drift to my brother again, a dreamy expression on her face. To his credit, he wasn't glaring daggers at me, even though I was the one standing at her side instead of him. His jealousy had been a big obstacle not too long ago, though he'd made big strides thanks to Addison's saintly patience.

"Got sleeping bags or blankets?"

"Sure, plenty. Should I grab some?"

I gestured to the garage. "If you leave a pile somewhere, people will use what they need."

"I think you're right." Addison shifted back into hostess mode, gesturing for me to follow her.

She stacked my arms with a mountain of blankets and sleeping bags.

"That'll do it."

We deposited them on the folding chairs arranged near the fire pit. She patted my arm in appreciation before heading in my brother's direction. His eyes were laser-focused on us. I gave him a one-fingered salute that tightened his mouth before making it lift in a grin.

Seeing half of the altercation, she glanced over her shoulder, catching me in the act.

"The two of you, I swear." Her laugh was carried away on the breeze as she went to him.

"Sorry!" I called out in apology.

She shook her head. Dennis, on the other hand, skewered me with an annoyed stare after she was close enough for him to pull into his arms.

Pushing my big brother's buttons would never, ever get old.

I lost track of them both for a while when I went back for another plate of food. When I got back to my post near the fire, I saw Dennis slowly lead Addison up the stairs to her place by the hand.

The sound was faint, but I heard her protest, "I shouldn't leave a party I'm hosting." Dennis leaned in toward her ear and said something. Addison complained, "Trina's supposed to crash on my couch. Not sure how that'll work if…" her embarrassment was obvious, though positively adorable.

Dennis looked over her shoulder, locking eyes with me. The idea of where they were headed and why made my guts clench, but I could take care of things while they were gone. I raised a hand, signaling to him that I had things under control.

He dipped low again, whatever he said convincing her it was fine. She glanced back a couple of times as they climbed the stairs, but didn't stop.

Trina joined me with a few friends near the fire, but it wasn't long before they started to drift away from the party toward their beds.

"C'mon, handsome. You owe me a dance." Trina reached out a hand.

My body flared with surprise. "I do?"

Her playful smile was impossible to resist. I accepted her hand, realizing all too quickly I should have put more effort into getting myself up instead of allowing her to pull me. She overbalanced and, to save us from landing flat on the pavement, I had to wrap my arms around her and twist. I took the brunt of the blow by landing on my ass, Trina sprawled across my lap in a straddle.

"Oops." Trina's laugh was a high-pitched giggle. "Sorry."

She wiggled and slid across my body in her efforts to get up. I was forced to sit for a long moment once she was on her feet, because my body didn't discriminate over where the caress was coming from; it just appreciated being touched.

"Can I still have my dance, please?"

"Yes, ma'am." I took a deep breath before climbing to my feet, dusting off my hands before taking hers in them.

The music was much more subdued thanks to the late hour, so I swayed with Trina in my arms, her floral scent filling my nostrils as she leaned her head on my chest. My body was sending out signals for either lust or distress; I wasn't sure quite yet. She smelled nice and felt good under my hands, but it was just a dance.

I repeated those words to myself a number of times.

"You're a good dancer, Dallas."

"Thanks, you are too." I spun her away from me then back again, her steps graceful despite her intoxication.

As the song ended, she gave me another bright smile and then dropped a kiss on my cheek.

"Appreciated, sir."

"The honor is mine. Need a drink?"

"I got it. Thanks though." She skipped toward the coolers, saying goodbye to a few guests on her way there and back.

The party was pretty much over shortly thereafter, and I was left with Trina near the fire pit in the quiet. She was clearly on the drowsy side of drunk.

"Where'd my bestie go?" Trina glanced around for Addison. "I haven't seen her in a while."

"I… I think she had an appointment." I smirked, handing her one of the fleece blankets.

She pulled herself out of the low-slung chair she'd been occupying so she could wrap it around herself before sitting back down.

Her deep exhale ended in a grunt as she leaned back against the chair, groaning, "My buzz is fading. That sucks." Her face screwed up in confusion. "Wait, an appointment? Who has an appointment this time of night on a Friday?"

I stared at her meaningfully, understanding slowly dawning on her face.

"Ohhh. A dick appointment. Got it. Good for her! She deserves it." She blew out a hearty sigh. "I wouldn't mind having one of those myself. *I* deserve it too."

The measured up-and-down assessment she gave me with her eyes made me throw up my hands in a defensive pose.

"I don't doubt it, but I'm afraid I can't help you."

She waved a hand, as though dismissing the thought altogether. "Thanks for the blanket."

I laughed at the way her thoughts bounced from one place to another. "You're welcome. Do you need some water?"

She nodded, pulling the edges of the blanket tighter across her bare legs. "That would be great, thanks. As much as I'd enjoy another cocktail, I'll probably get the spins if I drink more. I don't want to puke on you."

"I don't want that either, so I appreciate your choice."

I grabbed us both a couple of bottles from the cooler. After a while, some people stopped by to tell us they were leaving and I realized we were alone.

"Did you have a good time?" she asked, voice low as she propped her head in her hand.

"I did. Thanks for inviting me."

"You're welcome. It's Ads you should thank. She's the best." Her heavy breath told me she was going to blink out before too long.

"She's pretty great."

The quiet embraced us as the flames entertained us.

I recalled similar situations throughout the years in my parents' backyard. There were plenty of times we'd all crashed in sleeping bags under the stars after drinking too much or watching movies projected onto a sheet or the wall. Backyard camping was one of my favorite pastimes, and I hadn't done it in all the years since I'd left. Remembering a thing I'd loved so much warmed my chest with a very particular kind of calm.

Trina started laughing when she spotted Dennis and Addison rounding the bottom of the stairs, the raucous sound breaking the silence of the night.

Addison turned ten shades of red, her mortification visible even in the dark. My brother said nothing, just maintained a neutral expression as he cleaned things up.

I got to my feet so I could help him, gesturing for Addison to sit.

"Sorry," I heard Addison apologize as I strode toward the garage.

"Sorry? Hell no, you get it, bestie. I'm only a little bit jealous. It was my party after all—if anyone should have gotten some, it should have been me. But I'm still glad *someone* got lucky. Bonus points because it was you!" Trina's laugh carried on the night breeze as Addison took her up to the apartment.

I started putting all the leftover food into the garage fridge while my brother bagged up trash.

"Not a word," he warned, making eye contact as we crossed paths.

I held back a laugh. "I didn't say a thing."

As far as welcome home barbeques went, this had been a good one, right up to the very end.

CHAPTER SEVEN

Trina

GETTING CALLED INTO a private meeting with management less than two weeks after transferring to a new location was sure to raise anyone's blood pressure.

It took the rest of the weekend for my body to fully recover from my welcome home party, but I'd gone to work on Monday full of determination. Sasha would be visiting the Birmingham location for the week, thanks to the merger that had allowed me to move back, and I knew I needed to be on my toes.

I could only hope the amount of time between *the incident* and now would make things slightly less awkward. It was one thing to be polite via occasional email. In-person interaction was a whole different beast.

The summons to the conference room put me on high alert, and for good reason. It immediately went ass over teakettle, as my father was fond of saying.

My boss and a pasty older gentleman were waiting for me with a stack of papers between them. Incredibly, there was also Jesse, sitting a seat over from Sasha, tidy in a suit that probably cost a fortune.

"Thanks for coming so promptly," Sasha said, giving me a twisted smile that made my blood run cold. "This is the Bronson district supervisor, Mr. Franklin. This is our new CEO." She made a graceful gesture in Jesse's direction.

"Jesse Bronson, pleasure to meet you." He held out a hand.

My heart plummeted to my toes before rebounding into my throat. Mr. no-strings-hookup had been keeping some big secrets. Not that we'd talked about anything at all, but *yikes*. This was far messier than I thought.

"Nice to meet you." I shook out of shocked reflex.

The suit took over talking, spouting a bunch of words that sounded like they came directly out of a jargon thesaurus.

My boss, bored with his droning, interrupted.

"Thank you, Henry." She linked her fingers together on the tabletop, making the very large diamond on her finger wink under the fluorescent lights.

I choked on my own saliva, managing to turn it into a discrete cough. So Jesse had *really* apologized after stepping out on her, it would appear. The whole situation made me feel sick to my stomach.

"Trina, I'm afraid we have to let you go."

Sasha's words were English, I was sure of it, though they didn't make any sense.

"I'm sorry?" The words sounded muffled in my ears as my blood started to pound.

"The decision came from above me, Trina. You've been a great asset to the company, but with the acquisition by Bronson and the merger…" she trailed off, looking at the man seated beside her. Jesse wore an apologetic expression as he shifted uncomfortably in his seat.

Mr. Franklin, on the other hand, wore an expression so bland it was inscrutable. I'd wager he didn't give a single damn one way or the other because he didn't know me. He could have been any middle-aged white dude in a suit as far as I was concerned, and I was just another name on his list of people to fire.

"There are a significant number of redundant positions. Unfortunately, yours happens to be one of them," Sasha added.

"I'm *redundant*?" The words were meant to be cutting, I was certain. I also knew she felt there was a good reason to be smug about this development, but I was a damn good employee and one of her most talented designers. "You very recently transferred me back here. There isn't even a comparable department on the Bronson side as far as I'm aware. Is that correct?"

The pasty Mr. Franklin cleared his throat. He reminded me of a pufferfish with his beady black eyes and wobbly jowls.

"The fact remains your position no longer exists. It's been eliminated."

My boss' mouth broadened. I was guessing the word tasted as sweet in her mouth as it did sour in mine.

"You're of course also being offered a severance package for your years of service." The bloated suit handed me a folder, and I skimmed through the contents.

The numbers on the paperwork inside were not impressive. The money they were offering would only get me so far. Things like filing for unemployment and paying for extensions on my health insurance floated through my thoughts.

"Effective when?"

My boss unlaced her fingers, once again purposefully drawing attention to the rock on her hand.

"You'll need to collect your things when we're done with this meeting."

Pulse racing, bile rose in my throat. "I've got half a dozen projects I'm in the middle of. Surely I could have a few days to wrap things up—"

Mr. Franklin interrupted me. "We'll take care of all those details, no need for concern." His condescension disguised as comforting words burned. "Please be sure to read over the client confidentiality portion of your exit paperwork carefully."

My boss kept her stare on me, the feral grin starting to creep me out.

"I'm sure Ms. Lee is well aware poaching clients is illegal."

I wondered if she would also be shown the door after they'd made her do the dirty work of firing her employees. This guy was something else, and I'd bet Sasha would never see it coming, especially since she was in bed—literally—with the new CEO.

"Yes, I'm aware of the fact that both my artwork and the clients I was creating the projects for belong to the company. Recruiting them once I leave is against the rules." My thoughts were muddled. Thankfully, my organizational drive took over. "I just moved back from Memphis. I'm staying at the Home Lodge until I can find a permanent residence. Per the transfer agreement, the company was paying for it through at least the end of this month. Does that stand?"

His mouth narrowed. "Unfortunately, the transfer agreement is voided by the separation paperwork. We apologize for any inconvenience. You're paid through..." he flipped through a set of documents. "Friday. I'm sure they would be happy to extend your stay, though Bronson will not be responsible for the cost. We wish you the best in finding a permanent residence."

"How thoughtful," I muttered, numbness beginning to seep into my veins. "Especially considering a lack of stable employment is problematic when trying to sign a leasing contract."

His caterpillar eyebrow lifted a fraction. I forced a deep, slow breath, stifling any other thoughts that might get me into trouble.

"If you accept the package, we need you to sign off, Trina," Sasha nudged the paperwork toward me.

I blinked at her, trying to see through my rage.

"If I don't accept?" I met the steely blue gaze of the district supervisor.

"We are not prepared to make a counter offer at this time. Either you accept or you decline. Either way, you are no longer an employee of Bronson."

"Of course." The stabbing sensation in my chest intensified. It dawned on me after a painful beat it was my heart breaking. I *loved* my job. I was damn good at it. I'd interned with the company fresh out of college, so it had been my only full-time, adult job. Now, through no fault of my own, it was suddenly over. The unfairness of it all stung.

With a pen the supervisor offered me, I signed the papers with a shaky hand. When I tried to give the pen back, he held up his meaty palm as though warding it off. As though I, a mere peasant, were contaminated.

"You can keep it."

"Gee, thanks."

His eyes narrowed once more at my thick sarcasm. I was visualizing jamming the disposable ballpoint into his eyeball clear up to the printed Bronson logo.

As Sasha and the supervisor got to their feet, I stood, recognizing the dismissal.

"Someone in HR will be in touch by phone to conduct an exit interview. A member of security is waiting to escort you to your desk. You have half an hour to collect your things."

"Is this really necessary?" My tone held a sharp bite. I made the mistake of making eye contact with Sasha, who seemed incredibly satisfied with herself.

I met Jesse's apologetic eye for a brief moment. There was no doubt in my mind Sasha was behind this whole situation.

"It's standard procedure, Ms. Lee." The way the suit regarded me led me to believe he thought I wasn't above stealing something.

I yanked the heavy conference room door open. There was indeed a member of the security team there, ready to walk with me to my cubicle.

"Hi, Ron."

"Hey, Ms. Trina." He lowered his head, a hot blush forming on the dark brown hue of his skin.

I always made it a point to get to know the security staff where I worked. Ron was on the day shift and I'd said good morning to him each of the seven days I'd come to work at this building.

"Been a busy day?"

He shook his head, eyes downcast. "No ma'am, not for me. You're my first escort."

"Mmm." I stomped a little harder than necessary down the short hall. I hoped the frustrated clack of my heels told everyone in their drab little gray cubicles exactly what was happening.

Calling someone in at ten on a Tuesday morning to fire them, *after* making them attend the most boring project meeting on the planet, was downright cruel.

There was a single white banker's box waiting for me on my desk chair. Ron clasped his fingers behind his back, standing right outside the doorway of my cube, facing away from me.

Emotions surged as I filled my single, sad little box. I'd just brought my things in a few weeks ago, so packing up wasn't much of an undertaking. It wasn't difficult, but it burned.

My main complaint was the half-finished art files I was forced to abandon. They were *mine*, even though they technically belonged to the company and my—*their*—clients.

I wiggled the computer mouse to wake up the screen, briefly surprised when my password didn't work. Anger trailed shortly after the shock.

"They work really fucking *fast*, don't they?" I grumbled, glancing at Ron, who was embarrassed at having to be party to my removal. He didn't say a word, as he glanced at me over his shoulder, just nodded softly.

As quickly as I could, I shoved my personal effects into the box. I grabbed all the thumb drives in my drawer, unsure of which ones were new and which had artwork stored on them. I flipped through the items in my file cabinet, deciding I'd probably get in trouble for taking anything.

In the end, my box was still half-empty, and my rage had settled into cold heartache.

"I'm done," I grumbled, picking up the box.

Ron gave a short nod before leading me on the most epic walk of shame back through the office. My face burned the whole time. I'd done absolutely nothing wrong, yet here I was, with my box of things, being led out by security as though I were a criminal. He gave me an empathetic look as we rode down in the elevator together.

Sasha was waiting for us in the lobby, clinging to the arm of her new fiancé. Jesse's embarrassment matched her smugness.

Ron's eyebrows drew together, but he let Sasha approach. His intense gaze indicated he wasn't moving. He crossed his arms, widening his stance as he waited for us to chat.

"I'm sorry it came to this, Trina."

"I'd love to believe you, Sasha." There was no disguising the heat in my tone.

"Despite our personal differences, you are genuinely talented." She gave the compliment begrudgingly.

"Damn right, I am."

Sasha's eyebrows went straight up and Jesse stifled a laugh. I knew my worth. I'd be damned if I was going to downplay it, especially after losing my job.

"You managed to get me home, and I'm beyond grateful. No matter what else might have happened." I should have stopped there, but I couldn't help myself. "Congratulations, by the way." I turned my eyes to Jesse. "I'm sure she'll make you as happy as you both deserve."

They gaped at me, Jesse in amusement, Sasha in indignation. My money was on her getting dumped *and* fired before the month was out.

I met Ron's dark eyes. "I'm ready if you are."

"Yes, ma'am."

He took me all the way out to the parking lot, waiting until I was in the driver's seat of my car to go back inside.

Lucky for us both, I managed to contain my breakdown until he was safely on the other side of the lobby doors.

Once unleashed, my emotions bounced from rage to despair before veering to betrayal. It took me ten solid minutes to compose myself enough to be able to drive.

Addison was naturally my first phone call, but I got her voicemail.

"Those assholes *fired* me today! Can you believe it? I need a fucking drink. Call me when you get this, okay? This tea is hot and messy."

I made record time getting back to my motel, shucking out of my work clothes the moment I was safely inside as though they were on fire. I showered for the second time that morning before putting on my cozies.

It wasn't even lunchtime, and I was ready for bed.

As a pity-party extravagance, I ordered delivery from a nearby deli before powering up my laptop. While I waited for my food, I simultaneously searched for apartments and job openings, unsure how exactly everything in my life had fallen together so perfectly then completely apart all in the same month.

Not long after my food was delivered, Addison called me back.

"They fired you? What the hell! Why?" she asked, not even bothering with a greeting.

"They're blaming the merger. I know better, though. My boss had a brand-new gaudy rock on her finger and Jesse is the Bronson CEO."

"Wait. Jesse? Who's Jesse?"

"My MatchMaker hookup."

"Sasha's boyfriend—fiancé, whatever—is the *Bronson CEO*?" Horror suffused my best friend's tone.

"Yep. Convenient, right?"

"Oh, my God. She had to be looking for a reason to get you out, right?"

"Right? They said my position was *redundant*. There isn't even a comparable department on the Bronson side, but whatever."

"Aw, Trin. I'm so sorry! That's nuts. Want me to come over after work?"

I scrolled through some job listings, glancing around my sad little hotel room before responding.

"Oh, that's the other thing. They're not footing the bill for this place past Friday. If I want to keep staying here, I'm responsible for the bill. Can you believe it? Double. Freaking. Whammy. Anyway, this place is depressing, I don't want to be here any more than I have to be. Want to go out?"

"I could go with you for a drink or two. Do you want to just come to my place? The drinks are way cheaper. You know you can stay here, don't worry about it."

I mulled over the options as I chewed a bite of my antipasto salad. Addison took my silence as an opportunity to decide for me.

"Come over around five-thirty. We'll have pizza and champagne to celebrate your unexpected freedom from corporate restraints."

I couldn't help but laugh at her. I would bet ever since her failed wedding, she'd been waiting for a chance to help me as I'd helped her. Champagne was now known as cham*pain* between us because of how badly the hangover hurt after we'd overdone it. Junk food and rom-coms on repeat with periodical walks to sweat out the booze were the prescription of choice.

"Don't you have work in the morning? We can put it off until the weekend."

She *tsk*ed at me. "I'm disappointed in you. Did you forget I'm sleeping with the boss? I can work from home, Dennis doesn't care. Dallas can hold the fort down at G4 on his own."

The fact she was joking about her intimate relationship with a man who was also technically her manager told me she'd come a long way in a short amount of time. It hadn't been too long since they were both using that as the reason they needed to keep their distance.

Addison sighed at my hesitation.

"Get your ass over here in time for pizza."

"Yes, ma'am." I laughed so I didn't start to cry.

"I love you," she said sympathetically. "I'm so sorry this happened, but I'm sure there's a good reason. Something awesome is waiting on the other side."

My friend, the optimist.

"Love you too, Ads. I'll see you later."

I hung up, still stressed, but I at least had something to look forward to. Time spent laughing with my bestie over cocktails and snacks was the best kind of therapy.

CHAPTER EIGHT

Trina

"**I** WANTED TO SLAP Mr. Franklin right across his smug, pasty face." An errant black olive flew across the room as I bounced on Addison's loveseat, reliving my irritating dismissal from the dour district manager.

"He sounds like a whole bucket of laughs." She frowned as she handed me a paper towel.

I hunted down the olive and tossed it into the pile of trash we'd formed on Addison's coffee table.

"I'm so frustrated. I *loved* my job. It's not *my* fault Jesse's a cheating turd. I just *know* Sasha manipulated him into proposing. They deserve each other, I guess." I dropped the remaining half slice of pizza onto my plate, wiping my hands and my teary eyes with the paper towel. "I didn't even get to finish my projects. They locked me out of my computer before kicking my ass out the door."

"You rocked your job. I'm so sorry, bestie." Addison pulled me in for a side hug.

She'd handed me a very strong rum drink the second I came through the door, and I was currently working through my second one. The buzz I was riding left me warm but still coherent. Anger was the emotion making itself known at the moment, though it was subject to change at the drop of an olive.

"There's no way Sasha will give me good references, either. This complicates everything."

"We'll figure it out. You'll have your severance, and you can file unemployment if nothing works out right away. I know you too well to think you don't have savings on top of that, even if you don't want to touch them. There's bound to be an apartment out there for you. Did you talk to Stacey? Do her parents know anyone else like the Clarks?"

I slumped back, narrowly avoiding sloshing my drink onto my shirt. It appeared I was more buzzed than I'd thought.

Addison's landlords had been a lucky lead from another friend. There wasn't any of the same good fortune for me to grab, unfortunately.

"No, she didn't have any more leads. She said she'd check around, though. Being unemployed is a *problem* when trying to sign a new lease."

"I know all about that, trust me. We'll get it figured out. I know you don't want to camp out with me, because of your pride and all. It's always an option, though."

She patted my shoulder as she got up to put away our leftovers.

"I know and I love you for offering. But this love seat is absolute shit for sleeping. Besides, Dennis might get jealous if I spend too many nights in bed with his girlfriend."

Addison chuckled, tossing a grin at me over her shoulder. "Pretty sure he'd understand. He'd probably either offer up his place or try to convince me to stay with him after a while, but he'd get it. I'd make sure of it."

She returned from the little kitchen with her hands full.

"Rocky Road or Moose Tracks?"

"Impossible choice. Halvsies?"

Addison nodded, handing me one of the pints of ice cream and a spoon. She turned on *Legally Blonde*, my traditional cheer-me-up movie.

"You're the best," I mumbled over a bite, trading her ice cream containers.

"What, like it's hard?" she teased, tossing out one of Elle's best lines. "It's just pizza and ice cream. It's the least I can do."

I rolled my eyes at her self-deprecation, though I appreciated the reference.

We traded every few bites until the petite buckets of sugary cream were empty while watching a movie we'd seen at least a dozen times over the years.

When it ended, I slumped into the seat, feeling wrung out.

"I feel like I just went through a terrible break-up," I complained. "Which is awful, because while they definitely fucked me, I one hundred percent didn't enjoy it."

Addison barked a laugh. "That's kind of what happened, though. You lost the most consistent, longest relationship of your entire life."

I hadn't thought about it quite that way, but she was right. Sasha and some of my coworkers were part of my life every single day for years. I saw them way more than I saw my family or even my friends. Aside from Addison, I didn't have anyone else in my life who met such criteria. Certainly, nobody I'd ever dated.

"That's really sad," I mumbled, suddenly feeling much worse. The food settled heavily in my gut.

Addison patted my leg. "It is. You're allowed to mourn the loss of it, Trin. You're a badass who takes control nearly all the time, but you're still allowed to be sad sometimes. It's okay to need some help."

She reached over, taking my hand in hers. The gentle support she was offering proved too much for my fragile emotions and I started to sob.

"Oh, shit," I swore, frantically swiping at my tears.

"Let it out!" Addison laughed lightly, knowing I was mortified that my emotions were on the outside of my body. This wasn't how I normally operated, at least not with the darker, serious feelings. "Nobody here to see you except me. You need this."

I did. I didn't want it, but I needed it. I loathed crying.

For the next thirty minutes, Addison held my hand and hugged me as I let out all my frustration and sadness at the abrupt shift of my life's path.

When I was done, I felt completely drained. My eyes were red and swollen, my head pounding from crying.

"Go take a shower. You'll feel better."

It was getting late, but I knew she was right. Buzz fading, I gathered up my sleepwear and carried it to her bathroom, letting the steam melt away my stress before alternating for cold water to take away the puffiness.

All the lights were off in the main room when I came out, so I went into Addison's room.

"Feel better?" she asked, looking up from her phone.

"Much, thanks."

Her arm swept over the bed in a flourish.

"Your accommodations for the evening," she said. "Not fancy, but it's comfortable."

"I'm so excited." I sighed, exhaustion heavy in my bones. "My motel bed is absolutely terrible."

"Take these first." Addison thrust a couple of ibuprofen and a bottle of water into my hands.

"Yes, ma'am." She raised a threatening eyebrow at my sarcasm. Payback was a bitch. She was just doing for me what I'd done for her after her breakup. "I know you're doing this out of love—"

"Damn right."

"—but it doesn't mean I have to like it." I loved it.

"Shut up and let me take care of you."

I dutifully followed her instructions, swallowing the pills with plenty of water before plugging in my phone next to the bed.

"What now?"

"You're already in my bed," she teased, turning off the overhead light. "What more do you want?"

We were suddenly in rich darkness, the inky blackness cut only by a few slivers of moonlight peeking through the curtains.

"Ooh baby, ooh baby," I replied, totally monotone. "Should we prank Mr. truck-and-shovel?"

Addison shrugged, holding her phone up above us and taking a picture of our faces smiling at the camera, heads touching on her pillows.

She sent the photo to him via text, immediately getting a response.

"He says, 'have fun'."

"That's it?" I was impressed. No pervy commentary, no jealousy. "Damn girl. He's a good one."

Her grin was wide and filled me with warm joy for her happiness. "I know."

"Aww. Gross." I got a fluffy pillow to my face for my taunt.

Like we'd done a thousand times through the years, we giggled, talking in hushed voices, lying there in the dark.

"Why are we taking turns falling apart right now?" I asked, eyelids heavy as we settled down. I braided swaths of Addison's long hair where it spilled across her pillow.

"Pretty sure it's a thing. Quarter-life crisis?"

"Sounds about right. Everything was finally coming together, though. I had a good job, finally made it back home..." My chest heaved, heavy with a sigh that battled with a yawn for dominance.

Addison snickered. "I was supposed to be getting *married*, remember? Life doesn't care if you make plans. Sometimes everything has to fall apart so it can fall back together the way it's supposed to, you know?"

"I guess." I closed my gritty eyes for a long moment, mulling over her words.

Deep down, I knew she was right. She was the perfect example, even. Just a few short months before, she'd been left at the altar by her fiancé for her sister. Everything looked dismal for a while, especially because she'd canceled her lease and had to rush to find somewhere to live. She'd even decided to quit her job. I helped her get some things sorted out. Now, she was in a better job and stupidly in love with the perfect man for her.

I just couldn't figure out what the universe was pulling me *away* from, never mind pointing me toward. I'd just been treading water for the last few years, working and trying to figure out what exactly I should be doing with my life.

"Oh," I said out loud, realizing I may have just stumbled upon the answer.

"Hmm?"

"Nothing, just thinking how maybe this happened because I need some direction."

"Maybe," Addison said, sounding heavily drowsy. "I just hope the direction isn't away from Birmingham."

"No way. I just got back. I don't want to move again for a long time, but especially not away from home. It would have to be the *perfect* job and tons of money or something to convince me to move away. For now, the only thing I'm moving away from is dating apps. Remind me to delete MatchMaker in the morning."

"You got it." Addison yawned so wide her jaw cracked.

"Me too. G'night, Ads. Thanks for tonight."

"'Night. You're welcome. I'm serious, Trin. We'll figure this out. You don't have to do this alone."

"I know." Knowing I wasn't by myself kept me from breaking down all the way, earlier tears aside.

Addison's slow breaths filled the quiet room as she dropped off to dreamland. I continued to fiddle with the ends of her long hair, using it as a fidget toy. There were few drawbacks to keeping my hair in a tidy pixie cut, but stress twirling was one.

I blinked heavily, sleep pulling me under. She hadn't oversold the comfort of her bed.

One thought allowed me to relax as I started to drift. If I could reassemble her whole life, I could certainly manage mine too.

CHAPTER NINE

CHAPTER NINE

Dallas

ON TUESDAYS, ADDISON and I went to lunch. We'd kept up the traditions since she first started her job at G4, and it was always one of the highlights of my week. It was nice to get out of the office and have some time to talk with my friend.

"Just like that, five years at a job, down the drain. I feel so bad for her." Addison's expression sagged in sympathy as she filled me in on her friend's situation.

Addison was a generally positive person, but I could tell having Trina close enough to see daily brightened her already sunny disposition.

"That's rough. Trina seems nice, I'm sorry about what happened to her."

Addison raised an eyebrow, inviting further explanation. "Nice?"

I elaborated after taking a bite of my sandwich. "She was very welcoming at her party. We had some friendly conversation, and she even persuaded me to dance with her." I paused, my back reminding me all about how I'd twisted to keep us from eating pavement. How she'd felt under my hands was an echo I tried to ignore. "That's about all I know. I'm sorry to hear about her being fired. Sounds like an all-around shitty situation."

"At least she got transferred back here. They were supposed to be sending her to Auburn first, so this was at least one lucky part of the whole situation. Thanks for hanging out by the fire with her." My friend cocked her head to the side, digging for some non-existent dirt all while blushing furiously.

"You were busy. I'm pretty sure you wouldn't have wanted her passed out on your couch with my brother in your bed. Unless you guys are *really* close best friends? No judgment. I'm not sure Dennis would go for it though, he comes across as the completely monogamous, non-voy-euristic type." She wouldn't be the first girl to experiment with her best friend, but her sputtering, emphatic 'NO' in response confirmed my assumption. "I didn't think so. Anyway, it wasn't a big deal. I just kept her company until you could get back. You know, in case of predators, kidnappers, raccoons… other bad things."

"I'm still a little mortified about vanishing, but thanks." She dusted her fingers off, changing the subject. "How are the roommate applications going?"

I groaned, leaning away from my empty plate. "Terrible."

"Sorry to hear it. What's the problem?"

"I thought there were a couple of decent options at first, but everybody I've talked to has some weird requirement I'm not sure I want to deal with."

Addison laughed, stacking our plates before pushing them to the edge of the table so the waitress would bring us our check. "Like what?"

I scrubbed a hand down my face, ticking off the list of oddities I'd encountered so far on my fingers. "One guy wanted to schedule times we used the living room and kitchen. Granted, he offered to pay me higher rent than I was asking. But only being allowed in the main areas of *my* apartment during certain hours of the day, though? No, thanks."

"Yeah, that's weird." Addison's nose wrinkled up at the idea. "What else?"

"Another guy wanted to use the second bedroom plus the office, but not pay any more than if he was only renting the second suite. So, I had to give him a hard pass. The most recent applicant was Kosher. While I don't have any issues with it as a lifestyle requirement, he needed a bunch of things changed in the kitchen so certain things never come into contact and I know I'd fuck it up. I didn't want to make him sick or cross-contaminate his food or whatever, so there was another no."

"Where are you finding these people?" Addison's face was scrunched up in similar disbelief of the audacity I'd encountered.

"Craigslist." I shuddered.

"Well, *there's* your problem." Addison paused to thank the waitress for taking the plates, handing off the company credit card to pay the bill. "There's another option, you know."

"Just suck it up?" I suggested. "Be broke? Never retire and always be beholden to my rotten older brothers? Beg for a raise?" I smiled, knowing exactly where she was headed. I'd been thinking about it myself since the last round of interviews.

"Well, that, or… consider Trina?"

I let out a breath, my arms on the table. I leaned forward, looking Addison fully in the face. "Is she genuinely interested?"

"One way to find out for sure. I know she's super stressed over finding somewhere to go. Her company was originally supposed to cover through the end of the month. After the termination, they won't pay past Friday. Even if she found a place in her budget, not being employed is probably going to get her application rejected and she doesn't want to drop most of her savings paying up front. There don't seem to be any other magical above-garage apartments waiting to be scooped up. I offered her my couch, but you know how tiny my place is. I tried to tell her the other day that we survived our dorm room. She reminded me about how back then we at least had separate beds."

I sat back in the booth, my arm stretched across the back of the seat. It sounded like a great option. Especially after the crazy I'd dealt with so far. "If this is something she's interested in, I'm happy to entertain an interview."

Addison's face lit up with a smile. "How official," she teased. "I'll have her call you."

"You're not at all worried about something terrible happening? What if it doesn't work out between us, and it causes a rift in friendships?" The idea that I could be the wrecking ball that tore apart several good relationships made my chest tighten. It wouldn't be the first time, and it wasn't something I was interested in repeating.

She propped her chin on her hand. "Not really. You guys are a lot alike. I'm pretty confident if things went sideways, you'd be able to have a conversation about it. You'd either work things out or go your separate ways before it became a blowout."

Her confidence was astounding.

It was like she'd never met me.

I was the youngest of four boys, coddled as the baby even if I'd never admit such a thing out loud. They loved to call me *Baby Greene*. As much as it annoyed the hell out of me, it wasn't an inaccurate nickname. I was still figuring lots of things out, personal relationships most of all. I had a terrible track record for cohabitation, romantic or otherwise.

At least in this situation, since the apartment was mine, I wouldn't be able to run. Not like before.

"Fair. Tell her I'll be expecting her call."

"I think this is a great idea, for the record. I love it when a plan comes together."

Addison slid out of the booth, swinging her purse over her shoulder. Shaking my head, I followed her out of the restaurant, undecided about whether this was a good situation I was getting into or not.

"WE'VE MET BEFORE, so I know you understand how… candid I can be." Trina sighed into the phone. "I was actually going to say abrupt, or obnoxious. All are accurate."

She'd called me promptly at six, just as Addison said she would. I held the phone loosely between my face and shoulder as I opened a jar of spaghetti sauce.

"I do. Candid fits." I appreciated this about her, as a matter of fact.

"None of the places I've looked at are within my budget. Well, at least not the ones I'd want to live in. To be frank, I don't want to be in a situation similar to yours where I'm hunting for a roommate after I'm already locked into a long-term lease. I'm currently unemployed, so many places won't even consider my application. I'm getting desperate. My job being eliminated… *accelerated* everything."

"Understandable." I poured the sauce into a pan, giving it a quick stir before gripping the phone with my hand. All I needed was for it to slide out and end up in the sauce.

"If you think we'd be a good fit, the rent is manageable for me. I'm actively trying to find a job, by the way. Brutal honesty? You're the best option I've come across."

"Do you have any special requirements?" I asked hesitantly.

"Such as?" Confusion coated her tone.

"I don't know. Special dietary concerns? Particular scheduling issues you'd need to have accommodated?"

"Uh, no? And that's a bizarre but oddly specific question. Did someone you interview have those things?"

No point in lying. "Yes."

"Oh. No, to all of the above. I just need somewhere to live. I'm not always the tidiest person in the world, but I know how to clean up after myself. I can respect boundaries and won't eat your food unless you invite me to. I hate being late, so most of my bills are scheduled to be paid at least 48 hours early. When I have a job, I'm a workaholic, though I do enjoy some trash TV and a cocktail in my downtime."

I laughed, turning the burners off so the food didn't overcook. I remembered asking Addison if she enjoyed reality shows and cocktails once upon a time. Her positive answer was one of the things I knew made us compatible as friends.

"Would you like to come see the room?"

"I'd love to." The relief in her voice was palpable. "Is tomorrow too soon? I don't want to be overly anxious, but I'm about to get kicked out of this motel."

As the words crossed my lips, I wondered what had come over me, but there was no way to take them back. "I'm available now if you're in that much of a hurry. I made some spaghetti if you haven't eaten."

Trina cackled, her easy joy infectious. "You Greene men really are something else. Are you sure it's not an inconvenience? I'm in a hurry, but not *that much* of a hurry."

The more I thought about it, the better the idea seemed. If she liked the place and we got along over dinner, we could get the paperwork taken care of in time for her to move over the weekend. It was fast, but it made sense. Assuming we got along, anyway.

"No problem at all. I'll keep everything warm for you."

She took down the address, tone warm as she expressed sincere gratitude I could feel even through the phone. "Thank you, Dallas. I appreciate this more than I can say."

"The pleasure is all mine. And don't thank me too much yet. If we end up throwing food at one another over dinner, it probably won't work out."

"Noted." She chuckled. "I'll see you soon."

I disconnected, meeting the eye of my reflection in the microwave glass. "What? It's a good idea." I broke contact, shaking my head at myself. "Jesus, you do need a roommate. You're already talking to yourself."

I mixed the pasta and sauce before putting a lid on the pan to keep it warm. She probably wouldn't take more than fifteen minutes to get across town, but I didn't want the meal to be ruined. I shot off a quick text to Addison, thanking her for the suggestion and letting her know Trina was coming over to see it.

ADDISON: Fingers crossed! She's calling me
right now. Lol
DALLAS: Go talk to her, then, I'm sure she'll fill you in
on how it goes later.
ADDISON: She definitely will. Thank you again! For
what it's worth, I hope it works out.

As I gathered up plates and silverware, I realized the buoyant sensation in my chest was optimism.

Apparently, I hoped it was going to work out, too.

CHAPTER TEN

Trina

"THIS IS A great part of town." A smile spread across my mouth as I approached Dallas in the lobby of his building.

We were in an older area of the city undergoing both revitalization and expansion. It was far enough from the heart of downtown to have open spaces but close enough to the city center that you could easily find plenty of food or shopping.

"It is, I love it here," Dallas agreed, pressing the elevator button for his floor. "There was something about this place in particular, though. I breathe better here." He looked at me, something crossing nervously over his face, as though he'd said too much. I just smiled gently in response, familiar with the sensation he was describing.

My heart hadn't stopped racing since he invited me over to see the apartment. I knew being too excited wouldn't be good if this didn't pan out, but I couldn't help it.

"This is me." He unlocked the door for apartment 3-D, gesturing for me to go in ahead of him.

"Thanks. Oh, wow." I breathed a wistful sigh as I took in the spacious, open living room and kitchen. Everything sparkled like it was brand new. There was a suspicious lack of furniture in the living room, though a large TV hung on the wall.

"Your room would be this one." He led me down a short hallway, passing up a small bedroom and bathroom before leading me into an empty suite.

"This room is a wonderful size," I said, checking the closet before wandering into the bathroom.

"These units were designed as two master suites. My room isn't much bigger, but it has a better view."

Keeping a neutral face while I wanted to explode out of my skin with excitement was difficult. "It's very nice." *Nice* didn't even begin to cover it.

He showed me the empty third bedroom, which he intended to turn into an office, plus the hallway half-bath before leading me back to the kitchen and plating up dinner for us both.

I slid onto a barstool at the oversized granite island, awed by the chef's kitchen. It probably helped that the spaghetti he'd made smelled wonderful, and I was ravenous.

"What do you think?" he asked.

I held the fork loosely in my fingers. "It's a beautiful place."

"It's more than I need for myself, which is why I'm trying to find a roommate."

"You could make it work, but it's a little tighter than you'd like?" I guessed, accepting the plate he slid across the granite. I stifled the *that's what she said* trying to escape from my lips. "Thanks."

"You're welcome. And yes, that's exactly it. With a roommate, I'd be a lot more comfortable. I'm not sure why I thought I needed three bedrooms. Well," he dipped his fork. "I knew it was too big, but the view was perfect and it felt like the right place. Plus, the smaller units were all booked out so it was this or waiting. I didn't want to wait."

"I completely understand. I'm in a time crunch for a very different reason, but I can see why you fell in love with this place." I sampled the pasta. "This is delicious, thank you." I was hungrier than I realized, and the simple meal hit the spot.

"Thanks. I'm not much of a cook compared to my mom, but I get by."

"Addison and I were great roommates because we both have our strengths. She's a decent cook, I'm a good baker. It worked out very well for us when we lived together."

"It must be nice to have a good friend you've known for so long." He sounded wistful, which I found interesting. Someone as easy-going and charismatic as him surely had friends? This was where he was from, after all.

"For sure. I'm so glad to be home."

"Do your parents live nearby?"

I shook my head, pausing to chew a flavorful bite of pasta. "No, they live in an RV."

"Oh?" His eyebrows shot up. "That's… unexpected."

I completely understood the conclusions people jumped to when I told them my parents lived as they did. Even knowing better, I still often pictured a dated RV parked somewhere with permanent lawn ornaments and a very active community events center for retirees.

My plate was empty, so I blotted my mouth on a napkin and slid off the barstool to take my dishes to the sink.

"You don't have to wash your dishes," he protested, finishing up his last bite.

"It's the least I can do." I rinsed my plate before continuing my explanation. "I realize saying it the way I did implies they're broke or holed up in a trashy RV park somewhere. What I mean to say is, they travel the country in their RV, but it's their permanent residence. They don't have a house anywhere."

"I'll admit I was assuming the wrong thing there for a minute," he admitted. "It's a very… adventurous way to live. What made them want to do that?"

He brought his plate to the sink, handing it over with a chagrined expression. I ran it under the water, giving the red sauce remnants a swipe with the soapy sponge. Standing in such close proximity, it was hard not to have my full attention on him.

Dallas was shorter than Dennis, but he was still tall, broad in the shoulder, and gifted with the same bright blue eyes. His jawline was sharp, his careless dark hair artfully slumped across his forehead. It was no surprise his oldest brother, Devon, had successfully made it to Hollywood. Remembering the little tidbit about this family never failed to give me a thrill.

I snapped myself back to reality, diverting my gaze to the plates as I realized he was watching me right back, waiting for further explanation. I shared the same story about my parents I'd told many times over the years.

"They were both in the tech industry. I'm a late-life, only child, so when I came to Alabama to go to college, they took the opportunity to retire, downsize their house in Connecticut and start traveling." I missed my childhood home, but I didn't hold it against them. They'd lived in their RV for nearly a decade, loving every minute of seeing the country as they pleased. Besides, their rig was just as big and nicer than plenty of houses I'd been in.

"Wow." Dallas reached into a cabinet, pulling out some storage containers for the leftovers as I loaded the dishes into the dishwasher.

"It's not a realistic lifestyle for everyone. I'd hate parts of it." The thought made me chuckle. I'd be terrible at most parts of living the way my parents do.

"I feel like that's an understatement," he agreed. "Can I offer you a drink?" He opened the fridge, gesturing at an assortment of local beers.

"Water is fine, thanks."

Niceties depleted, we got down to business, going over the basic logistics of being roommates. I was just as comfortable with him eating pasta while discussing my parents' unconventional lifestyle as I had been at my welcome home party, and there wasn't even alcohol involved this time. I was betting on the whole, the Greene men were as easy to get along with as they were on the eyes.

"None of this sounds even remotely difficult." I nodded. His requests were just common sense. Things along the lines of no parties, no breaking lease rules—things I wouldn't do, anyway. "You've seriously had a hard time finding people who couldn't agree to these things? Where have you been advertising?"

He shrugged, opening a folder with the lease agreement in it so I could read the rules for the complex.

"Craigslist."

I grunted. "That's where you went wrong."

He grinned, blue eyes sparkling. "Addison said the same thing."

"Damn right." As I skimmed the document, he chuckled. "Nothing weird here."

Dallas took the papers back. "So where does this leave us?"

I shrugged. "I'm feeling pretty good about this if you are."

"I agree." His handsome face broke into a wide smile.

It was a potent thing to be on the receiving end of—all charming dimples and sparkling blue eyes.

A thrill ran through my veins. Excitement wasn't a strong enough word to describe the emotion I was feeling at the prospect of moving into this lovely apartment.

"I'll get some paperwork drawn up. Can you provide first and last?"

I nodded. "Absolutely."

Dallas stuck a hand out. I shook it reflexively.

"It sounds like we have an agreement."

A squeal made its way out of my throat, which made him laugh.

"Thank you! This is a *lifesaver*."

"Same. You're welcome to move in whenever you want. If you need help, I can probably convince Dennis to loan me his truck…" Dallas' eyes squinted as though picturing how such a conversation might play out.

"Truck and shovel guy? No way. He doesn't seem like the lending kind."

He looked a bit perplexed at my nickname for his brother, but didn't address it. "You're probably right. I bet he'd help, though."

"I'm sure he would, he *does* come off as the helpful type. If he weren't, I'd be doing everything in my power to talk Addison out of falling for him. Not that it would work, but I'd give it my best shot." Dallas grinned, a brief nod letting me know he and I were on the same page, which was reassuring. "I honestly don't need it. All of my stuff is safely packed in a container in a storage lot downtown. I'll need help after it gets delivered, but until then… everything I have with me should fit in my car."

"Oh. Well, when the time comes."

"Thank you so much, Dallas. Truly."

"My pleasure," he repeated, walking me to the elevator. "See you soon!"

I waved as the elevator doors closed, cutting off my view of him, all but floating the whole way back to my mediocre efficiency for one of the very last times.

Unable to rest after the excitement, I called the automated service for the container company and snagged the earliest possible delivery appointment, which–to my surprise–was Saturday morning. After texting Addison a message with about a dozen exclamation points, I sorted the few items in my motel room, getting them ready to chuck into the car.

I eventually crawled into bed, excitement bubbling under my skin. It was not the adventure I'd been planning to have, but it was one I was ready to begin.

"THAT'S IT?" DALLAS asked, he and Dennis mirror images of each other as they stood scowling at the small metal container holding all of my belongings.

"That's it," I confirmed.

"Huh," Dennis grunted.

The container was the smallest one available, so only my most precious or necessary items made the move. Everything extra was sold or donated. My parents taught me very well how to minimize when they hit the road.

"Trina is nothing if not organized. I'll bet this thing is perfectly Tetris'ed." Addison beamed, oddly excited to help unload my things.

My girl knew me so well and I loved her for it. "Damn straight."

"Let's get started then." Addison clapped her hands, rubbing them together to signal she was ready to dive in.

She'd brought over coffee and muffins from Mugs for sustenance. I, on the other hand, gleefully checked out of my efficiency first thing, breakfast the very last thing on my mind. I drove straight to the apartment, carried my luggage straight to my room, teary-eyed when I set them down. I had a place to call mine. It was a healthy first step toward getting my shit put back together.

I rolled up the door on the little cube, revealing exactly what Addison predicted. Things were stacked and squeezed into the space until there were no gaps, floor to ceiling. There was no telling how roughly they'd treated the little box, but as far as I could tell, nothing had shifted since I'd loaded it up in Memphis.

"This is the only time I regret not having a ground floor unit," Dallas grumbled, stacking boxes onto one of the hand trucks Dennis had brought. I was forever grateful for these men and their preparedness, never mind their willingness to help. Hauling one box at a time again, this time *up* the stairs, would be an absolute nightmare. My legs ached at the memory of how loading the container had gone—my old building's elevator had picked one hell of a day to go out.

"At least you can take the elevator with those. Some of this is going to need the stairs." Dennis grunted, lifting a box of books.

"What's in here as far as furniture?" Addison asked, handing me a plastic tote containing bathroom items.

"One big bookshelf, my desk, and my bed."

"Seriously?" Dallas looked doubtful. "Where?"

"In the back." I laughed. "This thing holds a whole one-bedroom apartment."

"I'm going to take your word for it." He shook his head, turning the fully loaded hand-truck toward the building, Dennis following with his own.

Addison and I got to work pulling out boxes, roughly organizing them in the parking space next to the one the container occupied while they were gone.

"I'll be so glad to quit moving for a while." I moved a few things around, so the heavier boxes stayed on the bottom.

"Moving is the worst." Addison turned a bright smile on me. "I'm so freaking glad you're home."

"Aw," I laughed. "Me too. You have no idea how much."

With both Dallas and Dennis on the job, we made record time moving all my things into the apartment. Nearly everything fit in the small elevator, after all. By mid-afternoon, I was arranging the pick-up of the empty container.

We ate the pizza Dallas had ordered for delivery while recovering on the plush carpet.

"Thanks for all your help today."

"Our pleasure," Addison grinned at me, her hand linked with Dennis'. "You pick out a couch yet?" she asked Dallas.

"No. Furniture shopping is a nightmare."

"What? Furniture shopping is fun!" I exclaimed. There were days I went to the giant furniture places just to see what they had and daydream.

Dallas took me in with a measured stare. "I welcome any help you want to offer in that department."

I beamed. "You got it."

After everyone was finished eating, Addison and Dennis got ready to leave. My bestie gave me a tight squeeze before the brothers shared some kind of weird secret handshake hug, which was fun to witness.

I showered, putting sheets on the bed before deciding to tackle some of the kitchen items. By the time I called it quits for the night, it was very late, but most of my room was put together.

My body was tired, but I felt lighter than I had since finding out I was being fired.

Dallas was right—there was something about this place that took worries away and I couldn't wait to start shedding all of mine.

CHAPTER ELEVEN

Dallas

TRINA WAS A hurricane of bright energy. She swept into the apartment on a wave of enthusiasm that didn't let up. Sure, she ran out of gas in the evenings and needed meals periodically, but for the most part, she was a wellspring of light.

Before I had a chance to blink, she'd completely decorated her room and mingled her kitchen stuff with mine so thoroughly it was like she'd always been there. She moved *fast* when she wanted something accomplished.

I learned within a few short days how coffee was not only very important to *her* wellbeing but also to *mine*—which honestly explained a lot—and how she appreciated order in an awesomely chaotic way. This was also an excellent metaphor for her as a person.

We were using the barstools at the island to sit on while watching the massive TV I'd mounted in the living room. Every time we did so, Trina alternated between scrolling through her phone and asking me questions.

"Do you have a budget you need to stick to as far as the living room furniture goes? I'm more than happy to help since it's a big purchase, but when the day comes where we move on to other living situations, we'll have to work out a shared custody agreement."

I laughed. I found myself doing so quite a lot when we were talking. It was such a change of pace from my previous living situation it awed me.

"Do you have something in mind?" I hated shopping for things like furniture. It was too big, too much of a commitment. It overwhelmed me just to look at the flyers included with the grocery ads every week. I used a plain metal bed frame so I didn't have to worry about a headboard and my dresser was something I'd found at a garage sale. The barstools we were sitting on had been the biggest commitment as they came from an actual home goods store. They'd been on sale. My standards were low. For now, they suited me fine.

She nodded, showing me her phone. "Based on what you've told me, any of these are probably a good choice. This company will do delivery, they're local."

Stunned, I scrolled through the detailed portfolio she'd assembled into a Pinterest board.

"This is…" I couldn't find the word I needed. There were couches, chaise lounges, and armchairs. Everything coordinated. She even had full-color palates of matching fabrics put together. "You're... good at this."

Trina shrugged. "Bored, more like it. Plus, my ass hurts from these cheap bar stools, so I'm motivated to get this couch situation managed."

I cracked a grin. Her honesty about everything was also very refreshing.

"Can we see this bigger?"

"Sure." she lifted one shoulder in a shrug. "We just need a computer."

I slid off the stool so I could grab my laptop from my bedroom. We turned away from the TV, using the island as a table to review her handiwork.

"I love the idea of this daybed," she sighed dreamily. I wouldn't have guessed that's what the deep love-seat piece was called, but it made sense. "One day."

"This sectional is nice," I said, opening up a folder she'd made for a large couch that could be reconfigured in multiple ways. It looked both comfortable and classy.

"Which color? The steel blue or the slate gray?"

"Blue," I said confidently, going with my gut.

"I like it. It matches the accents in the kitchen. And your eyes."

"It does?" I was blushing at her off-handed compliment.

Trina laughed at my shocked expression. "Yep. Do you not have a mirror? I'm sure you know just how blue your eyes are. Pretty guys like you usually do. Anyway, which kind of feet?"

"Pretty?" I snorted. I was immensely flattered but also humbled. I did know. Having her point it out so casually made me feel the tiniest bit better about my vanity.

She walked me through designing furniture from scratch based on their options, adding in a matching coffee table and rug for good measure. The result was a gorgeous couch we were sure would fit the living room because she'd already gone so far as to measure. I was dumbfounded by the tidbit of foresight. Admittedly, it wasn't something I would have thought to do.

"You want to go down there to sit on one? We probably should. Sometimes furniture is really pretty, but not comfortable."

"Sure. I can go after work tomorrow if they're open."

Trina checked the hours on their website. "That works. We can maybe grab dinner if it's not weird?"

"Why would it be weird?"

"I don't know. It's probably not. We've eaten here plenty of times."

Having dinner out with Trina felt like it might be as entertaining as my lunches with Addison usually were.

"I'll come home first, we can ride together. Want to go on my bike or do you want to drive?"

Trina beamed. "Motorcycle, please, and thank you. Do you have another helmet?"

"I do."

Her grin was infectious. My mood was somewhere

between sky-high and limitless as I packed the computer back up. I'd missed feeling this way.

"I will miss the ballroom, though." Her eyebrow raised and I found myself swept up as she waltzed me through the living room, humming a tune I recognized from one of my favorite childhood movies.

"Is that… the song from Sleeping Beauty?"

She laughed. "Yes! My favorite Disney movie. The new version of the song Lana Del Rey did is so gorgeous."

The weight of her in my hands was as pleasant as it had been at her party. The way she floated across the floor made me feel positively graceless, but she led like a pro. Her laughter echoed back at us from the walls as she put herself into a spin, then a dip.

"Look at you! This was fun, thanks." She winked at me as she straightened.

My pulse was up, and I was certain it wasn't just from the quick dance across the living room.

"This place isn't far. I'll check for places to eat nearby." Trina trotted down the hallway, leaving me standing there staring after her like a stunned puppy.

It was early on, but I had a feeling this living situation would be the one I'd compare all others to for a long time. It was a massive victory that the last one, the one I'd been regretting, was finally displaced.

"IT'S SO SQUISHY." Trina sighed happily, wiggling deeper into the seat of the model couch. "Good choice."

"Will a brand new one be as broken in as this one, though?"

Trina clucked her tongue at me. "No. I'm sure we can invite some people over to help us sit on it if we need to."

I'd invite the noisy teenagers from down the hall to jump on it if it helped. It was hard not to melt into the buttery cushions. The fabric was even softer than I'd pictured.

"Alright. Let's go order it." Trina's momentary relaxation flipped on a dime and she was bouncing up on her feet, ready to tackle the next thing. "Need anything else?"

I shrugged, overwhelmed by the number of fake rooms they had set up. Every single one was attractive in its own way. I couldn't fathom how most people made choices about this kind of thing, but I was decidedly terrible at it.

"Maybe a desk?"

"Those are this way." Trina grabbed my hand, pulling me along behind her as she speed-walked across the warehouse of a store toward the pretend office set-ups.

My fingers brushed the backs of leather chairs, the chrome of desk lamps.

"What are you looking for?" she asked, arms crossed and stance wide as she surveyed her new temporary kingdom. She was adorable. I'd never tell her so because she was also fierce. She was a tiny terror, but a terror nonetheless.

In my mind, I called her as much pretty regularly and had since the end of her first week in the apartment. She flew in, unpacked, and got situated; instantly becoming part of my life. It was equal parts amazing and terrifying.

Terror fit her better than Trina did much of the time.

"Simple," I answered, drawn back to her question among the sea of desks. "I don't need it to do much more than hold my laptop."

"Okay." She turned away from the elaborate completed room designs and bulky wooden behemoths with hutches, leading me instead to a section of minimalist tables. "Anything catch your eye here?"

I glanced between the options, all variations of a flat surface and all perfectly serviceable for my needs. I shrugged.

Trina groaned, rolling her eyes. "Okay, fine. This one matches the color of the cabinets. What do you think? It's simple, but it has a couple of drawers for random office crap and file folders."

"Perfect."

She grunted louder, even throwing her hands up. With her short spiky curls, she looked like she was about to sprout snakes and turn me to stone. I was wise enough to say nothing, even though it amused me.

With a flick of her wrist, she snatched the little card with the desk's information on it.

"Chair?" she asked.

"Minimal. Ergonomic. No arms, preferably."

Trina stalked around the area, choosing a new chair for each of us.

"Happy?" She asked, pointing at what she'd picked for me.

"Yep."

"You're difficult."

"Difficult? I answered all of your questions directly. Besides, I liked your *first* choices."

"I said what I said."

I laughed behind her as she led the way to the design desk.

Somehow, Trina and the woman behind the counter made me feel involved in the process, even though they clearly did not need my input.

Trina asserted some expert negotiation skills about the fabrics and, thanks to some kind of sorcery, the couch ended up being seriously discounted. Once they got the order built into the computer, the delivery estimate popped up. We'd have to wait a couple of weeks, but it would be worth it.

I offered the woman my credit card so she could ring us out.

"We'll figure out your chair later," I told Trina, who was digging around in her purse. I was genuinely unconcerned about her hundred-dollar chair after dropping what I'd spent on my stuff.

"No shared custody, then?" Trina asked, a bit crestfallen as we left the store.

"If it comes to that, we can talk about it." Her pout renewed the rumble of laughter in my chest. "Thanks. This was the most painless experience I've ever had in a furniture store. Ever think of changing career paths? You could sell the hell out of some couches."

She snorted. "I'll keep it in mind if things get desperate. And I'm glad to hear it wasn't too terrible for you." She strapped on my spare helmet. "Dinner?"

"Dinner."

I mounted my motorcycle, Trina settling in comfortably behind me with her hands warm against my stomach.

She'd chosen a nearby steakhouse that looked like it had been around forever. The 60's style sign wasn't updated, though it had been repainted. The inside decor was all dark wood booths and deep jewel tones.

"This place gives off going-steady date vibes." Her eyes widened in mock horror as she sipped at her iced tea. "Sorry. I just wanted a good piece of prime rib."

The waitstaff all wore full white dress shirts with ties, a wine-colored cloth napkin draped over their forearms. There was a gentleman tending bar who looked as though he may have been manning the post since they first opened.

"No worries." I scanned the menu, pleased to find any number of tasty options. "They must have good food if they've lasted this long."

"Hopefully." She dove into the basket of fresh bread as soon as it was delivered, displaying no hesitation at all as she buttered us each a slice. I hadn't realized it was something I'd be impressed by.

"Thanks." I accepted the warm bread she offered and took a bite.

"Sourdough." She smiled. "I'll have to add this place to my list."

"Because of table bread?"

She scoffed. "Table bread is a very accurate measurement of restaurant quality, I'll have you know."

"My apologies, I had no idea." I did my best to communicate repentance for my ignorance with a wide smile.

"Accepted."

True to her prediction, the meals we got were incredible.

Her slice of prime rib was as big as the plate, and she finished off every last bite. I was impressed in a way I couldn't define. Watching the petite woman enthusiastically consume a slab of beef hit several buttons for me I wasn't even aware I had.

My steak was also perfectly cooked. Not a single item we were served was anything less than delicious. I mentally noted that I should tell Dennis about it, since I was sure he and Addison would enjoy it.

"Table bread," I mumbled as we climbed onto my bike. I was so full riding was going to be a challenge, but it was worth it. "Who knew?"

"*Table bread*," she emphasized. "Ten out of ten times. And *I* knew." Trina confirmed, sucking in a tense breath as she wrapped her arms around me. "I promise not to squeeze you. I may throw up in sympathy if you do."

"Much appreciated."

As promised, her grip was comfortably snug.

I realized as I drove us back home that life with Trina was likely to be full of fun and surprises. There was a heavy measure of comfort to her personality as well. She seemed to be perfectly balanced, something I desperately longed to learn how to be.

It may have just been furniture, but the experience told me everything I needed to know about my new roommate.

CHAPTER TWELVE

Dallas

A S IT TURNED out, the merits of table bread as a gauge for restaurant quality was the tip of the iceberg when it came to things my new roommate would teach me in the early weeks of our cohabitation.

I learned in very short order the correct way to load a dishwasher, how not to wash her perfectly seasoned cast-iron skillet, (which I already knew thanks to my southern mother). She functioned best when supplied regularly with coffee and snacks. Her e-reader was a prized possession and even if she only paused to read for ten minutes at a time, it was always nearby.

Food was a top priority in Trina's life, and I wasn't upset in the least about it. Coming home from work to find her cooking or baking was not unusual. I learned quickly she managed her stress through baking, having spontaneous dance parties throughout the house, and cleaning. As far as I could tell—based on the number of cookies available at any given time, plus the shine the countertops had—job hunting was not going as well as she hoped.

The dance parties were super fun to watch, if nothing else. More than a few times, she'd convinced me to join in. It was incredible for my serotonin levels to let loose with her lithe form under my hands and just *dance*. Everything about it felt right.

All things considered, it was nice to have a considerate roommate who participated in cooking plus other areas of home maintenance. It was refreshing how opposite from my last situation everything about her was.

It was nice to be able to come home and… be myself. It sounded truly ridiculous, but I'd spent years stifling myself for the sake of someone else's ego. There was no reason to disguise how I was in my natural state with my roommate because she was going to see all of it no matter what. She was as over the top about things as I'd been accused of being. I'd accidentally found a kindred spirit.

I never imagined coming home would be so productive for renewing my sense of self. Parts of me I'd shoved way down were seeing the light of day for the first time in years and thriving from it.

Sitting down in the evenings together became a habit over the first few weeks. It was stilted and a little uncomfortable at first, though we quickly discovered we had a lot in common.

"I can't believe we were in Tennessee at the same time. It's a strange coincidence," Trina mentioned over dinner one night.

I happened to agree, though there was enough distance between Nashville and Memphis there was no real chance of us having crossed paths while we were there. I hadn't gotten out much aside from Reggie's country club circle while I'd been there, either. He'd isolated me away from anything that didn't revolve around him, so independence became my default. I hadn't even realized it was happening until it was already done. The dramatics involved in getting out of town to attend Devon's wedding was a blaring neon sign that it was time for me to leave altogether, it just took time.

I *hated* thinking about all the wasted time.

Trina's bright-eyed smile brought me back to myself. It was so damn pleasant to simply hold space with someone without walking on eggshells or having to manage their emotions.

"The universe is funny sometimes." I tilted my beer bottle in her direction and she responded in kind.

"It is. I'm still thanking the stars for allowing me to get transferred back before I lost my job." Trina's perky smile drooped. With a heavy breath, she got to her feet, trudging into the kitchen.

I wanted to offer words of comfort, but I wasn't sure what to say. She was doing everything right. Besides, losing her job the way she had wasn't her fault.

"Are you working over there, or are you playing?" Trina asked, offering me one of the cookies she'd retrieved from the kitchen.

"Working, unfortunately."

"It's almost nine pm!" She grimaced in horror.

A laugh warmed my chest. Point taken, I closed my laptop. My spreadsheet of doom for the next weeks' deliveries would wait.

"We've been very fortunate lately. We're much busier than expected."

"You should still give yourself permission for downtime. It's not healthy to work around the clock. Schedule in time for rest if you have to."

"Sounds like you're speaking from experience."

"Does it?" The coy smile she offered didn't fool me. She picked up her phone.

"Says my roommate who obsessively checks job posting boards and emails."

Trina's mouth twitched as she lowered the screen to glare at me.

"Ooh, he's feisty tonight. And yes, I know from experience. Even though I loved my last job, I had to make myself stop working all night after hours. It didn't get projects done any faster, or any better, and left me drained. Look." She flashed her calendar at me.

"You *schedule* your dance parties?"

"Damn right. What do we need to put on your calendar? I can help."

I laughed as I opened the calendar. It wasn't a bad idea, even if it sounded silly.

"I have no idea."

"Dates? Cookie breaks? A trip down to the gym? Personal 'shower' time?"

I coughed, but she was undeterred.

"Whatever it is, put it in there. Make a reminder. No judgment. Everyone needs a good release now and then."

Her playful nature brightened everything in the apartment. It manifested around the apartment in trinkets like the cat-shaped salt and pepper shakers on the kitchen counter. No matter the form, it made me smile. *Trina* made me smile.

I dropped in my evening runs so I had somewhere to start before changing the subject. Maybe dance parties would go on the list for later.

"Anything good lately on the job boards?"

Her deep sigh made me regret asking the question.

"No. It's a weird market right now. Fingers crossed something pops up soon." Her gaze snapped to mine, a flash of panic behind her dark eyes. "I'm fine, for the record. For money, I mean. For now."

I waved a hand at her, brushing off her concern. "I'm not worried about it."

"Well, I am," she groused. "I don't like not having a stable income."

"I understand, but I know you're good for it."

She leaned forward, reaching for the remote. "Do you still want to watch this? I'm going to bed soon."

Guilt pressed in. I'd just been making small talk, and my subject change had inadvertently chased her off.

"No, thanks. I can use the TV in my room."

Trina stretched, her shirt riding up, showing me a flash of abdomen. I should have looked away, but couldn't manage to avert my eyes.

"By the way, I was going to do all the floors tomorrow. If you don't mind me going in your room, I can vacuum and mop yours while I'm at it."

I paused, surprised by her offer. "That's fine. You don't have to, though."

This time, she waved me off. "It's way less effort to do them all at once. If I do everything at one time, it's easier. I'm a nosy bitch, but I promise to stay out of your stuff." She tossed me a wink.

"I don't have anything to hide. I'm afraid it would be pretty boring for you to go through anything of mine." Truth be told, I didn't have anything much to go through, but that was beside the point. "You really don't have to do any of the housework all by yourself. If you wait until the weekend, I can help."

"It's okay. I don't mind. Besides, I'm not doing anything else except copying and pasting my resume. Well, I do have to attend my regularly scheduled dance parties, but they fit just about anywhere I need them to. The mop makes a good dance partner, besides." She grinned, some of her mood recovered. "Goodnight, Dallas."

"Goodnight, Trina."

She wandered down the hall toward her room as I looked around the living room, unsure of what to do with myself. I wasn't ready for bed, though a few extra hours of rest would do me good.

I found myself standing in the doorway of the bedroom I'd intended to turn into an office. So far, it had become a catch-all storage room, the place half-empty boxes went to be forgotten. My desk and chair were moved in, though I'd never once used them.

"I should probably do something in here," I muttered to myself, trying to gauge the wall space with my arms.

The longer I stared, the more I realized there was plenty of space in there for both of us.

Trina was working from her bedroom, but there was no reason she couldn't have a space in here too.

With the idea percolating, I turned off the light and went to my bedroom.

While I was brushing my teeth, a text pinged. Adrenaline flooded my system as the unknown number popped up with a version of the same message I kept getting.

UNKNOWN: Need to talk. Please.

"Not today, Satan," I mumbled to myself, forcing a handful of slow, measured breaths while I deleted the message, blocking the number after taking a screenshot of the details. It felt more than logical that it was Reggie trying to reach out. I'd hired a company to lock down my online presence and hide as much of my personal data as possible, plus I'd changed my phone number. Changing my number was one of the hardest parts for me. I knew it was silly, but it was the number I'd always had. I wanted to keep it. I'd gotten one with a couple of the same digits, which I was now thinking was a mistake.

To burn off the excess agitation, I went through an exercise routine I'd practiced since I was a teenager, one handed down to me from my older brothers. We'd always called it the fab five. Crunches, push-ups, lunges, squats, and pull-ups. The only difference was now, I had a pull-up bar hanging in the doorway of my closet instead of having to go outside to use the pole on one end of Mom's laundry line.

Muscles burning and mind settled, I rinsed off in the shower again before finally crawling into bed. As I lay there in the quiet, my mind drifted erratically. I resolved to suggest the idea about the office sharing to Trina and seriously consider changing my phone number again.

Eventually, I was able to claim those extra hours of sleep I needed so badly.

CHAPTER THIRTEEN

Trina

"YOU DON'T HAVE to do that, you know," Dallas said, watching me scrub the stovetop. His eyebrows were drawn together, his mouth set into an uncharacteristic frown.

We were navigating the intricacies of having a roommate with gusto. His work schedule gave me free rein in a quiet apartment all day, so I tried to make the best of it. We'd already found a decent balance with chore division. Meals were our time to reconnect, and I was enjoying having someone to eat with.

"I'm the one who spilled half of the ingredients from dinner down here. I can clean it."

"You also bleached the sink and scrubbed the hall bathroom the other day. After you ran the vacuum and mopped *all* the floors. You went shopping yesterday and bought enough groceries for a month. Plus, you baked whatever those ridiculously delicious things with coconut in them are." He narrowed his gaze at me. "Is everything okay?"

Adrenaline spiked, a cold flash zipping through my veins. I knew very well he was just making an observation, but guilt was ever-present as he called me out.

My tone was sharper than I intended as I responded, "Are you complaining that I cleaned? I always ask before I go into your room. And they're called Magic Bars."

His hands went up, a silent plea for me to not shoot him where he stood. I took a deep breath, trying to cool the anger surging behind my shame-colored guilt. My gut rolled as I tried to silence the noise in my mind that sounded suspiciously like my mother and grappled with what *exactly* had made me feel this way in the first place.

Besides my period, anyway. Because such an answer was too easy and probably only part of the issue.

"I'm absolutely *not* complaining that you cleaned. I appreciate you asking before you go into my room, but as I've said, I don't have anything to hide from you. You know my position on the bars." He opened the fridge, pulling out a container of mixed fruit. "I'm only trying to say you don't have to pick up more than your share of groceries, cooking, or cleaning. That's not how this works."

"I'm home more, so it's no big deal."

Dallas pulled a face. "Trina. You're my roommate, not my housekeeper. I appreciate you doing all those things, don't get me wrong. I understand if you're doing them because you're bored. That's fine. I'll still feel like an ass when you clean or do things I should be handling, but I can accept it. Don't do it because you think you *have* to. Okay?"

I stared at him, thoughts too scrambled to respond properly. "Okay."

He nodded, maintaining the serious, unblinking eye contact for a moment longer before stepping forward and folding me into his arms.

"What… what's going on?" My body melted into the embrace even as I questioned what was happening. I breathed in the scent of his cologne, my arms moving to wrap around his back out of reflex.

"It's called a hug. You looked like you needed one."

His voice rumbled through his chest. He wasn't holding me tightly, just… securely. It was nice.

I punched back a surge of emotion with sarcasm. I didn't have time for tears, nor were they welcome. Stupid hormones. "Oh, is that what this is?"

Dallas relaxed his hold, staring me in the eye from arm's length. "Better?"

I wanted to argue, to toss out some snarky response. It would have been a lie, though. "Yes, actually. Thank you."

His mouth tipped up in one corner, the trademark Greene smirk making its appearance. "You're welcome."

As if satisfied with our interaction, he grabbed an apple from the cute basket I'd put on the counter and vanished into his room.

I finished up what I was doing in the kitchen, Dallas' words running around in my head. I was cleaning because it needed to be done. Surely that's all it was.

The question chased me for the rest of the afternoon, mostly because I didn't like the answer I kept coming up with. I was doing more around the house out of guilt. Or something *similar* to guilt, anyway.

My rent was paid. I wasn't short on any of my bills. But because I wasn't actively going to a job, I was compelled to do *more*. Because I could. Because I was home. Because if I didn't, I was being lazy.

It *was* my mother's voice I heard in my head. Hot frustration swamped my chest as I yanked my clothes out of the dryer before taking them back to my room.

I didn't appreciate the revelation even a little bit.

Thinking back to how my mom had always spoken about cleanliness and chore division occupied me as I folded. A quiet knock on my open door threw me out of my memories just as I was beginning to work up some steam about realizing I'd been conditioned to believe my value in the household was tied to the amount and type of work I was doing at any given time.

"Do you want to move your desk into the office?" Dallas' expression was thoughtful as he hovered in my doorway. His bright azure gaze dipped briefly from my face to the gauzy summer shirt I was holding.

It took me a moment to shift mental gears. I blinked a few times to organize my thoughts.

"Isn't *your* desk in there?"

My bedroom was plenty large enough to accommodate all of my furniture, but it would be nice to separate my workspace from my sleep space. Plus, if I moved the desk out, I could get a dresser or maybe a chair and another bookcase…

"I'm pretty sure we could both have a desk and it would be fine. We could put them on opposite walls." He gestured for me to follow him, so I abandoned the rest of the laundry on my bed to go with him.

He'd been busy moving around the boxes of miscellaneous stuff that had accumulated in the empty room. Instead of still being haphazardly stacked on the floor, they were tucked neatly into the small closet.

"I just figured neither of us has a huge desk. One of us could be here, and the other over there." He gestured again with his hands.

"Could work." I measured the available wall space with my arms, getting a rough idea of where my desk would fit. "You sure?"

He grinned. As usual, the sight of it lifted my spirits. He was as easy-going as they came. It didn't take much to spark his joy, and his smile was too charming not to respond to.

"Better for the room to be used than just sit here. Maybe I'd come in here to work instead of using my laptop on the couch or in bed if I had some company."

For some reason, this seemed like the highest kind of compliment. I couldn't resist the opening to poke at him, however.

"I thought you were going to stop working so much in the evenings?" His mouth opened to respond, but I laughed, interrupting before he could say anything. "Okay."

Dallas' handsome face lit up at my agreement. He clapped his hands together firmly. "Yeah? Okay."

As he watched me, I realized he was waiting for me to move.

"Oh. *Now?*"

"Yeah, let's do it now." He chuckled, leading the way out of the room.

I wasn't sure what had gotten into him, but I was here for it. The energy Dallas put out when he was motivated and playful at the same time was irresistible. I now understood why Addison was so easy to convince to go along with my crazy schemes when I was in a similar mood.

There was barely time to gather up my computer and notebook before Dallas lifted the simple wooden desk by himself, toting it into the office. I trailed behind him, setting my things down on the newly relocated desk before going back for my chair.

Dallas followed me, scanning for anything else I might need help to carry.

"That's it?"

"That's it," I confirmed, gripping the back of the chair with my hands.

A sly grin crossed his mouth. "Sit down."

"Why?"

His smile went wide enough to show me all his teeth.

The tip of his tongue poked out at the corner of his mouth. "Just trust me."

I narrowed my eyes at him, though I did as he asked. The moment I was seated, he sprinted down the hallway, not slowing until we were in the kitchen.

A surprised shriek popped out of me, but all too soon I was laughing. "Dallas! Oh my God."

He spun the chair, zooming me all the way back down the hall and into the office, leaving me a giggling mess at my desk.

"Do you want a turn?"

"Nah. I'm more of a giver."

"Oh?" I raised my eyebrows at him, which incited a wink.

Shaking my head at his playful shenanigans, I turned to arrange things on the desktop.

He was mumbling 'this will work' to himself as he organized a pencil cup, lamp, and his laptop on his own desk across the room.

While he fiddled, I plunked myself back down in the chair to finish a job application I'd been filling out before the laundry interruption.

"Do you work better with noise?" I asked. I needed something—music or a podcast or someone to chat with. Having someone in your same workspace who needed silence could be problematic.

"Always."

Relief washed over me. Silence and I were not friends.

"What's your office like at G4?" I spun in my chair so I could look at him and found him in a mirror of my position.

"No office. I have a little desk set up in a corner of the warehouse so it's always noisy." His hands fidgeted with a pen, wrists resting on his thighs.

"There's not an office you could use?" I tried to recall how Addison described the building, but was coming up blank.

"There is. I don't mind being out there, though. It's easier to get things done and I'm not a total douche trying to manage my team from another part of the building."

"You'd rather stay hot all day and go deaf than be perceived as a douche?" I was teasing, but he just shrugged. He would.

"I wear earplugs. It keeps my guys from having to go in and out of the office a thousand times a day, which Addison probably appreciates. I'm sure Dennis does when he's there." His lip curled in a smirk. He liked to give his older brother a hard time, though they were both very considerate of one another as far as I could tell.

"Huh. That's actually very smart, at least as far as the staff goes."

"Thanks, I think so too."

He waved a hand toward my computer.

"We can set up a different background if my desk isn't in a good place for your interviews. They have things you can unroll like projector screens or fabric ones..." His eyebrows pulled together as he pulled his phone out, I assumed to shop for one.

My heart squeezed. Dallas was a very different kind of man than I'd ever spent much time around. He worried about things even I didn't consider, which was saying something with my chronic overthinking habit.

"It'll be okay, thanks, though." I peered around. "We need some stuff on the walls."

"That's all you. Put up whatever you want."

Those were the magic words as far as I was concerned. I had plenty of art ready to hang and a fresh, blank space to put them on.

"This was a *good* idea."

He smiled back at me, getting to his feet. "I'll get you a hammer."

As I took in the room, mentally organizing the artwork I wanted to hang on the walls, I got an idea.

Once, I'd run a website of my own, freelancing little projects for people. Just something I started after college as a test to get my designing toes wet. Random infographics, humorous images, logos. It was never much, and I shut it down when my day job limited my free time… but it could be fixed up to be put back into service.

Inspired, I pulled my notebook over to start jotting notes down. I could take commissions while I waited for something permanent. I could revamp my page so that once the shopping cart was up and running, I only had to maintain it. Things like social media, which I generally despised, could be employed as advertising. It would take some effort to get things going, but it could work.

By the time Dallas got back with a hammer and some picture-hanging hooks, I'd put down a page full of scribbles plus a vague game-plan for a potential side hustle.

Mostly, I felt hope, which was something that had been starting to wane.

This idea felt *good*. I was a bit disappointed in myself it had taken so long to come up with, if I was being honest.

Dallas caught me grinning as he handed off the tool.

"Something I should know?" he asked.

"I just had an idea."

"Oh?"

I explained it to him as he shadowed me to my bedroom closet where my cache of framed art was stashed.

"That's a great idea. I don't know much about most of what you said, but you seem excited." He held his hands out to accept as many paintings as he could carry.

"Thanks. Going to take some work to get ready… but I feel good about it."

Dallas stayed the whole time I tested, moved, and hung art in the office. He was an excellent helper, offering some helpful suggestions when needed, plus a very effective extra set of hands.

More than once, I found myself comfortably caged between his warm body and the wall, a reminder I needed a date soon pulsing through my body.

"Looks awesome." He grinned at me before slinging his arm around my shoulders for a loose side-hug. "Thanks for helping me with the office. You hungry?"

I warmed, blushing from his flattery. He'd helped *me*, but I wasn't going to correct him. We'd been an excellent team.

"Sure." I followed him out of the room, taking one last glance back to admire our handiwork.

CHAPTER FOURTEEN

Dallas

"**O**H, GOD. NOT you too."

"Not me too, what?"

Trina was lounging on the couch with her glasses on, e-reader propped in front of her. Her short hair was tied up in an adorable, tiny ponytail at the very top of her head in a nubby horn.

She gestured aggressively at all of me. I was wearing basketball shorts with a loose tank top, nothing I would consider reaction-worthy. As she continued, I tucked my lanyard inside my shirt, the metal house key cool against my skin.

"You asked me if I wanted to go run with you like that's something *normal* people do. Addison still does her ridiculous 5k thing every weekend, even after she got backed into by a damn car. What's *wrong* with you people that you need to run? Nobody's chasing you. You know you don't *have* to run, right?"

I laughed at the disgusted sneer on her face.

"Just making sure when the zombies show up, I can get away. I only have to be faster than the person behind me."

"Nice. *I'd* be the person behind you. You know that, right? I can follow the logic, though. I eat brownies so I'm harder to kidnap."

I barked a laugh at her argument. "I'm not sure anyone's told you, but exercise is good for you, Trina."

She tilted her head, glare intensifying. "I'm well aware, *Dallas*." The way she swore my name made it sound anything but complementary. It still sent a flash of awareness through my body. "I do just fine wandering downstairs to the gym now and then to lift some weights if my YouTube Yoga isn't cutting it. Walking around the lake is admittedly pretty nice. I've done that a few times when it cooled off in the evening enough I didn't sweat my ass off the whole time. Running, though? I honestly don't understand the appeal."

"Make you a deal. I'll go run a few laps. If you want to meet me out there, I'll walk with you."

Trina sat up, tossing both her glasses and e-reader onto the coffee table.

"I suppose Poppy and Cas can wait a little while."

"Who?"

"My *book*. Maybe if you did more reading to escape reality and less running, you'd know more character references. Why are you so hell-bent on getting me to work out?"

Her fire was one of my favorite things about her. Her sass matched mine on a level I'd never expected, but one that proved we were incredibly compatible as both friends and roommates.

"Fair. I don't read nearly as much as I should. Is it a good story?"

"Damn right. I can make plenty of recommendations if you're interested."

"Noted. Anyway, you said something the other day about feeling guilty about how much you'd been baking, so…"

Her head tilted dangerously to the side, her mouth tight. I realized my error immediately. While I didn't give a single damn how much she weighed, I'd overheard her lamenting to Addison on the phone the other night about how many treats she'd been consuming. I loved that she knew herself and was confident in her skin. My suggestion seemed reasonable before I made it, though now I was second-guessing myself.

I rushed to clarify, hand defensively out in front of me. "I don't agree with you, not even a little bit. I selfishly very much love the products of your kitchen adventures. I don't believe food has to be earned. Food isn't a punishment, either. It should be *enjoyed*. Eat what you damn well please. I just thought maybe you'd enjoy getting outside, maybe moving a little. I run because it clears my head. It lets me focus on nothing more than my breath and my feet. I thought it might be something else you could use to try to help with your stress."

Trina's eyes narrowed as she processed my words. "Fine. I'll go change. But I'm sure as hell not running. Walking is the best I can do."

My heart thudded in my chest. I was careful not to outwardly display my excitement at having convinced her, though.

"Fair. I'll see you downstairs?" I double-checked to make sure my key was attached to my necklace, feeling for it through my shirt.

"Yeah, yeah," she grumbled the entire way down the hallway.

Feeling like I'd won a small victory, I went down to the trail I could see from my bedroom window and started to run my laps.

The breeze coming off the small, man-made lake was cool, which made it much more pleasant to run than I'd been expecting. Summer was in full swing, making it blistering hot most days by late morning.

I passed up a woman walking behind a stroller, a handful of joggers, and a couple of people walking their pets as I ran out some tension.

My head was pleasantly quiet, my body covered in a sheen of sweat when I spotted Trina approaching the entrance to the trail closest to the rear building doors.

She was decked out in a bright pink moisture-wicking shirt and gray compression leggings. Her spotless shoes matched the neon hue of her shirt.

"Let's get this over with," she muttered, pushing her giant sunglasses further up her nose.

I dropped my pace to match her stride as I took a deep drink from my water bottle.

"It's already stupid hot out here. Why is this fun, again?"

"You didn't have to join me," I teased her. "My offer was mostly me being polite."

"Yes, I did. I'm not getting my daily D any other way, I might as well get some sun."

I managed to catch myself before choking for a change, but grinned broadly as she met my eye.

"You do that on purpose."

"Of course, I do." She giggled. "It's no fun if people don't react to my ridiculosity."

"Is ridiculosity a real word?"

She skewered me with side-eye, lowering her glasses down her nose for extra impact.

"Did you for real just ask me if a word I made up to emphasize how over the top and ridiculous I am is *real*?"

"Point taken."

She shook her head as she settled the glasses back over her eyes. A wide smile spread across my face. This woman was an absolute riot, and I loved spending time with her. The fact that I'd fallen into the best possible roommate situation after rushing into it was not lost on me. On the contrary, I was grateful for it every single day. I looked forward to coming home from work to spend time relaxing, like anyone did, but I especially anticipated the time *with her*, because she made me happy. My blood fizzed pleasantly at our banter, pulse still pumping from my run. It was also elevated because of her proximity.

Trina increased her speed to a fast walk.

"Nice shoes."

"They're pretty, right? Been sitting in my closet for almost a year. Addison talked me into buying them when she dragged me to a shoe store one day. I guess I lied when I told her I'd never wear them. I'll have to call to apologize."

"I won't tell if you won't."

Her little unicorn hair horn was starting to fall out, the humidity making it all frizz. I found it adorable.

"Deal."

We walked in silence for a whole lap. I thought Trina would head right back inside after we made the circuit, but she continued, so I just followed her lead.

"How far is a lap?" She asked.

"Half a mile or so."

She made a thoughtful noise in her throat.

By the time we rounded the lake for the third time, I was grinning ear to ear, certain she was going to call it quits at any moment. To my surprise, she kept right on going.

"Two miles is a good goal," she said simply. "How many did you run before I came out?"

"Four."

"What do you usually run?"

"Ten."

"Five miles?" The horror on her face was hilarious. "How many times a week?"

"I try for at least three, though I don't always make it."

Trina bumped her pace again, her breath speeding up as she pushed.

"I'm quitting at four, but I see what you mean about it being good for your head."

"You never tried before?" I asked, careful not to gloat. Trina was as peaceful as I'd ever seen her outside one of her post-yoga sessions or baked-goods comas, and I didn't want to ruin it.

"Not really. Addison and I get too goofy when we try to work out together. Everything ends up with me trying to turn the moves into a dance routine or us falling because we're laughing too hard. Or, she gets completely exasperated with my lack of athletic skill and quits trying." She paused to take a drink, moisture from the damp air and sweat gathering along her collarbone and on her face. "This has been… nice?" She sounded surprised.

"Yeah, it has. How does it compare to baking?"

Her head tilted as she considered. I wished I could see her dark eyes behind the oversized glasses.

"This disgusting, hot, wet air doesn't hold a candle to warm gooey brownies, but it's worth doing some more extensive experimentation, I guess. Maybe I'll come out with you a couple of times a week. As long as we can do it in the evening so it's cooler."

"I'd like that."

A smirk appeared on her lips and she pointed a finger at my face. "I still think people who run for fun are weirdos."

"To be fair, I never said we weren't."

"I happen to love my weirdo friend Addison, so I guess it's okay."

"I love your weirdo friend Addison, too."

Trina's smile was gentle, her whole tone much more relaxed when she spoke. "I'm really glad she found you guys. She needed you after Mark."

Why those words made me feel shy, I wasn't sure, but they were powerful in their sincerity.

"I'm glad she found us, too. She's one of the best friends I've had in a long time. I'm not you, though. We're a lot alike, but not the same. I'm happy I could be there for her."

Trina's head bobbed. "I wish I could have been here to help her in person more. I'm relieved she had the next best thing, though."

Her compliment came with a shoulder-check she threw her whole body weight into. I jogged a few steps to the side to rebalance. It appeared as though I wasn't the only one who struggled with genuine compliments and deep feelings.

"You did everything you could. House, job… it was a lot."

She didn't answer, her gentle smile dimming before brightening again. "I did."

The cicadas in the trees sang loudly as the sun beat down on us. The gentle waves of the small lake lapped up on shore with a satisfying *slurp*. It was peaceful.

True to her word, Trina headed for the building as we rounded the lake for the fourth time.

"I'm going to finish my laps," I said.

"Okay. I'm going to shower, I feel sticky and not in a good way. Have fun."

"Thanks for walking with me, Trina." I gave her my most charming grin, which only resulted in her giving me the finger.

"I'll save you a cookie," she called.

I'd take it.

Trina

"NOT THAT I don't love going out with you, or Addison, or some of my other friends—" Friends who were largely absent since I moved back, which was something I hadn't anticipated, "—I just wouldn't mind going to a dinner that has the potential to end in orgasm, you know?"

Dallas coughed on the drink he'd taken. I internally cheered, overjoyed every single time I managed to make him blush or choke on my words.

"You still manage to shock me," he mumbled, dabbing at his shirt with a paper towel. "It's the damnedest thing. True talent. But I get what you're saying, I feel the same way."

"Were you seeing someone before you moved back here?"

He paused, gaze unfocused as he stared across the room. I wondered if he even realized he checked his phone before answering me. The motions were mechanical. Eventually, he gave a slow nod.

I tried to backtrack, feeling guilty that I'd mis-stepped. "Sorry, you don't have to answer. You can tell me when things are off-limits. I'll respect boundaries. I have a bad habit of assuming most people have as few boundaries as I do until they tell me otherwise."

The corners of his mouth twitched. "No, it's alright. It's just not my favorite thing to talk about. I did. I went through a couple of reasonably long-term relationships while I was away. Neither ended well. The most recent one, especially."

"I'm sorry to hear it."

"Don't be. It was definitely for the best. For what it's worth, I don't think your question is rude, though I am trying to forget most of it ever happened. What about you? Did you have someone in Memphis?"

My last *someone* in Memphis crossed my mind. I would regret that stupid swipe forever, it seemed.

"Nah. I'm a serial dater, never really been serious with anyone. Anything lasting longer than a few weeks is a mystery to me."

His eyes widened. "Seriously? Never?"

"Nope." I popped my *p*.

"I find that hard to believe. You're quite the catch."

I preened at the compliment. "Aw, Dallas Greene, you flatter me. Aren't you the sweetest? You're also one *thousand* percent correct, I'm a spectacular fucking catch. I just haven't managed to go out with anyone who sees my incredible potential in quite the right way. They all like how cute I am. Most want to carry me around in their pocket. Lots of them have told me I'm the perfect cute little pixie princess girlfriend until they realize I've got claws."

"And fangs," Dallas grinned at me.

"Keep sweet-talking, I love it. But you're right. They like how I'm petite and pretty, but most get offended by the fact I have a brain and confidence in my sexuality. It's bizarre how mad some guys get when they offer me a compliment and I respond with *I know*. Or when I bring out my personal use electronics during sex."

A warm laugh rolled out of him. "Personal use… electronics? You mean toys?" He gaped at me. "Wait. Guys have been offended when you suggested using *toys*?"

I gave him a wink and pointed finger guns at him. I was adorably awkward, but I embraced it. "You got it. Anyway, too many bad experiences, so I quit trying for more than a hookup. Easier to cut out the weird middle man. Even that backfired on me, actually."

He chuckled. "Well, if all you're asking for is dinner, drinks, and dick, why not hop on an app? It's what they're for, right?"

I groaned, my frustration with dating apps extensive. "The apps are all ridiculous. Full of catfishes and assholes. I've gone on some good dates, but never more than one with the same person. Besides, the backfire I mentioned? It was bad. Epic bad. I deleted my last app when I moved."

Dallas squinted at me. He was reclined on the chaise end of the couch, comfortable as could be, scrolling endlessly through God knows what on his phone. I hoped it wasn't work. He was trying to cut back but still hadn't managed to get away from it in the evenings.

"You've never gone on more than one date with someone?"

I tried to recall if I'd ever done a double-dip.

"Nope, never. I thought about it with a couple of guys. Unfortunately, they usually blocked me by the morning after which let me know I'd made a big mistake going on the *first* date, let alone consider a second one."

Dallas' face scrunched up in distaste. "What kind of men are you saying *yes* to?"

I snorted. "Clearly the wrong ones."

"Obviously. Maybe you're using the wrong app?" He suggested helpfully. "You're not using Craigslist, are you?"

I tilted my head to the side, rolling my eyes at his joke. "Ha, ha, mister. No, definitely not. Is there a right app? What are you using? Did you find your long-term mistakes there?"

His gaze met mine for a moment before his head tilted to the side. "No, I met them at a bar. Well, one was a bar," he clarified.

"Well, that's different, obviously."

He grinned. "The other was a country club, if you want to get specific." The smile slipped, his eyes dropping to his phone. I couldn't help wondering what he was looking at, but he'd started doing it much more often. "I suppose there isn't a right app. There might be a decent one, though. I mean, they're all pretty specific. If you're using the ones designed for hookups and wondering why you're not getting another date, then I can see why there was a problem."

"Nah, that wasn't it. I just attract the wrong types, somehow."

His bright blue gaze met mine again.

"Maybe someone else should do your profile. Then you're attracting the right kind of guy. Whatever that means."

The idea filtered through my thoughts, a tingle of interest making my fingers twitch. It wasn't a bad idea. Addison helped with some descriptions here and there. Perhaps having a man—a *good* guy like him, who knew some of the inner workings of my personality from having lived with me—in charge would be the key to better experiences.

"What about you?"

"What about me? I'm *also* not attracting the right kind of guy, if that's what you mean."

Something clicked, everything about him making a little bit more sense all of a sudden.

"Not that." I laughed. "We've both been talking about getting back out there, but I don't see either one of us doing a damn thing about it."

"How do you know for sure?" His lips curled into a smirk.

I rolled my eyes. "Trust me, I'd know."

He rumbled a laugh, sitting up so he could turn his full attention on me.

"You sound very sure of yourself. How ready are you?"

"I could have used a drink I didn't have to pay for and an orgasm not of the do-it-yourself variety weeks ago."

"Mmm. Well, there's an obvious solution then." He tilted his head to the side, a coy grin on his mouth. He was ridiculously handsome. I knew he wasn't hitting on me, though. We occasionally pretend to flirt with one another, but it was never serious.

I put a hand to my throat, unable to resist teasing him back. "My, my, Dallas Greene. Are you *propositioning* me?" Heat unexpectedly flooded my body at the thought. Thankfully, the feeling was fleeting and passed as quickly as it came, probably in part due to my momentary panic over the inappropriate notion where my roommate was concerned. I was reminded of how he'd felt pressed up against my back while hanging pictures and shoved the sensation away.

He laughed heartily as he sat forward, elbows on his thighs. "I'm afraid not, sorry."

"I appreciate you letting me down gently. I have a feeling you're about to suggest we help one another with the dating profile situation?"

"Indeed, I was. What do you think? Do we know each other well enough for it to work?"

I shrugged, reaching for my drink. "I'm sure I can't do much worse than some of the guys I've brought home in the past, so it's worth a shot. You live with me. You've seen me before coffee. Sounds to me like you probably have a decent amount of insight into who I am."

"I'll get my laptop."

"I'll get some snacks."

When he came back, we sat with our thighs touching on the couch, both of us looking at the screen on his laptop at the same time. To keep things fair, we agreed to sign up for the same app, one new to us both.

"Name, age, location…" Dallas typed in his general information. I was surprised when his age came up.

"Oh. I didn't realize I was older than you."

His eyebrow lifted. "How much?"

"Three years. When's your birthday?"

"August."

"August what?"

"You going to run my zodiac?"

"Nooo–" I tried to lie, but I knew I was already caught when he pinned me with his sharp gaze. "Yes."

With a sigh, he relented. "The twenty-ninth. I'm a Virgo."

"Fits you. I'm a Sagittarius on the Scorpio cusp." I wiggled my eyebrows. I didn't put too much stock into astrology, though the information I'd learned about where my birthday fell was honestly pretty accurate. I was outgoing, focused on organization, and unapologetically sexual. "My birthday is November twenty-third, so a lot of years I share my celebration with Thanksgiving because it's so close."

"I'm the baby of the family. You and Addison are both around my brother Daniel's age. The three of them are all about two years apart, but my parents waited a little longer with me."

I shrugged. "Three years isn't much once you get out of school. For what it's worth, I don't feel as though I should be labeled as an adult at all most days, so you're doing just fine." I patted his knee, the rasp of his jeans rough under my fingertips.

He chuckled as he finished up the basics. Frustration formed as we moved into the more detailed portion.

I groaned. "These are the worst. It sounds like a centerfold info sheet."

"How would you know? Aren't magazines way outdated?"

"Who *doesn't* know, even if they aren't called that anymore?" I mimicked an air-headed, cartoonish bimbo voice. "Turn ons: long walks on the beach at sunset and working out. Turn-offs: guys who make me open my own doors and cold espresso. Hobbies: Volunteering for the less fortunate and saving endangered animals." I shuddered. "It's dumb. Everyone lies."

"So let's make it worth their time." Dallas got a devious glint in his eye as he moved the cursor into the "*what I enjoy*" category.

I met his eye. "You're seriously going to leave this part up to me?"

"That was the deal. Don't let me down."

The dark humor areas of my brain engaged, absolutely up for the challenge he was issuing.

"Alright. Let's go."

HOURS LATER, WE were still laughing at the finalized profiles we'd created for ourselves.

"Trina Lee, digital art sorceress, master of eviscerating humor. Are you sure that's an actual word? Isn't it acerbic wit?"

"Do you want to go have drinks with someone who doesn't know what eviscerating is?"

His incredulous expression made me snort. "No, I suppose not. Are you sure this is the picture I should use?" He'd selected a random one from my camera roll where I was bent in half, laughing at something. My mouth was wide open, my body's flaws undisguised. I was pretty sure Addison was the person who had taken the dozen or so in the series.

"It's the perfect picture, trust me."

"If you say so. I still wonder if saying outright that I'm looking for someone who can get me off is too aggressive."

"Just going with the *'honesty is best'* policy. What about mine? Your highest praise for me was *'won't murder you'*, closely followed by *'will offer you an uncomfortable pancake breakfast if you accidentally sleep over'*."

"Hey, the murder thing is *really* important. Besides, I made sure to have you put how hot you are sitting on your motorcycle—which honestly should get you dates all by itself. Chicks dig guys with motorcycles." I glanced at him, realizing what I'd said. "Dudes too, I imagine. Besides, it's only fair since you put what I said as a *joke* down for me. I've never once saved an endangered animal or taken a beach walk at sunset."

"You're missing out. The gulf is awesome, maybe we should take a trip down there so you're not lying."

Dallas set the laptop on the coffee table before stretching his arms over his head. A yawn cracked his jaw wide, triggering one for me as well.

"That was fun." The smile wouldn't leave my face.

"Here's hoping it works, right?" He collected our snack debris as he got to his feet.

"I suppose. Could be we just opened one hell of a Pandora's Box on ourselves."

We did a companionable quick tidy of the kitchen before going our separate ways.

"'Night."

"Goodnight, Trina."

Once safely behind my bedroom door, I exhaled a happy breath. I hadn't enjoyed a night of entertainment quite like this… ever. Dallas was a good egg, and I was glad Addison had found her way to the Greene family so I could, as well.

After washing my face and brushing my teeth, I opened the dating app on my phone. My thumb hesitated over the activation button for a few moments. I pressed it before plugging in the charger and climbing into bed.

Time would tell if our ridiculous new profiles were good bait for the right kind of dates. Either way, I'd had a great time, and it was well worth getting to know Dallas more. It was not at all lost on me given the events of the evening, I'd say he was a great match for me.

Too bad it was still not only a terrible idea, but also completely out of the question.

CHAPTER SIXTEEN

Trina

I T TOOK LESS than a week for the new profiles to start yielding fruit.

Dallas warned me via text not to worry about him as far as dinner on Friday night. He had a date.

I appreciated the heads up, but I also wanted at least three hundred percent more information than what he'd given. I didn't have a chance to talk to him when he first got home because I was trapped in the office on yet another video-style interview screening that led nowhere.

He emerged from his bedroom as I was settling in on the couch after taking a shower to wash away the stench of my job-hunting failure.

"How do I look?" He asked, catching me staring as he got ready to leave. "I'll probably be home late."

"You look great." Which was the truth. He could pull off the dark-washed jeans and t-shirt as date clothes better than anyone I knew. "The new profile worked, then? Anybody I know?"

He smirked, one eyebrow raised. "It seems to have worked, though I've deleted more private messages than I've ever gotten before combined. You may have been on to something with the *'won't murder you'* thing. Not someone you know, this is a random swipe right situation."

"See, I told you so!" I giggled at how adorable he was, torn between embarrassment and excitement. "I should probably consider answering some of those messages myself." I didn't miss most parts of dating or all the mess it created. The build-up, the effort of getting ready… all to ultimately be let down in one way or another. Even with the new profile, I was a little gun-shy. Maybe if he went on a good date, I'd feel better taking the plunge.

"Well, good luck. Here's hoping this one is a hit. Where will you be? You know, just in case."

He stared blankly at me for a moment. "You going to be checking up on me?" His mouth twitched in amusement as he pulled out his phone.

I lifted a shoulder. "No, but these days, it's a good idea for *someone* to know where you'll be. Safety first, after all." I was unrepentant for asking, despite him finding it funny. I didn't care if he was a man, or if getting the information might make it seem like I was mothering him. Terrible things happened to all kinds of people, no matter their appearance. It was important.

"I texted it all to you." My phone dinged in confirmation,

so I glanced at it while he grinned expectantly at me. "Thanks for looking out." He double-checked his pockets after slipping his phone back in one, winking at me as he pulled the door open. "Don't wait up."

"Have fun!"

After he was gone, I ordered my favorite dinner from a little seafood restaurant down the street. I texted Addison while I ate and watched TV. The quiet was nice for a while, but I weirded myself out when I turned to joke with him about something on the show and remembered he wasn't there. It was around this point I decided it was probably best if I headed off to bed.

Around 11:30, there was an awful commotion. I'd been reading a perfectly delicious dark mafia romance when I heard the door slam. Pulse racing, I grabbed my bedside baseball bat with my heart in my throat.

I cracked my door open just enough to listen, prepared to defend myself with the bat when a grating sound rang out. It sounded very much like furniture was being forcibly moved across the living room hardwood.

All it took for me to relax my stance and close my door was the very deep moan I heard coming from down the hall. My pulse jumped in response. It wasn't a noise someone in trouble would make. The furniture wasn't being stolen, it was being *used*.

Realizing it was Dallas and his date, I closed the door as silently as I could before getting back into my bed. I snorted, realizing I was straining to hear what was going on.

"You perv." Shaking my head, I grabbed my e-reader off of the comforter, trying to get back into the story. As the story got steamier, so did the soundtrack on the other side of my bedroom door. I hadn't realized until now it would have been wise to invest in noise-canceling headphones before moving in.

I was sweating, hormones on high alert between the steamy scene I was reading and the moaning echoing down the hall.

Dallas' date's voice was deeper than his, the sound of the two dark tones clashing together as they rode a wave of passion with one another made me blush.

"Jesus, Trina. You absolute *hussy*," I scolded myself.

Unable to sit still any longer, I went into the bathroom, hoping the extra distance and insulation would muffle the extracurricular activities happening in the living room. I considered texting Dallas to see if he wouldn't mind moving to his bedroom, but kept deleting the messages as I typed them. No combination of words felt right for such a request. There was no way I was going to be that kind of cock-blocking roommate.

I didn't *need* another shower, but my blood was singing. There was no way I was going to get to sleep as warm as I was, noise levels aside.

I turned on the spray, leaving it as cool as I could stand it. I lathered on my favorite nighttime body wash, the lavender and vanilla scent filling the room as my hands roved over my skin.

Turning over the scene I'd been reading in my mind, I made a date out of myself as I soaped up.

My fingers dipped, teasing and stroking before pressing into my core. The sound of the water striking the tile muted my sighs of pleasure. I drove myself higher while pretending the touch belonged to someone else. Heat rose into my cheeks, tension coiling deep in my gut. I pressed my forehead to the cool ceramic, swapping my hand for the pulsing spray of the showerhead. It only took moments for me to come apart, my forearm in my mouth as I moaned out.

I slumped against the shower wall, breathing deeply as the rush subsided.

"You are a pervy bitch," I muttered under my breath, resuming the thorough washing I'd started. Shame made a passing attempt to settle in, but I scrubbed it from my skin.

By the time I was dressed in clean pajamas, my facial creams refreshed and teeth brushed for the second time, the noises in the living room had stopped.

Time would tell whether Dallas' guest was gone or whether they'd just moved into his bedroom. Either way, I was thankful.

A cold tendril of jealousy wound itself around my ribcage. As I lay in the dark, I tried to puzzle out whether I was envious of the fact his date had gone so well or if I was simply jealous.

Neither option sat well with me. We were friendly roommates, that was all. I owed him nothing, and he held no claim on me.

A grin spread over my lips as drowsiness claimed me. The precedent was set. If he could bring home dates, so could I.

STILL BLEARY-EYED, I stumbled my way down the hall the next morning, coffee my only goal.

I prepped my cup with creamer as the pot sputtered. In my defense, my brain was never fully functional until I was at least most of the way through my first cup, but I should have noticed the mostly naked men sprawled out on the couch *way* before I did.

No doubt Addison would be horrified by my dismal situational awareness. I did, however, register how the chaise end of the couch was about two feet from where it had started the night before. I hoped the new floor hadn't suffered too badly.

I was fine until the unfamiliar bronze face hanging off the arm of the couch sucked in a breath that was half snore and half growl. *That* made me squeal.

"Fuck!" I burned my arm with hot coffee when I jumped, swearing in a harsh whisper, as though it would undo the teakettle noise I'd already made.

Dallas' sleep rumpled head popped up from somewhere in the middle of the couch, his guest tumbling off the cushions altogether, hitting the plush rug that barely covered enough floor for the coffee table to sit on with a muted thud.

"Sorry! Shit. Sorry, sorry." I put my hands up defensively, backing down the hall.

Dallas scrubbed his face with his hands as his date got to his feet. Both looked quite a bit worse for the wear. It had been an *excellent* date, by all appearances.

"I'm sorry, I should have checked first."

Standing awkwardly on the far fringe of the living room with my coffee mug in my hand, shirt damp from where I wiped the steaming hot coffee off my now throbbing wrist, I was sleepily scrutinized by two men showing a whole lot of skin.

"No, no. It's my fault." Dallas yawned.

His date was wide-eyed, still immobile as he stood there staring at me.

Unsure what else to do, I raised a hand in a wave. "Hi. I'm Trina."

"Uh… Oscar."

"Nice to meet you, Oscar. Sorry about waking you up like that." After another moment of super-awkward silence, I couldn't stand it anymore. "I can make muffins?"

"Muffins would be great," Dallas said in a rush, ushering Oscar toward his bedroom. "We'll just… get dressed."

"Okay."

I detoured back to my room for my phone. Baking was one of my favorite distractions and it felt extra useful today. Dallas and Oscar were having a whisper-yell conversation behind his bedroom door.

My muffin batter hadn't even been properly mixed yet when Oscar hustled out of Dallas' room, one hand raised in a wave, the other messily tucking his shirt into his pants.

"Thanks for the offer, but I have to get going. Sorry, again. Didn't mean to startle you."

"Oh. That's okay. Nice to meet you!"

He looked completely mortified as he opened the door, vanishing out of it with a slam.

I cracked an egg into my mixing bowl as Dallas, now fully dressed, came into the kitchen and poured himself a cup of coffee.

"Sorry," I apologized again, sorry I'd run his date off.

"No need to be." He glanced over my shoulder into the bowl. "What flavor today?"

"Coffee Cake. Double streusel."

"Sounds delicious."

I resumed mixing up the cinnamon and brown sugar for streusel. Questions swirled around inside me as he leaned casually against the counter, sipping his coffee. My stomach was knotted. I'd never been in this kind of room-mate situation before. Addison and I worked out a system to communicate when we had company back in college.

After I shoved the pan into the oven, I refreshed my coffee, meeting Dallas' eye.

"Sooo… good date?"

He blinked slowly, as though reliving some of the better moments behind his eyelids. A sly grin formed on his lips as he raised his coffee mug to his mouth.

"Yeah, good date."

"I'm glad to hear it." Energy buzzed around inside my body. I'd probably never tell him how overhearing them affected me, but it wasn't in my nature to hold things back. "Speaking of hearing… sound travels pretty well around here."

His hand paused, coffee cup suspended halfway between his mouth and the counter. "Oh." A blush stained his stubble-prickled cheeks. "We *were* rather…" He scrubbed a hand over his face. "Wow. I'm sorry."

I shrugged, my face burning as I remembered how even *my* libido was super-charged by their enthusiasm. "It's not a big deal. Just wanted you to know."

"Still, it wasn't very considerate. You'd have gotten one hell of an eyeful if you'd wandered out for a drink of water or something." I blinked slowly, trying to keep my expression blank. Every word of that was absolutely true. "And there won't be a next time, I'm afraid. At least, not with Oscar." Dallas' face drooped into a frown.

Guilt pressed in heavily on my chest. My stomach rolled for good measure. "Oh, damn. I'm *really* sorry. Did I scare him off?"

Dallas met my eye, expression back to his neutral half-grin. "Maybe. I didn't think to tell him I had a roommate. Or that said roommate was female. It's probably for the best."

Apologizing again felt redundant. There was a stilted silence as we sipped our coffee and waited for the timer to go off on the muffins.

When it did, I carefully took them all out to cool on a rack before serving us. Muffin in hand, I sat at my favorite spot at the island.

"Sounded like you had a good time, at least." I blushed as the words came out of my mouth.

Dallas coughed over his bite of muffin, brown sugar streusel sprinkling the countertop. I pounded on his back to help him out, laughing.

"He definitely has some talents."

"Damn. Then I feel extra bad for accidentally chasing him off."

"Nah, don't be. Some things are meant to be once in a lifetime experiences."

I grinned as I ate a steaming bite of sugary coffee cake. If that wasn't the truth, I didn't know what was.

CHAPTER SEVENTEEN

Dallas

AFTER THE EXCITEMENT over Oscar on Saturday morning, we'd both indulged in a lazy weekend. I'd convinced Trina to join me for a walk both Saturday and Sunday evenings in trade for a movie marathon, plus some very limited work time. She told me I could only work as long as it took her to complete two applications, which seemed fair.

When she got up from her chair in the office, doing one of her yoga stretches that always made her body creak while giving me a peek of her skin, I saved my work and closed my computer as promised.

Her setting boundaries on my time and suggestions to put things on my calendar were working out far better than I'd thought it would. I went into the next work week feeling more refreshed than usual.

When I got home from work Friday afternoon, Trina was rushing around like a woman possessed.

Seeing her dressed up was an unexpected, although pleasant, surprise.

"Hey! Sorry to rush out. I'm already running late." Trina hopped on one foot while she slid into some shockingly tall black heels. She somehow multi-tasked grabbing her purse and a light jacket to go over her slip dress at the same time without falling over, defying all laws of gravity.

"Interview?" I pushed away the feeling of disappointment that crept in. I needed a break after my hectic week. I'd been hoping part of my weekend included a pizza and beer with her, but it was on me that I'd built it up in my head without asking her if she had plans.

She snorted, hand on the doorknob. "Cute, but no. I have a date. How do I look?"

"Very nice. Have fun." Even I could hear the lack of enthusiasm in my tone. I immediately felt like an asshole. She'd been plenty supportive of me when I said exactly the same thing a week ago.

She was stunning. While every day Trina was—without question—a force to be reckoned with. Trina in a red bodycon dress and heels was on a whole other level. Something stirred in my gut as she fussed with the finishing touches on her makeup in the small mirror over the skinny table by the door.

She'd been bringing home pieces of furniture and decor bits at a time. I didn't want to bring too much attention to the decorative towels or candles she'd sprinkled through the house, because I loved her additions and didn't want her to stop. The little table was one of my favorite things. Trina was turning our happy little apartment into a home. Her notion of shared custody for the furniture became something I wondered about whenever something new appeared. What would be left if we split things and went our separate ways?

I didn't like to think about it.

I crossed my arms, processing the concern that set in over the top of my appreciation for her appearance.

"Does someone know where you'll be?"

Trina looked at me through her eyelashes, her fiery expression cutting. She could give my mom a run for her money with such a perfect glare. Her lips curled into a smile and electricity zapped my veins. She was playing with me.

This woman was *trouble*.

"Naturally. Addison has all my deets and even my GPS location. No need to worry. I appreciate it, though." Her words echoed mine from the week before. She tapped out a quick text. My phone vibrated in my pocket.

"Of course." I grinned at her, unable to contain the amusement following her around like her favorite lily perfume. If she was going to watch out for me, I was going to return the favor. Truth be told, I would have asked either way, but she'd taken me by such surprise by asking the other night, there was no way I could skip asking her back.

"Alright, I'm off. Here's hoping James273 is as handsome in person as his profile picture. Don't wait up!" She wiggled her eyebrows suggestively, singing the words as she slipped out the door.

My gut twisted, something foreign slithering in my veins. It wasn't jealousy, though it was close. I rationalized it was some version of concern, mostly because she was a woman and strangers could be dangerous.

"She's your roommate, you idiot," I grumbled, making my way to my bedroom. I found a pair of basketball shorts to put on after my shower. "And a *friend*. You know where she'll be. She's a big girl, she can take care of herself."

Once I was clean, I scrounged up a dish of leftovers from the fridge. I didn't want to still be in the living room when Trina came back, especially if she ended up bringing him home.

The idea made me nauseous, which in turn made me angry. I had no right to feel like that. She didn't deserve a shitty double standard about hooking up on the first date. After all, Oscar and I hadn't even made it to my bedroom, and she'd gotten an earful. There was no room for me to be judging.

I grabbed my laptop, settling into bed with a fresh beer and a new project, completely in denial that I was waiting for Trina to come home.

The master delivery schedule spreadsheet I'd been prom-ising to Addison for weeks took shape on the screen in front of me. Nothing like a little vexation to motivate me to get the most tedious things accomplished. I ventured out to get one another light snack before calling it a night. As the clock ticked toward eleven, I glanced at my phone, half expecting a message, either from Addison checking to see if Trina was home yet or from Trina herself.

There were none.

Frustrated with myself, I took all my empty bottles to the trash, checked the door to be sure it was locked, and sequestered myself in my bedroom with a TV show I hoped would put me to sleep.

A handful of episodes in, I was barely drowsy.

I was waiting for her to come home. I was man enough to admit it. But it didn't mean I had to like it.

I wasted a ridiculous amount of time trying to find something else to watch and was just about to resign myself to a rom-com when Trina's giggling traveled through my closed bedroom door.

I heard a fleshy noise as a body bounced off of the couch and then something clatter off of what might have been the kitchen island before the laughter faded down the hallway. My stomach tightened. She'd warned me about how noise traveled. I didn't realize how well until hearing it myself. I kind of wanted to apologize again.

At least she was home safe. I could relax. The rest of it was something I'd have to deal with in the morning.

IT WAS A dick move, but I couldn't help myself. I wanted to see for myself if James273 slept over or if I'd missed his exit in the middle of the night after I finally passed out cold.

I'd woken up at six, and there was no way I was getting back to sleep. There was time to brew coffee, make bacon, eggs and even try my hand at flipping some pancakes before Trina and her date appeared. There was nothing in the world quite like malicious friendliness.

"Good morning! Can I get you guys some breakfast?" I asked, a little extra perk in my voice.

She cringed at my volume, a hangover evident in the squint of her eyes. "Coffee first."

The guy, a handsome enough brunette with mocha skin, took me in with wide eyes. I could only guess what he was thinking, seeing me standing in the kitchen with a bright smile, spatula in one hand, coffee pot in the other.

My lack of shirt may have had something to do with his speechlessness.

"Ahhh, thanks, but I'm good. Thanks for everything, Tina, I gotta jet," he said, dipping in for an awkward, chase kiss on Trina's cheek.

"So soon?" I asked, feigning disappointment. "It's *Trina*, by the way. You sure you don't want coffee or breakfast? I'm making pancakes." His calling her the wrong name made my blood pump, and not in a fun way.

The man glanced between a confused Trina and me, hastily backing toward the front door. It was not much different from how Oscar looked after she'd accidentally woken us up. He'd been shocked to find out I didn't live alone and was beyond horrified she might have heard us. I tried to convince him there was no way that had happened. As it turned out, he was right.

"I appreciate it, but no. See you around!" He unceremoniously slammed the door behind himself, making Trina wince. She didn't seem surprised or shaken by his sudden departure.

I slid a mug across the counter as she took a seat at the island. Patience was not my strong suit, but I was prepared to wait. I was also very amused by her bedraggled state. I continued to flip pancakes until the batter ran out as she cautiously sipped from her cup.

By the time I put a plate of food in front of her, she looked slightly less worse for the wear. She was finger-combing her short, spiky curls and swiping the smeared eyeliner out from under her eyes as I started eating.

"So?" I raised my eyebrows, hoping she would go for being prompted.

"Smells good, thanks." She poked her fork into some of the eggs, nibbling carefully.

"I wasn't fishing for compliments about my cooking."

"I know." Her mouth twitched as she chewed. "I thought we put the awkward pancake breakfast thing on your dating profile for *your* dates, not mine."

"I'm pretty sure we never specified." I should have known better than to assume she wouldn't recognize where I'd gotten the idea from.

I blew a breath out my nose, dragging some pancake through syrup on my plate, silently willing her to start talking.

She was halfway through her eggs when she finally loosened up. "As it turns out, James273 is not quite as handsome as he is in his profile picture. Photo filters on social media are getting way out of hand. Anyway, he was a decent date, bought me some good drinks, made me laugh, and made sure I came first. So…" She shrugged, stabbing at her egg like it owed her money.

The bite I'd taken got stuck in my throat. I gulped some orange juice to help it go down, the urge to laugh not helping at all. Why I wasn't expecting it was a mystery, because I knew Trina, but I was still unprepared for that level of candor.

"Well. Congrats? I'm not sure how to respond, honestly. He has somewhere to be this morning?"

Her eyes lifted from her plate to meet mine. "Probably nowhere special." Her head cocked to the side. "Shirtless was a nice touch, by the way. I like your tattoo."

I couldn't stop the grin spreading over my mouth. The words trailed over my ribs and down my side weren't something I flashed around—they were deeply personal. I was betting James wasn't paying attention, and she was too hungover to see the words clearly. "I thought so. Did you guys hit it off? Should I expect good ol' Jim to start hanging around, *Tina*?"

She scoffed into her coffee mug. "Nah. He was nice enough… nothing to write home about. He didn't even ask about a second date. It was good, but a reminder why I quit all those apps in the first place."

Perplexed, I reached for the full pot of coffee, offering her a refill. "Now I kind of feel like *I* need to apologize."

She stuffed a hearty bite of pancake into her mouth, then blotted her lips on a napkin before pushing the plate away.

"No need. That's a pretty standard date for me, to be honest. Besides, we're even. I scared yours off with my muffin, you terrified mine with your hot cakes…"

I leaned on my elbows as laughter rocked my whole body. Even half-dead hungover, this woman had one hell of a way with words.

Pushing my empty plate out from under me, I processed what she'd said, glad the smile had returned to her mouth.

"It's kind of sad. The standard date thing."

Coffee mug gripped in her hands, she shrugged again, rolling her shoulders a few times to loosen the muscles. "Maybe. But pretty normal."

I sighed. "We probably should have talked about this before, but maybe we could work out some kind of system if we're going to bring someone home? You were right, sound travels *really* well around here."

Trina's face went from surprised to carefully blank in the blink of an eye. I felt the slightest pang of guilt for not being specific. I hadn't heard anything once they'd gone to her room, though clearly, she'd heard *plenty* when Oscar and I were in the living room.

"Sure. What did you have in mind? When we were in college, Addison and I would try to rotate weekend days. We'd stay with a friend or at least plan to have our earbuds in. There was a red bra we'd hang from the doorknob."

"This sounds... complicated. Plus, I'm not sure the neighbors would appreciate lingerie hanging from our door."

She considered. "We could try to go to their places instead of coming here."

I grimaced. "I'm rather fond of my own bed."

Trina pierced me with a stare over the top of her coffee cup. "Well, then maybe we just don't get laid. This feels too damn complicated." Her uncharacteristic grumpiness wasn't something I wanted to continue to test.

"I'm not looking for anything long-term, anyway. We'll figure something out. We could probably do something easy, like send a text as a heads up."

Trina nodded, sliding off the barstool. "I need a shower. Thanks for breakfast. If you want to leave the dishes, I'll clean them up when I'm done."

"I got it. And you're welcome. Sorry about James273."

As I loaded the dishwasher, relief filled me at the thought of never having to see her wander through the house with another man again. Guilt rushed in that I felt this way, but I found myself smiling because it had been a treat seeing the dude's shocked face as I served up coffee and pancakes without my shirt on.

I was probably going to hell.

After a brief deliberation, I decided I was fine with the possibility.

CHAPTER EIGHTEEN

Trina

WE COMPARED OUR dating matches after dinner most nights, trusting one another's opinion to filter out the duds from the possibilities as a safety measure.

My standards weren't unreasonable, but I was already tired of jumping through hoops so I could go out for a single drink then come home alone. After James, I'd pulled way back on seeking out dates simply to get lucky. Neither of us was clicking with the people we were matching up with, and it started to feel like a waste of my weekends all too quickly.

I wasn't doing anything during the week, though I was sticking to an almost regular work schedule, putting in applications, and working on my website.

"What do you think of this one?" I tilted my phone to show Dallas my latest match.

His profile tags made me smile, which was more than I could say for most.

Dallas' mouth pulled to the side in a 'meh' gesture. "Sounds alright, as long as you are attracted to guys who believe misogynistic jokes are the height of humor."

"Fair." I deleted him.

Without a word, he showed me his screen.

I checked the shock I felt as I scanned the picture. It wasn't what I'd expected to see. Every match he'd made so far was a very attractive man. I didn't care one way or the other, it just surprised me. I might have even been a little jealous of the caliber of guys he was pulling. This picture happened to be unique since Dallas had yet to take out or bring home a woman. The fact that this particular woman he'd matched with was gorgeous in a lot of ways I wasn't, but could still be my sister, certainly was nothing to do with whatever the hot sensation in my chest was.

Probably.

"She's pretty. Sounds as though she's got some fire in her." I read through her profile. She also *sounded* a lot like me.

He met my eye before glancing back at the screen, no doubt trying to find the flaw he thought I'd seen.

"But?"

I tried as hard as I could to come across nonchalant. "You haven't taken out any women before. I guess I just wasn't expecting it even though we set up your profile to accept all options."

His expression went soft, almost dreamy as he scrolled through her photos. "Me neither."

Pushing whatever spicy emotion I was feeling to the side, I continued blandly, "Looks like a reasonable match. Can't hurt to go for a drink. What about this guy?"

I flashed him my screen. The corner of his mouth twitched. "Seems a little boring. Maybe he's a diamond in the rough. Go for it."

We both responded to private messages, making final decisions about meeting in person with our matches while we watched the latest zombie movie on Netflix.

"I'm going to meet with her on Friday," Dallas said casually, frowning at a text notification on his phone before tossing it over to the coffee table.

My match asked for a drink on Friday as well.

"We both appear to have a date then."

Dallas reached across me to get the bowl of chips, brushing my thigh with his arm as he did so.

"I'd have handed it to you," I teased, ignoring the rapid beat of my heart.

"I know." He winked at me.

All I could do was steady my breathing while I grabbed a handful of chips. I knew he wasn't flirting, the same as he knew I wasn't when I did things like that.

But it didn't stop my pulse from doing erratic things when he touched me.

INSTEAD OF MY normal enthusiasm for Friday afternoon, I was anxious and frustrated.

As I applied the final touches on my makeup, Dallas knocked on my bedroom door.

"Come in!" I called, leaning out of the bathroom as he cautiously took a step into my space.

"Hey," he said, scanning me from head to toe. His eyes burned a hot trail over my body. "That's… a nice dress."

I looked down at myself, smoothing a wrinkle out of the navy fabric. I'd put on a pound or two, thanks to the frequent baking and comfortable couch, but it fit me perfectly. If anything, I filled it out better than I had the last time I'd worn it.

"You don't like it?"

He tilted his head to the side. "I just thought maybe you'd go with the red."

I gestured for him to come in. Dallas leaned casually against the doorframe of my bathroom while I put on another layer of mascara then swiped on crimson lipstick.

"The red dress is for James273 situations. That's not what I'm going for tonight."

"Ah. I see. I feel as though I'm learning top secret information when you tell me those kinds of things." He leaned against the doorframe with his arms crossed, watching me.

Addison called it his model pose. I didn't disagree, but I'd seen it so much it had become one of his default positions in my mind.

"You have no idea. There's a whole system. We develop it early and stay consistent with it throughout our entire dating lives. Naturally, everyone's is different."

"What does red lipstick mean?" His bright blue eyes tracked my movements in the mirror.

He'd dressed in the pair of dark-washed jeans I'd never seen him wear anywhere except on dates. A red plaid shirt layered over a plain white t-shirt left unbuttoned. His broad shoulders filled it out well.

"Confidence mostly. But it's also a way to keep men's eyes on your mouth instead of your tits."

A slow grin spread across his mouth. He stared into the glass as though daring his eyes to stray from my face.

"I see. Does it work?"

"Maybe half the time. The problem is, they start to over-focus on your mouth instead and veer off into making innuendos about what your lips might look like around their dick. There's no winning."

He blinked at me, wide-eyed. I could see the moment he began struggling to keep his eyes on mine instead of dropping to either my mouth or my chest.

I snorted. "See?"

"Fuck. I'm so sorry." He was mortified, hands pressed together near his chin as though begging me for forgiveness, as he gave in to a short, chagrined laugh.

A chuckle rumbled out of me. "No worries. I kind of set you up talking about it. You don't wear certain things for dates? I've never seen those jeans unless you're going out. There's no deeper thought behind what you're putting on when you have a date? No special underwear? Which, by the way, is a whole conversation by itself. I'm not sure you're ready for it if you don't already know."

He tugged on the hem of his shirt.

"I don't really put too much thought into it. This was clean and it's nicer than the stuff I wear to work, so it passed muster for date quality. I guess the jeans don't get much other use. No special underwear."

"See?" I tossed a few final things into a small make-up bag for my purse in case I needed to refresh while we were out. "Though I will say, I'm a little disappointed that many men don't overthink every single part of their outfits like lots of women do."

Pushing past him, I slipped on the heels waiting for me near my bed and slung my purse over my shoulder.

"What's the deal with the underwear?" he asked.

"I'm guessing you already know."

"Matching set means you were hoping for us to see it? Black or red is a good sign?"

"Ding, ding, ding! See, you're well aware of our methods whether you realize it or not."

I led the way out of my room and down the hall, pausing by the front door to grab my jacket. It was hot as Hades' armpit outside, which meant businesses had their air conditioning turned down to arctic temps.

"Ready?" I asked.

"Ready."

We made our way to the parking lot together, separating at our vehicles.

"Good luck," he wished me as he pulled his helmet out of the saddlebag.

"Safe travels."

Despite the parting words, his motorcycle headlight followed me out of the parking lot and through town, veering off only blocks from the bar I was headed to. The gesture left me with a warm feeling in my chest.

If anyone asked me for one word to describe how Dallas made me feel, it would be safe. That felt important, but I couldn't quite pin down all the reasons why.

After a final touch-up in my visor mirror, I made my way into the bar.

I spotted my date at a tall table right away. He was handsome enough, all perfectly styled blonde hair and bright smile as he greeted me with an outstretched hand.

"Hi. I'm Chad."

"Trina. It's nice to meet you."

I got a whiff of clean linen as he shifted back into his seat.

It only took a second for the waitress to hustle over to get my order. Chad had a bottle of local IPA in front of him already.

"Can I get you a drink?" he offered, giving the waitress a polite smile.

So far so good.

"Absolutely. Vodka and cranberry if you don't mind."

Once she'd stepped away, Chad flashed his pearly whites at me.

I braced for what I knew was coming—the small talk portion of our evening. It was always the worst part for me. My stomach did a tumble, then settled. It went this way every single time. Like my body was telling me I didn't have to do this. Like feeling nervous was permission to stay single forever.

I was in this for the duration, my guts would just have to deal with it.

"So, Trina. You mentioned on your profile you're an artist?"

"Graphic artist, yes."

"Does that kind of thing pay well?"

I did everything I could to keep my eye roll strictly internal. *Here we go.*

Chad began to veer off track from his very promising start, but I would at least humor him until I could finish my first drink. I glanced around for the waitress, already impatient.

"Usually, yes. I was with a company that did marketing for some prestigious clients for a few years. I'm between jobs at the moment."

Chad stiffened. Whether because I'd made him uncomfortable with my honesty or because I was unemployed, I wasn't sure.

"That's too bad."

"I agree. I loved my job and was excellent at it. Unfortunately, when we merged with another company, my position was eliminated." The words had gotten easier to say, thanks to all the interviews I'd parroted them through lately. I didn't understand why I felt compelled to explain myself to Chad, however. Having done so left me feeling frustrated.

"Ah."

I glanced around for the waitress again as he took a swig of his IPA.

"You said you were in flooring?" I prompted, hopeful if I shifted the attention of the conversation to him, I could buy some time for our drinks to arrive.

"Yes, been with my current firm for a while. I specialize in tile and laminate." As Chad enthused about the intricacies of flooring sales, I allowed my gaze to travel the room.

He barely paused for breath when the waitress finally delivered my drink. I wasted no time sampling the cocktail.

At an appropriate pause, I said, "That does sound interesting."

It did not, in any way, sound interesting.

"Are you from around here?"

"Not originally, though I went to college nearby. I was away for several years, but this is home for me."

"Must be nice to see other parts of the country."

"I never went very far. I do recommend moving at least once, though, but I'm glad to be done moving for a while. It's rough."

Chad peeled his bottle label and there was an uncomfortable silence between us. This is what I got for saying yes to a date with a man legitimately named *Chad*. I took a drink of my cocktail, praying it kicked in soon.

"Can I be honest with you?"

My stomach pitched. Nothing good ever came after those words on a first date.

"Of course."

"I haven't done this kind of thing very much."

I lifted my half-empty glass to my lips. "No? Well, you're doing just fine." The lie rolled off my tongue almost too easily.

"Thanks, I appreciate it." He combed through his hair with his fingers, the nerves now obvious on his face. "I haven't had a chance to do much dating since my fiancé and I separated. Honestly, I never thought I'd have to date again, so I feel... out of my comfort zone."

Oh no. No, no, no.

"It's good to put yourself out there after a while." I wasn't sure what else to say, so I took a deep drink from my glass, the vodka leaving a sharp bite at the back of my tongue as I swallowed. Mentally, I'd already checked out. Chad was clearly not ready to be dating, but I'd committed to a drink and would do the best I could to give him a gentle letdown.

He continued on about his ex, how I vaguely resembled her except for my short hair, the fact they'd gotten together just out of college. How really, it wasn't anyone's fault things didn't work out, they'd simply grown apart.

As he rambled, I glanced across the bar. A man was grinning broadly at his pretty date, gesturing wildly with his hands. Whatever story he was telling made her laugh. They seemed ridiculously in love. A hot burst of melancholy emotion chased through my veins. I blamed the feeling on the alcohol finally kicking in and giving me a mediocre buzz for making me want what they had when I was stuck hearing about Chad's former fiancé.

"So, anyway. I thought I'd give this dating thing another chance."

I forced my gaze from the couple across the room to the man in front of me.

"Completely understandable." Something cold slithered through my gut as I put a plastic grin on my face for my date. This whole thing had been a terrible idea.

I drew in a deep inhale, bracing myself for what would probably be another hour of consoling Chad, trying to smile my way through the awkward conversation.

"Do you mind if we get something to eat while we talk? I'm starving," I said, interrupting him mid-sentence. Maybe if I was rude, things would end faster, I could get home to my cozies and a vibrator.

"Oh. Great idea. Their appetizer menu showed some interesting fusion egg rolls. Diana hated anything deep-fried. She was very into the holistic health lifestyle, so I've been exploring lots of new things since we ended…"

Outwardly I had a smile pasted on, but inside I was dying as he continued to tell me all about his amazing ex-fiancé, Diana. I heard her name so much it became one I never wanted to hear again. Only Wonder Woman herself could wear the moniker without me cringing. I had half a mind to delete the dating app altogether. For sure, I'd never again accept a message from anyone named Chad.

I could only hope Dallas' date was going much better than mine was.

CHAPTER NINETEEN

Trina

AT THE END of the night, Chad thanked me for listening and even picked up the whole bill, despite me arguing we should split it. I got a chaste kiss on the cheek after he walked me to my car. He took it very well that there wouldn't be a second date.

It might have felt like one of the longest dates of my life, but it could have gone a whole lot worse.

Dallas was in the kitchen with his date when I got home. I'd been one thousand percent ready to dive into my cozies and a bottle of wine when I realized I wasn't alone. I hadn't noticed his motorcycle in the parking lot, so I'd burst through the door of our apartment without any care for potential onlookers.

My fancy lace bra was dangling from my fingertips while I stared at a woman in my kitchen who could almost be my sister. She was giggling over something Dallas had said while eating a cookie. One I'd set aside specifically for myself. I'd been looking forward to it the whole drive home after surviving Chad.

Her pretty grin faded when I came through the door. I took a certain amount of satisfaction in seeing some suspicion and panic flit across her face when he smiled at me in greeting.

Something ugly flared inside me over the whole situation. I didn't like it one bit. I excused myself as fast as I could once I got my hands on a bottle of chardonnay, changing my plans to include a bubble bath.

As I soaked in the hot water, I realized the terrible feeling was *jealousy*. Which was stupid. Dallas had his life and I had mine. We were roommates. Just roommates. Friends, maybe. But nothing romantic.

Everything has been going perfectly fine until my emotions decided to get involved where they didn't belong.

"This is so *dumb*," I scolded myself.

Dallas wasn't hard to talk to, but the conversation I needed to have with him had me completely twisted up on the inside.

I let my hair down from the towel it was wrapped in. It was approaching an awkward length; if I didn't get it cut, it was going to get totally out of control and be unmanageable.

Good thing I didn't have anywhere to be. No dates, no job—no reason to have cute hair.

Checking my shitty attitude, I decided I would call a salon in the morning.

When my hair was short and easy to manage, I felt more in control. The more effort I was forced to put into styling it, the less I wanted to deal with it at all. Once I'd permitted myself to go pixie, I'd felt an immense amount of freedom. Besides, the super short haircut was cute as hell on me. I could use some self-care.

I tossed the tiny pot of anti-aging cream back onto the countertop more forcefully than I intended, frustrated with myself and the situation.

Interviews were going well, but nobody was making any offers. I was bored. My creativity was partially redirected to some little commission projects, but I wasn't sure it was ever going to be enough to sustain me, financially or creatively. I was tired as fuck of applying to places I had no real interest in working. My money wasn't endless, though. Something needed to give soon or else…

"*Stop.* It will work out."

Trying to get my train of thought back on track, I put on one of my favorite sundresses with red lipstick for confidence. Even though Sunday at home shouldn't have required it.

"Listen, I've been thinking…" I was very aware my opening sounded weak. I'd already tossed out "*we need to talk*" and "*hey, about the dating thing, could we not?*"

I applied a fresh coat of moisturizer to my face in my bathroom mirror as I rehearsed the imaginary conversation.

All too soon, I was out of things to apply to my face and was forced to leave the bathroom.

Dallas was on the couch, scrolling through an endless menu of movies.

"Want to order pizza?" He asked. His gaze tracked my body. "That's a cute dress. You going out?"

"Thanks. No, um, I'm not going anywhere. Pizza sounds great."

I sat stiffly on the far end of the couch, hands folded in my lap. He tapped around on his phone, ordering the food.

"You okay?" he asked, looking over once he'd finished. "You seem… tense."

"Fine." I even sounded uptight, and I knew it.

Dallas chuckled. "Okayyy…" Realizing I wasn't going to talk, he got up. A cold bottle of hard cider appeared in front of me. "Maybe this will help?"

"Thanks."

I was three gulps in before I loosened up enough to start the conversation. The fact I needed a drink to start the conversation worried me.

"I've been thinking…"

"That's dangerous," he teased.

"Maybe we do need some ground rules if we're both going to continue to date like we've been."

Seriousness clouded Dallas' normally playful features as he straightened.

"Rules?"

My skin was itchy. I couldn't figure out why this was so complicated. Feeling jealous had thrown everything off.

We were very much alike, and I didn't want to upset him. If he decided I was too difficult to live with, I was screwed.

"Nothing serious, but I think my last date was it for me. At least for a while. I just don't have the energy to deal with the Chads of the greater Birmingham area right now." My insides rioted as I continued. "And I... I'd appreciate it if you didn't bring people home without warning. Send a text or something," I rushed to add, mortified I was saying it out loud at all. It felt so petty, but I never again wanted to walk into my house and see my doppelgänger eating *my* cookies in *my* kitchen with *my* Dallas smiling at her. It made me feel a certain murderous kind of way. I didn't need that.

Dallas watched me carefully, nodding slowly.

"I'm really sorry Crystal ate your cookie. I didn't know you were saving it. It's my fault, I offered it to her."

My face flamed hot with embarrassment. He'd already apologized twice. It was such a stupid thing for me to have mentioned, but I had, complete with bitchy attitude, the next morning while I waited for the coffee to finish brewing.

"It was just a cookie. I shouldn't have even said anything about it."

He rubbed the stubble on his chin with the back of his fingers.

"Anyway. The first couple of dates were fine, but then... I was mostly saying yes simply for the sake of doing it," I admitted. "Like I was obligated since I was the one who activated the profile. I'm really not feeling it."

Dallas ran a hand through his hair, and if I wasn't mistaken, he was relieved.

"For sure. I went on a couple of good dates, but I'm not sure the time is right. It's a lot of work."

Guilt made me sit forward in the seat, nearly spilling my cider. "You don't have to stop on my account, you know. I just wanted to let you know I'm tapping out."

"I'm honestly pretty relieved we're on the same page." A warm, rich laugh rumbled out of him. "I was stressing myself out trying to find good matches. I enjoyed my date with Crystal the other night, but…" he shrugged. I hadn't asked what happened between them after I went to my room, and didn't plan to. I hoped they had a good time. Whatever that was. I did. Even if it made me want to vomit.

"We're ridiculous." I shook my head, taking a deep drink of my cider while he answered a knock at the door.

He brought our pizza directly to the coffee table. We'd arrived at the point of comfort where we ate straight from the box. So far there hadn't been any major accidents, but I could tell we were due a tragic spill on the clean area rug.

"No more rushed matches?" I prompted, wiping sauce off my fingers.

"Nope. Back to platonic couch dates unless there's someone on my app I feel like I need to have a drink with. After you've given them a second look to be sure."

"Agreed."

I settled back into the cushions as he scrolled with the remote. We'd started sitting next to one another instead of at opposite ends of the couch. I wasn't sure when that had changed. My spot happened to be the edge seat with the armrest to my right and his was the squishy center cushion next to me.

"What about the new sci-fi one? I heard it was good." I mumbled over a bite of pepperoni and banana pepper.

"Sure. Need another drink?" Dallas got up, grabbing some paper towels and fresh bottles.

"Thanks."

Tension slowly leaked out of my body as I filled my stomach and the alcohol soaked into my blood.

We sat there watching the movie, trading playful barbs and laughing together. It was the best date I'd had in weeks, if I was being honest about it.

"Really? I thought you and Chad hit it off pretty well."

I sputtered, setting down my bottle. "I said that out loud?" Mortification made my cheeks grow hot, my heart stuttering in my chest before finding a steady rhythm again.

Dallas chortled. "Yep. Honestly, I'm flattered. I've always wanted to be the gold standard of something. Might as well be pizza and beer dates."

"I guess I'm much more of a homebody than I used to be. Though you *are* the best pizza and beer date I know. Well, except Addison, maybe."

His eyebrows lifted. "Of course, I never doubted Addison held the top spot. I remember going out all night long, getting up in the morning, pounding an energy drink, then doing it all over again. Now? I just want to sleep."

I grinned. "Yep. Past eleven, I turn into a pumpkin."

Dallas held out his fist. I stared at it for a moment before realizing what he was doing and bumped his knuckles.

"Roommate pact. We don't bring home randos and if we do, we let the other person know first. Overnights are fine, but leave something on your doorknob as a warning. Text first, too. No sleepovers in the living room." He ducked his head, color rising into his cheeks. "For the foreseeable future, I'm not doing much more than grabbing a drink with someone, if that."

"Sounds good to me. Having to hear all about Chad's ex-fiancé Diana sealed the deal for me. Though the fusion egg rolls were delicious, as promised. After Jesse, I should have known better. I deleted my apps for a reason."

Dallas snorted.

"Crystal was a better date than Chad, but your cookie was probably the highlight of our evening. I guess Oscar got the one-night stand out of my system. Who's Jesse? One of the guys you met for a drink before?"

My heart pounded as I processed what he'd said and I mulled over how to explain Jesse. I'd conveniently neglected to explain about him before. Why did the revelation he hadn't slept with her make me so happy? It shouldn't matter who he was spending his time with but knowing his adventures were as selective as mine made me feel a lot better.

"Remember the epically bad hookup I mentioned?"

"Yeah." He lifted his beer bottle to his lips.

"Right before I moved, I got bored while I was packing. I met up with a guy for a quick hookup. It was fine. Good, even. He didn't seem keen on leaving right away, which was annoying. Then my boss stopped by."

Dallas' eyebrows pulled together, but he didn't interrupt.

"Turns out, the guy was not only the guy my former boss was in a relationship with but also the new CEO of the company my old one merged with."

"Ohhh shit." Dallas' eyes were impossibly wide. He carefully finished his drink and set the bottle down, never breaking eye contact with me. "That's bad."

"Yeah. Honestly, it explains why this job search is so fucking hard. There's no way she's giving anyone who contacts her anything more than the bare minimum about my employment there. Forget about a reference."

He whistled, blinking slowly a few times.

"That's rough."

"Yeah. Anyway… we may have wasted our time doing the profiles." I frowned.

Dallas shook his head.

"No way. I had a blast. Plus, we learned a lot about each other. No regrets."

I smiled, snuggling down in my seat, his leg touching mine.

No regrets.

CHAPTER TWENTY

Dallas

S MY FEET pounded the concrete on my way around the lake, I did my mental filing for the day. Things at work were busy. By itself, that was a good thing. Unfortunately, I was overwhelmed to the point things were slipping through the cracks. I'd get a grip on the three most urgent things, and two others would get pushed back.

It would be fine, I just needed to find a way to get ahead. I didn't want to let anyone down, my brothers especially. Not only would they give me a hard time, but failing them was infinitely worse than letting down a nameless boss somewhere.

The creepy unknown texts were coming more regularly, the words getting further and further under my skin. I knew they would have to be dealt with sooner or later, too. Later was more likely.

Breathe in for four, breathe out for four. The thud of my feet in time with my breaths was a meditation.

Trina convinced me to integrate some of her yoga stretches into my routine after our walks. She hadn't been exaggerating about her habit of turning group exercise activities into a game. She'd been wrong by assuming she would only get silly when paired with Addison, however. The first few times we'd tried, sitting with our legs spread wide on the living room floor, she'd gotten the giggles. Stretching was part of what we accomplished, though mostly we laughed so hard my stomach hurt without having done a single crunch.

I wiped some sweat from my forehead with the back of my hand, heart pounding in time with my strides, a smile on my face.

She was truly something else. I'd have to remember to thank Addison again and ask them to tell me some of their favorite college stories. I was guessing they were the best kind of outrageous.

Higher education hadn't been in the cards for me, but I was considering taking some online classes. When was the only factor I still needed to figure out. If I could get some of my workload cleared off, I could use evenings and weekends. Which brought me right back to where I'd started with my thoughts.

As I rounded lap number six, I put on a little more speed. The sun was beating down relentlessly. Trina was out getting her hair cut and spending some time with Addison, so there was no walking today.

I'd thought I'd gotten out early enough to beat the heat, but that was never really a thing in the south during the summer months.

After I'd finished my laps, I took the stairs up to the apartment as a final push. Dripping sweat, I stripped on my way through the apartment and immediately took a cool shower. When I got out, there was a message from my mom, asking if I was busy today. Dad was off playing golf with some friends, so she was hungry and bored.

I couldn't help smiling. Somehow, Mom always knew.

Texting back, I told her to put on something suitable for a ride on my bike.

"HOW DID YOU find this place again?" Mom asked, buttering a slice of sourdough from the basket on the table.

"Trina found it."

"Oh? Well, it's lovely. Reminds me a lot of a place your father took me when we were young and he was trying to impress me. He even wore a *tie*."

"Dad owns a tie?"

Mom grinned. "He used to. I'm sure there's one or two still in the closet, but your father when he was young? In a suit? Well. There's a reason we got married and went on to have the four of you."

"Ma."

I understood all too well why the women my brothers and I seemed to gravitate toward got along so well with her. Shelley Greene lacked a filter. Proudly so.

She chuckled her way through a few bites of the bread. There was nothing that brought her joy quite like making her sons uncomfortable.

The steakhouse was just as busy on Sunday at an odd time between lunch and dinner as it was during a full dinner service.

Mom fluffed her hair, worried the helmet she'd worn had destroyed her style.

"You look gorgeous, Ma. Quit fussing. I'm glad you wanted to go for a ride, but you might have bruised my ribs; you were holding on so tight."

She *tsk*ed her tongue at me.

"At least if I'm riding with you, I know you're being safe. So. Tell me what's on your mind, baby."

I sipped at my sweet tea before answering.

"What makes you think something's on my mind?"

Mom skewered me with her eyes, rumbling a laugh deep in her chest. "Want to try again, son?"

I shook my head, leaning back as the server delivered our plates. The salad Mom picked took up the same-sized plate Trina's prime rib had and appeared to be topped with nearly as much meat.

My sandwich was a similarly massive offering. My mouth was watering from the salty scent of the au jus.

"It's nothing, in particular, I guess. Just a lot on my mind."

"Hmm."

Mom's clever eyes assessed me as she worked dressing through her lettuce and I took a few bites of my sandwich. I knew she was waiting for me to start spilling my guts, but my guts weren't sure what part they should spill first.

"Work's good?"

"Busy, but yes."

"Too busy?" She guessed.

I gave a lopsided shrug. "I'm making do."

"But?"

"I'd like to feel as though I'm doing more than keeping my head above water most days."

"So, say that." Mom made it sound so simple.

"I'm still getting my ducks in a row, Ma."

"Don't wait until you're drowning, Dallas. Your brothers will understand. Did you forget how long I was in the office with you all? Speak up. There's no shame in saying you need help."

"I hear you. I do."

She grunted at me, the noise a simple chastisement. "I know you hear me. *Act* on it. Anyway. How are things with your new roommate? She sounds sweet from what I've heard."

"I'm not sure sweet is the best descriptor for Trina. She's... feisty."

This made mom beam with joy. "Oh, wonderful! She's a good match for you then."

I pinned my mother with a look, expressing my exasperation with my eyes. "Mom. It's not like that. You know why."

"Baby, I love you. And that's not at all what I meant, though it's interesting you jumped to dating all on your own."

Shock rocked through my system. Assuming she was telling the truth, and she'd just been claiming Trina was a good match for me in general terms, it *had* been me jumping to something more.

"I didn't—"

"The last time I checked, you were the walking, talking embodiment of *love is love*. I don't care who you date, so long as you're happy." The mischievous grin on her lips didn't fade even as she stuffed her face with salad. "Either way, I'm glad your apartment is working out. I worried about you because that's what I do. It sounds as though it's all working out swimmingly, though."

"It is. Thanks. Can we talk about something else?"

"If you insist. This is delicious, by the way. How's yours?"

"Fantastic."

Mom waited out my little burst of temper, a placid smile on her mouth as she nibbled on more bread.

"I've been considering taking some night classes."

Her smile cracked wide.

"Wonderful, baby! How about you take the money you think you owe us and put it towards classes instead?"

"Mom, I know *you* say I don't owe you anything, but I *do*."

"No, you don't."

My eyes were fastened on my plate, but I looked up at the forcefulness in her tone.

"I mean it, Dallas. Forget it. I don't care. If going to school is important to you and you're delaying because of the money, I don't want it. We've already had this conversation. I'm not discussing it with you again."

"I'll think about it."

She reached across the table, gripping my chin in her hand. It struck the same chord of fear in me it had when I'd been a child. I was now bigger than her by at least a foot and outweighed her by at least forty pounds, but the terror wasn't diminished one iota.

"Dallas Kyle. You'll do more than think about it. I insist. For me. Okay? It's important. That money kept you *safe*. You are my son. It's my *job* to keep you safe, at the bare minimum. Please." There were tears in her eyes. I realized how scared she must have been for me. Deep down I'd already known, but she never let us know when she was afraid because she didn't want us to change our plans to accommodate her emotions. It was important to her we all lived our lives for ourselves, not for her.

"Yes, ma'am."

"Good." She released me, blinking back the shimmer in her eyes.

A surge of adrenaline flowed through me and I flagged down the waitress to order matching slices of chocolate cake.

I couldn't promise my mother I'd go to school or even that I'd consider the debt resolved, even if I quit paying it back. What I could do is treat her to a lovely lunch and a giant slab of dessert.

CHAPTER TWENTY-ONE

Trina

ADDISON CALLED TUESDAY morning to invite me to join her and Dallas for lunch.

"Isn't that your special work friend slash boyfriend's brother bonding time?" She'd video called me from work to extend the invite and was currently getting an eyeful of me using wax strips on my chin hair. I had an interview later and I didn't want to be distracted if I happened to spot one of the spiky bastards in my mirror right before walking into the building.

"Yeah, but he won't mind. I want to see you. Plus, it's the one day this week I'm sure I'm getting away from my desk to be properly social. It's been super busy lately." She sighed and I could hear the tiredness under her buoyant tone.

"Yeah, Dallas has been working in the evenings a lot lately." He'd been coming home, grabbing a bite to eat, then logging back in while we watched TV more evenings than not. True to his word, he always made time for our evening walks. They were growing on me, too. "I could come over one evening. Or you could come here. I can always bring you lunch at the office."

"I know, but this way *you* get out of the house too. I know you're not going anywhere you don't have to."

"You say that like it's a bad thing. Plus, I go get coffee sometimes. I hit the grocery store occasionally. I walk a few nights a week."

"I said what I said. I know you, Trina. I know you're enjoying being home a lot even if you don't want to admit it."

I groaned. I hated how she could call me out so accurately. Well, hate-loved. It was nice to have someone who pretty much walked around in my brain with me sometimes. It could suck when she called me out, but I needed it as much as she did sometimes. We were a good team that way.

"I don't hate not having to get all dressed up to go sit in an office that's twenty degrees too cold where I have to smile at people I don't like. I do miss some of my work friends, though. I hate how no matter what, everyone just stops talking when you leave a job, it's weird. Makes me feel as though I wasn't actually friends with any of them. Like I experienced a five-year-long hallucination. I do miss the paychecks, though."

Fueled by my rant, I yanked the wax strip off with determination, exhaling a curse as it yanked my unwanted facial hair out by the root.

"Feel better?"

"Fuck off. Yes." I wanted to be grumpy at my best friend, but she was good at playing therapist and I did feel better having gotten it off my chest.

"Anyway. We usually go to this little diner, you'd love it. Besides, you're getting all made up for an interview, right? Might as well show it off as much as you can."

I fidgeted with the wax strip before throwing it away. I was out of excuses and we both knew it. "Clear it with my roommate first and I'll seriously consider it."

"Why do I need to ask him?" She giggled at me.

"Because it's your thing, the two of you. I don't want to intrude. Though, I would bet he wouldn't tell me no if I asked."

"Fine. I'll check and text you later. Your new haircut is gorgeous, by the way."

"Yeah? Thanks, it was way past time to get it cut. Anyway, bye, bestie. Have a great day."

My interview was at ten, so there was ample time to fuss with my makeup before heading out.

The company I was interviewing with was a competitor of Bronson's, so for petty, selfish reasons, I wanted to nail this one. The position was not quite what I was hoping for, but if I could get in the door, I might be able to maneuver myself into a position similar to what I had been doing before the merger and subsequent firing.

I went with red lipstick and bold eyeliner wings. I made sure my shaggy pixie cut gained some structure by adding mousse to tame my curls as much as was ever possible. My lip color matched my heels and the subtle paint splatter pattern on my white blouse. The black suit jacket pulled everything together.

With my portfolio in my hand, I left the apartment, feeling confident. The music I picked in the car kept my energy up and I arrived at the building ready to conquer the world. The job was mine, I just had to go claim it.

I tried desperately not to lose my good energy when I saw the crowd of people waiting in the lobby. We all shared a common expression of exasperation, every single one of us qualified for a job that may or may not even exist.

I'd been wrangled into a cattle call. Again.

After taking a deep breath, I checked in at the desk and took a seat.

I tried to take a quick headcount, though I lost track after I got to thirty. Half a dozen more people came in after me, one of which turned right back around and left when he saw the crowd.

To my surprise, they were moving through people pretty quickly, calling people back in groups before separating us into smaller offices from there.

I was in the third group to be called landing in an office with a man who reminded me so strongly of the district supervisor who'd fired me at Bronson, I had to consciously make an effort not to frown at him.

"Thank you for coming in, Miz… Lee."

"My pleasure," I lied.

"They were interested in your qualifications for the graphic design department?"

"Yes, that's my understanding." I patted the portfolio I'd propped up against the legs of my chair.

He scanned my resume, leaving me in awkward silence for a moment.

"You seem to have a very nice history with your employers. Why did you leave your last job at… Bronson?"

"When they merged with my former company, I was downsized." Simple was best. The way he asked the question, I could tell they hadn't done any research yet.

"I see. What would you say were your biggest accomplishments in your time there?"

I launched into a well-practiced routine about clients, dollars, and visibility. It was all true, but shoveling the same bullshit was getting old. I'd wondered more than once if anyone genuinely cared about those things.

"Where do you see yourself in five years?"

I knew where this was going. Unfortunately for us both, my patience was up with this kind of game after so many weeks of applying, interviewing, phone calls, and overall ridiculousness.

"May I ask if the position I applied for, and came here today in good faith to interview for, is currently available?"

The man gazed down his nose at me, surprised by my abrupt question.

"I'm not at liberty to say."

"You're not allowed or you don't know?"

He set my resume down on the desk blotter. He was a generic man, sitting in a generic office, in a generic building. There was nothing about him that communicated any kind of emotion aside from annoyance.

"There are quite a few positions open at the moment and we've seen quite a few people here today. I'm obviously not the only person interviewing potential applicants—"

I stood, snatching my portfolio before putting my hand out.

"Thank you for the non-response. I have no interest in working for a company with this kind of approach to interviewing because I can only *imagine* how that would translate to actual personnel management."

Unsure what to do, he shook my outstretched hand as he gaped at me, mouth opening and closing soundlessly.

"May I have your HR director's name?" I asked.

"For what reason?"

"So I can call to complain about your unscrupulous hiring tactics."

"Miss, I hardly think that's necessary—"

"Never mind, I'll get it from the receptionist. You will never find good, loyal employees this way. Please stop wasting people's time, it's rude and disgusting. Also, fraud is illegal."

"Ms. Lee," he called after me as I yanked open the door, leaving the same way I came. "Ms. Lee!"

I flipped him the finger as I barreled out into the lobby.

"If you're here for the graphic arts position, it's probably not actually available. Honestly, if you're here for any job, I'd recommend you quit wasting your time." My voice carried well in the open atrium-style lobby. Several people shuffled nervously, including the receptionist. "Get out while you still can."

I didn't bother stopping at the desk on my way out the doors—I had Google. I could complain without anyone's help.

I was fired up, hoping that more than the three or four people who'd gotten to their feet as I threw open the double doors to exit the building saved themselves the time and trouble this kind of interview was worth.

Once I was in my car, I let loose a frustrated scream, hand pounding on the steering wheel.

"Why?!" I yelled, frustration humming through my body.

I texted Addison to let her know my interview was a bust.

> **TRINA:** Another fucking scam. I'm so pissed! I put on my red patent heels for this!
> **ADDISON:** Aw shit. I'm so sorry! You're still coming to lunch, right?
> **TRINA:** What did Dallas say?
> **ADDISON:** He's fine with it. One sec.

I glanced around the busy parking lot, mentally cheering the people who were also leaving. I hoped they hadn't sat through the entire interview before getting out.

ADDISON: Since you're done, want to do
brunch instead?

I blinked, surprised by the suggestion.

TRINA: Sure? Can you guys do that? I don't want you
to rearrange your whole day because of me.
ADDISON: No, it actually works better because I
have a call at one. We can meet you there in 30?
TRINA: Do they have alcohol?
ADDISON: No idea. I do know they have amazing
waffles. And pie. Carbs may do just as well until we
get to the other side of noon, right?
TRINA: Okay, you convinced me. I'll see you soon.

I let out a breath, trying to force my frustration to leave my body with it. I started my car, plugging in the diner's info on my GPS.

"What a fucking waste," I grumbled, backing out of the lot, glad I'd never see the ugly glass building again.

CHAPTER TWENTY-TWO

Trina

THE 50'S STYLE diner lifted my spirits the moment I pulled up outside.

The sparkly red vinyl booths and chrome everything were the kind of comfortable nostalgia I needed after my shit-show of a morning. I was eyeballing the rotating pie display full of mile-high meringue when they walked in, barely a minute behind my arrival.

Addison didn't hesitate a moment before she pulled me into a hug.

"Still homicidal?"

I snorted against her shoulder. "Nah. I told the guy off. It helped some, then I warned everyone in the lobby waiting like suckers to get the hell out as soon as they could. Now I'm just pissed."

Dallas met my eye over Addison's shoulder and grinned sympathetically, hands tucked into his jeans pockets as he rocked on his heels.

"Group hug?" He suggested, opening his arms wide.

"Sure."

His wingspan was broad enough to adequately squeeze us both, the breath I got of his citrusy cologne another layer of familiar calm. He gave a squeeze, making Addison and I both laugh.

"Can I help you kids?" The waitress asked.

I felt a decade younger being addressed in such a way, and it turned my frown right upside down.

"Booth for three, thanks." Dallas took control, breaking the hug. He turned his bright grin on her and she winked back at him.

"You're here a little early today, yeah?"

We filed along behind her, Dallas bringing up the rear.

"Emergency brunch meeting," Addison told her as she and I slid into a booth together.

"Coffee? Water? Or your normal tea?"

"Sweet tea, please," Addison confirmed.

"Same," Dallas said.

"What about you, honey?"

It felt weird to ask this sweet lady for booze, so I settled for a lemonade.

"I thought this was supposed to be *the one*." Dallas frowned as he put the menu aside, having already decided what he was going to order.

"Ugh. Clearly not. It was another bait and switch cattle call."

"Gross. How can they do that?" Addison asked, stacking her menu as well.

"I have no idea, but I'm going to complain to… someone." I sagged, realizing they probably didn't care. "No, I won't. They don't care. Anyway. What's good here?"

"Everything," they said together.

"Super helpful, thanks, guys."

I closed my eyes, randomly pointing to something; happy with my tactic when it ended up being chicken and waffles my index finger landed on.

The waitress brought back our drinks and took our food orders. It didn't take any time at all for me to realize why my friends made it a point to come to this restaurant at least once a week. It was comfortable in a way that spoke directly to my soul. The waitress, Dorothy by her name-tag, had probably been there at least twenty years.

"Can I be nosy? What's your meeting about this afternoon?" The lemonade was the perfect blend of sweet and tart on my tongue.

"Call with the family, actually," Addison said, smirking at Dallas.

"Oh?"

Dallas took a deep drink of his tea.

"What's going on?"

"She's being dramatic. Nothing serious. Dennis thinks he found a good location for a new animal shelter, so we have to have our obligatory vote to be sure we all agree it's a good option. Everything at G4 has to be voted on unanimously by the members of the board, which is us four brothers."

"Makes sense. You're the four G's in G4, after all. Another shelter? That's good, right?"

"Very," Addison sighed, leaning back in the booth. "When Dennis is in the office a lot, things tend to get… tense."

"He's been around a *lot*," Dallas agreed, eyes wide in emphasis.

I couldn't help laughing. "Aw, you guys are adorable." I accepted the side-eye from them both, which only made me giggle harder. "Does Dennis know you bond over his… overwhelming presence?"

"Yes," they answered together again.

I was still giggling when the sweet waitress delivered our plates.

My waffles were crispy and the chicken had an edge of spicy heat. It was perfect.

"So, what happened this morning?" Dallas asked, his fluffy omelet similarly delectable.

I took a bite before answering. "When I showed up to the building, there were dozens of other people there."

"Oh no." Addison shook her head, stabbing a red potato in her skillet.

"Yeah. *Lots* of people. They called us back in groups. All around a bad situation." I sighed, poking some of my waffle into the syrup.

"You said you told the guy off?" Dallas asked, eyebrow raised, a playful grin on his mouth. He looked as though he'd thoroughly enjoy witnessing my temper boil over, as long as he wasn't the target.

"I did. I'm not even embarrassed about it either. He started asking me the generic questions they put on every interview script ever, so I lost patience with the whole mess. *What are your weaknesses? Where do you see yourself in five years?*" I made a gagging noise. "I wanted to know if the job I was interviewing for was actually available. He couldn't tell me. Well... whether he couldn't or didn't know is still a mystery. I got up and left after telling him he was disgusting and wasting people's time." I knew I was leaving plenty of details out, but it was enough. I took a drink of lemonade before cutting up the rest of my food. "I spoke loudly about my complaint as a warning for the other applicants on my way out." I popped a bite of chicken topped waffle into my mouth. "No regrets."

"Well, you're hot," Addison said, bumping shoulders with me.

"Thanks, bitch." I bumped her right back.

"Your outfit is very... powerful, Trina." Dallas grinned at me. "I bet the poor guy nearly swallowed his tongue."

I wasn't sure whether Dallas meant because I looked sexy or because of what I'd said. I was taking the compliment either way. Both may have been accurate since I had a pretty good idea the pasty interview guy didn't get much excitement in his day-to-day life.

"He looked like he was about to have a stroke when I stood up. Just asking about the job made him stumble all over himself." I smiled, remembering his wide-eyed expression. "I appreciate the compliments, though. I felt badass when I left this morning and was pissed it was all for nothing. If nothing else, I'd found out early enough to not waste any more than a few minutes of my time on a company that doesn't deserve me, anyway. This place is out of this world, by the way." I gestured to the diner. "I'm glad you talked me into meeting you."

"Tuesday lunch is important for mental health. Or brunch. Whichever." Addison grinned at me as she took a bite of her food. "Maybe we should make another day of the week for all of us." She motioned between the two of us with her fork.

"I'm good with that. This place is cute. Plus, this food is amazing."

Addison smiled brightly at me, then tilted her head, eyes squinted as she looked me over.

"Wait. You do fancy web design stuff, right? And you—" she gestured toward Dallas with her fork. "—need someone to carry some of the load for that, right?"

Dallas stopped chewing, bright blue eyes shifting from me to her.

"I wouldn't mind some help." He swallowed, a nervous grin tugging on his mouth.

Feeling put on the spot, I glared at my friend. "Be straight with it, bestie. What are you suggesting?"

Her face brightened. "Just thinking there may be a decent solution for both of you in there somewhere. You could freelance some time to help with the G4 website, which would take a little bit of work off of Dallas."

"It's… not a terrible idea," Dallas said, thoughtful as he pushed some food around on his plate.

They weren't wrong. It made me itchy to consider all my eggs tied to the Dallas basket, but as a freelance project, it could be a quick injection of cash, which I needed, plus a new item on my resume.

"I could help with that, sure."

Addison beamed. "Great. Send me a proposal. I'll get it approved."

Dallas snorted at her, though relief colored his features. "You'll get it approved?"

She was unbothered by his sarcastic tone.

"I attend the Monday board meetings, same as you. I'm the office manager–this kind of thing is in my job description."

I lifted my glass, gesturing it in a toast to my friend. She was one smart cookie.

"I can give you a general idea of what needs to be done when I get home?"

"Sure." I turned my attention back to Addison. "I'll email you something after I get a briefing, I guess."

"Perfect. I do love it when a plan comes together."

She winked at me, and I realized we were even. She'd helped me find a place to live, then maneuvered me into a way to make money with G4. The imaginary debt she thought she owed me for helping her after her life fell apart was now fulfilled. I winked back, laughing. Dallas glanced between us, pleased but uncomfortable.

"I'll explain later." Addison waved her hand in a dismissive gesture.

"Sure."

By the time I left, my stomach was full, my volatile mood soothed. I couldn't have asked for a more dramatic turn from the way the day started.

DALLAS POPPED HIS head into the office after tapping on the wall outside. I appreciated his habit of letting me know he was there, so I didn't get startled. The very last thing I needed was to spill something on my laptop.

After brunch, I'd come home, done some yoga, then had taken a long shower to relax. Feeling much more centered, I jumped into working on one of the commissions I'd gotten from my website and hadn't gotten up from my desk chair since.

"Hey."

"Hey, what's up?" I closed my computer, grateful for the distraction. Cleaning up my website was proving more labor-intensive than I'd hoped, but already having a handful of commissions with the site at less than a hundred percent was highly motivational. Doing something—anything—other than returning to a corporate setting was becoming more and more attractive the longer I tried to get back into that kind of job.

"My mom just called. She invited us to dinner on Saturday. I said I'd check with you. I thought you maybe wouldn't mind a home-cooked meal. Do you want to come with me?"

Mild discomfort surged in my chest. I'd never really gone home with a guy to meet his folks. This, of course, was different, though still outside my comfort zone.

"Um…"

My hesitation amused him. He grinned as he leaned further into the doorframe, arms crossed. A supermodel pose, but he did it with more flair than I'd ever seen in a magazine and completely without cockiness.

"Addison and Dennis are probably going too."

Breath flooded my lungs, my chest instantly looser. "Maybe lead with that next time? Pretty sure I had a miniature panic attack. Yes, dinner sounds… nice."

"You don't sound so sure." He was grinning at me, but I could see the twinkle of concern in his eyes.

I got to my feet, ready for a snack with some time away from resume adjusting, job board posts, and website coding.

"I honestly don't know if it will be nice or miserable, so I'm afraid it's the best I can do. Addison has spoken very kindly of your mom, and you're not so bad…"

He sputtered in fake offense as I passed him, headed for the kitchen. There were some leftovers and at least one brownie with my name on it.

"*Not* so bad? Not *so* bad? Not so *bad*?"

I laughed, rounding on him at the island. "You asked. Seriously though, I like you fine. It will be interesting to see where you come from. Parents and I are… a little complicated."

"You'll fit right in, if you want my opinion." He leaned on the cool stone of the island, watching as I retrieved enough food for the both of us. "Mom will be thrilled, she loves the company, especially when the estrogen levels nearly balance the testosterone. Besides, she's been waiting to meet you."

I snorted a laugh as I scooped out my dinner onto a plate. "Good to know. What are we bringing?"

"She didn't mention anything. I can ask."

"I can make whatever. Tell her we'll handle dessert."

"It's cute you believe I can *tell* my mother things."

The microwave beeped, and I swapped his hot plate for my cold one.

"You're the baby of the family. I assumed if anyone could, it'd be you."

"You'd think so, but no. Shelley Greene does much better with things offered or suggested to her." He chuckled, firmly shaking his head.

"Okay, then politely suggest I would be happy to bring dessert if she'd appreciate it."

"Nice." He grinned as he tapped out a text. "You're good at this."

"I was quite good at crafting emails for cranky customers."

Once my plate was hot as well, I slid onto my barstool. The timing was good because a response text flashed across his phone screen just as I peeked over while I got situated.

He glanced at it before showing it to me.

> **MOM:** How sweet! I'd love that. Can't wait to see you both.

"Nicely done," he complimented, nodding with wide, impressed eyes.

"Thanks."

After we were done eating, I searched the cabinets while Dallas washed the dishes.

"Blondies?" I queried, holding up a bag of white chocolate chips.

"Sounds perfect."

I felt better with a plan. Baking helped too. If I was going to show up armed with my best friend and baked goods, everything would be fine.

CHAPTER TWENTY-THREE

Dallas

TRINA PARKED HER little sedan alongside Dennis' truck in our parents' driveway. I glanced over to find her fingers tightly gripping the wheel.

"Hey. You okay?"

Her dark gaze flicked to mine. "Fine." Her response was too short, her eyes too wide.

"They're mostly harmless, you know. Addison comes here frequently of her own free will. No horror stories yet."

Except for a couple of really rough meals early on when she and Dennis first started dating, at least. He and I hadn't talked about the situation with his ex back then, but his jealousy was out of control. He didn't realize it at the time, but it was because he was catching feelings for Addison and projecting on me. Trina either already knew about all that or didn't need to know. Especially not right now.

"I know. Parents and I…"

"Complicated?"

"Yes. Like, this shouldn't even be strange because I'm just coming to dinner as your roommate. It's not as though we're dating."

It was odd but also amusing to see my normally bold roommate nervous.

"Come on. I'll even hold your hand if you want."

Trina huffed as she opened her door and climbed out, reaching into the back seat for the pan of Blondies she'd made.

"Get real. If anyone's going to hold my hand, it's going to be Addison."

"Noted." My chuckle managed to give the corners of her mouth the tiniest lift.

Dad came around the corner of the house from the back as we approached, little dogs running up to greet us with yips and cold noses.

"Hey, guys!" I dropped into a crouch, accepting the affection bomb from the dogs to spare Trina from their overly enthusiastic jumping.

"Thought I heard you pull up. Welcome," Dad said, shaking her hand.

"Thanks for inviting me along, Mr. Greene," Trina replied.

"My pleasure. A friend of Addison's is welcome anytime."

"She's my friend too, old man." I rose, the dogs running off at my dad's whistle.

"Of course she is." He winked at me before clapping me on the shoulder as I walked past him toward the backyard.

"The other ladies are in the kitchen," Dad gestured to the sliding door leading into the kitchen from the wooden deck.

"Thanks." Trina wasted no time heading in that direction. "Hi, Dennis."

"Trina." Dennis inclined his head at her as he glanced up from the barbecue.

The sounds of both my mother and Addison greeting Trina followed shortly after. There was an odd twinge in my chest at hearing their voices all melded together. It was the same warm, homey feeling when my sisters-in-law joined in on our video calls.

"The roommate situation is working out?" Dad asked casually as he took over the cooking. His eyes were on the food, despite the very pointed question.

"So far," I confirmed, sitting down at the picnic table. I missed the dogs and the comfortable feel of my parents' home since moving out, despite the love I'd found in my own space. "She's going to be helping me with a few projects for the foundation, too."

"Good, good." Dad nodded, briefly making eye contact with my older brother.

"I told you it wasn't worth betting on," Dennis muttered, handing me a bottle of beer he'd retrieved from a cooler as he joined me.

I chuckled. It was always a bet with my parents, and they'd passed their penchant for gambling on things on to us. Personal lives, serious issues, major decisions—bet.

"Let me guess, *someone* may have decided my situation was similar to yours?" I asked my brother. I recalled our conversation about it at lunch. I'd have to call her bluff when we got a moment to ourselves.

"I cannot confirm or deny, but it sounds a lot like something Mom would think."

Dad snorted. "You know damn well your mother saw you getting a roommate as an opportunity for cupid to strike."

I raised an eyebrow, Dennis' head tilting briefly in what amounted to a shrug as I met his eye. Whether or not Dad knew my dating history was up in the air.

"I'm sure she did."

As I chuckled, the sliding door opened and Mom carried out multiple dishes of food.

"You need a hand, Ma?"

"We got it, thank you, though." She winked at me.

Addison carried a bottle of wine and glasses while Trina supplied a massive bowl. I could only hope it contained my mother's macaroni salad.

I did miss meals at home, too. Mom had the southern cooking thing nailed.

Getting to my feet, I greeted my mother and Addison both with a quick hug.

"It's so nice you all could join us." Mom was positively bubbly, in her element as hostess and probably frothing for some fresh gossip.

Dad scooped the burgers off the grill, joining us at the rectangular glass table. There was organized chaos as things were passed around and plates filled.

"As always, this looks amazing, Mrs. Greene." Addison smiled.

"Shelley, dear. Just call me Shelley. We've been over this." She gave Addison a friendly side-eye.

"I know, I know. Sorry."

Trina was quiet, watching the interactions with a clever smile on her mouth. She'd sat across from me, between Addison and Mom.

"How was your interview?" Addison asked Trina.

"Same as the last dozen. Lots of pointless questions from someone who doesn't understand what it is I do. I'm not sure what I'm doing wrong. I'm still hopeful the right thing will come along soon."

"I'm sure it will," Addison said, pouring Trina's glass of white wine extra full.

"What is it you do, Trina?" Mom asked brightly as she smeared mayo on the bun for her burger.

"Graphic design. Specifically for marketing, but I dabble in infographics, web design. A few other things too."

"How lovely. You and Dallas must have plenty to talk about then."

Trina nodded, unable to respond to the clever comment due to the forkful of macaroni salad she'd put in her mouth.

"We do. She's helping with a few projects for the G4 website, actually," I interjected. Trina sent me an appreciative look.

"Oh? How lovely! How nice that you get along so well you can both live and work together."

"Did I tell you? The lot I was interested in over by the airport is going to work out after all," Dennis offered, redirecting Mom's matchmaking line of questioning.

"That's great, son. I know you were having a hard time with this one. I'm glad to hear it." Dad was, as usual, heavily invested in Dennis' animal shelter projects.

"You're welcome to come out next week if you're interested."

"I'll take you up on that. Let me know when you're headed out and I'll meet you."

Retirement was something my parents were still adjusting to.

"Your macaroni salad is delicious, Mrs. Greene."

"Thank you, dear." Mom beamed at Trina's praise.

"It tastes a lot like Angel Eggs." Trina looked at Addison who nodded in agreement. "Is there dill or capers in your dressing?"

"Well, I don't share the information with just anyone, but since you figured it out on your own, I can confirm there are a few things most people don't use…"

Mom went on to detail how the salad was made. I

honestly couldn't have cared less about what the secret ingredient was, but Trina and Addison both appeared genuinely interested. Too late I realized if I'd been paying closer attention, I might be able to recreate it for myself.

"Can I get your recipe, Ma?"

"Of course, baby."

"You never give *me* any recipes," Dennis groused. I could see the crinkle to his forehead though, a tell that he was kidding.

"You never *ask*, dear. Is there something you wanted to know how to make?"

"No. You know I don't really cook."

Mom swatted at him playfully. It was nice to see Dennis smiling. He'd gone years without doing so and I still held some guilt about my part in the cause of it.

The conversation drifted to how close my brother Devon's wife, Stephanie, was to delivering their first baby (very), then Mom turned her attention to Dennis and Addison as though expecting an engagement some-time soon.

"You know Daniel and Phae are probably closer to that than we are, Ma." Dennis shifted uncomfortably in his seat, Addison blushing.

"I'm just saying, it seems like you two—"

"Ma." I gave her my most adoring look, lacing it with a warning. The tension level had ratcheted up at least a dozen notches from her question. For whatever reason, me and my oldest brother, Devon, were the two best suited to defuse her tangents. Dad was the master, though he usually waited a little too long to jump in because indulging her was his favorite thing to do.

She knew the subject of engagements was a touchy one with Dennis. It went a long way back, but his first serious relationship ended badly after he proposed and she declined. For years, he thought something happened between her and me, which was not how things had gone down. There was also the fact that Addison herself was left at the altar by her ex. Marriage was likely quite a way off for them; if it ended up being in the cards at all. I worried Mom's well-intentioned pushing might backfire on her.

"I know, I know. I'll quit."

"You don't want to know about *my* recent dates?" I put a hand to my chest. "I'm broken-hearted."

Mom brightened, probably expecting a much different answer than I was about to provide. "Oh? Are you dating again, dear?"

I laughed. "Not seriously, Ma. I did start using apps again, though. Trina and I helped each other make new profiles."

Mom looked from me to Trina with her eyebrows raised. "Oh? That's an interesting way to go about things, isn't it?"

Trina smiled. "Definitely. I wasn't having much luck finding good matches on my own. Nice to get a fresh perspective on things, you know?"

Mom took a sip of her wine, amused. "Well, if it works, I suppose it's well worth it."

Addison grinned at her best friend over a mouthful of food, turning her smiling eyes on me next.

"You guys seem to have lots of fun," Dennis teased, his wording suspect.

"Tons," I confirmed, wiping my mouth with a napkin.

Eyebrow up, he said nothing further. He stared deep into my soul before finally blinking. It reminded me of a few interactions from our childhood, the playful glare stirring some old memories. Even if it was at my expense, it was nice to see him casually happy.

"Remind me before you go, Dallas. I'll write down that recipe, plus I have some mail for you." Her gaze locked onto mine, her serious expression making my stomach swoop.

"Okay, Ma."

We sat at the picnic table through dessert with a cup of coffee, long enough that the sun set and the bugs came out to take their turn feasting, which was our signal to start wrapping things up.

"Wonderful as always, Ma, thanks." I kissed my mother on the cheek as we prepared to leave, Dennis and Addison doing the same.

"You know we miss the house full of you lot," Dad said, clapping me on the shoulders as he gave me a quick embrace.

"Enjoy the peace and quiet, old man."

He chuckled, gesturing behind him to the dogs. "What's quiet? I don't know a thing about it."

"Oh! Your mail." Mom dashed back to the kitchen, reappearing with a couple of envelopes and a hand-written recipe for the macaroni.

"Thanks."

Trina glanced at the paper. "Is it alright if I use your recipe?" she asked.

Mom positively beamed. "Yes, of course, dear. It's no family secret, or at least not one worth keeping. Recipes should be shared and enjoyed. If you have questions, just give me a call. I wouldn't mind swapping for your Blondies, if you like?"

It was Trina's turn to light up. I loved seeing her smile, it was a nice reversal from her nervousness when we'd first arrived. "Yes, of course."

Trina waved as we strode down the walk, my hand going to my pocket to prevent it from going around her shoulders. She wouldn't have minded, but I didn't want to give my parents the wrong idea.

They lingered on the front porch as we got into our vehicles.

Trina fired up the little sedan to take us home, following Dennis' big truck down the street as I waved out the window at my parents.

"You survived. Flying colors," I teased, seeing the relief on her face.

"They're pretty great. For parents, anyway." She grinned back at me.

"They like you."

"What's not to like?" She chuckled. I was glad to see her back to her normal, snarky self.

"Nothing. Nothing at all."

I'm sure she thought I was exaggerating to placate her. Hell, even I may have thought I was exaggerating. But the words rang true, which made me smile all the way home.

CHAPTER TWENTY-FOUR

Trina

DEEP, THROBBING HEADACHE settled behind my eyes.

I was moving through some yoga stretches as I mentally replayed the recent interview conversation in my head. Since it was the second round of phone screening for a job that had potential, I couldn't help nitpicking how the discussion went. If I was doing myself a disservice by putting off employers, I needed to figure out how, and fast.

As I inverted myself into downward dog, I remembered mentioning I had the capability of working either in-office or from home. Saying how the salary wasn't quite what I was looking for, though the option for stocks plus immediate health coverage kind of made up for it ran through my mind as I stood in tree pose, taking deep cleansing breaths. Child's pose while inhaling the rubbery scent of my yoga mat. It reminded me I'd told what was probably a borderline inappropriate joke while trying to lighten the mood.

Shit. There it was.

The music I'd been using stopped, replaced by the tone for an incoming call. I answered quickly as my mom's avatar popped up on the screen.

"Hi, Mom! Where are you today?"

"Hi, honey! We're in Maine."

While they were always stressful, I did genuinely love the chats with my parents when they checked in by phone instead of email. Mom's weekly emails were always detailed, but I missed hearing their voices.

"Maine?" My eyes scanned my planner. Maine wasn't on their normal route. I expected her to say Washington D.C. or Boston, same as every other July. They loved being in D.C. for the fourth. "What are you doing in Maine?"

"Staying cool," my dad chimed in. "High in the seventies today, it's glorious!"

"Hi, Dad! Sounds great. It never drops into the seventies here until fall. You guys don't normally go so far north. What made you decide to change your route?"

"I wanted to see some beaches. Lighthouses. Eat my weight in seafood and enjoy temperatures under eighty degrees," Mom listed, tone dreamy.

A glimmer of travel envy sliced through me. It sounded perfectly wonderful to me, every single part.

"Sounds fun. How long will you be there?"

"Another week or so. Then we're headed to Vermont for a while before we head back down toward Boston. How's the weather there?"

"Super hot. I'm ready for fall already."

My dad laughed. "Does it ever cool off there?"

"No, not really. Not like that, anyway. We do get some reasonably cool nights in the winter." Unfortunately. We did get some weather changes, but it was warm and humid most of the time. I sometimes missed having all four seasons, though I didn't miss driving in the snow.

"Are you having any luck finding work?"

The gentle tone with which my mother asked me the question belied her absolute persistence on the subject. She'd asked me the same question every time we'd talked.

"Not anything full-time yet. I've sat plenty of interviews, even second interviews, but no offers yet, which is frustrating—"

"You need to expand your search, maybe. Or agree to take less money."

A strangled laugh came out of my throat. "That's not the issue, Mom. I'm getting plenty of interest—"

"Don't let your pride get in the way of a good job, Trina. You can't afford to be out of work in the long-term. Gaps on resumes can make it even harder to find work later."

I closed my eyes, holding the phone away from my ear as she ranted. Nothing she was saying was new information. I'd even agreed with her on all points, multiple times. For some reason, she thought I was sitting at home, slacking off and letting all the reasonable jobs pass me by.

My mind spun back to the conversation Dallas and I'd had about my overzealous cleaning. I realized, after he'd pointed it out, exactly why I was doing it. I was trying to make an effort not to repeat the pattern when I started to feel like I wasn't pulling my weight.

My worth wasn't tied to my job. It was a new mantra, one I knew I had to get used to telling myself. I'd spent far too many years judging myself based on my salary and the number of overtime hours I was putting in. Society as a whole repeated the idea constantly, also. I knew it was a completely false construct, but it didn't change a damn thing.

I took a deep breath before answering my mother, who finally stopped chattering about things I should do to land a job.

"Mom. I *know.* I literally just got off a call with a good option, my second round of screening. It's hard right now. I'm not refusing anything, there haven't been any offers—"

"You know I love you, baby, but you always do this. You think you're too good for things. If you have to, go work at a restaurant. A store. Something is better than nothing."

I was already exasperated, on the verge of screaming or crying, or both. Frustration burned down the back of my throat.

Thankfully, my dad finally piped up, "Tori, my love, leave the girl be. She's doing her best. You getting all worked up about it doesn't help."

"Worked up? Worked up nothing, Hiro. She needs to get *motivated* before she loses good opportunities!"

My eyes filled with tears. I cleared my throat to get rid of the lump that was forming. I wasn't sure how my mother wielded the magical ability to make me feel like I wasn't making any effort at all when I knew damn well I'd been working my ass off trying to find a new job.

"That's not true, Mom," I said weakly. It was my only defense and it felt totally useless.

My mom huffed and puffed in the background as my dad tried to smooth things over. How they got along so well being such opposites never ceased to amaze me.

"Don't stress too hard, baby. We know you're doing everything you can. Someone will come along with the right offer soon, I'm sure of it."

"Thanks, Dad. Are you driving right now?"

"No, we're stopped. Been in the same campground for a few nights. We'll be moving on tomorrow. We wanted to call while we had good service and a few minutes to chat."

"I'm glad you're seeing new things. I miss you guys. Will you be coming through around Thanksgiving as usual?"

"Yes, of course. Wouldn't miss it for the world, it's your birthday! We can't wait to see you."

Mom still hadn't come back into the conversation, but I could hear her muttering to herself in the background. I was sure she was carefully using a volume I would be able to hear yet not be able to make out whole words with.

"I'm looking forward to seeing you, too. I can't wait to show you my new apartment. I think you'll get along with my roommate. He's fantastic. His whole family has been very good to me."

"That's another thing, Trina. A male roommate? Are you sure this is the kind of girl you want to be?"

"Mom." My forehead landed in my palm with a fleshy *smack*.

"What? I'm just saying. How will you ever find a good husband if you're living with another man?"

"Honestly, Mom? It hasn't been a problem. We've both brought home dates without any issues. Plus, I'm not looking for a husband. Let's get that out in the open right now."

My mother gasped. "Trina! This is not how I raised you!"

"Then where, exactly, do I get it from, Mom? You raised me to be a strong, capable, independent woman. That's what I am. I'm not ashamed of my dating life. I'm doing the best I can to find a job in my chosen career path worth my time. Meanwhile, I'm freelancing multiple projects, all of which provide some income and look good on a resume. It bothers me how you don't see *any* of that." I barked, shocked I'd finally snapped and was giving such impassioned back-talk to my domineering mother.

By all accounts, both of my parents were similarly stunned, a hollow silence stretching out across the phone line.

After several stressful moments, with my heart pounding in my ears and my cheeks growing hot out of a strange mix of terror and horror, my dad started to chuckle.

"Well, there you have it, Tori. She's not wrong. The verbal spanking she just delivered has been a long time coming."

A laugh tried to burst free at my father's words, but I wisely held it in.

I heard my mother mutter something about me being disrespectful, which my father also shut down.

"Respect is *earned*, my love. You can't expect to continually tear her down and question her choices without any consequences. She's a successful young woman, she's simply going through a setback as far as her job. Leave her be."

My adrenaline crashed, making my hands shake. I couldn't believe I'd told my mom off. Not that she didn't deserve it, because she had, for quite a long time. It wasn't unusual for my dad to take up for me when I needed him to, though I was still amazed I'd snapped articulately.

"We love you, Trina. We'll talk soon, okay?"

"Okay. Love you too, Dad."

I wondered what kind of wrath he would be facing after not only shutting her down himself but also approving of me doing the same.

For the first time in my life, I worried about my parents' marriage. Though honestly, I didn't see much of it, so maybe this is how it had been for a long time and what worked for them.

I sat in my room for a while, going over the conversation. While I hated how she couldn't stop repeating herself, my mother's words were at the core of my worries about being jobless. It was obvious her voice was my internal monologue about it. I didn't know how to break free of it.

Stressed, I made my way to the kitchen, on the hunt for something to bake.

Dallas was watching a sci-fi movie on TV. He turned to look at me over the back of the couch. His eyes shifted to the butter and sugar I'd gotten out, his expression growing concerned.

"You okay?"

"Fine," I snapped. I regretted the tone the word flew out with—this wasn't Dallas' fault.

He joined me, an abundance of caution in how much distance he gave me. I appreciated it, while simultaneously wanting a hug. Maybe I'd drive over to Addison's for a bestie squeeze with a side of cocktails.

"Want to talk about it?"

"Not really." I slammed the mixing bowl on the counter, glad it was my stainless steel one instead of my beloved vintage Pyrex.

"Okayyy. Want me to make you a drink?"

I nearly asked him to pour me shots. On second thought, the way my stomach was roiling like I'd swallowed a bath bomb, alcohol probably wasn't a good idea.

"No, thanks. I'm fine."

"Trina." He approached with long strides, gripping my shoulders in his warm hands.

"What?"

"You're not fine."

The empathy in his clever blue eyes broke me. I tried to shove all the emotions away, but they ganged up on me, attacking me at my weakest. Jerks.

"Sure I am," I croaked. "I yelled at my mom for badgering me about not having a real job. First time I stood up to her without it being a joke. I nearly puked."

"I'm proud of you?" Dallas responded uncertainly, head cocked to the side.

"Thanks. I'm proud of myself too. She's scary."

"Scary? Compared to you? Or… compared to Dennis?"

"Is Dennis scary?" His question made me drop my guard a bit, softness returning to my tense muscles.

"Dennis is *terrifying*. Devon's the oldest, but he's a softy. Dennis is the grumpy one."

"Huh. Interesting. I tend to forget all about Devon, to be honest. Anyway, I get it from my mom. My dad's a teddy bear. Where did you think *I* got it from?"

Dallas chuckled, dropping his hands but lingering within my personal space bubble. The scent of his cologne was oddly comforting. The longer we talked with him near me, the more my tumultuous stomach settled.

"I had no idea, honestly. I like your brand of feisty, though. You're a tiny terror."

I'd already started venting, so I decided I might as well get it all out. If nothing else, Dallas was well equipped for my vent sessions.

"She's not wrong, though. I need to try harder to find something. The longer it goes, even with unemployment, the more broke I get and the harder it's going to be. Nobody actually wants me, though! They want to string me along through multiple shitty interviews, but they don't want to hire me. Is it me? Am I too demanding? Do I come across as a terrible employee? Sasha's probably not giving glowing recommendations, which I get. I just don't understand…" Without any warning at all, I fell apart. Dallas wrapped me into a tight hug as I sobbed into my hands.

"Shh. Hey, it's okay," he shushed me, offering comforting words and encouragement as I cried myself out into his shoulder. "It hasn't been all that long. A few months is nothing. You'll find something soon. You've been a Godsend for me." His fingers stroked up and down my spine, setting butterflies to swarming in my stomach.

Horrified, when I was able to pull myself together, I stepped back, out of his embrace.

"I'm *so* sorry."

Dallas chuckled, giving me one of the kindest, gentlest smiles I'd ever seen. It was soft and made my embarrassment vanish. I wanted to curl up in his arms and cuddle at the sight of it, and I wasn't a cuddler.

"No need to apologize. We all fall apart once in a while. Tacos do it all the time and everyone still loves them. What are we baking?"

Somehow, it was exactly the right thing to say. My heart warmed with his sweet words, a wet laugh replacing the sobs at his ridiculous—if accurate—comparison. Besides, he'd immediately suggested baking. How could I refuse?

I looked around at what I'd already gathered for ingredients.

"I have no idea. What do you feel like?"

"You don't have to bake for me, Trina. But I know you do it as a stress reliever, so if you need this, I want to help."

I felt a throb in a part of my body that should absolutely not be reacting to Dallas in the way it was. I rushed to respond so I could focus on something else.

"Something chocolate."

"Naturally." His easy grin usually helped me relax. It must have been *screw with Trina day*, though, because this time it made me wonder how soft his lips would be against my skin.

"Cookies?" I offered, willing myself to be distracted by baking instead of my handsome roommate.

"Hey, I'm just helping out, this is your show."

"Cookie bars. They take less time." Less was better as I needed to get the hell back to the safety of my room since, clearly, I'd lost my mind.

"Sounds great."

The routine motions helped me find my center again and let go of the sneaky spicy thoughts trying to take over my heap of confused emotions.

Dallas was an excellent helper as I assembled chocolate chip cookie bars. He'd trained under a master—he took directions like a pro. Once the dough was layered in a pan and set in the oven to bake, he pulled out some leftovers to make us both a plate for dinner.

"Why are you single again?" I asked as I shoved a forkful of the reheated chicken casserole into my mouth. If I'd timed it right, the cookie bars would come out right as we finished eating.

"Fatal flaw, remember?"

"Right. Which is what? It certainly isn't your ability to be kind. Or cook. Or take care of a girl dangling over the edge of mental breakdown."

He shook his head, the slightest blush on his cheeks.

As further proof of my argument, he cleared the dishes, washing up the mess I'd made baking when we were done—the most direct way to the hearts of millions around the world. He sealed the deal by getting out a pint of vanilla ice cream I wasn't even aware we had to serve with my bars.

Once they were out of the oven, I cut the gooey, steaming tray into reasonably sized cookies, but they didn't want to come out of the pan without falling apart because they were still too hot.

"Here," he said, scooping a bite of ice cream into a spoon, then dipping into the pan for some cookie to go with it. He offered it to me, his mouth opening in a mirror of mine, his hand cupped under the spoon to catch any drips. "You should have the first bite."

The gesture hit a number of my *'holy shit, that's sexy'* buttons, which put me right back where I'd started. My emotional state was already haywire, I didn't need any help to feel out of sorts. A handsome, sweet man literally spoon-feeding me dessert? I was *doomed*. It didn't matter that until this moment we'd been strictly platonic, my body was fully on board with whatever he was offering.

I chewed carefully, sighing as more of my tension dissolved in the sugar.

Dallas used the same spoon he'd offered me to get himself a bite, licking it upside-down after making appreciative noises.

"So good," he said, low in his throat. He repeated the whole routine, feeding me a bite before taking one for himself.

One spoon. Throaty noises. Sugary treats.

My body was sending out tingles to places that made me clench my thighs and struggle to stifle noises I usually reserved for the bedroom.

When he licked a smear of chocolate from his thumb, my brain short-circuited.

This man. He was as close to perfect as I'd ever seen, met, or had the pleasure of conjuring with my fantasies.

Before I could stop myself, I stood on my tip-toes and crushed my mouth to his. For a second, his body was stiff. I nearly panicked and pulled away, every alarm bell in my brain going off full blast. Before I could, he not only loosened up, returning the kiss, but he also threaded his fingers through my short curls, giving a slight tug that snatched a moan from my throat. He opened his mouth, and we traded sugary breath as his tongue cautiously probed at mine. I enthusiastically returned the gesture, banding my arms around his center.

All previous boundaries vanished as we stood there in the kitchen doing very un-roommate-like things with our bodies pressed together.

Even knowing there would be serious consequences to my lack of impulse control, I couldn't bring myself to regret my split-second decision to kiss him for even a moment.

CHAPTER TWENTY-FIVE

Dallas

FIRST, MY FEISTY friend of a roommate laid one hell of a kiss on me.

Then, I did a crazy thing and kissed her right back. Because it felt right.

Her lips were sweet, the moment all ours. We were in our kitchen, surrounded by the scent of those damned cookie bars.

It was perfect.

I still wasn't quite sure how we'd ended up sweaty and naked in my bed, but here we were. I wasn't complaining, though I did worry we'd have some serious concerns about it later.

She let out a sigh as my fingers coasted over the curves of her hips that made my cock swell and I knew there was no turning back.

"Trina, are you sure this is…"

"Don't stop."

"I just don't want—"

"Shh. I want. I *definitely* want." I could see the need reflected in her dark eyes. The breathy quality her voice took on made my blood pound.

I couldn't effectively argue with her, because at the moment, I wanted as well. More than I should. The consequences for this departure from simple friendship would be waiting on the other side of our tryst, of that much I was certain. Still, it wasn't enough for me to pull the brakes.

With a thick swallow, I allowed myself to touch more of her naked flesh. She was a compilation of everything I adored about the female form. Her curves fit perfectly in my hands, her labored breaths matching mine while we moved from cautious exploration to heavy petting.

Her fingernails scraped my stomach as I leaned over her to lick along her collarbone, the muscles contracting under the tickle.

"Tell me," she said breathlessly. "Tell me what you like."

I grinned, turning to run the tip of my tongue along the shell of her ear. "I like everything. I thought you knew that already?"

Her lips quirked into a grin, but all I could see was our mutual lust. It was clouding everything up, even with all the lights on.

"Fine. Then we'll do what *I* like."

My brain malfunctioned at her words, lust roaring in response.

"Can't wait."

She pulled me down by the neck for another ferocious kiss, this one involving her teeth and nails. Blood pounded in my ears as I tried to give back as much as she gave, nipping and tasting as her body reached for mine.

Her hand wrapped around my hard cock and squeezed, causing me to break the kiss so I could breathe.

"Hold on." I reached for my nightstand drawer, sanity momentarily returning. "Safety first."

"You are one of the most prepared people I know. We only need it if you want, though. I have an IUD. My doc records are digital. *I'm* actually the most prepared person I know."

Trina's coy smile heated my blood. The sharp left turn we'd taken in our relationship left me stunned, but I wasn't doing any take-backs.

When she saw I was ready, she stood at the edge of the bed, her back to me. Her legs were pressed together, her torso leaned forward, flat on the mattress.

"Jesus," I swore. I could see she was swollen, slick, and ready.

"Don't make me wait," she said, looking at me over her shoulder. "Please. I want you, Dallas."

Her words burned through me as I positioned myself at her entrance and pressed in slowly, her heat wrapping around me, chasing intense pleasure down my spine.

Trina made a throaty noise as she pressed her forehead into the sheets, adjusting her stance slightly to meet my height as we found the perfect angle. A warning throb had already started at my base, so I waited a moment before drawing out of her. Her damp core gripped at me as I moved out, trying to draw me back in.

"Fuck," I groaned.

"Yes, please." Her muffled words spurred me into movement.

Trina's hips pressed back into mine, countering my motions and ensuring I went as deep as possible.

I gripped one hip with my fingers, leaning forward with my chest pressed to her back so I could wrap my other hand around her throat. I didn't apply much pressure, just gripped at the sides of her neck. The salacious grin she gave me, turning her head to press a violent kiss to my mouth, told me I'd guessed one of her kinks correctly. I briefly wondered how many we shared, but didn't have time to think about it. Her body didn't stop moving against mine, and her throaty moans spoke to something deep in my gut.

I didn't want to embarrass myself, but the pace she'd set was too perfect for me to last very long.

"Trina."

"Don't slow down, it's fine."

She used one of her hands to cover mine, pressing my grip around her throat tighter as her other arm disappeared underneath her body.

Blood pounding fiercely, I matched her demanding rhythm, closing my eyes as sparks flared in my blood.

"It's fine, it's fine, it's fine…" she chanted the words, her hips bucking as she chased her release.

Her body squeezed mine, pulsing as she crested her climax. She sagged into the mattress and I sped right after her, my body going rigid as sensations hit a brutal peak, sparking through every part of my body.

I didn't dare move for a moment as dizziness threatened. As blood flow returned to normal, the floaty sensation in my head passed.

Carefully, I separated us. Trina rolled over in bed, eyes wide as she stared at the ceiling.

"Holy shit," she swore, a broad grin on her lips.

I agreed. As I washed up in the bathroom and dampened a towel to take back to her, reality started to set in.

Had we just screwed everything up?

We'd definitely screwed.

Hopefully, those consequences I knew were going to show up soon weren't too damning.

TRINA WASN'T A post-coital snuggler.

I usually was, but these were special circumstances.

We'd made our way back to the living room, settling into our normal spots on the couch. One of our favorite reality TV shows was playing, but neither of us were paying even the slightest bit of attention to the drama unfolding on the screen.

"What's going on in your head?" Trina asked. Her eyes were stuck wide open, as though she were shocked by our behavior.

"I'm wondering if that was a terrible idea," I admitted. "Don't get me wrong, it was shamefully good. Definitely unexpected. Incredible, though."

Her mouth quirked to the side. "Same. I think… I think it's going to be okay. Don't you?"

I didn't want to worry her. My tendency to overthink had nothing to do with her, or even what happened between us, but I'd already gone over several worst-case scenarios should things implode as a result of what we'd done.

"I'm not a great authority on this kind of thing. I've never slept with someone I lived with who I wasn't also already dating."

"Do we need to be dating?" Her expression changed to perplexed.

"No, I'm saying that's all I have experience with."

"Would you… would you want to do it again?" She blushed. "Or do you want to just forget it ever happened?"

I smiled back at her, the rosy hue of her cheeks as endearing as it was humorous after how in charge she'd been in the bedroom. "Definitely no forgetting that anytime soon, Terror. So, hell yeah, I'd do it again. Wouldn't you?"

"I would. But not if it makes things weird." Her anxiety was palpable. How she hadn't figured out I wasn't going anywhere was a mystery to me.

Then again, I suppose I was still settling into the idea myself.

"Well, what if we agree it won't make things weird?"

Trina scratched her cheek, watching me with clever eyes. It often felt as though she could see right through me. I couldn't decide if it was terrifying or thrilling. Maybe it was both.

"Sounds reasonable. Almost too reasonable." Her eyes narrowed. "Is it that easy? *Deciding* it's a certain way makes it true?"

"It's a reasonable possibility." I was flying by the absolute seat of my pants while trying to convince her of my confidence. I hoped she couldn't see right through me. "Do you feel different? Like it's going to be awkward now?"

"No, not really." She leaned her head into her hand. "No strings, right? Just sex?"

"Is no strings what you want?" I purposefully kept my tone as bland as possible. I couldn't tell if she was asking or stating. No strings was probably better in my opinion, though I was biased because of my past relationships. We worked well as friends, so I didn't see why we couldn't add sex to our current arrangement. In some ways, it felt like a natural step. Where feelings would end up in the mix of things was an unanswered question.

"It's probably the best way, don't you think?"

"Honestly, I have no idea. As I said, I've only ever habitually had sex with roommates I was already dating."

Her eyes drifted around the room as she thought. "Okay, but we should probably keep it just between us, if we don't intend on going full-blown relationship, right?"

"Probably. There would be questions if people found out."

"What if… what if we agree to add those kinds of benefits to our friendship, as long as we keep it on the down-low and only until one of us starts dating someone else."

"Okay. It's an arrangement that stays within these walls. And only happens if we're not seeing anyone else on the side."

"Agreed," Trina said, very matter-of-factly as she shoved out her hand.

Shaking to solidify the agreement was somehow the weirdest thing that happened between us all night.

"It's this simple?" She tilted her head to the side as though expecting something else to happen once we'd let go of the handshake.

"Look at us being all grown up," I teased. "Pretty sure, yeah. I'm no authority, though."

"This is so bizarre, but I'm here for it. You're something else, Dallas Greene. I knew so from the moment I met you."

"Oh yeah? What else did you think when you first met me?" I wasn't sure what I was expecting, but her answer surprised me.

"That you were as handsome as your brother. Way less serious, though. How you were smoking hot, dismounting your motorcycle, and your ass looked amazing in your jeans. I thought you were quite charming, to be honest."

"You've got one hell of a list." My smile was unrestrained at the genuine compliments she offered. If there was one thing I never doubted about Trina, it was her sincerity.

"Well, ask and you shall receive. I told you most of that when we were setting up your dating profile."

"Yeah, but I believe you mean it now."

Trina's eyes rolled a little, her mouth pulled into a sweet grin.

"Plus, you hung out with my drunk ass when Addison ducked out to hook up and then you let me come live with you. You dance with me. I'd be stupid to skip over what just happened in there," she said, gesturing to my room. "All things considered, what's not to like?" She paused, making an exaggerated shrug. "What about me? What did you think about me when we first met?"

"I had a feeling you were going to be trouble," I said, which earned me a raised eyebrow with a wicked grin. "I was right. You might be small, but you're mighty. I wouldn't want to be on the wrong side of your storm, that's for sure."

"You didn't know the half of it. Poor little Dallas from a few months ago. He was in for one hell of a shock."

She was one hundred percent correct. And I didn't regret a damn thing.

CHAPTER TWENTY-SIX

Dallas

"**W**E'VE GOT A big dry goods donation coming in today. Food, bedding, you know the drill. Push the truck first, then we can come back to resetting racks eighteen through twenty-five. Good?"

My team of five guys stood in a rough semi-circle around me. I could identify each of their unique wide stances in my sleep—they were the same every single morning. We all showed up in jeans and t-shirts every day, ready to work. Cal carried around his massive cup of coffee as though it was his lifeline (it probably was), and Drum compulsively cracked his knuckles while pecking keys on the keyboard to make shipping labels. When one of them saw me without my phone, they asked if I was feeling okay. It made me cringe because that meant I was taking on very Dennis-esque traits, but as a manager, it was something I needed to deal with. Every last damn one of us tensed up when Dennis came out into what I considered my territory. On the other hand, when the guys spotted Addison, they softened like butter on a hot day. I had zero complaints about any of them or their productivity or attitude; as far as I was concerned, I was living the workplace dream.

"I made a map for the reset, it's taped to the racks. Get the truck unloaded first, we have six different shipments going out needing product to fill them."

They all gave a gentle nod as they mumbled and yawned, gearing up to go their separate ways to start the workday. I rarely had to do more than give them a plan to start with, which was a blessing in and of itself. There was a mountain of logistics to manage, so while I helped where I could, much of my energy was spent taking care of the details while they pulled off the actual physical labor.

Not long after, the beep of the forklift horn and the sound of pallet jacks being dropped to the concrete floor began making the familiar music of my day, Addison came rushing out through the double doors.

I happened to be standing in the center aisle, so I saw her wide-eyed, startled expression. My heart instantly dropped.

"What's wrong? Is Trina okay? Dennis?"

Addison's face broke into a bright smile.

"Everyone's fine! Sorry, I probably looked scared, right?"

"Terrified."

"Sorry! It's urgent but fine. Better than fine! You're about to be an uncle."

"Oh." The startled response was the best I could manage. My brain instantly went to any number of worst-case scenarios involving injury or worse. I wondered if Addison noticed I'd asked about Trina first, as I obediently followed her into the office. My feet must have been moving slower than she liked, because, by the time we got to the conference room where my brother Daniel was already connected via video call on the projector, Addison was dragging me by the hand.

"You're about to lose your title, Baby Greene," he teased.

"Thank God." I was too nervous to sit in a chair, so I leaned my ass up against the edge of the table. "What's going on?"

"Stephanie's water broke around two this morning. They're already at the hospital. Devon's been updating me by text, but we thought this might be easier." He frowned at his phone. "It's Mom, she's having a hard time getting connected, gimme a sec."

"Sure."

Addison was pacing along the side of the table, texting in rapid bursts.

"Dennis should be here in a minute." She set her phone down on the table, arms crossed. "I'm not sure what we should be doing right now."

"Me neither."

"Doesn't labor take a long time usually? Especially with a first baby?"

"I have no idea."

She took a seat next to me, both of us straightening up as Daniel returned and a screen with my parents popped up.

"Oh my goodness, this is so exciting!" Mom wiggled in her chair, an exuberant expression on her face.

"Are you going to fly out to California, Mrs. Greene? To help out for a little bit?" Addison asked, thrilled at the prospect of having a project to tackle if only some online travel booking.

"Yes, that's the plan, but there's nothing set yet. We were waiting to see if they were going to choose to recover at the condo in the city or drive back to the studio in Santa Barbara before buying a ticket."

"If they come back here, we can all rotate bringing food and helping out. Maxwell and Nora are right next door, plus Phae and I are only about ten minutes away," Daniel said, frowning at his phone. "I'll be back." His video screen went black.

"Let me know and I'll get your tickets set up," Addison offered.

"How sweet of you, dear. I hate having to wait until the last minute, they're going to be so expensive." Mom's face pinched.

I laughed at her. "Ma, Devon is a literal millionaire. I'm sure a last-minute plane ticket for you is completely manageable."

She waved a hand, dismissing my words. "Still. Money is money!"

"Just don't worry about the cost, okay? You going too, Dad?"

My father shook his head. "No, I'm going to stay behind and hold down the fort with the dogs." The expression on his face was less than enthusiastic. I tried to remember the last time my parents went on an actual vacation. The only thing I could come up with was when we all went to California for Devon and Stephanie's wedding. "You should go. I can take care of the dogs." I heard myself make the offer before I fully finished thinking about it. "Go see some things. Meet your grandbaby, then go somewhere fun."

My parents looked at one another, hope in their eyes. "It has been a while…"

"It's been years," I said.

"We're nearby too. We can help! You definitely should go. You've more than earned a vacation," Addison added.

Daniel and Devon both popped up on the video screen while Addison was doing her very best to help me convince my parents to take a trip. Devon was standing in a long hallway, grinning like a fool.

"Take a couple of weeks. We can manage the dogs and housesit." She nodded enthusiastically, her excitement translating to my mother.

"I suppose we are due some time away." The way my mother was gazing at my dad made my chest warm. The adoration there never faded or dulled, not even after all these years. I was pretty sure there was a photo on their fireplace mantle from decades ago, with them staring at one another the same way.

"Definitely," Devon added, amused at having come into the conversation where he had. "Say the word and I'll get a private jet reserved."

"No, no," Mom argued. "That's too much."

"Why, Ma?" Devon asked.

"It just is. Where's your lovely wife? How is everything going?" Changing the subject when she got uncomfortable was a tactic she'd mastered.

Devon shook his head but didn't press the subject.

"She's doing great. Everything has slowed down for a second, so I ran out to get a coffee while they check her. I'll see if Alan's cabin is available if you want to hang out in the mountains."

"We'll talk about it later." Mom flapped her hands again in dismissal of the topic. "Tell Stephanie we love her!"

Devon's whole demeanor warmed at the very mention of his wife. There were dark smudges under his tired eyes, though exuded pure joy.

"I will. I'll update as soon as I can. If you want to keep the call open, that might be easiest. No need to sit around waiting. This could take a while."

"First babies usually do." Mom's smile was warm and nostalgic. "After that, it's a crapshoot. The first one is the hardest."

"I think she's fishing for an apology," Daniel teased Devon.

"You, hush. You took the longest," Mom admonished him.

"I was the best labor, the easiest baby… you guys know I'm the favorite," I teased.

"Keep telling yourself that, Baby Greene." Daniel laughed. I flipped him off.

We'd all heard her war stories over the years, but she loved to tell them, so we all listened no matter how many times they got repeated. Devon was the hardest labor, Daniel the longest. Dennis was the biggest baby, and I came so quickly they barely made it to the hospital.

Dennis rushed through the conference room doorway, eyes wild. "Did I miss it?"

"Nah," Devon shook his head. "You didn't all have to rush in, but I appreciate it. Steph does too." He looked off to the side, nodding to someone out of the camera view. "I'll check in soon, sounds like the nurses are done with her for now."

There was a messy chorus of well-wishes and Devon dropped off after briefly showing a tired Stephanie waving from her hospital bed.

Something surged in my chest. I was well aware our family was one of the most functional I knew, but this was further proof. Emotion clogged my throat. I'd stayed away for a few years and I'd missed this without realizing how much. Everyone was all in, no matter the event. Having a group of people perpetually on your side was something I hoped I never took for granted again.

"I'm going to grab my stuff so I can work in here," Addison said, sliding off the table.

My brother intercepted her, so I looked politely away while they shared a hello kiss.

"Good idea," I agreed. "I'm going to check on the guys, then I'll join you."

We separated to gather our things for a day of working in the conference room. It would be interesting, especially if my parents just stayed on the line, but we'd make it work. We were nothing if not adaptable.

Mom and Dad left their laptop logged in, one of them checking in every once in a while as the rest of us worked, treating the day like one long meeting. Daniel's girlfriend, Phae, joined him at the office in California, the video feed becoming a comical collection of people all working on their own electronic devices while sporadically chatting with one another.

Addison worked on tentative travel plans while I maneuvered through my list of incoming shipments. Dennis fiddled with his detailed spreadsheets for planning and outfitting a new shelter.

Not long after Addison retrieved our lunch order from the lobby, Devon's video box changed from black to an image of his smiling face.

"Everyone still here? We'd love to introduce you to someone."

Mom and Dad's screen only showed an empty couch, so Dennis called out to get their attention. After only a moment, they came rushing into the frame.

"Is it time?" Mom asked, breathless.

"The gang's all here," Dennis confirmed.

Devon nodded, holding the camera at a distance so he

could lean in to put his face next to Stephanie's. They were smiling, the beatific grin unique to new parents. She was beautiful even in her exhaustion, and there was a tiny bundle wrapped up on her chest.

"Everyone, meet Eleanor Rose. Ellie, this is your family."

Mom made high-pitched noises, starting to cry while smiling more widely than I'd ever seen.

My throat clogged, tears unexpectedly filling my eyes. I took a quick, nervous glance at my brother, finding him similarly speechless, blinking quickly. For a stoic grump, it seemed he too was susceptible to the unyielding power of newborn babies. I guess the same held true for me, which was unexpected. It took three attempts to clear the lump out of my throat.

Addison was staring wide-eyed, a hand on her cheek. "She's so beautiful," she said. "Congratulations, you guys." Babies were a somewhat touchy subject for her, as her former fiancé and sister were expecting soon. Dennis took her free hand between his, allowing her to breathe normally for the first time in several long moments.

"Welcome to the family, Baby Greene," I said. Some of the weight of the nickname slid from my shoulders. I welcomed passing the moniker to another member of the family. I didn't believe for a moment my brothers would actually quit calling me by it, especially because they knew it bothered me, but I would happily share, especially with someone so cute.

"How are you feeling, Stephanie?" Phae asked.

"I feel pretty good, all things considered." She smiled, gazing down at the sleeping cherub on her chest with awe.

"She's perfect," Phae sighed, Daniel kissed her temple. The way he looked at her made me suspect Mom wasn't far off in her assessment about him proposing to her indeed being just a formality.

"Congratulations, you guys," Dennis said.

"Thanks, man." Devon gazed at his wife and new daughter.

We all sat on the call a moment longer, greeting the tiny new member of our clan before disconnecting. There was a sedate silence once the west coast half of our family was off the line.

"Wow. That's…" Addison said, a little bit flustered as she tried to collect herself. She never did get around to finishing her thought. Maybe there wasn't one to be had.

Dennis linked his fingers with hers, giving her a patient, understanding look. I was an awkward third wheel sitting there during their sweet interaction. I was glad to not only see how my brother cared for my friend, but also the love my friend gave him in return.

It was not at all the day I'd expected to have when I got to work, but it was one of the best I could remember.

CHAPTER TWENTY-SEVEN

Trina

THE WAY DALLAS bounced in the door after work, a beaming grin on his face, made my heart dance.

"Good day?" I asked, pausing the show I was watching to greet him.

"Yeah, today was great." He dropped his keys and travel bag. "Stephanie had her baby today. I'm an uncle!"

He threw his arms wide, the excitement he radiated was unexpected but adorable. There'd never been much talk about her pregnancy or how he felt about becoming an uncle, despite the media coverage about it. So his feelings about the topic were largely a mystery until now.

"Aw, congratulations!" Addison had already texted me, but I didn't want to steal the thunder from his announcement.

"She's cute. Ellie is her name." He took a deep breath, as though getting that out had taken it out of him. His eyes were as wide as his smile for a moment. Reality was sinking in. I wondered if maybe he'd needed a little time to get used to the idea of his brother having a baby. It probably wouldn't be completely real until he saw the little nugget in person.

"You seem surprised." Laughter rumbled in my chest as I got up to join him in the kitchen.

"I guess I kind of am. I mean, we all knew Stephanie was pregnant. I've only met her in person once, though, at their wedding. Her having a baby and me becoming an uncle to an actual tiny human was an abstract concept until today."

He opened a beer and took a drink, standing at the island like the revelation left him stunned. I felt vindicated that my suspicions were correct.

"Well, I'm sure you'll be a great uncle. You're pretty fun."

His eyes sparkled as he looked at me, an electric current running through my blood in response to the energy I found there.

"You think so? As the youngest brother, I didn't get any practice at caring for someone smaller than me like my brothers did."

"Sure." I shrugged. "I don't believe you Greene men know how to be bad at things for the most part, if I'm being honest. But you're all naturally skilled at the family thing. I'm guessing since she's the first grandbaby and the only girl in the bunch, she's going to be spoiled rotten."

"Oh yeah," he agreed enthusiastically. "I'm sure Mom is absolutely frothing to start buying her all kinds of things.

Devon asked that nobody send them anything until they knew what they needed, but once the call goes out, I can see it spiraling fast."

I laughed again, the vision of an all-boy mom being set loose in a store to buy anything and everything she wanted for a girl running through my mind.

"Speaking of which, I may be dog sitting for my parents for a couple of weeks."

"Oh?" I busied myself with getting out the rest of the ingredients for dinner as we talked.

"Yeah, Mom wants to fly out to help with the baby and we're trying to convince my dad to go with her so they can do that and take a real vacation."

"Aw. How nice of you guys."

Dallas saw what I was doing, quickly washing his hands before grating some cheese as I shredded up the chicken I'd made in the crockpot for tacos.

"They need a vacation, to be honest. I'm pretty sure the last time they went anywhere was Devon's wedding."

"I'm not sure I'd be much help. I'm happy to do whatever if you need something, though."

Dallas quirked a grin. "I appreciate it. I'm going to miss my bed if that happens because those dogs are needy as hell, but it's the least I can do."

"Did Dennis volunteer too? Or just you?"

He squinted as though trying to remember.

"I'm pretty sure Addison volunteered Dennis, but don't quote me on that."

"Sounds right." I laughed, turning my attention to dicing up tomatoes and shredding lettuce.

We mutually assembled our plates, not even bothering to sit down before crunching into the shells I'd made.

"I fucking love taco Tuesday," Dallas mumbled over a full bite. He swiped a lingering smear of guacamole from the corner of his mouth with a thumb.

"It's Wednesday," I corrected.

"Don't care. This is awesome."

The praise warmed me.

"I appreciate your appreciation." I joked, handing him a paper towel. The chicken hadn't sat quite enough time to soak up the sauce and there was a drip running clear down his arm.

"Thanks." He licked the length of his forearm before employing the towel.

My stomach dipped into my toes at the innocent gesture.

He caught me staring.

I blushed as he grinned at me, the casual shake of his head giving me butterflies.

"I thought *I* was bad," he said, using the paper towel on his fingertips before reaching to assemble more tacos. "You might be worse."

"Is it really worse? Or is it equal?"

"Fair point. It's probably equal. Don't get me wrong, I don't mind being looked at that way at all, it just still surprises me sometimes."

"The same way me saying shocking things—which I do *all* the time, by the way—surprises you?"

He pushed his remaining half of a taco into his mouth before responding. "Yep. Same thing."

I didn't know what to say, so I finished eating my food without comment.

We'd arrived at a place in our comfort with one another that meal prep and cleanup was a silent dance most of the time. He started putting away the leftovers while I rinsed the dishes. Most nights, after dinner, he collected drinks for us both, then led the way to the living room while I trailed behind with dessert.

It should have been strange. Instead, it was incredibly soothing. It was the same level of intuitive friendship I had with Addison, just with some added… spice.

Instead of moving off to the living room while I wiped the stove and countertop down, he scrolled through his phone, the same frown I'd noticed a few times appearing at a text notification.

"Everything okay?" I asked.

He nodded slowly, closing out all of his apps before setting the phone as far out of reach as possible.

"Yeah. Work stuff."

I could tell he was lying but didn't call him on it. Whatever was going on was his business. If he didn't want to share with me, that was okay.

"Can I help?"

Dallas turned a grateful, gentle smile on me. "No. I appreciate the offer, though."

"Sure."

"I'm going to go take a shower."

"No run this evening?"

He looked up, but not directly at me. His gaze went to the front door, and I wondered what it was that had his attention so diverted. Not for the first time, I noticed he seemed tired. Usually, the suggestion of exercise was enough to snap him out of his funk.

"No, not tonight, sorry. Were you looking forward to our walk?" His brows drew together. It was as though he worried that choosing not to take his run was problematic for me.

Trying to put him at ease, I put some extra brightness into my response. "No big deal. Really. I'm not upset about skipping for a change."

Dallas' face was closed off as he left the room, the humor of our discussion over tacos having completely evaporated.

Since he was taking a shower, I waited to choose a show or movie. We didn't always buddy up for our evening entertainment, but it was fairly common.

It was only Wednesday, and my week accounted for three more useless phone screenings, plus a handful of new applications. Since I had time to kill and stress to feed, I decided I'd made some peanut butter kiss cookies.

I chose a music station on the TV, hosting my own private dance party in the kitchen as I put the dough together.

My trusty stand mixer creamed the butter and sugars while I sang along to the pop ballad at full volume, a wooden spoon as my microphone. I carefully dropped in the egg and vanilla to get mixed in as I swayed my hips to the beat, shedding the worries of the day right off my back. I mixed all my dry ingredients in my favorite giant measuring cup, as usual wearing nearly as much of the flour as I poured safely into the container.

I kept my eyes closed as I sang and rocked my body, rolling little perfect balls of dough between my palms. When I opened my eyes, I found Dallas standing near the fridge, watching me with a smirk on his handsome face. He was drying his hair, casually leaning up against the wall in just a pair of sweats.

My pulse spiked at the sight of him, embarrassment be damned.

I continued as I was, but used my eyes to tell him if he was going to stare, he could at least be helpful.

He tossed the towel he'd been using on his damp hair off to the side and opened the bag of chocolates, carefully pulling the flag to unwrap the foils.

"I need a dozen of those, please." I stopped singing long enough to make my request.

Dallas said nothing, just pinned me with those bright blues and popped chocolate into his mouth.

The heat in the kitchen suddenly had absolutely nothing to do with the preheating oven.

I rolled out twelve cookie balls, swirling them through a plate of sugar before putting them on a cookie sheet. I stashed the remaining dough in the fridge.

Once the tray was in the oven, Dallas closed the distance between us, taking one of my hands into his and wrapping the other around my hip. The station changed over to a more ballad-like tune. While I was all enthusiasm and no skill when it came to dancing with a partner, he one thousand percent knew what he was doing. We'd danced together before, but never like this. We usually bounced along to the music in our own separate ways, even if his hands were on me.

This was a whole new animal and I was here. For. It.

He pulled me tight to his body, my focus on his face as I tried to keep from trampling his feet. He maneuvered me around our kitchen, somehow keeping me from bashing a hip bone on any of the corners of the island as he moved our bodies in time to the pulsing beat.

With a small adjustment of his arms, he pulled me flat against his chest. I could feel his heart racing against my cheek. My pulse was pounding in kind, from my throat clear to the hollow between my thighs. His hand slid from my waist to my ass and I made a noise when I exhaled that had him echoing with a low growl in his throat. As the song ended, he pressed me up against the wall.

I stared up into his eyes, our mutual lust resonating in our heavy breaths.

"Can I kiss you, Trina?"

I nodded hastily, and he captured my mouth with his, one hand guiding my thigh over his hip, the other at the side of my neck, his thumb resting on my jaw. I melted into the embrace, as he cautiously nipped at first, before diving in whole-heartedly to devour me.

A noise rattled through my chest as need pulsed through my body. As our kiss deepened, tongues mingling and breath trading bodies, his hand traveled the length of my thigh. My leg muscles trembled as his fingertips lifted at the edge of my panties so he could gain purchase on my bare ass cheek.

He pressed his full weight into me, my back flat against the wall. He was hard against my center, and it felt like I was mere moments from combusting out of my skin with need. He didn't voice his request out loud, but I could see what he wanted in his eyes. I wanted it too.

"Hurry," I gasped. "Please."

With some quick handiwork, the barriers between us disappeared, and he slid me up the wall with his hands under my legs. I locked my ankles around his waist as he pressed inside me in one thrust, breath hot against my throat as we began to rock together. I moaned out as he pressed his lips back to mine, stealing my breath as he caressed my tongue with his in a rhythm that matched what his hips were doing. It was steady at first, then the same punishing beat the song playing distantly in the background held.

My brain became pleasantly empty as sensation took top priority.

It was as though Dallas couldn't get close enough to me. He guided my hands over my head, pinning my wrists to the wall with one of his as he pressed in even further, melding his chest with mine as his hips drove against me. I worried briefly about the integrity of the drywall, until suddenly it didn't matter. Nothing did.

The current building in me broke free. I cried out as climax claimed me, electricity pulsing through my core to my extremities. Dallas' motions became stilted, and he grabbed my mouth in one final kiss as he crested the apex of his arousal.

"You are cute as hell when you dance around the kitchen, Terror."

"Who knew cookies were an aphrodisiac?" I panted, grabbing up my discarded underthings.

Still trying to catch my breath, I wobbled on unsteady legs into the kitchen. I pulled the tray out of the oven and without a word, Dallas helped me plunk a chocolate into the center of the warm cookies.

They'd gotten a little overcooked, but neither of us minded. We nibbled our way through at least half the batch as we watched a movie, curled up on the couch together.

It was a surprise to me to learn that I was feeling touch-starved. I couldn't come up with any other way to describe how we both were acting following our lustful interlude. It was different from any other time we'd hung out, and it satisfied a need I wasn't aware I had. I wasn't a cuddler, but this… this I wanted.

Our bodies casually tangled together on the couch, Dallas' fingers trailing along my bare legs. My hand was in his hair, twisting through the strands, trying to massage out some tension in his neck with my thumbs.

My eyes scanned his tattoo, then my fingers. *It takes courage to grow up and become who you truly are.* He tensed under the tickle of my touch but smiled at me as I grazed the words. It sounded like E.E. Cummings or one of those other stately old poets. It was also a thousand percent perfect for him.

Talking was overrated. I was sure both of us dozed off at least once.

If monogamous relationships were like our evening had been, I could almost understand why they were so attractive to people.

CHAPTER TWENTY-EIGHT

Dallas

SOMETHING HAD SHIFTED between Trina and I. It was foolish to deny it, especially after we spent the evening cuddling on the couch.

I wasn't complaining, I just didn't know if I needed to call attention to it or take some kind of action. Things had been completely normal between us in the couple of days since, but I couldn't quit thinking about how sexy she'd been dancing around the kitchen. How relaxed I'd been with her fingers in my hair, and how well I'd slept afterward.

Things at work were starting to get the better of me, however, even with Trina managing the updates to our website. More things were slipping through the cracks. Nobody liked to make mistakes; I was no exception.

Dennis was in the office late Friday afternoon, so I made a point to pull him aside to talk about it.

"I need someone else managing the website full time if I'm in charge of the warehouse and logistics. Trina's doing great with the updates we paid her to do, but it's not enough. I thought… well, I thought wrong. I thought that part would be enough. Growth is outpacing what we're currently staffed for. I can get it all done, but it isn't comfortable. I don't want to be here all day, then go home to log more hours. It's not fair or sustainable. We need to tweak some things. Again."

It hadn't been too long ago we'd shifted a bunch of the workload around when we opened the second location in California, then again when Dennis hired Addison. The foundation was growing exponentially, however, and things required another adjustment. I knew I wasn't asking too much, but deep-seated fear made me brace for my brother's response.

My brother stared off, considering what I'd said. He tipped his water bottle up, taking a deep drink before responding.

"Did you have someone in mind?"

"I don't see any reason to reinvent the wheel. Trina's already doing a great job with the parts I've asked her to help with."

Dennis smirked. It still took me by surprise when I saw it come so easily. He'd gone years without so much as cracking a grin for anyone, except maybe Mom.

"She has. I'm sure Trina would be a good investment if you feel like she's up to the bigger assignment."

My main concern was that Trina would believe my offer was out of pity.

I'd overheard one of her last follow-up calls. My heart hurt for her over the rejection because she'd been so sure she was a shoo-in for the job and thought the interview went well. She'd been casual about it, but had immediately taken out butter, sugar, and flour when she emerged from the office. I knew she was in a rough place the moment she started piling ingredients on the counter.

Brownies loaded with mini peanut butter cups took shape as she commented about how it was *fine*, it wasn't the best fit, the salary was a step back, the location wasn't great, plus some other things that eased the sting of being denied the job.

"Let me write up the new parameters, then we can call the Tweedles."

"Tweedles?"

"Yep. Tweedle-Dev and Tweedle-Dan."

Dennis snorted at my new favorite nickname for our other two brothers. "Your brain is a terrifying place sometimes." He shook his head, mouth pulled into a wide grin as he tossed the empty bottle into the recycling bin.

"All the time," I agreed, forcing myself to stay light about it. If I let the shadows creep in even a little, they liked to make themselves at home. I didn't have time for that.

"Go home. Put together a little proposal, and we can go over it during the call Monday morning. Make sure you send it to Addison, though; she's in charge of the office."

"Yeah, I know."

I knew all too well if I went around Addison, especially with something involving her best friend, I'd be in deep shit with her, which was not somewhere I wanted to be.

"You okay locking up, or should I hang around?" Dennis asked, shifting as though impatient to leave.

"I got it. Go home so you can get ready for your date."

"How do you know about my date?" He grumbled.

"I know all and see all." He just glared at me with an eyebrow raised. "Addison told me. Say hi to her for me."

He muttered to himself as he crossed the parking lot toward his truck, flying one middle finger high.

As the warehouse staff headed out for the day, I took care of my closing duties. Making sure the lights were off and the office was locked down were all part of a routine I was getting used to doing.

If anyone told me a year ago this would be my life, I'd have laughed right in their face. Now? I was close to enjoying the stability, and it was a novel experience for me.

Once everyone was gone and I'd locked up, I rode my motorcycle to my favorite Thai takeout place before heading home.

I didn't know what Trina had planned for her evening. I was hoping some pineapple shrimp curry would make her feel a little better about not getting the latest job, though. We didn't talk in-depth about her financial situation, but if her tight-lipped sighs when she looked at her phone were anything to do with it, she was getting to a point of discomfort as far as her bank account, despite the trickle of income from freelancing. I understood the position very well.

The sun was brutal even through the visor on my helmet as I made the final turns toward the apartment complex. My saddlebags were heavy with containers of food and I was anxious to change into my cozies—as I'd started calling them thanks to Trina.

It hit me as I got into the elevator that we had *habits*. Not uncommon for roommates, but unlike every other time it started happening between myself and the person I lived with, I wasn't unhappy about it. She and I had good synchronicity, or at least we'd gotten some since our initial frustration over one another's extra-curricular activities. Once we narrowed down the ground rules for having guests over, everything smoothed out and we developed a strong friendship.

My stunned reflection split in half as the elevator doors opened. I gave myself a rough mental shake as I walked down the hall. The scent of banana bread teased me as I opened our door.

"Smells amazing." I smiled, spotting Trina in the kitchen. Her focus was intent as she inverted the metal pan onto a cutting board.

"Thanks. We had some bananas right at the perfect stage of decay." She barked a laugh at the grimace that crossed my face from her description. "I added chocolate chips and pecans, just because."

"It'll be great for dessert." I set the two bags of Thai takeout on the island and her eyes lit up.

"Is that..." Dark eyes wide, she reached for the containers.

"It is. I'm going to take a quick shower, then we can eat?"

"Yes!" Trina clapped her hands together, all vestiges of yesterday's sadness gone. "Get your cozies on. I'll go change and get this ready."

My heart bumped in my chest. She was adorable, and I was glad something as simple as a take-out dinner cheered her up.

"SHE'S TRASH. I'M glad he didn't choose her," Trina groused, dusting banana bread crumbs off of her fingertips.

"What? You're crazy. They're a perfect match!" I'd discovered bickering with her over obviously scripted matchmaking shows was one of my favorite past-times. Even when we agreed, we sparred. I'd never tell her so because I valued my life, but she was cute when she was angry.

"Perfect match? In what universe?" Trina clucked her tongue at me in disgust as she collected some of our trash, disposing of it in the kitchen.

I gathered the rest, tossing it before washing my hands.

"They're perfect for each other. He's never happy and she lives to complain about things. She can whine *Parkerrrr* at him every time she's not satisfied for the rest of their lives and he can puff his chest like the eternal frat boy he is."

Trina glanced over at me, hip leaned into the counter, her arms crossed. "I hate to admit it, but you might be right." She squinted, mouth quirked to the side.

"That does happen, occasionally." I chuckled, offering her a hard cider from the fridge.

She accepted with a huff and we returned to the sofa for another episode.

By the time the ciders were gone, Trina went sleepy on me, leaning heavily on a hand propped up by the arm of the couch. She sighed deeply at something on her phone.

"Good news?" I joked.

"I probably shouldn't tell you this, but I'm about to be really fucking broke." Her eyes widened, darting to my face. "Don't worry, I can make rent. Things aren't looking too hot for my long-term savings, though. Or my short-term ones."

"You'll find something," I reassured her, not wanting to reveal the offer I was going to make until I got a chance to run it by all of my brothers and Addison.

"I hope so. I feel… itchy without a job."

It was a sensation I knew all too well. Not having a foundation or a direction was infuriating. I always felt a low-level buzz under my skin, like a hornet had taken up residence when that was my state of being. Restless, with extra attitude.

"Everything is temporary," I recited the words my mother repeated to me at least a thousand times over the years. She hadn't been wrong, though it was impossible to see it while you were still in the middle of things.

"Yeah." She sighed. "If it weren't for our current arrangement, I'd think maybe I just needed to get laid."

I snorted. "Happy to be of service?"

The edges of her lips lifted as she sat up, her shoulder giving a mighty crack as she stretched. Her shirt showed off a sliver of her stomach and I swallowed against the surge of hormones it gave me.

"I'm done. You?"

"Yeah, I should get to bed."

"Goodnight, Dallas."

"'Night Trina."

She walked sleepily down the hall, but I knew I wasn't going to bed any time soon. I had a job to create and a proposal to draw up. To hell with the fact that it was the weekend, my brothers and I could have a conversation.

CHAPTER TWENTY-NINE

Dallas

THE VIDEO POPULATED slowly on my laptop, three dots dancing in the small boxes as they connected. Dennis was first to appear, his expression set in a neutral frown.

"Morning," I greeted him.

"I'm not sure why I have to be here since we already talked about this and agreed on *Monday*, not Sunday, but good morning, I guess."

Addison popped into frame, a coffee mug in her hands. It looked as though they'd had a sleepover based on her rumpled t-shirt and yoga pants.

"Morning Dallas!" She moved quickly out of frame.

"Hey, Addison. What's up?"

Her head popped back into frame. "I hereby give my full approval, by the way. The paperwork looked great to me. I think Trina will be pleased with your offer. I don't get a vote, but you have mine anyway."

A weight lifted at her words. It was nice to have an early voice of approval.

"Thanks."

Both Devon and Daniels' video connections changed, their faces popping up on my screen.

Dennis' scowl evaporated, his gaze tracking her as she walked out of the room.

"I gotta change for my run. Have a good talk!"

"Be careful!" To his annoyance and my amusement, Dennis and I said the words at the same time.

"Aw look, they're getting all matchy-matchy on us," Devon said. As usual, using his humor to enter the conversation.

"Cute," Daniel teased.

Dennis shook his head, already over our usual nonsense. We all slipped into our roles instantly. Time and distance made no difference for our group calls.

"What's happening, Baby Greene?" Devon said, face morphing into an exaggerated shocked face when he realized what he called me. "Oh wait. That's not you anymore."

To punctuate the fact, my niece was heard softly crying in the background.

"Fuck off," I grumbled, a warm feeling in my chest despite my words.

"You need to go help Steph?" Dennis asked, frowning.

Devon shook his head. It was obvious how tired he was. Happy, but exhausted. "No, she's fine. Ellie is fighting her morning nap. Growth spurts are rough."

"I'll keep it as short as I can," I said, glad to move the conversation forward and get us all on our way since it was the weekend. "I need help."

"We've been saying that for years," Devon sighed, waving his hand.

"Yes, well… I mean specifically at G4, asshole."

"Ah."

Daniel chuckled, and even Dennis cracked a grin.

"I emailed over the proposal I want to make to Trina. Did anyone look at it?"

Daniel nodded, Dennis was scrolling around on his phone, and Devon waved a hand.

"I trust you," Devon said. "Can you give me the short version?"

"Sure. I want to offload the entirety of the website maintenance from my duties. Specifically, I want to offer a contract position to Trina. I'd like her to take over the website maintenance and design stuff so I can focus on the logistics. Doing both is too much. Her work doing our visual updates has been stellar so far. She's also versed in marketing, so we may be able to utilize that as well."

"Sounds good. I'm assuming all the salary stuff is in the email?"

"It's here," Daniel confirmed. "Sounds good to me."

"Great, shall we vote?" Devon glanced over his shoulder, grinning at the silence that had replaced the earlier fussiness.

"That's it?" Shock jolted through me.

"Should there be something else?" Devon frowned. "Is there something else, Dennis?"

I sighed, frustrated how my older brothers were checking with one another, but not surprised. I'd been the baby my entire life; they'd always done this.

"Not as far as I know. Addison is doing well with the office workload. She already approved the proposal as well. I'm out in the field more. Dallas mentioned his work balance has gotten thrown off again and he needs help. It looks clean to me. I know Trina well enough to trust her with this position." He shrugged one shoulder before relaxing back into the couch. "We can vote unless you have questions."

"I don't have any questions. It's a yes from me, that's fine." Devon's eyes shifted to where I was guessing Daniel was on his screen.

"Sounds like a good solution. Yes, from me too," Daniel confirmed.

"I already answered, but yes." Dennis gave a long-suffering sigh. "We good?"

"I… ah…" I wasn't expecting a fight, but the ease with which the conversation happened had me at a loss. "No, that's all. Thanks, guys."

"Hopefully, she accepts. I'm sorry you're feeling overworked again." Devon's sincerity came through the screen as he locked eyes with me, his fingertips rubbing the stubble on his chin. "How's the roommate thing working out?"

"She's great." I'd turned away to put my printed copy of the proposal away. When I looked back, they were all staring at me through the screen, three pairs of eyes watching me. "That's… creepy."

"Any concerns this will cause problems? Work and home life crossing, I mean?" Devon being serious was a rare and powerful thing.

I choked back a strangled laugh. If they only knew how crossed our boundaries already were. But it was a valid question. We'd had the same concerns already, Trina especially.

"I don't think so. I'll be mostly in the office, while she'll be working from home unless she wants to go in." I tilted my head as I realized she might want that, especially with Addison there. "Which would also be fine because I don't spend a lot of time off the floor. We're a pretty good team."

Devon's mouth twitched up into his signature smirk. It was the very one I'd seen in modeling photos and on TV.

"What?" I prompted.

"Nothing, nothing."

Frustration bubbled under my skin. Sometimes, I hated being the youngest brother. Or a brother at all to these three smartasses.

"Out with it."

"He's wondering if you're going to date her," Daniel piped up. "You know, Dennis and Addison part two."

"Hey," Dennis grumbled.

I laughed. Did I tell them we'd already skipped a few steps, or did I keep it to myself?

"As yet undetermined." It was a safe answer.

"That's not a no." Devon was pleased.

"It's not a yes, either." Daniel shook his head. "You haven't won. I'm not paying up until it's a definite."

"Of course you guys are betting on it. Fuck off, all of you." I shook my head, laughing as they debated among themselves what my answer meant.

"Hey, while I've got you, do you know someone named Reginald Peters? I got a weird letter the other day." Daniel's eyebrows were drawn together as he flashed an envelope to the camera.

My amusement evaporated. It matched one of the two Mom had given me after lunch the day Trina went with me.

"What did the letter say?"

"Some nonsense about you abandoning a lease in Tennessee. I wasn't sure why they were sending it to me or how they found *my* information, though. Seemed sketchy."

"For what good it will do, can you send it to your lawyer, Dev?"

The whole feeling of the meeting changed at my words. Everyone grew serious.

"I can. What's it about?"

I shook my head, hands shaking. I met Dennis' eye in the camera. I understood from the expression on his face he'd follow my lead. I'd never held a real official coming out conversation with anyone but my mother before the blow-out conversation he and I had about his ex, Shantel. It was necessary to let him in on the fact that I was bi-sexual, since me dating mostly men was pertinent to what she was claiming happened—in reality, what *hadn't* happened at all—between her and I.

"He's my ex."

Silence greeted the three simple words. Three familiar sets of blue eyes blinked at me. Dennis was the one who broke first, looking down at his hands, then out the window. Devon tilted his head to the side slightly, as though seeing me clearly for the first time. Daniel wore the tiniest of smiles on his lips.

Encouraged, I explained, "He's a spoiled country club kid who grew up to be an abusive alcoholic who can't keep a job. It's a money grab. The lease in Tennessee was never in my name; I don't owe any money there. I imagine he does, though. Let the lawyers handle it."

"Okay," Daniel said simply, nodding in reassurance.

Nobody said anything for a long moment. The silence made me want to crawl out of my skin. I was ridiculously uncomfortable with their intense focus on me.

"Tennessee?" Devon scrunched his nose. "Gorgeous in places, but the humidity is worse than at home. Yikes." His levity allowed me to breathe past the bricks piled up on my chest. "The whole time? Like *years*?"

My mouth twitched. "Most of it, yes."

"His real name is *Reginald*?" Devon's incredulous expression made me laugh outright.

"Yes. Reginald Charles. His parents are very… traditionally southern." My grin faltered. I'd called him Charlie once. *Once.* I'd thought it would be a cute nickname for him. He'd gone from laughing about it to pushing me into a wall hard enough to dent the drywall. It was the first of many incidents I brushed off as an accident or a one-time occurrence.

"His parents must be something."

I couldn't refute the statement. They were both snobbish, racist enablers. There was no question as to where Reggie had gotten most of his issues from.

"So dating Trina is off the table." Daniel nodded. "The women in our lives might be a little disappointed. There's been hopeful gossip about another member joining their little coven."

"I didn't say that."

Their eyes all snapped to me again. This time, I took a heavy measure of satisfaction in their shocked stare.

"Oh." Daniel blinked.

"*Oh,*" Devon intoned, mischief on his face. "That makes a *lot* of sense."

"Does it?" I asked.

"It does." The expression on his face was something akin to pride. My chest warmed in response.

"I've dated mostly men since high school, but there have been a few women in the mix too."

"Why did you never say anything? How did none of us know?" My silence displeased my oldest brother. "You were worried about telling us?" Devon appeared offended by the notion.

"Yeah."

"The fuck?" He was *definitely* offended. "Why?" I shrugged, no valid response forming in my brain. "Well, stop it. You're no different today than you were yesterday, and I don't really care who you date. Unless their name is *Reginald*. Or they're an asshole. Particularly if it's both."

"Did you seriously worry about that?" Daniel looked pained by the thought.

I shrugged again. "It was just one more thing that made me the weirdo of the family. You all had girlfriends. You fit the mold. I… didn't."

"What fucking *mold*?" Dennis asked. His voice was quiet, but his tone was cutting. "Devon is an actor. Daniel loves numbers. I'm a masochistic workaholic. We're *all* idiots. I told you before, I don't give a single, solitary fuck about who makes your dick hard."

I coughed over a laugh.

"I'm remembering it very differently. You didn't say those words, exactly. Thank God too, Addison was standing right there." Sarcasm could cover any number of sins. We all knew that extremely well.

"Sentiment stands. I don't care. You're my little brother. I may not like you sometimes, but I still love you."

Hearing those words from my grumpy, big brother made my chest squeeze in an almost painful way. He wasn't big on words or even acts of affection. I took those words directly to heart. There was a chorus of agreement from the other two.

"Wait, Dennis already knew?" Devon's affronted expression multiplied on itself.

"It was necessary at the time."

"Do Mom and Dad know?"

"Yes. Well, I assume Dad does because Mom's known for years."

"Years." Devon's mouth turned downward.

"Hang on, you dated in high school?" Daniel interjected, sidetracking the conversation.

"Yes, I dated multiple people in high school."

"You never brought anyone home. Not that I remember." Daniel's expression was perplexed.

"Sure I did. I just wasn't dumb about it like you guys. I never got caught, and I wasn't stupid enough to run them across the living room roof to sneak them into my bedroom window."

"How was I to know Mom and Dad could hear it?" Daniel argued.

"It's common sense, numb-nuts. Feet on a roof make noise in the room down below—"

"Well, thank fuck *that's* all finally cleared up," Devon interrupted. "Anyway, you guys want to see Ellie while she's sleeping? She's ridiculously adorable. Let me see if

Steph's up for it…" Devon babbled on, carrying the phone with him down the hall.

He panned around, showing his lovely wife curled up with our gorgeous niece in a cozy chair. For a bunch of big tough dudes, we all melted into big gooey puddles when shown a baby.

My head was buzzing, and I was feeling pleasantly numb as the conversation went on around me. After the call was disconnected, emotions ran rampant through me. It was a long time coming, and the relief was intense as it worked its way through my body. I laughed, then I cried. Big fat grateful tears ran down my face, soaking into my comforter.

I was out. My brothers didn't care. Everything was fine, and now I had some powerful help to fend off Reggie's crazy if I needed it.

There was a job I could offer Trina.

Things were looking up.

Or they were… until all of our phones went crazy with an alert that the fire alarms were going off at our warehouse.

CHAPTER THIRTY

Dallas

A WIRING ISSUE APPEARED to be responsible for tripping all of the alarms.

Dennis spent the bulk of the day making calls to his favorite tradesmen and talking to the fire inspector while I checked over the warehouse for anything missing or damaged.

The massive fans in the warehouse had also gone out halfway through the day for some unknown, although probably related reason, so I'd baked trying to finish up. There were lines of salt across the chest of my shirt from how sweaty I'd gotten. With some luck, the repair service would show up in the morning. At the very least, I'd been able to take a few breaks in the air-conditioned office.

Addison cornered me at one point, asking if I'd like to make the offer to Trina or if I wanted her to.

"It's technically my job," she said, handing me a freshly printed copy with everyone's signatures on it. "But you live with her."

I took the folder from her, debating.

"I want to do it if you don't mind."

Addison smiled. "Of course, I don't mind. I think she'll appreciate that it came from you."

She winked at me before dashing off to help my brother make phone calls, and I was left wondering whether or not I'd actually decided anything about this situation after all.

Trina was in the office when I got back home. I quickly dropped off the take-out I'd grabbed so I could rinse off before we ate.

"Hey!" I called, stripping off my leather bike jacket on my way to my room. "I brought egg rolls! I'm gonna rinse off real quick."

I took the fastest shower possible and returned to the kitchen about the same time she emerged from the office.

"You read my mind. I've been dreaming about these spicy veggies all day long." She poked around in the collection of boxes. "Noodles?"

"They should be there, I got both lo-mein and chow mein."

She groaned appreciatively, her eyes rolling back in her head. It shouldn't have sent a spark into my blood, but it did.

"You're the *best*. Why are you single again?"

I chuckled at her quip. "Fatal flaw, remember?"

"Oh, that's right. I keep forgetting. Well, let me know when you figure it out. Anyway, this is awesome. Thank youuu." She dragged out the syllables as she spun away from the island, hands full.

I joined her on the couch. As she scrolled through to find the show we were currently binging, I pulled the coffee table a little closer.

"How was your day?" She asked.

"Not terrible, all things considered. At least not until the fans went out."

Trina gasped. "It was a hundred and five today! That sounds miserable. I was planning on complaining about the ridiculous number of dead-end phone interviews I have scheduled, but I don't think I will now." She crunched into an egg roll.

"Nah, you definitely still can. It's not a competition."

My heart began to pound. Had I covered all the bases with our offer? Would she find it insulting?

Her attention became focused on the TV as she scooped up noodles with chopsticks. I wondered, not for the first time, if she realized she did a little happy dance when she ate. At the island, it was a gentle sway on the barstool; on the couch, just a little bounce. It was adorable, but I knew if I ever pointed it out, it was likely to disappear forever, so I kept my mouth shut.

The evening progressed as it often did—with the pair of us laughing and bickering at the characters on the TV. When Trina brought me a fresh drink, I took the opening to hand her the paperwork I'd left in my messenger bag before she could sit back down.

"What's this?" Her eyes scanned the paper. "I mean, I can see what it is… what is this?"

"A job offer. You have some availability at the moment for freelancing, right?"

Trina snorted. "You know damn well I do. I'm free as a fucking bird right now."

"Well, as you've been so kind to point out lately, I'm overwhelmed. I'm not enjoying being overworked. This proposal solves that. Well, part of it, at least. I need help with all the web stuff. Not just updating, which you've done brilliantly. You do web stuff. See where I'm going with this?"

"I hear you, I do. But… wouldn't this muddy things? I mean, that's… a couple of *big* boundaries to leap over, all at one time."

I crossed my arms. "You'd be welcome in the office, of course, but I figured you'd be mostly working from home, whereas I usually go there. Your projects would be pretty self-contained. Sounded like a win-win. Besides, I'm not your boss in this scenario. Technically, Addison is."

She snorted at the idea, looking from me to the paper again. I could see the gears turning behind her eyes. She wanted this, and I wanted to give it to her.

"You'll be the person in charge of both my home and my job, if only because I'll be learning it from you. Plus, we're sleeping together. It feels…"

Discomfort swirled through my gut. Put that way, it did feel like a weird power move for me to be in control over some important aspects of her life.

"No. No, no, no. I mean, yes, technically yes, but I don't want that much control over your life, Trina. We can take the sub-let directly to the leasing office if you want. Then, I'm only your roommate, not your landlord. I don't sign the checks, Dennis does. Well, for now, anyway. It's going to be one of the Tweedles' responsibilities soon. Since Addison is the office manager, she'd actually be your boss."

She snorted again, amused by the description of my brothers and the idea of her best friend as her manager. Still, relief chased across her features. The paper trembled in her grasp, telling me exactly how nervous she was about the proposition.

"This is legit? Not some kind of pity offer?"

"Do I seem like the kind of guy who would give you a pity offer?"

Her nose scrunched up as she scanned the paper once again. "No, but—"

"No buts. I mean, yours is spectacular, but it's not why I went to the board with a proposal to hire you as the web coordinator."

She tilted her head, skewering me with a sarcastic look.

"If anything, I would have thought my magical va-jay would've done it, but fine. Seriously, though. I know I've complained a lot about the way things have been going with my job hunt. This isn't because of that?"

I met her eye, aiming for total seriousness with my expression, which was difficult after her commentary.

"You need some work, I need some help. Anything that happens at G4 is done by unanimous vote. *All* of my brothers agreed with this offer. If one of them had objected, you wouldn't be holding that piece of paper."

Her wide eyes blinked heavily before she turned laser focus on the paperwork.

"Can the foundation afford this?"

It was my turn to feel a little insulted. "The offer wouldn't have been made if we couldn't."

"I…" She pursed her lips, eyes focusing on something across the room. "Is it alright if I think about this for a day or two?"

"Of course."

Thinking about it meant she was serious. I could only hope it meant she was considering it.

"It would be pretty awesome to work with Addison," she muttered, the paper in her vision once again. Her mouth twitched as she fought a grin.

"She is a kick-ass co-worker. Tuesday lunch has become an institution. You haven't started joining us yet, though you would of course be welcome to, if you wanted." I genuinely looked forward to our weekly lunch out. Addison might be Dennis' true love, but she and I were platonic soul mates.

Dennis *hated* when I called her that, so naturally, I made sure to do it as often as possible.

"You truly don't believe being… *involved* in every part of our lives is a recipe for disaster?" Her expression bordered on pained. I understood all too well she was envisioning everything around her going up in flames. It had happened to me before, too. Losing everything was a very different feeling than walking away from everything.

"Nope. We're both pretty outspoken. I don't see why that should change."

Trina chuckled, pushing off the back of the couch with her free hand. "You obviously haven't read many romance novels."

"What?" The laugh shook me. "I'm not sure what that has to do with anything."

"This kind of thing is exactly what every fated couple says before setting off on a harebrained scheme that ends up with them either banging like bunnies, falling in love, horribly broken-hearted, or all of the above."

My pulse surged. Whether it did so out of nervousness or excitement was a mystery even to me.

"Well, good thing we're not in one of your smutty books then."

"Be a lot more fun if we were," she muttered under her breath. "Where do you think I get some of my more creative bedroom ideas?"

I choked out a laugh. "Well, be that as it may, and I'm thankful, don't get me wrong. I honestly believe we'll be fine. I'm confident if something starts to go sideways, we'll be able to catch it. I enjoy living with you, Trina." Her eyes met mine. The admission was true, and I wanted her to hear how heartfelt it was. "You're a good match for this job. I know you're dedicated to your work. I have no doubt you will be an asset to G4."

"Aw, what a good pitch!" Trina sang, tears glistening in her eyes. "Aren't you the sweetest thing? Look, you got the waterworks running. Well done. Addison is usually the only other person able to manage it." She blew out a breath, swiping the scant moisture from under her eyes with her fingertips. "Alright. I'm going to seriously think about this. By that I mean meet Addison for a drink so she can repeat everything you just said."

"You won't see me arguing." This woman was honest to a fault and funny. There was nothing about her often brash personality I didn't find endearing.

"Okay. Thank you, Dallas."

"My pleasure, Trina. Let me know what you decide when you're ready. Either way, it'll be fine."

"You're right. It'll be fine. Totally fine."

We both should have known better, but as far as famous last words go, they were pretty good ones.

CHAPTER THIRTY-ONE

Trina

"EXPLAIN TO ME again why this is something you have to consider so seriously?" Addison frowned at me over the rim of her massive strawberry swirl margarita. "Would you be this far in your head about it if I'd been the one to hand you the paper?"

I'd called in my bestie consult session at our favorite Mexican restaurant. We'd discussed the finer points of the exceptionally well thought out job offer over a basket of warm chips scooping up chunky guacamole they'd mixed fresh right at our table.

"Because if I accept, Dallas is my landlord, my boss kind of, and…" I caught myself. "That's weird." I crunched a chip to disguise my almost-flub.

Addison scanned the paper again before handing it back to me.

"Okay. He offered a solution for all of those things, right? Because I'd be your boss, he'd just be training you for the position. The leasing office can take over whatever they need to."

Indignant, and unsure why I had my heels dug in so hard about a flaw in this plan, I mumbled a vague, "Uh-huh."

"So, the person in the way here is you?" Addison's eyebrow rose, her head cocked to the side.

"That's not—"

"You're the *only one* who has an issue with this arrangement. Right?" She grumbled, "It's almost as though I attract people with this specific personality flaw."

I narrowed my eyes at my best friend, glaring at her as I slurped a massive gulp of frozen margarita through the straw. I understood the comparison perfectly well. She'd gone through this same conversation with Dennis not all that long ago. Lucky for her, he'd gotten the hell out of his own way or she'd still be single and he'd probably want me to bury him somewhere with his shovel after he ran himself over with his truck.

"You're a rude, insightful bitch and I don't like you."

She laughed at my sarcasm. "You're welcome." Her clever hazel eyes bored into me. "Why are you fighting this so hard, bestie? It's a good offer. You can work from home. I know you'd rather be doing things on the artistic side full time, but it's a job. A job you can kick major ass at and are very qualified for. Where you could see me as much as you want. You can take this to make money, plus keep doing the artsy stuff for fun."

"I know." In full pout, I slumped back in the booth.

"So…" Addison prompted, pushing her drink off to the side so she could lean forward across the table to peer into my soul.

"So, I don't know," I admitted, making a face at how stupid it sounded.

"Think about it. I'm sure they'd probably allow for some kind of trial run if you asked."

"Maybe."

Our waitress dropped off our meal, which was a giant platter of appetizers to share. The most important reasons to come to this particular restaurant were the chips and the drinks, and those were already on the table.

"You don't want to work from home?"

"Are you kidding? I'd love to. Who doesn't want to do that? Working from home kicks ass."

"I know," Addison agreed enthusiastically, swiping a quesadilla triangle through some guacamole. "Those few days I did were magical, I screwed myself by voluntarily going back to the office so soon. Okay, so it's not that. Is it the pay? Is it not competitive enough?"

"Well, it's a vast improvement over the zero dollars and zero cents I'm making now. And no, it's right where it should be."

"Then it's the content?"

I groaned as I stuffed a mini taco in my mouth.

"No," I mumbled over the food. "It's not the content. I looked at the site, it's very well put together; it needs some love though. Dallas has done a great job with it."

"So it's Dallas? You're afraid he'll be a demanding boss or something? Or maybe I will? Or that it will change things at home?" She scrunched up her nose. "I don't see him as the domineering type, but who knows."

I coughed, remembering all too well his bossy side. I sucked another long drink of my margarita through the straw to cool myself off. I grimaced as brain freeze hit, making it feel like someone had shoved an ice pick through my skull.

When the sensation let up, I shook my head. "No. I'm not worried about him. Not really. I just…"

Addison's eyes widened. "Oh, my God. You're sleeping together."

I choked on the bite of miniature chimichanga I'd taken. "What?"

"You *are*!"

Panicked, I glanced around the restaurant. "First of all, lower your damn voice."

The gleeful expression on her face dampened my frustration instantly. She looked like a cartoon character with her bright grin spread ear to ear with her eyes bulging wide.

"Since when are you *shy* about your sex life?" She cocked her head to the side, eyes sweeping my face. "Holy shit. You are. For real. Oh, my God. I was kind of kidding, but now? Definitely not. You two hooked up."

I said nothing as I avoided eye contact, occupying myself with my drink.

"Trina Louise Lee. How could you keep something like this from me?!" she demanded, fist slapping the tabletop, silverware, and plates jumping noisily. "From *me*?"

"Hush!" I barked, glancing around again to see if we were drawing attention to ourselves. Thankfully, nobody was looking in our direction. "Addison Grace Weatherly, don't you *dare* go full naming me." She was completely nonplussed by my threatening tone. "We agreed to keep it quiet. I was respecting that."

"Since when do you agree to those kinds of rules?"

"Since I live with my current friend with benefits and he's related to *your* boyfriend."

"I'm *so* disappointed in you. Keeping secrets? Pah." Addison crossed her arms, the expression on her face the epitome of a disappointed parent… aside from the wide smile.

"Shut up." Cheeks hot with embarrassment, I put a hand on my forehead and started to giggle.

"How long has this been going on? You better believe now that I found out, I'm going to need to know everything. You wouldn't let up on me for a hot damn second if the tables were turned."

She was one hundred percent correct, so I didn't dare deny it.

"Not long." I sighed, swiping a chip from the basket. "It just... happened." The words sounded so weak, but they were true.

"How long is not long?"

"A few weeks. The night I talked to my parents on the phone, he... comforted me and fed me ice cream and cookie bars..."

Addison made a squeaky noise in her throat.

"Well. Son of a bitch." She shook her head firmly. "I can't believe you both kept it a secret from me." Her eyes fell to the table. She gathered a few more items onto a separate small plate before sipping at her drink.

There was a tinge of genuine disappointment in her tone. I got a pang in my chest. She was my best friend. She was also a good friend to Dallas. Even if she understood, it probably did sting that her two closest friends were keeping something so big from her.

"Hey."

Addison looked up from her plate. "Hmm?"

"I'm sorry I didn't tell you."

She took a deep breath, studying my eyes before nodding. "I get why you didn't. It makes total sense why you're making a big deal of this job offer now. Your whole life would be attached to him; and only a couple of months ago, you didn't even know each other."

I eagerly agreed, happy she understood what I was having such a hard time grappling with. We both mulled things over while we made our way through the platter of the appetizers. By the time the plate was nearly empty, the waitress stopped by to replace our still half-full margaritas. It was going to be one of *those* nights.

"If it bothers you, do what he said. Run your paperwork through the leasing office. Talk to Dennis or even Daniel about the money. Separate what you can. For the record, I don't think this is as scary a risk as all that."

"No?"

Addison shook her head as she fished around for another chip.

"Nope. This whole family is good people, Trin. Plus, you'd get to work with me!" Her eyes were bright again as she chirped the words.

"I know. That alone almost sold it for me."

"Then take it. Or make some counteroffer so you're more comfortable. Remember when you talked me into applying at G4?"

"Of course I remember. How could I forget? Your life was in pieces. We were putting them all back together again."

"Exactly. This is the lifeline you've been looking for. Imagine it, no more job applications or terrible interviews. No more putting on your gorgeous fake smile and telling some guy you'd be great for a job he has no intention of giving you."

"Ugh," I groaned, the prospect more attractive than I had words for. "Say less, my friend, say less."

"There you go. If you have a concern about the offer, counter. Otherwise, you'd be an idiot not to take it."

"That's rude."

Addison laughed at me. "But it's true. Now, drink up," she said, gesturing at the frosty glasses in front of us both. "I want to order dessert, so we need to get these bad boys gone; especially if we don't want to have to call someone to come drive us home."

We made a solid effort to empty our glasses quickly, sliding them to the edge of the table. The remaining food didn't last long and by the time the waitress stopped by to clear, we were feeling the tequila much more than we had been.

Addison ordered their dessert assortment as I put the paperwork back in my bag.

"I'm going to say yes," I mumbled, watching a flaming pan of fajitas being delivered to a table across the room.

"Good. So are you going to tell me anything more about you and Dallas?"

"No."

"What? Why not?" Addison threw daggers at me with her eyes. "I even waited until your buzz got going to ask again."

"There's nothing to tell, honestly. He's a great roommate. He's an amazing person. We happened to kiss one night… well, to be fair, I kissed him, then we ended up doing more than a kiss. A few times." My mouth widened to elaborate on those few times, but I reeled it in. "We agreed not to make a big deal about it. It's not about feelings even, just… sex."

Addison blinked at me, annoyance plain in her expression. "That's painfully little information."

"It's all you're getting… for now."

"You suck."

"Sorry, babe."

She shook her head. "Nah, you're not, but it's okay. You'll tell me, eventually."

I snorted as I tossed a piece of the parsley garnish at her. "You're probably right."

"Oh, I'm absolutely right, that's how we roll."

We plowed our way through the rest of our drinks and dessert, giggling while teasing one another like we always managed to do.

"Hey, Trin?" Addison asked, eyes glossy as she slumped in the booth.

"Yeah?"

"This was super fun. Unfortunately, I'm so full I can't move, I have to pee, and I'm too drunk to drive home."

"Aw, shit. Me, too."

We dissolved into the giggles before getting brave enough to leave our tip on the table and go as a pair to the restroom.

We took a seat on the brightly painted wooden bench out front afterward, debating what to do. They were piping the music from the inside of the restaurant to speakers on the outside, and we both swayed to the beat as we sat.

"Should I call Dennis?"

"Probably. I'm not sure I could sit on the back of Dallas' motorcycle right now without falling off and road rash doesn't sound very fun. Plus, it wouldn't go with my outfits."

Addison nodded, movements ungraceful as she pulled her phone out to dial. I smiled, remembering this exact version of us from our college years.

"Can you come get us, please?" she pleaded sweetly.

I stifled a snort in my arm as Dennis' voice came through her phone. "Aw, hell. Are you both that drunk?" If I wasn't mistaken, he sounded amused by us being in such a predicament.

"We only had *two*," she insisted.

"Two is clearly too many though, babe. I'm grabbing my stuff, I'll be there in a few."

"Thank you, love you."

"Love you, too."

She was grinning like an idiot as she hung up.

"You guys are adorable." I made a gagging noise, which ended up being more dangerous than I'd predicted. "I see we've progressed to the 'L' word quite nicely."

"Shut up. We could be in-laws if you're not careful."

"You shut up."

I smiled though, hope flaring bright. Addison was already my sister from anister mister, but related for real? That would be something else.

Dennis pulled up in his big truck a short while later, Dallas in the passenger seat. My stupid, drunk heart did a little bounce in my chest as I got to my feet. Everything swayed as I got vertical.

The two handsome men approached, shaking their heads. Dennis wore a softness to his grin, one he reserved only for Addison. Dallas looked torn between amusement and jealousy.

"I get to come next time. No debate," Dallas said firmly.

"You gonna ask? Or just start throwing demands around?" Addison put her finger in his chest, the pressure she applied shifting her back precariously instead of moving him. Dennis protectively curled an arm around her shoulders so she wouldn't fall.

"Can I *please* come get messy with you next time?" He even batted his long eyelashes at her.

"Of course." Addison smiled broadly as she patted him on the head.

I was drunk, but she was *drunk*.

"Come on. Let's get you two home," Dennis said, pulling her to his side.

"Thanks for dinner," I said, reaching out to squeeze her in an uncoordinated hug before she was spirited off by her boyfriend.

"Anytime." She blew me a kiss from her fingertips as they left.

Dennis put a hand to her lower back and guided her toward the truck, her giggle loud as they walked away.

"Got your keys?" Dallas put his hand out.

"Yup." I dug around in my purse, locating them under a lipstick tube and a tin of mints. I dropped them gracelessly into his palm.

"Alright. Let's go, Terror." He threw his arm around my shoulders, kissing my temple.

My heart pounded as we crossed the parking lot toward my little car. I wanted to blame the alcohol, though I knew it was more than that.

CHAPTER THIRTY-TWO

Dallas

'D SEEN TRINA drink too much before, but tequila tipsy appeared to be a whole new animal. Usually, she got loud, a little extra swear-happy, then tired. This? This was nothing like any of that. She was already near passing out and we'd barely made it out of the parking lot.

"Thanks for coming to get me," she cooed drowsily from the passenger seat.

"No problem. You seriously only had two drinks?"

"Mmmhmm. The cut-off there is three, whether you're a big dude or a tiny chick. They mix 'em *strong*."

"Sounds like a ringing endorsement. How's the food?"

She groaned, eyes dropping closed. A smile painted her lips as she elaborated, "The best chips. Super thin and crispy. Warm, salty..."

She was talking about chips when my mind instantly went to something else matching the description. It was perhaps wholly inappropriate, but the image I got at her words started a pulse behind my zipper.

"Sounds delicious."

"Mmm." She relaxed in her seat, likely a few short moments from sleep. She looked similar to how she had the night of her welcome home party.

The apartment wasn't terribly far, but she was indeed sawing some alcohol-soaked logs by the time we pulled into the parking lot.

"Hey," I whispered, a hand on her thigh, giving a little shake. I was sorry to interrupt her nap but didn't want her to get a kink in her neck from sitting in such an awkward position or wake up feeling nauseous and vomit in the car. "We're home."

She made noises that might have sounded like words in her head but weren't intelligible as her eyelids lifted barely enough to allow her to see.

I propped her up as we crossed the parking lot successfully, though we nearly lost our momentum near the elevator.

"How long ago did you finish your second margarita?" I asked. Worry tightened my shoulders. She seemed much more intoxicated now than she was when I first picked her up.

"'Few minutes before we peed. Then we called you." She booped the tip of my nose with her finger as she dissolved into giggles. She was adorable but very, very drunk.

"I think it's just now starting to hit you."

The elevator dinged, and I steered her toward our apartment, her feet shuffling across the carpet.

She melted down my body as I paused to unlock the door. How a human being could spontaneously turn into a liquid was beyond me, but she managed it. With no small amount of effort, I managed to wrangle her inside and onto the couch.

"Sit there for a minute, okay? I'll get you some water."

"M'kay." She sighed, already slumping down, the armrest pillowing her head.

I texted my brother as I pulled out a bottle of ibuprofen to go with the bottle of water.

> **DALLAS:** Hey, is Addison acting way drunker than when we first got there?

I opened the water and took it to Trina. I helped her sit up as I waited for his response. With some help, she took a few swallows without spilling it all over herself.

> **DENNIS:** For sure. The second drink hit her hard about halfway home.
> **DALLAS:** Trina too. Trying to push water now. They had a good time, I guess.
> **DENNIS:** Looks like it. I understand why they have a limit on their margs.
> **DALLAS:** Appreciate the ride. The hangovers are going to be brutal.

DENNIS: Tomorrow is going to be rough for sure.
No problem.

I pocketed my phone, debating the best course of action to take. I could snooze pretty easily on the couch myself, but there were better options. I didn't like the idea of putting Trina in her bed, alone, in case she needed something in the middle of the night.

Which left my bed.

"Trina? Hey. I need to ask you a question."

"Yeah?" she slurred, eyes struggling to open.

"Would you be okay with me putting you in my room to sleep?"

"Sure."

I wasn't feeling great about how capable she was of making decisions. I was very glad she was home safe with me and not still out with friends or on a date. The idea made my stomach twist. For a split second, I pictured my sweet baby niece as a teen, rolling her eyes at her father plus three overprotective uncles. If nothing else, she had an army of people to call if she ever felt uncomfortable.

"Alright. Upsy daisy." I scooped her into my arms bridal style and carried her to my room. "Do you need the bathroom? Feel sick at all?"

"No, 'm 'kay." She breathed the words, eyes not wanting to open.

"Can you drink a little more water? You're going to be miserable tomorrow."

"'Mmhmm."

She sipped slowly as I held the container, dribbling a little and giggling.

"You're a giant mess, tiny Terror." I let out a heavy breath, helpless as she snuggled down into the blankets, her hands pillowed under her face.

While she snored peacefully, I watched some TV, waiting for any sign she might be about to project tequila all over my carpet.

Eventually, I gave in to sleep myself, the bathroom light half-illuminating the room, Trina's heavy breathing a soft invitation to join her in dreams.

I WOKE UP to find myself tangled around another body.

A very warm, very soft body.

As awareness snapped me fully into consciousness, I carefully extracted my limbs from Trina's form.

She made a cute noise as she rolled over, returning to her earlier position of facing away from me.

"You need to pee yet?" I asked, heart-pounding and cock throbbing.

"No, not yet." Her head popped up away from the pillow as she looked around through a single squinted eye. Her makeup was smudged, her hair wild from sleep. "Am I in your room?"

I swung my legs off the side of the bed and pulled on my sweats.

"Yeah, you tried to pass out on the couch. I thought this was a better idea. I asked if it was okay, but you were pretty out of it."

She slumped back down. "No big deal." She groaned, a hand flying to her forehead. "Fucking tequila."

I chuckled. "The second margarita took you girls *out.*" My worry from the night before surged, and my humor evaporated. "Seriously though, I was worried. You went from playful to passed out. I can't imagine what would have happened if you guys hadn't called for a ride." I met her eye. "Or if you'd been with someone else." Coming around to her side of the bed, I handed over the water and ibuprofen I'd left on the bedside table. "Take this, you'll feel better. I'll go start the coffee."

She grunted some kind of affirmative response as I left.

I added grounds to the filter and poured water. From the noises coming from my bedroom, Trina had changed her mind about needing the bathroom. There was no retching, though, which was a good sign.

Just about the time the brew was ready to pour, she ambled into the kitchen.

"Thank you." Her sigh was profound as she accepted the steaming mug.

"Did you puke?"

She inhaled some of the steam before answering. "No, but I kind of want to."

I barked a short laugh, copying her leaning gesture against the island.

"I've done that a few times. It usually helped. Want something to eat?"

"Sure."

"This feels a lot like the morning after your date with James what's-his-name." I teased, pulling supplies out of the fridge for breakfast.

"Definitely not. Addison was a way better date, I slept a thousand times better in your bed than I did on my own with him there. This hangover is absolutely *brutal* compared to that one."

"You really are a mess." I chuckled as she gave me the finger. "I'll still make you breakfast."

"You're a prince. Charming, even. I'm going to go shower."

I caught myself staring at her ass as she made her way down the hall to her room.

"Not the time, asshole," I grumbled to myself as I cracked eggs into a bowl.

I lost myself in the motions of cooking while the shower ran. My phone dinged a single time, showing an unknown number and an increasingly familiar text.

We need to talk.

No, we didn't.

I reported the number, then blocked it, deleting the text.

By the time she emerged, hair still damp and eyes much clearer, my haphazard breakfast was done.

"Refill?" She gestured to my cup.

"Sure, thanks."

We sat down to eat at the island. I blamed her hangover for being unusually quiet. When we were finished, she loaded the dishes into the dishwasher, hesitating by the sink.

"You doing anything today?" she asked.

"No big plans. I have a few little things I need to work on. Nothing urgent, though. Why?"

"Can you show me a complete overview of the web stuff? I want to take a look before I give you my final answer."

My pulse leaped. She was definitely considering it. I tried to temper my excitement so I didn't overwhelm her.

"Sure. Just let me know when you're ready."

Her eyes shifted from me to her coffee cup, then to the nearly empty pot.

"Let me make more coffee first."

"No problem. I'll go grab a quick shower?"

"Okay."

I went through the motions under the hot spray, daring to get my hopes up about her saying yes. It could change everything, both for my work life, for her outlook on finances, and our dynamic.

She was waiting for me on my bed when I came out of the bathroom, remote in one hand, coffee in the other.

Her eyes flashed with a bit of panic when I stopped short at seeing her so comfortable in my space.

"Sorry, is this okay?"

"Yeah." I smiled at her. I genuinely didn't mind it. The feelings around seeing her there were much more complicated than how simple those words were. Grabbing my laptop, I settled in as well. "You ready for this?"

"You bet." Her grin warmed my blood.

"Alright." I fired up the computer and walked her through the dashboard of our current web platform. She asked several pertinent questions, but seemed familiar enough with the way things worked.

"How many hours do you spend on this, usually?"

"No more than ten or so a week for maintenance. I figure you'll be doing more like twenty, at least at first to help get some new things developed."

Trina nodded thoughtfully. "Okay."

"Okay?"

"I accept."

My fingertips tingled from the surge of adrenaline those words provided.

"You do?"

She chuckled. "Yes, I do. I left the papers in my purse, but I'll sign them later. I think this is a good use of my freelancing time."

I couldn't contain my broad grin. I dropped down, planting a thorough kiss on her mouth. "I'm so damn happy to hear you say that."

Her eyes went serious as I held her cheek in my palm, a breath away from kissing her again.

"Dallas, Addison…"

My heart dropped. "Is she okay? You guys were both completely out of it last night—"

Her hand held my wrist. "She's fine. I texted her while you were in the shower. Last night, she figured it out."

"Figured what out?" I had a feeling I knew what she was about to say, but waited.

Trina sat back, putting some distance between us. I didn't like the cold swirl of emotion that sprang up when she did so.

"She guessed we'd slept together."

"Oh." Emotions mixed messily in my chest. It was hard to distinguish the relief from the tension. While we'd agreed to keep our personal lives personal, we'd both also guessed how at some point, our friends and family might guess we were more than friends. "And?"

"What do you mean *and*? Cat's out of the bag."

I shrugged, trying to defuse Trina's anxiety. At least one of us could feel better about things. I was nervous about the revelation, but I could mask it. I was good at that.

"It's just Addison."

"Which means Dennis also knows."

A grin crossed my lips. "That will probably confuse him a little."

"Why?"

"You know as well as I do you're not my normal type."

"You took out a girl not so long ago."

I shrugged. "As I said at the time, it was a unique event."

"There's also *me*. That's nearly the beginning of a pattern."

I laughed. "I would argue you also fall into the *unique event* category."

She smiled, her brows pulled together.

"Dennis knows your type?"

"Yeah."

"Does the whole family know?"

I bobbed my head slowly. "My brothers and I had a conversation not too far back. Mom knew a long time ago, but she was the only one for quite a while. Dennis found out during the blowout we had when Addison first came into the picture."

"Oh."

She still looked caught somewhere between puzzled and stressed. Her dark eyes were troubled as she nibbled on the inside of her bottom lip.

"It's okay," I reassured her.

"Is it?"

"Why wouldn't it be?"

"I don't know. We agreed to keep it quiet, and she figured it out without me spilling even a single bean. Plus, isn't it weird? Dangerous? Cliché? Insert any of my concerns about having you involved in every single part of my life here. Plus, there's the whole inexperience with relation-ships lasting longer than a single date thing."

I laughed, swooping in for another thorough kiss. I pressed my mouth to hers, making her smile before I deepened the motions enough to elicit a moan from her throat.

"All of those things, probably. Doesn't mean it's wrong."

"No?"

"No."

She breathed a few beats, staring deep into my eyes. "Okay. I'm trusting you."

The words sank deep into my flesh, resonating long after she'd said them.

I heard echoes of them as we snuggled into my bed for a movie. Then again, as she told me a ridiculous joke over dinner. I heard them loudest of all when she came back to my room after getting ready for bed and crawled between my sheets.

I desperately hoped I wouldn't let her down as we rocked together under the moonlight streaming through my blinds, her soft moans clawing their way into my permanent memories.

CHAPTER THIRTY-THREE

Trina

I T WAS A gorgeous Saturday morning and I wanted to bake muffins.

Naturally, since I was trying to make as little noise as possible, everything sounded ten times as loud as normal. The metal muffin tin clanged off the granite counter like a gong. The sound of the spoon hitting the side of the bowl seemed as loud as the dishes breaking in my kitchen back in Memphis.

Sipping my coffee, I mixed the wet ingredients until everything was smooth. By the time I was stirring in the dry ingredients, I was in my groove, humming a tune under my breath.

I slid the tray into the oven just as I heard the shower turn on in Dallas' room.

A gentle smile lifted my lips as I pictured him under the spray. It wasn't hard to get a full image, thanks to our recent stress-relieving interludes.

Since he was up, I pulled out bacon and eggs to round out the meal. I was whipping eggs in a bowl for omelets when his bedroom door opened.

He was lust on legs as he came my way, dark hair wet, dressed only in his favorite gray sweats.

"Morning," he grated, voice still rough from sleep as he made his way to the coffeepot.

"Morning."

"Smells good." Dallas dropped a kiss below my ear on his way past me to get creamer from the fridge.

"Muffins are almost done. We're both about to find out whether or not I can flip an omelet."

My temperature rose as he watched me intently from the edge of the island, his forearms holding his weight, coffee mug cradled between his hands. As the tip of his tongue appeared at the corner of his mouth, I had to look away. My insides were threatening to liquefy, and a pulse started beating between my thighs.

There was no reason for a single person to be so gorgeous, especially when they were also as talented as he was at procuring orgasms. It wasn't fair.

I saw him shift out of the corner of my eye as I poured the scrambled eggs into a buttered skillet. I added a special blend of spinach, cream cheese, and artichoke hearts, motions faltering as the warmth of his body shifted behind me.

"What—"

"Shh. Keep cooking." His words were low and heavy, the heated breath of them caressing my lower back, his palms on my hips.

His hands slid down the outside of my legs, then under the hem of my nightshirt, fingertips stopping as he discovered I wasn't wearing panties.

"Naughty."

I couldn't see his face, but I could feel his smirk. He pressed a kiss to my sensitive inner thigh. Which meant… he was on his knees. Behind me.

As my slow brain processed this information, Dallas' warm tongue found my center without error, his strong fingers gripping my thighs.

"Oh, my God." Uncooked egg splattered the counter as I dropped the rubber spatula. Lust roared through my body as he worked my core with his mouth, my eyes dropping closed, pleasure whipping through my body.

"Don't you dare burn my eggs, Terror. I'm starving."

His words blazed through me like fire. I forced my eyes open, a moan escaping my lips as he latched on, suckling my sensitive nub.

"Shit," I cursed, trying to remember how to breathe as I grabbed for the spatula. "If I burn myself, it'll be all your fault. Mmm." I squeezed my eyes shut as sensation pooled where he was sucking. It took mountainous effort, but I managed to stir the eggs before he started lashing me with his tongue from front to back, removing all thought from my brain.

"*Dallas*." He took my desperate moan as encouragement, using a finger to pump in and out of me for a moment before canting my hips to his liking so he could bury his face in-between my thighs completely.

Orgasm lingered just out of reach as he alternated suckling and flicking my clit with the tip of his tongue, licking down my wet seam over and over again, his hands busily caressing whatever they could reach.

Remembering my assignment, I hastily flipped the mass in the pan. It might be the ugliest omelet ever made, but it would be edible. I spun the burner knob, turning the flame off as the one inside me grew uncontrollably. I planted my hands on the edge of the counter, bruising my palms. Pushing back into his mouth as climax took me over, a loud moan flew from my mouth. A matching one also rumbled through his throat, the vibrations traveling through me.

"Fuck." I gulped air, legs shaky as he gave some final slow licks and got to his feet.

His clever eyes met mine as he wiped his mouth on the back of his hand. I still couldn't do much except hold myself upright. His arousal was more than evident in his sweats and it was all I could do not to reach a hand out toward him. The only thing holding me back was knowing I might face-plant the stove if I did.

"What was that?"

"You don't know?" One eyebrow raised as he smirked, peering over my shoulder into the pan. "You didn't burn my eggs, did you?"

"No." I gestured at the skillet with green speckled scrambled eggs in it, grabbing for a hot pad as the muffin timer went off. I adjusted my stance to be sure I was stable enough to take care of the oven.

"Good. I really am starving, I just wanted dessert first."

Heat surged through my already soaking center. He was infuriating in the best way. I set the hot pan of muffins onto the stovetop. I could see cockiness radiating from Dallas' every pore as he watched me.

"Is that so?"

He said nothing as he widened his stance, arms loose at his sides.

I stepped into his body, drawing his face down to mine with a hand on the back of his neck.

"Are you going to finish what you started?"

"You didn't finish? I could swear that's what happened."

"You know I did. Doesn't mean I'm *done*." I crushed my mouth to his, and like we'd rehearsed the moves a hundred times, he gripped my waist, carrying me to the side of the island where the barstools were without breaking the kiss. My bare ass hit the cold granite, and I hissed, prompting him to nip at my lips with his teeth.

He stepped as close into the cradle of my thighs as he could after dropping his pants to the floor. I locked my legs around his trim waist, moaning into his mouth as he pressed into me. With one arm around my upper back and another gripping my thigh, he rocked in a steady rhythm. The angle was delicious for my g-spot and I sped toward climax for a second time as we continued to devour one another with our mouths.

"Goddamn." He gasped, tipping his head back. He surged deeper as my walls clenched at him.

"Dallas," I warned, pulses starting low in my abdomen.

He responded only by pressing his mouth to the side of my throat and groaning, his thrusts hitching as he climaxed. I could feel him throb inside me, which set me off for the second time. I sighed, mumbling incoherently as his hips slowed. Breathing heavily against my neck, he laughed. The sound was rich and warm, hitting deep in my ribcage.

My heart beat wildly at the sound, and I held him as tightly as he clutched at me, ignoring the warnings blaring in the back of my mind as I rode the wave of post-orgasmic bliss.

BREAKFAST WAS LATER than planned and messy, but still delicious.

Dallas lifted me off of the counter so I wouldn't fall, my legs still shaky on my way back from getting cleaned up. While I was gone, he'd served up the food and poured fresh coffee for us like a true gentleman.

"Have a seat," he invited, motioning toward the barstools.

"I can't."

"Why not?" His dark eyebrows pulled together.

"I know it doesn't make any sense, but I can't put my plate where my ass was."

At my side-eye, he wiped down the counter with bleach wipes so we could sit and eat, chuckling the whole time.

Appeased, I slid onto the barstool next to him as he scooped his eggs into his mouth, scrolling his phone. A smile tugged at my lips as I broke my muffin into four parts, smearing butter over as many surfaces as I could.

"Dessert first?" I teased.

He didn't look over, though he did grin. Strange electric pulses tingled through my body.

"Best part of the meal."

"You're a mess, Dallas Greene."

"You're *welcome*, Trina Lee."

After the dishes were cleaned up, I went to get ready for my day out with Addison. My shower fantasies returned while I was lathering up, but I forced my horny thoughts away, turning it into a mini spa routine instead, using my overpriced salon products to exfoliate and pamper myself.

Dallas stared blankly at me from the couch when I emerged.

"Need anything?" I asked, fastening an earring.

I'd dressed in a simple sundress with sandals, but the way he was looking at me, I might as well have been in lingerie.

"Yes." The grit was back in his voice and while my lady parts were definitely up for what he was laying down, I didn't have time for that.

"While I'm *out*. With Addison."

The lust cleared from his expression at the mention of our mutual friend. "Oh. Then no. Later, maybe."

I laughed at him as I grabbed my purse from where it hung by the door.

"I'll be back later. Text me if you think of anything."

Dallas tossed me a wink as I left, and my stupid heart soared, which left me worried, wondering when my heart had gotten involved with our amorous activities. Despite my confusion, I floated on the silly gesture for the rest of the night.

CHAPTER THIRTY–FOUR

Dallas

MY PARENTS TOOK our suggestion to heart and booked a trip to California for the two of them a few short weeks after our big family conversation. It was agreed I would take point on dog-sitting, but Dennis could take over for a day or two if needed.

Since there were four dogs to care for, it was easiest to stay at their place. I took care of things at the office Monday morning while Dennis took our parents to the airport. I skipped out after lunch so I could let the dogs outside and decided to work from home the rest of the day. My schedule was no doubt going to be erratic while my parents were gone.

Returning to my childhood home, my old room with the furniture I'd outgrown and left behind-twice-struck an unusual chorus of emotions.

I lingered for a few long moments, peering around my old bedroom after dropping my duffel bag on the bed. Everything about the house felt familiar but strangely distant. I wondered if this was what it was like to realize I'd fully moved on with my life.

After a round of fetch in the backyard with my parents' hounds to wear them out, I took them all inside where they filed to their favorite couch cushions or fluffy dog beds for a nap.

Mom being Mom, she'd thoughtfully left a fridge full of food, for which I was grateful. Between her and Trina, I'd gotten very spoiled eating well nearly all the time. Things were arranged on shelves based on meals she'd planned out for me. I needed to figure out some kind of gift to give her for taking care of me, even in her absence.

The week was a frenzy of restless nights in my old twin bed, working hectic mornings at the foundation before coming home early to give the aging dogs some relief. I was working longer hours thanks to having nobody around to monitor my laptop use in the evenings. Trina had taken up the website work like a total champ, which freed me up to do some projects that kept getting put on the back burner. It was a blessing and a curse.

We sometimes exchanged texts, but we were mostly an in-person friendship. It was odd not to hear her laugh or share our normal banter while watching TV. As I ate some reheated shepherd's pie by myself at the family dining room table on Thursday night, I got an idea.

Grinning, I went around the house making sure all of the supplies were in order, the younger two of my parents' four dogs trailing me from room to room, all of them joining me as I trekked out to the garage and back.

Once everything I needed was accounted for, I dialed Trina's number.

"Dallas? Everything okay?" She sounded stressed and, I realized, it was ten o'clock.

"Fine, sorry, I didn't realize it was so late."

"It's okay. What's going on?"

"Do you have any plans tomorrow night?"

She snickered. "No. I mean, unless you're referring to me gorging myself on junk food and sprawling out on the couch. I might talk to myself a bit more than normal since you're not here. It's really quiet here alone, by the way. Why?"

"Want to come over? My parents aren't home," I whispered the last words, injecting as much playfulness into them as I could.

Trina's infectious laughter warmed me as it coursed through the phone.

"Sure. What are we doing? Should I bring anything?"

"A change of clothes or two, plus your cozies. I was thinking you might want to sleep over."

"Okay." Humor still colored her tone.

I closed my eyes, trying to decipher how the sound made me feel. It was ridiculous, but she felt like rainbows.

"Come whenever you're ready. I plan on trying to finish up work as early as I can."

"I don't have anything much going on, so I should be able to come over mid-afternoon. I'll text you when I'm leaving."

"Sounds good. Sorry to have given you a heart attack when I called."

"It's fine. And Dallas?"

"Yeah?" I made a few notes on a pad my mother kept in a kitchen drawer, making a list of supplies to grab.

"I'm glad you called. When I say it's quiet around here, I mean it's way too quiet. I ate the whole last batch of cookies by myself. I've missed you this week."

My heart thudded behind my ribs. This conversation felt dangerous, pushing the boundaries of our no-strings, roommates with benefits arrangement. I'd missed her too. The blurred lines of where our friendship ended were getting harder and harder to see.

"Me too, Terror. I'll see you tomorrow."

I hung up and collected the hounds, trying to make the hours move faster.

"YOU NEED ME to take over house-sitting for a day or two?" Dennis asked, handing me the coffee creamer out of the fridge in the office kitchen the next morning.

"No, I'm good. They get home Tuesday evening, so I should be fine. I miss the hell out of my cushy new mattress, but Mom kept me fed and the dogs are no problem."

"She left you shepherd's pie?"

I smiled. "Damn right."

Dennis grunted.

Mom's shepherd's pie was everyone's favorite meal. She'd made an entire pan and frozen it for me. I'd enjoyed every single bite, especially since I didn't have to share it.

He watched me as he sipped from his mug.

"Everything okay?" he asked.

I glanced around the room suspiciously.

"Fine. Why?" I'd done nothing wrong, but having my older brother asking me questions like he was trying to parent me put me on high alert.

Dennis shrugged his broad shoulders, leaning back against the countertop with a hip. It was all the indication I needed to know he was settling in for a chat.

"No reason. Just checking in with how everything's been going since Trina started."

Oh. That's not what I'd thought he was asking about at all.

"And with the Reggie situation."

There it was.

I took up a similar pose against the wall opposite him.

"Trina's great. I'm finally getting around to some of the extra projects you and Daniel asked me for. As for the other..." I gestured with my mug. "Devon's lawyer is managing things."

I'd gotten a few more texts, but as instructed I'd just forwarded them to the attorney, then blocked the numbers.

Dennis' heavy gaze assessed me for a long moment before he finally decided I was being truthful. He rose from the counter, starting to make his way toward Addison's office. I followed at a safe distance.

"Alright. Let me know if you need anything. Addison and I can take over for a couple of days if you want to go home."

"I appreciate it. I'm fine, though. Trina's coming over tonight so at least I'll have some company."

He nodded, burying his face in his cup before veering into her doorway.

"Morning, Addison," I said, waving on my way past.

Dennis dropped into the single chair across from her desk. She gave me a bright smile.

"Morning, Dallas."

My brother only had eyes for her as I walked past. He'd come a long way since she dropped into our lives.

We all had.

I hustled through work, assembling my team of guys to give them instructions as fast as I could so I could get the rest of my paperwork done and go.

On my way back to my parents' house, I hit the grocery store for a few things, then the real work began.

When Trina wandered into the backyard a few hours later, everything was nearly assembled.

"Oh, my God. Dallas! What is all this?" She giggled, hands to her mouth as she looked around.

I was a hot, sweaty mess after making what I thought was the perfect outdoor theater setup for us.

It was the backyard camping of my memories, but better. I took a few photos to send to my dad, along with a note of appreciation for how much effort some of my favorite memories must have taken on his part.

I'd rigged up Dad's movie projector on a stand, using the back wall of the house as the screen. Using some of his old tarps and tent poles, I'd made a shade canopy. Under the canopy were two air mattresses I'd tied together to make one giant bed surface, covered in every spare blanket, sleeping bag, and pillow I could find. I'd filled a small cooler up with drinks and a bucket with movie snacks.

"This is amazing." Trina was wide-eyed as she took it all in. "What are we watching?"

"You choose." I handed her my phone, trading her for the overnight bag in her hand. "I need to shower real quick. It's still hot though, do you want to come in for a little while?"

"Sure."

I opened the sliding door, allowing her in before I invited the dogs. They'd all decided to take a nap under the shade of the canopy. Somehow, I'd managed to keep them off of the mattresses.

Trina followed me through the house and up to my childhood bedroom. Nervousness about having a girl in my room showed up from somewhere and I tried to squelch it. Some habits died hard.

"We can get anything on that website," I explained. She scrolled through the page on my phone as I grabbed some clean clothes from my duffel. "I'll be out in a few." I gestured to the hallway where the bathroom was.

"Okay." She smiled at me, a slight blush in her cheeks. "Do your parents know you have a girl in your room?"

I chuckled, pausing in the doorway. "Nope."

"Secret's safe with me." Trina winked at me.

I moved through the cool shower as quickly as I could, pleased with the outcome of my efforts.

When I got back to the bedroom, Trina's eyebrows were pulled together as she stared at my phone. She was using hers as well, which confused me. She glanced up and my stomach dropped.

"I swear I wasn't snooping. A text came across while I was scrolling through the movies."

I waited for a beat before responding. It wasn't her fault, so I wasn't upset with her. I did feel a hot mix of rage and shame as I took the phone from her outstretched hand.

"It's okay."

"You get a weird expression on your face every time your text notification goes off. You have since I moved in. Is that why?"

"I do?" I was confused again, opening the message she'd gotten.

The message popped up and shock jolted through me.

UNKNOWN: It's urgent we talk. Please?
Message me back.

Trina stood up, getting as close to me as she could without standing on my feet.

"You can tell me about it if you want."

My stomach churned. Telling anyone about my biggest shame was the last thing I wanted to do. But I had a feeling Trina would get it. She wouldn't judge me. She would just listen.

"Okay."

She bobbed her head. "Okay."

I led her down to my mother's kitchen. This kind of conversation required alcohol and food.

CHAPTER THIRTY-FIVE

Trina

DALLAS SUPPLIED BOTH of us with some kind of casserole from the fridge and a healthy pour from a bourbon bottle. Purely based on how inward he'd turned, I could tell whatever he had to tell me was a big deal.

"It's okay if you don't want to tell me," I tried to reassure him, but I could see he'd already dug in his mental heels.

"It's fine. I should've told you all about it when you first asked about my past relationships."

I waited, butterflies swarming in my stomach. He took a couple of bites before starting.

"You know why I left home, right?"

"Yeah. The misunderstanding about Dennis' ex-girlfriend, right?"

Dallas nodded, pushing his food around on the plate. The sun began to descend, the bright late afternoon sunshine lighting up his face.

"I felt like I was in the way, or responsible somehow. Like my presence was the issue. So, I removed myself."

"That wasn't… that's not how those things work. You know that, right?"

He nodded, a pensive expression holding his handsome face tense.

"I do now. I went to Nashville because I had a friend there who offered to help me out, give me a place to stay, all that. G4 was still barely getting started, so I still held down other jobs besides managing the website. I met Jack at a bar one night, and we burned brighter than the sun for about six months, then we fizzled out. It wasn't long after I met Reggie."

Dallas swallowed and paused, taking a long drink of his bourbon. I distracted myself by eating a little bit of the dinner he'd heated so it wouldn't be wasted.

"My friend knew someone who worked at the country club. He'd sneak us in to use the pool." Dallas smiled. "We felt like hot shit pulling one over on those rich families. One day, I bumped into Reggie while getting a clean towel in the locker room." His gaze went distant, whatever he was seeing in his memory causing the smile to fade. "It was downhill from there."

"Spoiled country club kid?" A thought occurred to me,

and while I would normally tease about it, now was not the time. "Wait. Or one of the husbands?"

Dallas still saw the humor in my question. The corners of his mouth twitched before he tossed back the remains of his drink.

"My age, though there were lots of thirty-somethings I wouldn't have said no to. At first, everything was great. Day drinking at the pool, spending our days in the sun, and our nights wherever we could manage to sneak off to together. We spent hours making out on furniture that cost more than I'll ever make in my lifetime. It became our favorite game to find new rooms to sneak into at the club. Debauchery was the name of the game and the riskier the situation, the better. My friend was leaving town for a job, so I moved in with Reggie. Everything was perfect. Until it wasn't."

The heaviness to his words wasn't like the Dallas I'd grown to know. I felt bad he'd been carrying around such sadness.

He continued, "I realized pretty quickly all the money Reggie was spending wasn't his. He couldn't hold down a job for very long and the credit cards his parents kept open for him were always maxed out before bills got paid. My money only went so far. He drank all the time. Instead of being fun, he was getting mean. He could go from joking to angry in a flash." Dallas snapped his fingers. "He wanted to live the same upscale lifestyle he'd had at home, but he didn't have any way to pay for it. Which is where I came in." Dallas shook his head. "When things were good, they were *so* good. When they were bad… Every time was always the *last* time he was going to get upset. He never *meant* to throw the punch that put a hole in the wall. He was perpetually looking for a better job. I'd already started to see the light when I flew to California for Devon's wedding. It was unreasonably difficult to get away. I realized how much he was isolating me. How much I was allowing it all to happen."

I could guess the ending to this story. My heart thudded painfully in sympathy.

"He never got a job."

"No."

"He hit you?"

"Yes." Dallas looked down, shame darkening his features.

"Hey. *Hey*." His blue eyes met mine, full of regret. "You didn't deserve the way he treated you. You never have to make yourself small so someone else can feel big. None of what happened is your fault."

His eyes welled up as he studied me. Slowly, he reached across the table and took my hand in his.

He rubbed a thumb across my knuckles as he continued, "I know. I do. Thank you. The straw that finally sent me back home was when he stole a computer from one of our mutual friends. Brand new gaming laptop. Thousands of dollars. When the guy pointed a finger, because it was obvious he'd done it, he blamed me. He'd already pawned it and spent the money on God knows what."

"Holy shit. Did the friend figure it out?"

"Eventually, yes. But I was already gone. I'd borrowed money from my parents a few times to pay rent, among other things. Our friend demanded I pay for the laptop, so I did. Reggie and I had a blowout fight. I left with what would fit in my backpack, my bike, and lots of bruises."

"I'm so sorry, Dallas."

He nodded slowly.

"Fatal flaw," he said after a moment of quiet.

"What?"

"That's my fatal flaw."

"What is?"

"Running away. Being a magnet for drama. Being the problem. Take your pick."

I scoffed. Dallas was shocked by my reaction.

"Bullshit. You realize it's all bullshit, right?" He stared at me. I got to my feet, dropping his hand so I could grab our plates. "You just told me how in both situations, you blamed yourself. In neither of those situations were you actually to blame."

"I suppose."

Shaking my head at my stubborn, idiot friend, I put all of our dinner dishes in the dishwasher, then stood next to where he was sitting.

"Come here." I opened my arms in an invitation for a hug.

Instead of coming to me, he pulled me to him. I straddled his lap as he clung to me for several long minutes. I breathed in his citrus body-wash scent and ran my fingers through his hair. He was well on his way to converting me from anti- to situational cuddling.

"So, he's trying to get in touch with you?"

"I don't ever answer, so I'm not sure it's him, but I think so. He's sent letters claiming I owe him money for a lease I was never on. Devon has his attorney involved."

I pulled back, looking him full-on in the face before offering a smile and planting an obnoxious, exaggerated smooch on his mouth meant to shock him out of the melancholy.

"Thank you for telling me. If the texts don't stop, you need to get the police involved."

"I've been considering it."

"I find it hard to believe between your mom and your brothers, he hasn't simply gone missing."

Dallas gave a genuine smile.

"It's possible they've threatened him and that's why he wants to talk. I doubt it, though."

"Well, good. As it should be. So… want to show me this movie screen?"

IT TOOK QUITE a while for the sun to go down enough to start the film, but once it did, I was doubly impressed with the whole setup Dallas had put together.

"Is this how your dad always did it?"

"No, we used to use ratty lawn chairs. I thought the tent was a good idea for shade, but also in case we wanted to do a double feature and passed out or something."

"Ooh, good idea."

"Mom and Dad used to just toss out blankets and sleeping bags. I remember plenty of times where all of us crashed out in the yard. I loved it. Your party reminded me of it, actually."

I was glad to see him remembering something that brought him some happiness after wading through the heavy relationship shit.

"It does sound like a pretty awesome time."

The dogs all joined us under the makeshift canopy. While it was still hot, the longer it went after sundown, the cooler the edge to the breeze blowing through.

Dallas started the movie I'd chosen, one based on one of my favorite romance novels.

"This… this story sounds like us," he mused, getting comfortable on the air mattress.

"I told you how roommate hookup situations happened in romance novels."

"That's fair, you did." He slid the bucket of assorted candies my way. "What have I missed you baking since I've been gone?"

"Oh, my God. I made a new recipe, you'll love it. Chocolate shortbread cookies with an Andes mint in the middle. They took forever and I was so sad I didn't have you there to help me roll out the dough. You would have enjoyed using the little circle cutters, too. Anyway, they rocked. I ate the whole freaking batch by myself."

"I'm really sad I missed out." He took a deep breath, eyes finally breaking away from my face. "I can't wait to get home to my bed." He winked at me, clearly feeling more like himself. "And your cookies."

We settled in for the movie, the heaviness of the earlier conversation lifting. After the first rom-com, we took an intermission before turning on a terrible sci-fi movie we quickly agreed to abandon. We settled on a mutual, long-time favorite fantasy, and I was fully immersed when it began to rain about halfway through.

"Should we go inside?" I asked, trying to gauge how much water was falling and how quickly.

"We'll be okay." Dallas dashed out to prop an umbrella up over the projector to shield all the electrical connections.

This particular summer storm brought a nice cool rain with lots of distant lightning.

Once we'd settled back in, I caught Dallas looking at me instead of the screen. The tilt of his mouth and the glint in his eyes sent sparks tingling through my lips, where his gaze was focused. In the next breath, he pinned me gently under his body, hands cradling my face as he used his mouth to sip from mine. Blood roared through my veins at his gentle ministrations, but I let him take what he needed.

His lips traveled from my mouth across my jaw before trekking down my neck to my collarbone. He suckled on a spot he knew made me squirm before kissing me again. His tongue tangled with mine, the whole pace slow and measured, as though we had all the time in the world.

Maybe we did.

The rain was softly falling onto the tarp, pattering gently all around us. The movie was playing in the background, but there was just us, making out like kids.

It was magic.

Definitely the best date ever.

"I'm flattered. Are you sure this counts?" Dallas mumbled into my hair. "As a date, I mean."

"Seriously? Are you sure I'm saying things out loud and you're not reading my mind?"

He chuckled, the sound vibrating through my chest.

"I'm positive."

"Well, it's not pizza and beer, but you knocked it out of the park. I'm not sure how you negotiated the rain, but well done."

"We aim to please."

Please he did. His hands wound their way under and inside my clothes, his need to consume me spreading over us like fire.

Hours later, we fell asleep right there, wrapped up in one another and the blankets, the rain still falling.

Everything had changed. I wasn't sure what it meant, but I was too at peace to care. We slept right there under the stars, cozy in our little nest. The rest of the world could wait.

CHAPTER THIRTY–SIX

Dallas

THE FIRST NIGHT back home in my own bed, I basically died.

When my alarm clock went off in the morning, it took half an hour for me to swim into consciousness enough to turn it off and remember where I was.

By the time I was showered, dressed, and desperate for a cup of coffee, Trina had already assembled my extra-large dose of caffeine and a muffin for me to take with me.

"Running behind this morning?"

"A little, yeah. Thanks." I accepted her offering gratefully, noting her warm smile as I dropped a kiss on her forehead. I held the flutters the simple interaction gave me close as I headed off to work.

The rest of the day passed in a blur of forklift beeps and shouted instructions.

By the time I got back to the apartment, I was ready to fall back into bed.

Trina came shrieking out of the office not long after I got out of the shower. I was about to dig through the fridge when she emerged.

"Oh, my God! Oh, my God!"

"What's going on?" I laughed at the enthusiasm with which she raced into the kitchen.

"I just heard from Animax. They invited me to come out for a job trial!"

Shocked, I stared at her for a moment. She was bouncing on the balls of her feet, face radiant with glee.

"I'm guessing that's something important. Come out where?"

"Orlando. I submitted my portfolio forever ago, but I didn't really expect to hear back. One of those jobs too perfect for mere mortals, you know? I spent half my afternoon talking to Colin about my portfolio and qualifications. Basically, it was one very long interview. They want to fly me out for a week-long trial. This is my *dream* job. I can't believe it."

The stars in her eyes made my heart squeeze. One thing, in particular, held my attention.

"Colin?"

"The guy who would be my manager if I get the job. He seems like a nice guy."

Heat flared in my chest. The thought of her going made me so itchy I could hardly stand it.

She went on a very excited rant, detailing every way in which it ticked every last one of her perfect job boxes. Pay, benefits, parameters, growth opportunities—they matched every item she'd put on her wish list.

Sounded suspect to me, but I was no expert.

I found myself instantly trying to come up with reasons why this job wasn't the only choice for her.

As she helped me compile some leftovers for dinner, I not so casually suggested the vague possibility of G4 bringing her on with a much more full-time position.

Trina was excitedly planning her last-minute trip for this trial while talking to this Colin guy, and I was epically failing to be happy for her. All I felt was pressure in my chest when she brought up the possibility of moving to Orlando to work for the marketing branch of one of the big animation companies.

"When are you leaving?"

"Tomorrow afternoon, if I can get this flight booked."

Absolute panic set in. Nothing about this seemed routine.

"Is it strange they're flying you out for almost a week? I've never heard of a company doing something like that before."

"I honestly haven't ever heard of it before, I've never had any involvement with a company like this either, though." A smile crossed her lips. "But they're the big guys. They can do whatever they want. I wonder what they're going to have me doing…" She looked across the room as she daydreamed about the possible tasks they might have for her during what amounted to a week-long internship.

"Do you really want to move again? Surely this isn't the only thing out there."

Trina scoffed.

"Hell no, I don't want to move. And it may not be the only thing out there, but right now, it's the only thing out there with any interest in *me*. Besides, it's everything I've ever wanted. Everything I've ever dreamed of having in a job." Her gaze turned shrewd, and she pinned me with it. "What exactly are you trying to say?"

I held a hand up.

"Nothing. It's just an unusual situation. Do you trust everything they're telling you is on the up and up? You're not flying into a trap for human trafficking or something?"

She snorted. "That's dramatic. And unlikely." Trina saw I was serious. "I'm sure it's not a trap, I swear. I did my homework and I'll leave you all my information. Addison, too. It's an amazing opportunity."

So she'd said. At least a dozen times.

I dropped the topic; instead, I took her into my bedroom to watch movies and soak up her physical touch while I still could.

Unfortunately, the seed of frustration about her leaving festered all night long while she rested peacefully next to me and I lay awake. It continued to follow me around all day while I was at work.

I came up with a dozen schemes to find her more hours with the foundation so she didn't feel like G4 was a sideline.

By the time I got home, she was getting ready to leave, and I instantly went into hyper-adrenaline mode.

It was a sensation oddly reminiscent of how my body reacted when Reggie drank. I was instantly uncomfortable. All I'd wanted to do was enjoy the few minutes I had with her before she left, but instead, my stress levels were making me panic and choose all the wrong words.

It was probably projection on my part, but I'd felt compelled to ask, "Are you sure this is the one? Are you sure you have to pursue *this* one?" While she gathered a few things from the kitchen to stuff in her purse.

Trina's expression turned icy and she stalked down the hall without responding.

Cautiously, I followed her.

Frustration bogged me down with heavy emotion as she went through a final check on her luggage. Even lingering in the doorway of her room, I could feel her intense anger. It'd been the wrong move to start this conversation while she was literally on her way out the door. I'd known it before I'd even opened my mouth, but I couldn't make myself stop. The thoughts that had been circling my mind all day long needed an outlet.

She tossed an extra jacket into her bag.

"I can't do this right now, Dallas. I *have* to go. This is the most promising job opportunity I've gotten in *months*. You know as well as I do how hard I've been looking, how many things have amounted to exactly nothing. People wait on lists for *years* to get this kind of opportunity. It could not only be my dream job but a huge bump for my career. This is *not* something I can take a pass on." Her words pelted me like heated stones. She slammed her suitcase shut, flinging the zipper closed. "It's completely unfair of you to ask me to."

I was flustered. The words I was trying to say weren't coming out right at all.

"I'm not asking you to give up on your dream. I would *never*. I just don't understand why *this* has to be the one." My argument was weak and I knew it.

"What other one has there been? I've done dozens of interviews that haven't amounted to a damn thing. This is promising. This is *more* than promising. I have to go."

I chased her as she speed-walked down the hall.

"I don't want to hold you back, Trina, I swear. But out of state to chase your dream? Is it the only way? What about your website? What about G4? There are plenty of things we can adjust to make it work. We can even tweak the arrangement between us if it's the problem." Panic was starting to rise. I was throwing anything out that might stick. Fight or flight set in. "None of this means anything to you? Me, the commitment to G4, your sublease? You can just up and leave? You'd treat… whatever this is—" I gestured between us with a shaky hand. "So… dismissively?"

I flinched at my own words. I didn't mean that. I didn't mean any of what I was saying. I knew better. It was like my mouth had forgotten it was attached to my brain. Things were getting real, and I was being careless. The very thing I'd tried to accuse her of being. Questioning her commitment to things was a tactic her mother always used to get under her skin, and I knew it. It was unfair—cruel even—to exploit such a soft spot of hers. I felt terrible I'd stooped to that level.

I also knew that since I'd used her weak spot, she'd go for mine. It was only fair.

"For someone who worries so much about being the problem, Dallas, you're *actively* being the problem right now."

"Trina, I—"

"No. No, thank you. I can't even tell if you're trying to push me away or keep me close, but talk about being dramatic and selfish." Eyes full of tears, her lip quivering, Trina pulled her purse over her shoulder and threw open the front door. "No part of this is about *you*. You approving this opportunity, or liking it, or *whatever* isn't required. This is *my* chance at something great and I'm taking it."

Her words, even expected, gashed a hole in my chest.

I was too stunned to stop her as she strode out the door, slamming it on her way through. I heard the elevator ding but was frozen in place.

My chest ached. I listened to my ragged breaths for long minutes as I replayed her words in my head, wondering what the hell was wrong with me, starting the conversation as I had.

Eventually, I made my limbs function enough to sag into the couch. I cradled my head in my hands, replaying the conversation over and over in my mind. What the hell was wrong with me? More importantly, how much had I broken things, and could I fix them?

CHAPTER THIRTY-SEVEN

Trina

I HATED LEAVING DALLAS the way I did.
After our fight, I'd needed to go directly to the airport. My makeup was still running down my face as I navigated my little sedan through traffic, sobbing to Addison over the Bluetooth speaker.

"I'm sure that's not what he meant." My best friend tried to soothe me, but I wasn't having it.

"It's exactly what he meant, Ads. What else could *'can't you wait for the next one'* and *'why does it have to be this one'* be interpreted as?"

"Hell if I know, Trin. Are you okay? Are you driving?"

"Yes, I have to get to the airport."

"I would have taken you! Why didn't you have me come get you or take a freaking Uber?"

"I already booked a parking spot. It's not a big deal. My flights were at weird times so I thought this was easier!" I found myself shouting. Nothing happening today felt like the right decision.

"Alright, alright. Don't holler at me, I'm not the one who pissed you off."

I took a deep breath. "I know. I'm sorry."

"I know it's impossible, but don't worry about it right now. Get on your plane, get to your job trial thing, and try not to think about the fight or what's going on back here. I bet… maybe some feelings are getting caught up where they aren't expected, Trin. It would explain lots of things."

"We agreed that wouldn't happen," I argued.

Addison wheezed a laugh. "It's that simple? Can you come up with any other reason he'd pick a fight with you? Because I can't."

"It's not impossible." My tears slowed, my body regulating a little bit. Shame rushed in after the rage started to cool. Addison was going on about the Greene men and their issues with expressing their emotions. I was only half-listening but it all sounded reasonable.

"I said some *terrible* things, Ads."

"Did he also say some awful things?"

I replayed the conversation in my mind. My words kept coming up as the damaging ones.

"Not like I did. He made some… unkind accusations. I was the one flinging hurt around at the trauma buffet, though."

"He picked a fight and you responded, that's all. Things happen sometimes. It'll be okay."

I wanted to believe her, but she was repeating it so much it was worrisome.

"I threw things he told me about his last relationship directly in his face, Addison."

"Well, it makes you a massive bitch, I guess, but it's not unforgivable. Did he do the same?" She asked again.

"I mean… I guess. He poked at a sore spot my mom always picks at."

"See? You're both assholes. Big deal. You fought, you both feel bad. Apologize. It'll be okay."

"It's not so simple, Ads."

"Yes, it is. Dallas isn't like this. I've only seen him upset or angry one other time, and it was about the misunderstanding between him and Dennis over Dennis' ex. He's gotta know you called me about it, too. I'll try to talk to him."

"Okay. Thank you, Ads."

"Of course. Deep breaths. You're a bad bitch, right? You're going to nail this. I'm excited for you."

"Bad bitch. Nailing it," I repeated, focused on making a turn into the airport. "Excited."

"I love you. Let me know when you land, okay?"

"I will."

I hit the disconnect button, putting all my energy into following the signs directing traffic around the terminal.

By the time I'd parked and gotten on a shuttle, I was dry-eyed and almost functioning normally.

Orlando was far enough away driving wasn't my best option, but was also such a short flight, it might have made more sense just to drive. Nothing was easy.

Between the excitement over the possibility of having found my dream job and the absolute mess of mixed emotions that came with considering moving again, I was a disaster.

Exhaustion set in deep by the time I got through security. I couldn't even keep my thoughts on a single track while I waited for my plane to board. They jumped from wondering what this test run would contain to worrying about booking another container and packing up my stuff again.

The pain in Dallas' eyes when I said those hurtful words haunted me. I hadn't been callous with him as he'd accused, but we were both raw. I didn't blame him for lashing out, even if his timing was absolute shit. I had every right to be angry at him for asking me to give up on this opportunity, but my body was too tired to be mad anymore.

I moved through the security line, trying to compartmentalize everything in my brain. Once I got through the scanner, I carried my single bag toward my gate, stopping only for a bottle of water that cost as much as two full cases anywhere else.

From my seat near the gate, I watched people, some rushing, some meandering. It was an odd kind of peace, feeling so small and unimportant as I waited for my flight to board.

More than once, I checked my phone, lying to myself about how I was only checking the time and not looking for some kind of message from Dallas.

By the time they called for my flight, I was sick of myself.

"I'm so sorry," I apologized to the flight attendant manning the desk as they scanned boarding passes. "My day hasn't been going well, but there's no reason it should overflow to you." My ID slipped out of my hand and we'd both ducked to retrieve it at the same time, foreheads painfully ramming together.

"It's okay." She gave a gentle smile, fingertips rubbing the spot where we'd made contact. "Have a good flight. I hope your day gets better."

"Thanks." My documents safely back in hand, I joined the long queue going on doing the jetway.

By the time I got to my seat, my head was pounding. I dropped into my seat with my small backpack, digging around for my travel container of ibuprofen. I swallowed the pills with a gulp of my expensive water.

Airport terminal prices were extortion.

"Excuse me. Sorry." A young woman apologized for bumping into someone taking up way more space than they should have been in the aisle. Red-faced, she slid into the seat next to me. I gave her my most reassuring smile as she pushed her backpack under the seat in front of her with the toe of her Doc Marten boot.

Her brow was dotted with sweat, her hands in constant motion until they finally latched onto the white fibers in the center of rips in her jeans.

Unless I was way off, she was nervous.

"First time?"

Her bright light brown eyes rimmed in heavy liner widened. "Is it obvious?"

"Only a little."

She let out a breath, making a tiny 'o' between her crimson lips. I understood as well as the next girl that her makeup application had likely veered bold for courage. "Second flight, actually, but I'm just as nervous as the last time."

"It gets easier. I'm Trina."

"Jasmine."

"Nice to meet you." We shook hands quickly before she ducked down to pull something out of her bag.

I retrieved my e-reader as she dug around in her bag.

She gave a light laugh as she held up a matching device, same protective cover and all.

"Well, look there. We were destined to be seat buddies. Once we get in the air, can I buy you a drink?" Jasmine's face went carefully blank, making me worry I'd misjudged her age. "If you're legal to drink?"

Still, she only blinked at me, and I realized that perhaps she was misunderstanding my offer.

"Listen. You're gorgeous, but I'm simply trying to make you feel better about the flight. I'm not hitting on you. I mean, I totally would, because you're stunning, but you're not my type."

Jasmine squeezed out a tight laugh, riotous blush in her cheeks. "Oh my God, I'm so sorry. How embarrassing. I appreciate the offer. And I'm 25, so yeah."

"It's a plan."

Encouraged it might be a good flight, after all, I scrolled around on my phone until they announced it was time to turn electronic devices off. Jasmine was already reading.

To our mutual shock, nobody took the empty aisle seat.

As the flight attendants demonstrated the safety features, Jasmine carefully unbuckled and slid over into the aisle spot, attention rapt as she alternated between watching the safety video on the seatback in front of her face and the flight attendant down the aisle a few rows.

Eventually, the plane backed away from the gate and began to taxi down the runway. I could see Jasmine fidgeting so I reached over, patting her hand where it gripped the armrest.

"You okay?"

Her other hand was hovering near her mouth so she could nibble on her nails. "Yeah. I think so."

"Just give a squeeze if it will help." I left my hand available in case she needed it, returning to my book.

My comfort with flying was somewhere between my current feigned confidence and how Jasmine felt. There was something about my brain that allowed me to take charge and do the thing, whatever the thing was, if someone else was in a more vulnerable place than I was about it. It was both a blessing and a curse.

Take-off and landing were my least favorite parts of flying, but landing much more so. Coming in hot with only little wheels to catch the plane defied logic to me. Take off at least was always equal parts terrifying and magical.

As the captain hit the gas so we could become airborne, Jasmine hastily grabbed my hand and gripped it fiercely.

"We're okay," I said reassuringly.

Her eyes were wide again, her entire body pressed firmly into the seat. She squinted her eyes shut as we lifted off the ground, relaxing once we hit a decent altitude and the cabin leveled off.

"Sorry." She looked panicked and embarrassed as she let go of my fingers.

"It's okay. Better?"

"Much. Thank you." Jasmine blushed.

"My pleasure."

We both turned to our e-readers, but I wasn't really taking in any of the words on the page. Without comforting Jasmine as a distraction, I was right back to being stuck in the argument Dallas and I had right before I walked out the door.

"HE SAID THAT, then you *left*?" Jasmine gaped at me, her rum and coke forgotten on the tray table.

"There wasn't much choice. I had to leave to make the flight."

We were well on our way to being friends. We'd already worked through one drink, exchanged phone numbers, and learned enough about one another to be sure the other wasn't a serial killer.

Probably.

"I don't know this guy, but it sounds to me like he caught some feelings and was total shit at expressing it."

A smirk tugged at my lips. "That's what my bestie said."

"Well, she's smart as hell." Shaking her head, Jasmine took a healthy gulp of her cocktail.

"She is." Addison had reassured me the Greene men all had issues with emotional constipation and struggled to express their real feelings until confronted with losing the people they loved the most.

The big fat 'L' word startled me enough to dry my tears. It has also pushed me from emotional overload into focusing on what my next steps should be.

"You're going for a job, right? What if you love it?" Jasmine's features pinched, animated face drawn tight as she shifted around enough to face me.

"I don't know. That's the big question right now."

"Hmm." Jasmine thoughtfully finished her drink, folding up her tray and pushing the cup into the seat pocket. "That's tough. I hope you guys can figure it out."

"Me, too." The sigh I released felt cold as it left my lungs. Deciding between a job and Dallas was not something

I'd been expecting to be doing. If nothing else, at least I'd found a new friend.

Jasmine and I continued to chat until the plane dived into the final descent. At that point, Jasmine had her eyes pinched shut again, my hand in hers with a squeeze so firm it made my fingers go numb.

As we waited for our turn to deplane, she sent me a practice text to be sure we got the right numbers saved. Near the end of the jetway, loss pressed in on me. We were about to part ways, but I wasn't quite ready.

"Call me when you get back to Birmingham, okay? We can have a drink or something."

"Sounds great. Thanks again." She dipped in for a quick, awkward hug.

"Have fun!"

Jasmine waved as she wandered off toward the exit and I glanced around for where to pick up a cab. I was ready for a nice soak in my hotel room bathtub, some room service, and a nice long rest.

As I shot off a text to Addison to let her know I'd arrived, I wished the feeling of regret would lift so I could find the excitement I should be feeling about this adventure.

CHAPTER THIRTY-EIGHT

Dallas

THE APARTMENT WAS too fucking quiet.

My nerves were strung tight. They had been since Trina had left for her job trial. The new, plush carpet rustling against my feet in my bedroom was irritating. The whisper-quiet fridge ran too damn loud. There was no water running in the pipes from her end of the apartment. The kitchen was too empty all the time and the dishwasher took forever to get full. There was nobody to watch trash TV or drink too much or get flirty on the couch with.

Nothing was right without her sparkle and sass all over it.

My gaze dipped toward the island where we'd enjoyed most of our meals… and plenty of *dessert* as well. Echoes of Trina chased me around the empty rooms. I wanted to tell her how I missed her, but I also didn't want to get in her way if she was supposed to be taking this job.

Frustrated with my sentimental self, I slammed some things around inside the fridge while hunting up something quick for breakfast. When this resulted in a broken jar of pickle relish, I cursed a blue streak while dramatically using half a roll of paper towels to clean it up.

By the time I was ready to leave for work, I was exhausted. I already had one massive issue to deal with that I was responsible for. My tantrum just made me feel bad.

Dennis hadn't done more than offer sympathy for my mistake at work, but I was feeling like total shit over having made such a careless error, anyway. I would fix it. It would be fine. I didn't enjoy the fact that I'd screwed up any more than the next guy, however.

I wandered away from the kitchen with the intent of leaving for work, but I found myself standing in her bedroom doorway, breathing in her lily lotion scent while staring at her bed like a total creep.

"Jesus Christ."

I was going insane. It was the only explanation.

The last time I'd been anywhere close to this was the first few months with Reggie. I'd fallen hard and fast for him. He'd *consumed* me. Everything about my life revolved around him for a time, but it wasn't love. I found out shortly after I moved into his apartment it was nothing more than lustful infatuation between us. Everything fell apart just as quickly as we'd fallen together.

This… this was different. Trina and I had a foundation in friendship. Even though we were a lot alike, there was enough about us that was different to keep things interesting. We were compatible in all the ways I thought mattered and many I would never have thought to look into.

She was my Terror and I was her Charming.

Hand out to pull my keys from the rack by the door, I stopped, my whole body broken out in a cold sweat.

I was in love with her and she didn't know. Hell, *I* hadn't even known.

Concern that I'd pushed her too far swamped me. My hands shook as my body processed my revelation. The argument about her going for the job trial suddenly seemed ridiculous. Had I intentionally been pushing her away so if she wanted to go, it wouldn't hurt so much?

The adrenaline subsided, leaving me worn out. I sat on the couch, staring blankly at the dark screen of the TV as I fell into full existential crisis mode.

If I was a few minutes late, it would be fine. I was not safe to drive in this state and I was proud of myself for being aware of it.

I may have pushed, but she'd still left. As usual, I was too much for a single person to handle and she needed some space to explore her options.

I tried to dislodge the destructive thoughts piling in. Trina wasn't like that. That wasn't what was going on. I was the one who felt like I was too much for everyone and every situation—this wasn't on her. If she was finding herself through this job trial, I would support her in every way I could, but I couldn't apologize for being upset about it. I wanted her close. I needed her near me in ways I hadn't realized or acknowledged before she'd gone.

While my thoughts spun out of control, I texted Addison I was running late. I knew she wouldn't care, but it seemed like the responsible thing to do. At the very least, if my brother was in the office, she could pass the message. He wasn't my keeper, but it would never stop feeling like he was maintaining tabs on me because I was the youngest out of the four of us.

I scrolled to Trina's name on my phone, but couldn't make myself tap out a message. What could I say?

Sorry I picked a fight, I didn't realize I was in love with you? How's it going? Is it your dream job, after all? Are you coming home soon?

None of those felt right. Not after how we'd fought before she left.

Fuck.

It was only Wednesday, and I was ready to be done with the week altogether.

"GODDAMMIT!" MY PHONE hit the conference room table with enough force I heard it make a sickening *crunch*. Knowing I'd broken yet another screen protector only intensified my frustration.

"Things are going well, I take it?" Addison stood in the doorway, an eyebrow raised.

I scrubbed my hands over my face, forcing myself to calm down. Addison took the opportunity to join me. She steepled her hands, elbows on the table as she watched me with a calm grin.

"Anything I can do to help?"

I pushed a slow breath out between my lips. "No. Not unless you can figure out how to make me stop screwing things up."

She reached for my phone, head tilted to one side.

"I'll order you another screen protector. I should probably just buy them in bulk the way we all go through them." Her kind hazel eyes bore into mine. "Did you talk to Trina today?"

"No." My sharp response surprised my friend.

"Not today or not at all?"

"Not since she left."

"She didn't text you when she landed?" Addison's brows pulled together in confusion.

"No." My chest hadn't loosened up since I'd opened my mouth that night. The last message I got from her was just a forward of her itinerary.

"Well, she's fine, in case you were curious. Got to Orlando right on time. She called me after she made it to the hotel. Sounds like they put her up in a super nice place."

My heart sank into my gut. I silently repeated the words I'd been telling myself for days. She was going after what she wanted and I was an asshole if I stood in her way. She deserved to be happy. If this job was what she wanted, I'd have to let her go.

"She seriously hasn't texted you?" Addison asked, head tilted to the side.

"No." Not in days. I never sent a single one of the dozens of messages I'd tapped into my phone to her, either. Not even the apologies. Everything sounded too simple. Trite.

"Huh. You don't have anything to say about it? You don't care?"

I absolutely did. And I would wager any amount of money Addison knew that and was either being kind or she was trying to provoke whatever reaction she expected out of me.

"You could call her, you know."

Anger rose up, my tone much harsher than I ever used, especially with Addison. "Why would I call? I wouldn't want to interrupt. She's off *pursuing her dream job*." The heated words tasted shameful. I let my head droop, chin briefly tapping my chest.

"Feel better now that you got that out?"

"Not really."

"Can I help you fix whatever is messed up here, then?"

I squeezed my eyes shut. "No. I've got it. I wasn't being careful and now we have overlapping deliveries, so everyone is going to be stressed. We'll probably owe some kind of fee. Not the end of the world, just something that could have been avoided if I'd been paying attention." Emotional distraction was responsible for a great number of mistakes in my life. I was sick of it.

"Well, if you change your mind, I'm excellent at strongly worded emails and sweet-talking a vendor into doing what I want while making them think it was their idea."

I smirked, knowing she wasn't exaggerating. It was good penance for me to clean up my mess, but I appreciated her offer.

Addison slid my phone within reach and slumped back in the padded leather chair.

"Call her."

"What would I even say?"

"*Dallas.*" Addison was exasperated, my name crossing her lips as a huffed curse. "Why are you all so freaking *stubborn*?" She crossed her arms.

"Blame Mom."

My friend snorted, the tension around us easing, allowing me to breathe a little easier.

"That part is probably true, but she uses her superpowers for good and not evil. The lot of you boys seem to need convincing that simply digging your heels in isn't the right way to go. It's just so… *dumb* sometimes. Completely counterproductive."

A similar conversation sprang to mind. Daniel's girlfriend Phae laid it all out for Dennis in a similar way when he was on the verge of messing everything up with Addison.

"We can't help it. Also genetic, probably from Dad's side."

"I promise to never tell Frank you said so. Also, quit it. She's coming home in about a week. Then what? What if she takes this job? Are you prepared to let her go so easily? I didn't have you pegged for being that guy, honestly. You clearly have feelings for her, even if you don't want to."

"I don't know," I admitted. I felt deflated, sagging in my chair.

"Do I need to schedule a conference call with the whole family? From what I hear, it worked for Dennis." Her lips curled. "I appreciate it, by the way."

I cringed. "You're welcome, but definitely not."

Addison chuckled. "Fine. You get a few more days, then I'm calling in the heavy cavalry as reinforcements."

"I hear you."

"Good." She pushed away from the table. "*Call. Her.* Text, at least. You guys were friends. Lots more than that. I know from personal experience you're both the best kind of friend anyone could have. So, get your shit together."

"I *hear* you," I repeated, returning her gentle smile.

Addison disappeared down the hall as I sucked in a deep breath, my sore chest protesting. I would call her. Soon. And I would tell her how I felt.

I would.

Just not today.

CHAPTER THIRTY-NINE

Trina

THE SHUTTLE TO my hotel was a very plush mini-bus.

Despite the very densely populated airport, only one other passenger made the trip with me to the hotel. I considered striking up a conversation, but he was far too involved in whatever was going on inside his phone to even make eye contact. Instead, I texted Addison and argued with myself over whether or not I should message Dallas I'd arrived.

In the end, I didn't, even though it felt wrong.

The hotel was luxurious, the lobby a classy compilation of vanilla marble and cherry woods. My room was a similarly high-class suite, the deep soaking tub calling my name the moment I laid eyes on it.

Room service was first on my list, however, so I called down an order right away. I hung up a few things to straighten out the wrinkles as I waited, then I flipped through the channels on the TV. My brain was thoroughly zapped of any useful energy, thanks to traveling.

Once the food arrived, I started the water running in the massive tub. Addison would surely scold me for eating my expensive room service pasta and salad while standing at the bathroom counter. What she didn't know wouldn't hurt me.

Leaving the slice of cake I'd ordered for after the bath, I submerged my body, forcing my brain to stop spinning.

White noise from the exhaust fan helped me relax as I floated in the water. I lingered in there for the better part of an hour, muscles relaxed by the time I finally climbed out.

My mind could be a terrifying place, I realized. As I'd emptied it, Dallas had popped up continually. His laugh. The way he watched me. How he smiled when he thought I was being ridiculous. How he'd choke on air when I said something especially inappropriate. All the ways he mastered touching my body to drive me crazy.

I was new to all things *relationship*, but it was becoming very clear what we had was something special. It was more than either of us admitted. It was something I wasn't ready to walk away from.

As I ate my cake, I typed out and deleted a dozen more text messages. I couldn't get the words quite right. Besides, it wasn't good timing to tell him whatever it was I was trying to say.

It was much better to do it in person.

On top of it all, despite the exhaustion, I was still upset with him. He could stew for a few days while I figured some things out. Or… he could reach out to me. I didn't care one way or the other, but I wanted to talk in person and that had my stubbornness showing.

Convinced I wouldn't rest in the plush hotel bed, I turned on a movie after setting multiple alarms for the morning.

The joke was on me though, because I didn't even make it through the opening credits before dropping off. The next thing I knew, those alarms were going off, and I felt oddly rested.

"WE'RE SO GLAD you could join us," Colin said, shaking my hand as he greeted me in reception. "Your portfolio was very impressive."

"I appreciate having a chance to come down to see everything for myself." I followed him through the office and into a conference room. To my surprise, there were three other people in there, one of which I'd seen at the hotel getting breakfast.

Colin closed the conference room door as I took a seat. The four of us assessed one another, confusion and discomfort evident on all our faces, barely masked by politeness.

"Now that we're all here, I want to officially welcome you to what we like to call the artist wars."

His welcome sounded… ominous.

"The four of you were hand-picked by multiple members of our team based on your artistic styles and skill level. The recommendations we received about you were positively glowing. Each of you has a unique work history we believe would be an asset to Animax. Unfortunately, we only have two positions available. There are four of you."

The youngish blonde man across the table from me smirked. I was still focusing on the glowing recommendation. Surely, *I* hadn't gotten one.

"So, you're testing us?"

"Not exactly." Colin's face was comically smug. "We're allowing you some time to work with the team so you can decide if this is a good fit for you. If it's not, there's no reason for either of us to continue and we ask that you remove yourself from the running. But yes, we're also checking to be sure you are a good fit for us."

"Why invest so much time and money into applicants then?" The other woman of the group, a willowy blonde, asked.

"Good question. Because it's worth it. Plain and simple. We have found this approach yields much more satisfying partnerships than what I'd consider to be the more traditional hiring practices. It's worth some upfront travel costs to find someone willing to be a dedicated, long-term employee." He looked around the room before clapping his hands together sharply. "Shall we start with a tour?"

Colin led the four of us around the building, pointing out

important rooms and introducing us to a dizzying number of people. The size of the campus alone boggled me. My fingers itched with the desire to play with the fancy tools. The other three candidates seemed as frustrated as I was at having been misled, though we were all stuck playing along… for now.

By the time lunch rolled around, I was ready to take a nap. The conference room was stocked with a tray of catered sandwich boxes while we were getting our tour.

"We've got a few videos while you eat," Colin said, grabbing a box for himself as he turned on the projector.

I was having doubts already, but the videos nearly did me in. I wondered how soon I could raise my hand to tap out without embarrassing myself or letting Sasha down. My need to uphold commitments kept my ass stuck to the seat, however, vowing I'd at least see the trial through.

Day one finished up with a trip through the art department in detail, some practice with the digital equipment, plus a whole lot of paperwork to sift through.

Back at the hotel, I skimmed the binder worth of documents as I enjoyed room service for a second night. If I weren't so tired, I would have ventured out to one of the local restaurants, as they were plentiful; I just didn't have it in me. Addison and I sent a couple of messages, but that was it.

I tried not to focus on the lack of messages from Dallas. The crater in my chest filled with cold regret every time I thought about our last words with one another. To be fair, I hadn't messaged him either.

Days two and three weren't any better. We were challenged with creating a piece of unique art, each of us mentored with a separate employee as we did so. Using the latest software was a bit of a learning curve and, while I appreciated the desire to see whether we could produce good marketing art quickly, my heart wasn't in it.

The four of us were often put in the same room without any real opportunity to speak to one another. It was all very bizarre.

By the end of day three, I'd more than made up my mind. This was an outrageous opportunity for someone to be offered. Unfortunately, that someone was simply not me.

I'd called Addison from my hotel room, already leaning toward my decision, but wanting to talk it out in case I was being unreasonable. As usual, she was the perfect rational voice.

"If you hate it as a trial, you'd hate it as a paying job."

"They invested so much to get me here, though. It feels… ungrateful to leave early."

"Who cares? They said this is normal for them, right?"

"Yes." I paced around my hotel room, yet another tray of room service waiting for me on the bedside table.

"Then don't worry about it. Tap out and come home. You have other opportunities here. You went, you saw, you didn't like it. It's okay, bestie."

I sat heavily on the bed, the heavy cover crinkling under my weight.

"It's so much money though."

"Trina." Addison sighed, exasperated with me. "Is the money worth how miserable you already feel? The benefits? Getting to work with the new fancy equipment?"

Eyes squeezed shut, I tried to hear my own inner voice over my mother's.

"No. I can do okay with my side commissions if I put some effort into trying to find more clients. G4 pays well for the work I'm doing for them." I took a cleansing breath. "This job would make me very comfortable, but at the cost of being miserable."

"There you go."

"I'm throwing away the same opportunity I fought with Dallas over needing to pursue."

Addison was quiet for a moment. I knew her well enough to guess she was carefully managing her words.

"You're not throwing it away. You are respectfully removing yourself from the list of potential candidates. As far as Dallas…"

I interrupted her long pause, unable to keep myself from asking.

"Has he said anything to you?"

"The two of you, I swear. I could strangle you both sometimes."

"I'm sorry. You know I love you. So, has he?" I nibbled on a fingernail, waiting for her response. Just the thought of him made my stomach knot. I missed him. I wanted to talk with him about this the same as I wanted to go over it with Addison.

"We talked after you left. He told me you didn't even let him know you'd arrived safely?" There was an edge of irritated accusation in her tone.

"I was mad." I sounded petulant and I knew it.

"Well, the two of you have to sort your shit out. For two adults I assumed were capable of talking things out, you sure are acting like stubborn ass toddlers."

"Hey!" I was offended but knew she was right. "You aren't wrong."

"I know I'm not. Since he clearly never called you, and you aren't going to call him, I guess it can all wait another day." She let out a breath. "He hasn't been himself at work. That's all I'm going to say though."

Guilt swamped me, regret at having dragged out the silent treatment weighing heavily.

"Thank you. I'm going to quit this trial first thing tomorrow. Then I'll be on my way home."

"Good. Keep me posted so I know you're safe. You guys will be okay."

"I hope so."

I bid my friend goodnight, eating my room service while I rehearsed what I planned to tell Colin in the morning. After I was settled on a good speech for turning down the job, I started on how best to apologize to Dallas in the afternoon.

It was the least restful night I'd spent in the plush hotel sheets. I couldn't wait to get home to my bed.

CHAPTER FORTY

Dallas

LOST IN MY thoughts, I parked my bike and was nearly to the double doors of my building before I processed the familiar form leaning against the bricks.

Everything in my body locked up. I noticed the grin on his deceptively handsome face when he realized I'd spotted him. Gathering all my courage, I continued my approach, steeling myself against his fake charm. He was dressed in his country club best, as usual. Instead of disguising his slime factor, it seemed to enhance it.

"What the fuck are *you* doing here?" I asked, the harsh tone of my words making him flinch.

"Well, that's no way to greet an old friend."

I couldn't help snorting as I pushed past him and entered the building.

"Friend? Is that what we're going with?" I glanced over my shoulder. He was sauntering behind me, his loafers whispering against the carpet.

Fight or flight had taken effect. I was terrified, but couldn't show him any weakness. He was too good at exploiting them. He smirked, catching me looking.

"Aw, come on, Dallas. We were good once. *Really* good. Don't you have five minutes to talk to me? We used to love each other. Isn't that worth something?"

My heart dipped, doubt rushing in. I knew better than to fall for such a plea but still found myself agreeing. Probably for the same stupid reason I hadn't left him leaning against the wall outside.

"Then it *was* you sending me texts?"

He shrugged. "Desperate times, you know. I needed to talk to you. I wasn't sure what else to do."

I wasn't sure why leaving me the hell alone never crossed his mind. Common sense never had been one of Reggie's strengths.

"Five minutes."

For reasons unknown, I nodded.

As he smiled, I knew it was a mistake. Regret for giving him even a second of my time cast a shadow on my confidence.

The overly bright, veneer-laden grin set all my mental alarms off. Adrenaline coursed through my veins, giving me hot flashes. I should have either turned around and left when I realized it was him or locked him on the other side of the entrance doors.

The elevator ride was uncomfortable. No matter how close to the wall I got, he still took up all the available space. The cologne he'd always favored clung to my nostrils. He also insisted on filling the time with inane small talk, which made me want to scream.

"You look *good*, Dallas. I mean it. Being home is treating you well. It's hotter here than I expected, though. When I got to town, it took me a minute to get my bearings; Birmingham isn't set up at all like Nashville. Though I expect you didn't have the same problem since you grew up here."

It didn't matter one iota that I wasn't answering. He carried on a full conversation all by himself. Once upon a time, it was a charming aspect of his personality. Now I knew it was just another layer of his mask.

When the doors finally opened, relief washed over me in a warm wave. I couldn't get out of the suffocating little box with my ex fast enough.

I wished I'd had the forethought to only agree to talk with him down in the lobby. I didn't want him in the home I'd built with Trina. His presence could taint everything I loved about the space that was wholly ours.

"What is it you want, Reg?" I entered the apartment in front of him without holding open the door, manners be damned. I figured Mom would forgive me, given the circumstances.

"Damn. It's like you're not even glad to see me."

I rounded on him as he chuckled at his terrible joke, hastily pulling a beer out of the fridge for myself. I needed both the courage and the weapon the bottle afforded me.

I didn't offer him one. This too amused him.

"Can't imagine why that might be." I kept my tone as neutral as I could.

His smarmy expression chilled my blood. I took a deep pull from the beer before setting it on the island.

"Your five minutes started—" I consulted my watch. "—two minutes ago."

Reggie's handsome features dipped from confidently sexy to strained. He swallowed, turning his palms toward the sky in a conciliatory gesture.

"C'mon, babe. I wanted to see you. Is that so wrong? I missed you. I know you probably don't want to hear it, but I realize I screwed up. I apologize."

"You apologize." My hands were shaking, a rough pounding of blood in my ears as I processed the paltry words. Words I had desperately wanted for such a long time. They now seemed completely meaningless. "You apologize? First time for everything, I guess. Do you think an apology makes everything okay?"

"Well, maybe not everything, but I thought, you know, I maybe owed it to you after everything."

"*Maybe?*"

"No, I did. I owed it to you." His hands were steepled in front of him like he was begging my forgiveness.

I scrutinized his expression, seeking the disingenuousness I knew was sure to be there. He was never sorry for anything unless it gained him something. I wasn't clear about what he was after, but I was damn sure not about to fall for his tricks.

"How did you find out where I lived?" I was fairly certain my online footprint was as locked down as it could get, thanks to a service I paid for every month without fail.

His grin spread wide and made my blood run cold.

"Lots of things are public record if you know where to look, lover."

If he could find my address, what else could he find? Panic settled deep in my bones.

"Don't call me that. I haven't been your lover for a long time. In fact, I'm not anything to you. Are you stalking me, Reg?"

Flight took over as he stepped toward me. I moved backward in response, which made him laugh. The sound slithered around me and sent my heart racing. Nothing had changed. He wanted something from me. He expected he'd be able to get it by faking nice. He hadn't even lasted the full five minutes.

"I really wanted to see you, baby."

I froze as he raised a hand, cupping my cheek. His overwhelming scent filled my lungs and I tried to breathe evenly as my mind spun a thousand directions.

The front door opened, time stopping as Trina came in, her smile bright.

I'd been wrong when I thought things couldn't get much worse.

"Dallas? Surprise! I'm home!" The joy on her face melted right off when she realized I wasn't alone. "Oh. Hi."

My heart tripped all over itself at seeing the woman I'd accidentally fallen in love with walk in. Her dark eyes scanned the pair of us, Reggie still touching me. I was sure from her angle, it looked like we were in a passionate embrace.

"Sorry, I didn't mean to interrupt." Surprise and embarrassment were written clearly on her face as her eyes went anywhere but at me and she rushed toward her bedroom.

"Trina, stop. Please. This isn't what it looks like."

She barked a wet chuckle as she halted at the edge of the living room. "Classic."

I broke away from my ex, frustrated his invasion might cost me Trina as well as my comfort giving me a burst of bravery.

"This is *Reggie*. And he was just leaving." I pushed ice into my words, staring at him as I said them. I prayed she understood the depth of what I was saying. His name tasted sour in my mouth.

Undeterred, he gave a rueful laugh.

"It's like that? I apologized, Dal, can't we go have a drink or something? I want to talk. Catch up, you know?" His smile was all teeth. He was like a deranged Ken doll in his khakis and polo. He even had a full face of makeup on, as though talking to me was a quick stop he was making on his way to a modeling gig.

"No, thanks. Your five minutes is way over. And so are we." I took long strides to the front door, opening it wide. Trina being home gave me a burst of confidence. My heart was pounding in my chest, but I knew I needed to remain as neutral as possible outwardly or he'd take advantage.

He glanced at Trina before taking a few steps toward me. His anger was simmering under the surface; I could feel it rolling off of him in a bitter wave. I was reminded of the brutal fights we'd had before I left and how low I'd felt. Our furious love affair ended with me broken, doubting everything. His love was toxic. I understood now just how much.

"Ohhh, I see. You got yourself a *girl*friend. She knows about us?"

"She knows everything."

His expression morphed into surprise. His eyebrows shot up, his mouth opening and closing a few times without sound. He glanced between her and I.

"Is that right? Does she know *everything* about you? What about how you can't help but ruin things, even the ones you love?"

I choked on his words. They were a futile attempt to get one over on me and they weren't true—I knew as much—but they still hurt. Thanks to lots of therapy, my mom's unwavering support, and Trina, I'd realized I wasn't at fault for everything he and I'd gone through. I wasn't at fault for even a fraction of what I'd dealt with.

His narcissism was showing already, mere minutes after he tried to love bomb me into forgetting everything he'd put me through. Plus, he was insulting *her*, which was completely unacceptable.

"I'm afraid we haven't properly met," Trina said, striding boldly across the living room with her hand outstretched. "I'm Trina. Dallas' roommate."

The neutral label made my chest ache, but her icy tone made the hair on the back of my neck stand at attention. Danger lay thick in the air. I wasn't sure which of them was of bigger concern.

Reggie snickered, gazing down at her as he shook her hand. "Nice to meet you, Trina. Are you seriously going with the roommate schtick? We did that too, once upon a time, didn't we, babe?" His eyes grazed me. I did everything I could not to flinch from them. It took everything in me to remember that while he'd been in control most of our relationship, I was still capable of removing him from my home. With physical force if necessary.

"Not that it's any of your business, but yes. We live together. We're friends."

My heart sank again. She'd obviously done some soul searching while she'd been gone, same as me. Unfortunately, it looked like she'd ended up with a far different conclusion than I had.

"Well, don't let him drag you down, Trina. He's got a bad habit of doing just that."

"Drag me *down*?" Trina crossed her arms. I could tell she was gearing up for a verbal confrontation. She was comically short compared to Reggie, who was well over six feet. I didn't doubt her ferocity, though, and he was almost certainly underestimating her. If he thought he had an ally in her, he was dead wrong.

"You should go, Reg," I said. "Your time is up."

He put his hand in my face to silence me. The childish gesture irritated me. It *infuriated* Trina.

"Don't do that to him."

He smirked. I recognized the danger there, but Trina was undeterred.

"No? What are *you* going to do about it?"

"Are you threatening me?"

"Does it sound like I'm threatening you?"

"It does. I'm honestly more interested in why you're in my house, harassing my friend, though."

"He invited me in." His eyes cut to me, I wanted to slap the smug smirk right off his face more than anything in the world.

Trina turned in my direction, asking for confirmation of his claim. "Dallas?"

I gave a regretful nod. "I did. He was waiting downstairs when I got home. I stupidly agreed to talk to him for five minutes."

"This is the guy you told me about, right? The one who stole a bunch of money from you? Well," she tipped her head to the side, rolling her eyes to the ceiling. "Stealing is a harsh word. More like spent and spent when there wasn't anything to spend, trying to keep up appearances. To stay loaded. This is him, right? The one who put holes in walls and bruises on skin and blamed passion for it? Or whatever other bullshit he claimed?"

My cheeks flamed hot, hearing her say it so plainly right in front of him. I refused to live in shame anymore, however.

"Yeah, that's him."

"Now wait, little girl. That's not the whole story—"

"The same guy who stole from your mutual friend, then sold their property and tried to frame you for the whole thing?"

Trina took measured steps toward him as she spoke, and to my amazement, *he* was the one backing up.

"Yes."

"Dal! You know that's not how it went down." He turned a pleading expression my way, a nervous chuckle grating out of his throat.

"I'm pretty sure that's exactly what happened, Reggie. You need to leave."

"Yeah. You *definitely* need to leave." Trina cut the distance between them, attitude making her seem larger than her actual petite size.

Reggie, flailing, laughed. It carried a forced, hollow quality. My skin rippled, reacting to the darkness there.

"Fine. I did all those things. Sure. It's all my fault, right? It doesn't have anything to do with your incessant need to be the center of attention or your victim complex. Both of which I'm sure have to do with you being the baby of the family and your beloved mother." I blinked hard, his words landing as fierce blows. "You've stooped to *this*, then? A man willing to let a woman he's not even fucking fight his battles?"

"Who said we're not fucking?" Trina spat.

Reggie gaped, mouth opening and closing without a sound.

Trina continued, "He doesn't need *anyone* to fight his battles for him, by the way. He does just fine on his own. Last I checked, theft and fraud are criminal offenses. So you might want to worry about yourself." She showed him her phone, which displayed a voice recording app.

"What the fuck? You bitch. I can't believe—" it was a terrible swing, but Reggie swatted at Trina. I roared, all but running towards them, but she didn't need my help. She ducked away from his arm, stepping further away from his reach.

"You need to go *right now*, or I'm calling the police to remove you," she said, the words like icicles. "I'm not half as generous as Dallas is. This recording is going straight to an attorney. They can do with it what they need to."

"Now wait, I—" Reggie sputtered.

Trina was undeterred. "Never come back. Dallas no longer exists to you. Birmingham is a place you visited once. Nothing special, no need to ever return, not even passing through. Understand?"

He considered briefly before throwing his hands into the air. "Fine. *I'll* be the bad guy."

"Seems to me you *are* the bad guy in this scenario," she insisted, arms crossed. "I bet a psychologist would have an absolute *field* day with you."

"Whatever. I'll remember this when you come crawling back to me, Dal." Disdain dripped from his words, but his hands wouldn't still, which was one of his tells when he got nervous. I also wondered if whatever he'd been high on was starting to wear off the way he was ticking his head to one side.

"Never gonna happen," I said firmly.

I could hear him cursing the whole way down the hall, even after I slammed and locked the door.

Adrenaline fatigue set in, making me slump against the wall. "Holy shit."

"Are you okay?" Trina closed the distance between us, hurriedly checking my face for marks.

I stilled her warm hand with mine, pressing it to the place where he'd touched me, erasing the sensation of his skin on mine with hers.

"I'm okay." I took a deep breath, calming as her scent filled my lungs. "I'm so glad you're home." With my free arm, I pulled her against me.

"Me, too. I wanted to surprise you. To apologize. I had a whole speech planned."

I breathed in her scent, letting go of her hand so I could wrap both arms firmly around her body.

"Well, mission accomplished, but I'm afraid it may have backfired a little bit. I have no idea how he found me. I was an idiot for telling him I'd talk to him."

"Don't blame yourself. I'm glad I took the flight I did."

"Me too, Terror."

She stepped back, a sweet grin on her lips as she stared into my eyes. "He was scared of me."

I couldn't help laughing. "*I* was scared of you. You're terrifying."

"Only when some asshole is threatening someone I love."

My grin faltered as something released in my chest. I could breathe deeply for the first time since she told me about the job in Orlando.

"You love me?"

"Of course, I do, you idiot. Why do you think I'm home so early?"

"Addison told me you hated the job, so…"

Trina laughed. "Really? That's it? Are you going to leave me just hanging here on that confession? You don't have anything else to say?"

"Oh. Absolutely. I love you, too, Trina Lee." To prove it, I kissed her mouth soundly, pressing all my feelings about her into the way I held her against my body, the way my lips moved against hers. I filled my senses up with her, welcoming her home the best way I knew how.

CHAPTER FORTY-ONE

Trina

MY FIRST REACTION to seeing a tall, blond man in our kitchen with his hands on Dallas was shock. Finding the willpower not to beat him to death with his own limbs once I realized who he was ran a close second.

I'd pay good money to see the expression on Reggie's face after I asked who said Dallas and I weren't fucking again. It was pure poetry, the way every perfect feature on his face contorted in confusion.

I kissed Dallas again before pulling away.

"It kind of feels like we need to cleanse this whole place now," I grumbled, grabbing water from the fridge. The flight had completely dehydrated me, plus with adrenaline finally waning, I needed something to rinse the sour taste from my mouth.

"It's not a bad idea." Dallas' eyes went blank for a long moment. "I can't believe he found me."

The haunted look in his eyes broke my heart. I was disappointed in myself for how I'd thought, even for a moment, he was hooking up with someone in the kitchen when I first came in. I knew him better than that.

"How *did* he find you?"

Dallas put his hands on the island on either side of me, caging me in, making my pulse spike.

"He said he found it online. I'm going to have to call SafeLock to complain. I pay them way too much for this shit to happen."

I gazed into his bright blue eyes, offering a small smile.

"I missed you," I confessed.

"Me, too." He dropped a light kiss on my nose. "We've got some things to talk about."

"Oh?"

"Yeah. I'm sorry. I shouldn't have picked a fight with you like I did."

"No, you shouldn't have. I cried all the way to the airport."

He sagged. "I'm sorry, Trina. It was a total dick move. I shouldn't have said any of those things, I know they aren't true," he apologized again, staring into my eyes so intently I blinked against the intensity. He brushed his fingers through some of the wild curls near my temple. "I was just… confused. I realize how cliché it sounds. But I didn't know how to tell you how I don't want you far away from me." My heart pounded wildly at his admission, my eyes tracking the way his Adam's apple bobbed as he swallowed. "If you need to take the job, we can work something out. I can work remotely again, or fly out whenever I can, or—"

"Shush." I silenced him by putting my mouth on his, sparks flying under my flesh as his fingertips burned through the thin fabric of my sundress. I needed him to touch me as much as he wanted to. If his skin on mine was the comfort we both craved, I was happy to strip down right here in the kitchen.

"I'm not taking the job."

"Thank fuck." He sighed, scooping me up with an arm securely under my bottom. I locked my legs around his waist as he carried me off to his bedroom.

"You good?" he asked, pressing me into the mattress with his body.

"Perfect, now."

His smile was bold and bright as he pulled his shirt over his head. The text of his tattoo shifted over his ribs, making me bite my lip. I had no explanation for why it was so sexy.

"You going to help, Terror?"

I grinned at him, sliding the bright yellow sundress up my legs. His body blocked any progress above my knees. I pushed gently against his chest so he would raise his torso enough for me to finish pulling it up my body and over my head.

"You *flew* this way?" He demanded, scanning me head to toe but finding no undergarments of any kind under the dress.

"Hell, no. I changed when we landed. I left Orlando in jeans and a t-shirt." I chuckled at his hungry expression as he palmed my breasts. "The underwear stayed on until I pulled into the parking lot."

"That's a lot of effort." He dipped his head, kissing the swell of one breast and then the other before drawing the nipples into his mouth one at a time. He blew a tantalizing breath over them, making them tighten. "It's not unappreciated."

"You going to lose those sexy jeans any time soon?"

He smirked, shucking them one-handed.

"This isn't how I planned on welcoming you home." He sank to the floor off the side of the bed, pulling my body right to the edge. "I was going to grovel. Apologize. Beg if I needed to. But I suddenly find myself starving."

My blood sang as he lowered his mouth to my core, licking a solid swipe along the seam before concentrating on the tight bundle of nerves with suction and a quick-flick of his tongue. This man and his dirty mouth.

"Aren't those all the same thing? This seems like a really… ohhh." It took a moment to gather my thoughts. "Like a super valid, successful tactic for those things, actually." I moaned again, pleasure spiking hot through my veins.

He knew exactly how to play my body; alternated licking, suckling, and touching, my need becoming frenzied.

I was on the verge of coming, unable to form a coherent thought when he finally pressed two fingers into me and sucked hard on my clit.

The sound I made came from deep in my chest and echoed around his room as I fell apart.

"I fucking love that." He smirked, wiping his mouth on his hand as he rose over me.

"Not as much as I do," I breathed the words, thoughts still scrambled.

"We'll have to agree to disagree."

He lowered his mouth to mine, the salty flavor of my arousal shared between us as he carefully worked his way between my thighs, the tip of him sliding through my wetness as I lifted my hips in welcome.

Dallas moaned into my mouth, rocking his hips to seat himself better as I chased his movements with my body.

He pulled his mouth away long enough to trail kisses from right below my ear all the way down my neck. Arms locked straight, his eyes slid closed as he rocked into me, his face turned toward the ceiling.

The expression on his face made me feel powerful.

"It should," he confirmed, a devilish grin on his mouth as he dipped down to resume light kisses all across my collarbone before lavishing my breasts with attention. "You have no idea how much you own me, Terror. It's dangerous."

"I seriously need to get a grip on this whole out loud or in my head thing."

He chuckled, adjusting our bodies so he could lift one of my legs over his shoulder.

"Don't worry about it on my account. I happen to enjoy the parts of your inner monologue you accidentally share with me."

"Of course you do." My witty comeback was interrupted by a moan of pleasure thanks to the position change. The angle he was pressing in at sent starbursts blooming behind my eyelids. I wouldn't last long if he kept it up, especially when he suckled his thumb and lowered it to where we were joined, slowly rolling my clit under the soft pad.

Sweat broke out on his forehead as his thrusts became more demanding. My thighs were screaming from being braced to counter his motions. When he moaned out, I saw stars, falling apart again, my core clenching and back arching. Dallas thrusted sharply a few times before letting my leg fall to the mattress, leaning down over me.

His damp forehead rested near my cheek as we panted together.

"Damn, I'm glad you're home."

I smiled, kissing his cheek gently, the stubble rough against my lips.

"Me, too."

DALLAS CALLED FOR delivery after we got cleaned up.

"I honestly didn't mean to jump you the second you got home," he said, scooping rice onto a paper plate. "It wasn't in the plans at all. I planned a big speech and was going to confess how I had a come to Jesus breakdown after you left. I hate that we fought before you got on the plane." He frowned, and I felt bad we didn't clear the air while I'd been gone. "Poor Addison's been hearing the two of us bitch and moan. She's had a rough time trying to set us straight."

"She's been tolerating it all with her usual grace for sure." I laughed. "We'll have to send her some flowers or something."

"And chocolate," he added helpfully.

"I'll bake her something every day if I need to." There was a brief silence as we slid onto the stools. "We're both a little stubborn," I admitted, knowing how much of an understatement it was. "And a lot alike, which may be problematic in lots of cases. I had the same realization, to be honest. I was super pissed at you, but I was also sad we fought." I remembered my seatmate on the plane. "On the bright side, I made a friend, and she helped me talk it out before I even ever got to Orlando."

I showed Dallas the picture of Jasmine and me from my phone.

"You're something else." He shook his head as he took a bite of his food.

"Damn right. I'm sorry I didn't at least text to tell you so though."

"What, that you'd made a new friend?" He smirked, trying to get a rise out of me even while we were having a serious conversation.

"No, idiot. That I regretted leaving like I did."

He kissed my temple.

"I know. It was my fault anyway. I shouldn't have picked a fight while you were on your way out the door. It was…" He shook his head. "Below the belt. We're good. Right?" The naked vulnerability that crossed behind his eyes made my chest squeeze.

I realized I was staring at a glimpse of my future if this crazy thing between us lasted. Jokes, sarcasm, and other deflective coping mechanisms while we had healthy, adult conversations. Lots of laughter. Great sex. Most importantly, a foundation in friendship.

It sounded pretty good.

"We are." I realized I was smiling at him again and wondered if this was what Addison felt like when she looked at Dennis. Fizzy, light. Free.

Love.

The four-letter curse I was certain I'd never feel for someone other than my best friend and my family. Not always my family, even.

Who could have seen that coming?

Trina

DALLAS HADN'T BEEN lying about the beauty of the Gulf Shore.

How I'd managed to avoid going the entirety of my college career still astounded me. I usually spent my summers working, so even weekend trips were out of the question. My one big trip a year—if I took one at all—was usually to meet up with my parents somewhere. I'd wanted to get to the ocean for years. Getting to do it with Dallas for the first time felt appropriate and special.

We'd driven down and played in the warm surf all afternoon, then curled into a blanket on the tiny little front porch to watch the sunset and the moon rise. Fall was around the corner and the evening breeze coming off the water was cool as we laughed our way through identifying constellations before making use of the couch. And the shower. And the plush queen-sized bed.

I woke up in our little rented cabin right on the beach, already tasting salt as the sunlight streamed through the slats in the wooden blinds.

Dallas, sensing my movement, groaned and pulled me closer into the curve of his body.

"Coffee?" I suggested. "We might be able to catch some sunrise if we get up."

"Not yet. Still tired." He brushed his nose along the shell of my ear and I let out a squeak from the tickle.

"Five minutes. But you have to make the coffee."

Pleased with the agreement, he snuggled even closer. My eyes slid shut, body relaxed in the firm grip of his arms. Unfortunately, my brain was already active; going back to sleep was not in the cards for me, no matter how comfortable I got.

"What do you want to do today?" I asked quietly.

"Sleep," he grumbled.

"After that?"

He gave a resigned sigh, loosening his hold across my body.

"You're not going to stop, are you?"

"Probably not. I'm awake, kind of have to pee, and want to go put my toes in the water as soon as possible."

"Fine," he sighed. "I'll make the coffee."

He rolled out of the bed, pulling on some shorts before making his way toward the kitchen. I detoured to the bathroom, the smile on my mouth a permanent fixture since… I couldn't even remember. It had been so long thanks to him.

Dallas handed off a mug when I emerged. Without discussing it, we went out the front door of the cabin, headed toward the set of lounge chairs belonging to our unit. They were yards from the water, but close enough to feel the breeze and smell the salt.

"It's gorgeous here."

"It is."

We exchanged a glance and settled in, the morning sun soaking into my skin.

When the cups were gone, he stood, offering me a hand.

"Where are we going?" It was impossible to tell just how playful Dallas was, but I knew him well enough to be cautious.

"You're taking a walk on the beach."

"Didn't we do that yesterday?" I hauled myself to my feet, linking my fingers with his as he led me in a sedate stroll across the sand.

"Yes, but this time, you're doing it with intention."

"Ah. Why?"

He tilted his head to look at me, blocking the sun with his hand.

"So you aren't lying on your dating profile."

My heart sank.

"It said I enjoy walks on the beach at sunset, not strolls along the surf mid-morning. Am I going to be *needing* my profile?" I could hear the horror in my voice.

Dallas laughed, pulling me close enough to the water the waves lapped over my toes. The water was chilly this early, but still pleasant.

"Not at all. I just remember you were quite bothered by the fact you were fibbing. I can't do anything about you saving endangered animals, but I can make sure you take a walk on the beach."

He dipped down and kissed me, every nerve ending standing up at attention as he did so. This man wrecked me, in all the best ways.

"Thanks, I guess."

"You're welcome."

We wandered quite a distance down the shore, picking up shells and pebbles that drew our attention. The sun was strong, reminding me how I needed another layer of aloe on the places that were already burned by the time we got back to our little cabin.

Dallas left me near the beach chairs to go refill our coffee cups.

I watched the waves lap at the shore as my thoughts wandered. Some intrepid children from a nearby cabin lead their parents to the water so they could splash and build sandcastles. The seagulls seemed a bit put out that their space was being invaded, but I was betting they'd be assuaged by the crumbs those kids left after eating lunch.

Dallas returned, setting down our cups on the little wooden table before sinking back down in his chair. He stretched his arms out and pulled me down into his lap.

His lips brushed over my nose, then seated firmly over mine. He broke the kiss before things got too indecent. The kids were plenty far away, but still.

"You good, Terror?"

"I'm wonderful, thanks for asking."

He smiled, arms banded around my middle. "What time are your parents coming in?"

"Around dinner, Dad said. They're bringing the food and I promised to make dessert."

"Sounds perfect."

My mom and I had come to an understanding after a very tense conversation. They'd rearranged their itinerary to meet us at the beach as a compromise. Whether I'd see them again in a few months for Thanksgiving and my birthday was a mystery. I was excited to see them for now, either way. Sometimes new traditions had to be made.

I climbed off of his lap as his phone buzzed in his pocket. I grabbed my mug, sinking down into my own seat as he smiled his way through whatever messages he'd gotten.

"Ellie's getting so big already."

"Babies tend to do that."

"Devon is asking if we want to come out there for Christmas."

I understood the pensive look on his face as he glanced at me. Thinking months down the road wasn't something either of us was familiar with doing when it came to relationships.

"I've never been to California before. Is he inviting everyone?"

He nodded. "Yeah. He says they might have a connection to rent some neighboring houses on the beach where they got married for a week or so."

I sat back, sipping at my coffee and watching the waves before responding.

"No complaints here. I think it sounds really nice, actually. The beach has my vote and I've only been here a day. The logistics of closing the warehouse are more complicated, but I bet you guys can figure something out."

Dallas grinned, already typing out a response.

"For sure. I'll let him know. It sounds pretty awesome, honestly. I can't remember the last time we were all together for a holiday." His phone went off moments after he replied. His smile broadened. "Devon says to start working on Addison so Dennis will agree. And he can't wait to meet you."

I blushed at the thought.

"Tell him me, too. Honestly, I bet Addison's already all in."

"Probably." Dallas nodded, texting furiously for a few moments.

"And thank him again for his help."

Devon's attorney had been quite enthusiastically receptive of my recordings as well. The last we'd heard, Reggie was facing a number of charges even his parents' money couldn't get him out of. He wouldn't have any choice but to remain in a tiny sliver of Tennessee for the foreseeable future, which was just fine by us.

They continued texting for a few more minutes, and then he pocketed his phone again, both of us quietly watching the surf with the wind in our hair.

"What are we baking?" he asked, a particularly devious gleam in his eye.

The smirk on his mouth made me smile. "Does it matter?"

"Nah. I'll eat your dessert anytime, anywhere, Terror."

"You're trouble, Charming."

He winked at me. I shook my head.

I loved us.

We weren't conventional, but we were still perfect.

ALEXANDER

Want an exclusive bonus scene with Trina and Dallas?

Sign up for Lily's newsletter to get special
bonus scenes and exclusive short stories!

http://bit.ly/ALANewsletter

Who is *Lily* reading?

Danielle Keil
Shain Rose
Victoria Anders
Katherine L Evans
Penelope Freed
LK Farlow
AK Mulford
Hollee Mands
KK Allen
CC Monroe
Molly McLain
Brittainy Cherry
Saffron A Kent

*NOTE: And MANY, MANY, MORE. Some of the best books
I've read all year I found on TikTok*

WHAT'S NEXT?

Image Destroyer – Image Series Book #3 – 2022

SNEAK PEEK

"ONE OF THE first steps into true recovery is making amends with those you have hurt or wronged."

The perky, well-spoken therapist was the embodiment of everything Olivia hated about rehab.

She didn't even belong there for starters. There was nothing wrong with her-she wasn't addicted to drugs or alcohol. There were no anger management issues. Sure, she'd made some bad decisions when it came to men, but she wasn't a damn junkie.

If it weren't a condition of her probation for the unfortunate sex-tape debacle she couldn't quite bring herself to regret, she wouldn't even be there. Not for a second.

Her eyes met the aqua ones of a man she recognized across the circle of chairs.

Unable to stop herself, she winked at him.

Ollie Parkinson.

Now there was someone who should be in rehab. Olivia had heard all the terrible stories about him floating around; everyone had.

"Olivia? Is there something you'd perhaps like to share today?" The pretty enough therapist smiled at her, and Olivia felt the urge to claw her eyes out of her skull rise suddenly. Intentionally folding her hands in her lap, she appraised the doctor. She was brunette but reminded her enough of that bitch Nora that Maxwell was still seeing that it made her blood rush.

"No, thanks."

The therapist's face dropped a bit, but she recovered quickly.

"That's alright. Sharing is never mandatory, but it can really help the process. Maybe next session."

Olivia felt her face form a pretend smile that she hoped came across the same as if she'd flipped Dr. Feelgood the bird.

After the painfully long feelings-sharing session finally ended, Ollie boldly approached her before she could slip out of the meeting space and return to her tiny cell of a room.

"Hey, Olivia, right?"

"Yeah," she snapped, not trying one bit to mask her impatience.

"Look, I know we don't know one another, but I think we have some… acquaintances in common. I've been here for a few weeks, and I can tell you that it gets easier." He seemed genuine, and for some reason that was worse than him propositioning her like she'd thought he might.

"Okay. Thanks."

He ran a hand through his sandy hair. There was no denying he was handsome, but Olivia wasn't interested. See? Who needed rehab for sex addiction? Not her. She was fine. There was nothing wrong with her at all.

"You want to grab something to eat?" Ollie deployed what should have been a very charming lopsided grin.

"Pass," Olivia said, pushing her way past him and out into the hallway.

"If you need anything…" he trailed off behind her.

"Sure," she said, glancing over her shoulder as her feet carried her quickly down the hall toward her room.

As if.

She was here to do her time and get the hell out, not make friends with the likes of Ollie Parkinson.

Looking for Dennis and Addison's story?
Catch up with

HOLLYWOOD CONNECTIONS BOOK TWO

HER FIANCÉ LEFT HER AT THE ALTAR.
NOW, HIS BEST FRIEND IS HER BOSS.

ADDISON'S life turned upside down when her fiancé sent his best man to tell her he wasn't coming to their wedding minutes before walking down the aisle… and then he eloped with her sister. She needs a new place to live, new friends, a new job and if her best friend has any say, a new man. When Dennis, the best man, suddenly fits at least two of those categories, he's not so off-limits anymore.

DENNIS' life centers around work, but he's running on fumes. Reluctantly, he agrees to hire an assistant but it's proving to be more hassle than help. When Addison walks through the doors, he knows he's in trouble. Not only is she overqualified, she's nearly perfect in every way.

He refuses to mix business and pleasure. She needs to live a little. He's come to her rescue more than once and she's the breath of fresh air he's needed for years.

Can they find a balance between their personal connection and their work relationship before everything falls apart?

Spring Breeze is available at Amazon
and other major book retailers!

Did you accidentally skip Daniel and Phae's story?
Catch up with

HOLLYWOOD CONNECTIONS BOOK ONE

BEST FRIENDS. ONE WEEK.
A ROAD-TRIP THAT COULD
CHANGE EVERYTHING.

PHAE is ready to hit the road and find herself somewhere
along the highway. There's a new life waiting for her in
Santa Barbara and she'd love to be there by Christmas.
Her original plan was to make the drive solo, but her best
friend Daniel has other plans.

DANIEL has been totally captivated by his friend Phae
since they first met. When he hears that she's planning to
drive cross-country alone, he can't help but invite himself
along. She'd never stop to smell any of the metaphorical
roses without a nudge from him, and distance is about to
be a big issue.

Stuck in close-quarters, they are confronted with the notion
that they might be meant for more than just friendship.
Will their bond survive all the big life changes happening
at once or will their relationship become a casualty of
the move?

Winter Bloom is available at Amazon
and other major book retailers!

Curious about Stephanie and Devon's story?
See how it all started in Image Adjuster!

RULE #1:
DON'T FALL FOR A CLIENT.

STEPHANIE'S job as the Celebrity Image Adjuster to play the perfect A-list girlfriend to the bad boys in the business. A former actress, her Hollywood royalty last name and squeaky-clean reputation are great for helping actors move get onto the A-list. It's all a paid transaction- they follow a script and go their separate ways when the contract is up. No risk, no feeling—just acting.

DEVON'S star is rising thanks to a hit prime-time show. He's got a smoldering smirk and massive… ego to match. He also has a heart of gold and just needs a little PR push to put him and his show over the top. A real girlfriend is out of the question – he's never had much luck in love and what you see is never what you get in Los Angeles.

Their chemistry is off the charts- and off the script. Why do their dates feel like more than acting? What happens when the contract ends and the feelings don't?

Image Adjuster is a standalone contemporary Hollywood romance. Perfect for you if you like intense friends-to-lovers chemistry, a guaranteed Happily Ever After!

Image Adjuster is available at Amazon
and other major book retailers!

Did you miss Nora and Maxwell's story?
Read

IMAGE
Protector

NOTHING IN HOLLYWOOD STAYS
A SECRET FOR LONG.

NORA CHASE is a good girl. Her carefully cultivated public persona is under lock and key—the price to keep it that way has been steep. Minding her image at every turn is a small price to pay to continue her reign as the sweetheart of the small screen. Unfortunately for Nora, her emotions pay no attention to the moratorium she's put on relationships where Maxwell, an acquaintance through mutual friends, is involved.

MAXWELL CAINE is an entertainment attorney at the top of his game at one of the biggest firms in town. He's just not sure that law is where he's actually meant to be. Temptation to overhaul everything he knows walks into his conference room one day, and her name is Nora. Falling for her may be the final push he needs to leave the law behind and chase his own dreams. He can tell she's hiding something big, however, and she won't let him get close enough to help her.

Maxwell's steadfast presence gives Nora comfort she didn't know she was seeking and isn't sure she deserves. Nora is everything Maxwell didn't know he was looking for. They're a perfect match—but can he stand by her when her past is exposed?

Image Protector is a standalone contemporary Hollywood romance. If you like red hot chemistry, a guaranteed Happily Ever After and a dash of suspense then you'll love this steamy beach read!

Image Protector is available at Amazon
and other major book retailers!

A NOTE FROM
The Author

FIRST AND FOREMOST, thanks to you, the reader! I appreciate you taking a shot on me and reading my words. That's a tremendous gift and I am truly grateful. <3

This book, much like the one before it, took much longer than I thought it would. In the end, Dallas and Trina stole my whole heart! I hope you love them as much as I do.

Writing is a solitary art, but also… no it's not. As always, this book wouldn't have happened without Shain Rose and Danielle Keil holding my hand the entire way. If you're not reading them already, you should be! My husband also deserves credit for being my first idea sounding board, editor and often, my hero inspiration.

Huge thanks to my betas, ARC readers and anyone who shared the promo! I couldn't do this without you either. <3

The team I have for cover, edits, proofreading and formatting is unbeatable! Annie, Abby, H.C. and Stephanie - You ladies are amazing! Thank you for helping whip this book into the best version of itself as usual, in a hurry. The pretty details both inside and outside make me feel like my vision for a story truly came to life and that's thanks to you!

If you loved the book I'd really appreciate if you could take just a minute to leave a review. Reviews help both authors and readers!

https://bit.ly/SummerStormGR

ABOUT THE *Author*

LILY IS A Colorado native enjoying the fantastic climate of Southern California with her family and cranky cats after surviving more than a decade in hot, humid places where hurricanes get their own season and Winter is a myth.

The written word is her favorite thing—reading or writing, she doesn't discriminate. That HEA is a powerful drug!

Find Lily on social media HERE: